Never Say Die

Praise for *Never Say Die*

"Never Say Die delivers everything a discerning fan of the genre could desire: a tough, engaging heroine, plenty of suspense and romance, and a complex mystery that stubbornly refuses to be solved until the final pages. Add to that a fascinating insider's view of the grueling sport of the triathlon and it's clear that Kris Neri has penned a winner."
~ William Kent Krueger, national bestselling author of *Ordinary Grace*

"*Never Say Die* starts with a twist, and the tension never ends. It is a fascinating foray into the world of the triathlon, interwoven with a superb story of suspense."
~ Linda O. Johnston, author of *Oodles of Poodles*, a pet-rescue mystery

"Neri clearly did her research before penning the mystery...savvy readers will recognize Neri's descriptions of the book's training grounds in San Diego and Boulder, and the novel, with a catchy plot and the familiarity of its sports-obsessed heroine, should make a good read between workouts when the body's too tired to take another page of Moby Dick."
~ Sarah Toland, *Inside Triathlon*

"The opening of *Never Say Die* rocks."
~ Martha Powers, author of *Conspiracy of Silence*

"*Never Say Die* is a real page-turner, easily Kris Neri's best book to date."
~ Barbara Seranella, author of the Munch Mancini crime novels

"…Combining the rigors of training for a major iron person competition, with a whodunit, Kris Neri…provides her readers with a captivating sports mystery… The twists will surprise the audience who swim, bike, and run along side of Zoey as she tries to stay alive."
~ Harriet Klausner, Genre-Go-Round

"*Never Say Die* opens with a bang, almost literally, when its protagonist, Zoey Morgan, is struck by a car and, briefly, declared dead… The fascinating insights into the lives of the competitors in this sport, and the sport itself, added to the whodunit and why of the well-written tale, make this a very good read."
~ Gloria Feit, 4 Mystery Addicts

Books by Kris Neri

Samantha Brennan and Annabelle Haggerty Magical Mysteries
Magical Alienation
High Crimes on the Magical Plane

Tracy Eaton Mysteries
Revenge on Route 66
Revenge for Old Times' Sake
Dem Bones' Revenge
Revenge of the Gypsy Queen

Standalone Thrillers
Never Say Die
Devil's Gambit – Devil's Due

Short Stories
The Rose in the Snow

Never Say Die

Kris Neri

The Well Red Coyote
Sedona, Arizona

Never Say Die
Copyright © 2005 by Kris Neri

Never Say Die is a work of fiction. Names, characters, places, and incidents are either the product of the author's imagination or used fictitiously. Any resemblance to actual persons, living or dead, events, or locales is entirely coincidental.

Second edition 2014

ISBN 13: 978-0615981833
ISBN 10: 0615981836

Cover Design by Kris Neri
Cover Photo: Tunnel run: © CanStockPhoto.com / Tawng

Published by:
The Well Red Coyote
Sedona, Arizona
www.welledcoyote.com

To Ruth, who lit the way out of the darkness, with boundless gratitude.

Acknowledgements

While writing is a solitary activity, no one completes a novel without the help and support of others.

For a sedentary klutz like me to depict the specialized world of triathlon, I needed insider information. I am indebted to triathletes Sue Latshaw, Joy Leutner, and Terry Martin, who generously shared their knowledge and experiences. They are not only great athletes, but really terrific women.

I appreciate the feedback writers Claire Carmichael, Susan Casmier, and Larry Hill gave me during my manuscript's earlier stages. You helped me to shape it into the book it has become.

At a Left Coast Crime charity auction, Vicki Smith bid to choose a character name in one of my books. Rather than have the character named after herself, she decided to use her daughter's name. I'm grateful to Vicki and her daughter for the character who became known as Alicia Salaz. Alicia, I hope you like what I did with your name.

As always, I'm indebted to my dear husband, Joe, whose belief in me dwarfs Mt. Everest.

And special appreciation goes to Ruth Sidney Segel, Ph.D., to whom this book is dedicated. But for you, my life would be lived in a much darker place.

One

ZOEY MORGAN HAD once heard the cynical adage, "Any day you don't wake up in a chalk outline is a good day."

Yeah? Zoey thought. *What if that's precisely where you wake up? What kind of a day is it then?*

Obviously, your last.

But the jury was still out on whether Zoey would die that day. They hadn't drawn the final ring around her yet. Though they were about to leave her for dead.

"Breathe, baby, breathe," one of the paramedics muttered.

She *was* breathing. Couldn't he tell? The measured beats of the CPR rolled through her body like waves, cresting at points along her nervous system in sensations too raw to be anything less than real. Her chest felt sore from the pounding, though it reassured her when it began again. It meant they hadn't given up.

"She's gone, Bob," the other EMT said.

"Not yet, Garry," Bob argued, before pinching Zoey's nose and breathing along with her.

Damn right—not yet. This had to be some kind of mistake—isn't that the cliché people use when they can't comprehend what's happening to them? One minute Zoey was running down the street; the next, she was ready for a body bag.

Bob pressed his hand to her carotid. "Come on, honey, beat for daddy."

"She's DRT, bud," Garry said.

She'd been around enough medics to know DRT meant *dead right there.* Fear clutched her throat when Bob's sigh of surrender dissolved into silence. Deadly silence. How funny that she knew the fear so well. She'd spent so long denying any familiarity with weakness, Zoey convinced herself she wouldn't recognize it again, yet she and fear were instantly one.

What was happening here? This wasn't some after-death experience she was having. No light at the end of the tunnel. Though Zoey couldn't open her eyes, all her other senses registered with startling clarity. She felt every throbbing muscle in her body, even if she didn't recall what had happened to make them feel so battered. She heard the traffic sounds in the street, the hushed whispers in the crowd that had gathered around where she lay on the pavement. She knew damn well this was the here and the very now.

An atheist in danger of being buried in her foxhole called out to her Maker. *Please, God...if you're there...don't let me die. Not this far from the finish line.*

However simple the entreaty sounded, it was hard for her to form. Appeals didn't come easily to Zoey. Especially when the last time she needed help this badly, no one heard her cries.

She waited. Nothing. Disappointment washed over her, though not surprise.

Then footsteps approached. "I'm Detective Luis Peña, San Diego PD Homicide," a man said. "And this is Dale Terry. We were passing and thought we'd see if you needed any help."

Garry laughed. "This girl needs your help more than she needs ours now."

Funny man.

Someone gasped. "Lou, look—it's her!"

"*Carajo!* You're right, Dale," Lou sputtered. "It *is* her."

"You know this woman?" Bob asked.

"We don't exactly— " Lou began.

But his partner cut him off. "She's not dead, is she?" that Dale-guy demanded. "She *can't* be dead."

"There's no one who can't be dead," Garry said with a sardonic chuckle.

Dale must have grabbed him. Zoey felt Garry's body yanked

across her own. "Listen, pal, you don't know who you're talking about," he insisted. "This woman's body will still be going strong when yours and mine are dust."

Finally, someone who believed in her. *Remind me someday to have this guy's baby, shake his hand—something,* Zoey thought. Thanks to him she might actually have a someday.

"Look, I'm sorry you had to find her like this," Garry said, rushing the words together. "But trust me, she's ready for a tag."

It still came down to her. Summoning every bit of her indomitable will, Zoey threw it all into one effort to attract their attention.

"Did you see that?" Dale asked. "She moved her foot."

"Hey, man, they twitch," Garry said.

"I'm telling you, she moved," Dale said, stronger now.

"Detective," Garry began, "maybe your friend— "

"I saw it, too," Detective-Lou said, though even Zoey could hear in his voice that he hadn't.

"Look, I'll settle this," Garry snapped. "I'll stick a catheter in an artery, then you'll see. When they're dead, nothing pumps. Get it?" Garry threw all his anger into shoving the needle in. That bruise would prove she was still alive—if they didn't embalm her first.

Silence again. This time less deadly.

"Shit, Bob! She's got a pulse," Garry shouted. "She's alive!"

Relief was a drug. She'd be addicted for life.

Garry shouted for everyone to clear the area and prepped Zoey for transport to the hospital. With her job was done, she allowed her mind to drift off. The cops who happened to pass just when she needed them—was that chance? Or had someone finally heard and answered her prayer? And though she felt churlish and ungrateful, she couldn't help but wonder, *Why now, and not then?*

What did it matter? She was alive. Sucking down the oxygen that flowed through the mask they slipped over her face, Zoey thought that nothing would ever worry her so much again.

Except what she overheard when they pushed her gurney into the ambulance.

"Detective, I saw the car that hit her," some quivering old-lady voice said. "You'll never guess who was driving it."

"Someone you know, ma'am?" Lou asked.

"Someone *everyone* knows. And it wasn't an accident, either. I'd swear he was trying to kill her."

Two

SLICK WITH SWEAT and promise, the hard-body blonde with the beauty queen smile beamed at Zoey from the glossy cover of *Triathlon* magazine. The cover tease read: "Zoey Morgan's Masterful Streak to the Ironman."

Didn't resemble anyone she knew. When she came to earlier that day, surprised to find herself in a hospital bed, a fog as thick as cotton filled her head. Somewhere within that fog a hammer clanged against an anvil with painful regularity. Her hunger was so deep and ravenous, she could have eaten the mattress of the empty bed next to hers and enjoyed it.

Despite that fragile state, the giddy physician fidgeting next to her bed stuck a gold Cross pen in her hand. "Make it out to Laura. That's my wife. She's not going to believe I treated Zoey Morgan."

Zoey's slim fingers tightened around the pen, and a surprisingly bold autograph flowed across the page. Maybe the resemblance was closer than she thought. The doctor chattered proudly about his wife's amateur successes in the sport where Zoey made her living. She figured he was either an insensitive slob, babbling on like that to a dying woman—or she was actually on the mend.

Once he moved on to discussing her condition, Zoey suffered through his report on her CT scan, but cut him off before the rest of the tests they'd performed while she was out of it.

"Bottom line, Doctor: am I going to make it?" She held her breath.

He closed her chart with a decisive snap. "Don't worry, Zoey, you're not going to die. I wouldn't have moved you from ICU if you weren't out of danger."

"Die?" She responded with a short laugh, struck as she often was, with how out-of-synch her idea of what mattered was with everyone else's. "I *meant:* am I going to make the Classic?"

The Touchstone Classic was the career-making half-Ironman race that had brought her from her home in Colorado to San Diego, and it was now just two weeks away. She'd been performing her own tests on her body since she awoke, to gauge the extent of her injuries, but given how hazy things were, she hadn't trusted her findings.

The doctor shrugged, jiggling the plastic nametag on his white coat that identified him as Dr. Stewart. "There's no medical reason why you can't. But it wouldn't be sensible."

With a grateful sigh, Zoey waved that objection away with a toss of her hand. If she wanted sensible, she'd find another life. She looked through the tan mini-blinds at the window, to the world beyond that antiseptic cocoon, where the race of her life awaited her. It was only the sun's glare that made her turn away, she felt sure.

"Do triathletes have publicists?" Dr. Stewart asked.

He was obviously confusing her income with his own. Zoey glanced at the pleasant hospital room, with its pale green walls and faux walnut trim, and wondered what all that was costing her. Convinced now that she'd just taken a tumble, it seemed like overkill.

"You made the newspaper," he went on. "It'd be a shame not to get some mileage from it."

He pulled a rolled-up paper from his lab coat pocket and tossed it open on her lap. On the front page of the City & County section of the San Diego *Union-Tribune* was the story of an unnamed woman who, after being struck by a car and declared dead yesterday morning, came back to life.

She felt a new tightness in her chest, unrelated to the injuries. Struck by a car? Declared dead? So much for convincing herself she just slipped on the road and had a bad dream when she knocked herself out. The memory of having fought for her life came flooding back.

Zoey's voice squeezed through a throat closing against her will. "They were awfully quick to kiss me off, weren't they? Why did they think I was dead?"

The doctor answered with a sheepish grin. "Simply put, there's a state that mimics death so well, we can't always detect it. Most of the time it's merely a precursor to the end, but every now and then, someone pulls back from it. I once read about a woman who woke up in a morgue drawer. Now you." He shrugged. "The phenomenon isn't without precedent. We've all heard of those Eastern mystics who can reduce their metabolic function below our abilities to measure them."

"I wasn't meditating, Doctor, I was trying my damnedest to tell anyone who'd listen not to assign my race bib number to another athlete. You said it yourself—I'm not hurt that badly. How could I have been at death's door?"

He hesitated, as a troubled look stole over his face. "My guess, Zoey, is that something out there scared you all the hereafter."

She laughed to show how absurd that was—only it came out as a strangled gasp. She tried to remember the accident, just to prove him wrong. She couldn't. Yet she *felt* what happened in some peculiar wordless way. Her heart began beating faster than it did during a neck-in-neck rush to the finish line.

What the hell was happening to her?

Three

ALIVE? HOW COULD she be alive? Doug Tomaso thought.

He hurled the newspaper at the knotty pine wall before him in disgust. The article didn't name the woman who had risen from the dead, but it had to be Zoey. What were the odds of *two* women being mowed down in that neighborhood yesterday?

He caught sight of his own face reflected in a window by the sunlight streaming through the trees. *What now, Dougie?* he thought, needling himself with the name he continually tried to leave behind, but which stuck to him like a burr.

He couldn't believe he'd blown it again. It should have been so easy. She was always zoned out in her training, drifting along in her "timeless space," that he'd counted on her not hearing the car's approach until it was too late.

It almost worked. Zoey turned toward the car when it came at her, but she froze in place like a pig at the slaughterhouse door. Despair had twisted her features. Then something ignited in her. She leaped from the vehicle's path. Her reflexes were excellent, but she had waited too long.

Or so he thought. He'd heard the thud when the car clipped her. But she fell alongside of it, instead of bouncing down the street like a soccer ball, as he'd planned.

Once he hit her, the car he'd used was too hot to be seen in. Yet he couldn't race away without knowing for sure. He stashed it on a side street and ran back to the scene, burying himself in the crowd that gathered around her, until he saw them give up on her.

Now she was alive again. Wouldn't you know it? He should have counted on her natural impulse to rise to any challenge. That bitch never knew when to quit.

She never knew when to butt out, either. She was all that stood between him and the biggest score of his life. He could still pull it off—but only if his secrets died with her.

Next time, Tomaso vowed, no way would he miss.

Four

ZOEY THREW AN anxious glance down an empty corridor on a lower floor of the hospital, wishing she could dismiss as crazy the sensation that she was being watched. She felt so vulnerable standing there in the open, that she gave herself a pep talk. *No one would think to look for you here, Zoey. You're safe.*

For how long?

She'd found the women's locker room as she planned, but it was being used by a couple of women who seemed intent on taking their own sweet time changing. Zoey stalled as long as she could at the water fountain and made inane chitchat with a perky magazine cart volunteer, desperately hoping nobody else came along to use the room before she could get in there. She could hardly pass herself off as an employee while wearing a gown with a breezeway. Besides, what she needed to do demanded privacy.

At the first window of opportunity, she slipped in and tried all the scratched brown metal lockers in that sizable room until she found an unlocked one. Someone always considers a combination lock too much trouble. She should know. To grab a few extra minutes of track practice as a kid, she had to leave her own locker unlocked if she wanted to make her bus on time. Got ripped-off regularly, too. She felt a guilty pang now that she was changing sides.

Unfortunately, the only person who took that shortcut here weighed considerably more than her, though by stuffing the woman's bulky yellow sweatshirt into her dark cotton pants, she managed to hold them up.

When she turned up the sleeves, she noticed the knuckles of

her right hand were badly scabbed and slightly swollen. She must have rolled over on it during the accident. She tracked down a mirror and let out a little gasp when she stood before it. The wounds were more extensive than she'd realized. She'd acquired some major facial road rash, along with what she'd already seen on her leg and hip. No question, the right side of her body had taken the worst of the damage, though by no means all. Strange that the scabs on her right hand looked older than the others. What odd healing.

Zoey wished someone had left some make-up scattered around. Just so she would look less conspicuous, not because she cared how she looked. The truth was, she felt uncomfortable about being considered attractive. Normally, she gave makeup a pass, and she kept her hair short and styled it by running her fingers through it. Despite her lack of effort, people still commented on the striking combination of her sun-streaked blonde hair and brown eyes, and that with her bones, she ought to be a model, not an athlete.

Sure, she knew there were worse problems. She'd lived with one for a long time; in some ways, still did. Good-looking women always get used by someone, she believed, even if only themselves. If she allowed herself to think of her body as anything more than a piece of equipment, she'd never survive.

The door flew open, admitting an explosive blast of women's laughter into the room. Zoey held her breath until the two intruders in hospital greens passed behind a bank of lockers. Time to go. She couldn't risk meeting the owner of the clothes she wore.

She looked again at the locker where she found those garments so she'd remember the number. She would slip back after she had them dry cleaned, stuffing a little money in the pocket to ease her troubled conscience.

But what could she do? Before he left her room, the doctor said a friend was waiting in the visitors' lounge to see her. An alarm went off in Zoey's head, sending a new wave of panic through her. She couldn't explain it—she was working blind. But the warning felt too strong to ignore.

No one she knew had any reason to think they'd find her there. Dr. Stewart said the police just ask to be informed when a hit-and-run victim emerges from unconsciousness, but no one had called yet. And her name hadn't been printed in the paper.

Denial and flight—her tools for survival. They had always gotten her through the tough times, and this one was no different.

Thinking fast, she asked the doctor to have the person wait, letting him believe she was too embarrassed to use the bathroom with someone just outside the door. What a joke. After you learn to pee on a bike, nothing matters. Then she made her escape.

Zoey remembered what that woman said when they put her into the ambulance—that someone had tried to kill her. She didn't intend to wait around there until he managed to get it right.

Five

A MAN STARED down a hospital passageway in desperation. *Where the hell was she? So many corridors, danged place was like a maze.* If he lost her now, he'd never find her again in time. Jeez! He couldn't believe how stupid he was, just letting her walk away.

Walk away...? He changed direction, speeding toward the exit.

There she was, slipping out the door, in clothes so baggy, they looked comical. He stopped and tried to catch his breath, only an involuntary sigh of relief left him so depleted, he nearly choked.

Shee-it! She was as slippery as an eel on algae. He wouldn't make that mistake again. Zoey Morgan held the key to everything that mattered to him.

The man stuck a toothpick in his mouth and nearly bit it in two. He took a deep breath. *Don't blow it now, boy.* He fell in step behind her, debating when to make his move. He had to get it right this time. There was too much riding on it.

Six

THE BLINDING LIGHT the afternoon sun sent into her eyes made Zoey trip down the concrete hospital steps, further disorienting her. *Keep going, Zoey—keep going!* Fighting down wooziness, as she sometimes did in races, she left the hospital and whoever had tracked her there, as fast as she could without drawing attention. She didn't stop until she'd gone a couple of blocks, when she paused to orient herself.

She knew this area. It was Hillcrest, a neighborhood north of downtown San Diego. She must have started her workout with a run through Balboa Park and cut over to Hillcrest when *it* happened.

While professional triathletes live all over the world, triathlon has two homes. One Mecca is Boulder, Colorado, where Zoey lived, which offers athletes the advantage of training at altitude. The other is its birthplace, San Diego, California, and the area beyond the city limits known as North County, which is blessed with a climate perfect for year-round training.

Zoey knew most of the cities where she raced better than the average tourist, but given its place in her sport, she knew San Diego the best. And Hillcrest had always been her favorite part. Maybe because of its funky quality, so reminiscent of Boulder she couldn't feel homesick. Zoey never missed a chance to scour its used bookstores, tiny little storefronts jammed floor-to-ceiling with enough cheap books to wile away hours. Nor its hole-in-the-wall restaurants, where even a competitive athlete could fill up in style without breaking the bank. Her home away from home. She stifled the irrational sting of betrayal.

She started moving again, her focus as intense as in any race. Until she perceived her own unacknowledged purpose. Even as she put as much distance as possible between herself and one danger, she was zeroing in on another.

Zoey realized she had to see the place where she almost left her life. The need felt too great to resist. As well as too suicidal to believe. She wasn't even sure whether she'd know it, more than a day later. Yet she did, judging by her racing heart. She knew it instinctively, as if the spot had been imprinted in her.

The accident had happened alongside a drugstore on Fifth, near Robinson. A skid still marred the street, though it wasn't the mark of a car screeching to a halt, but of one jerked sharply to the right. As if she had slipped from his sights. *A car actually hit me. Intended to, maybe.*

Luckily for her it happened before the workday began, when parked cars might have filled all the spots along the curb instead of just some. If she hadn't had that space to slip into, she would have been squashed like a bug. Given the angle of the skid and the need to make a fast getaway, if any car had been parked ahead, her assailant would have clipped it making his escape. No glass there now. *Why are the bad guys always so much luckier than us good ones?*

Though harried pedestrians kept brushing into her, Zoey went to the opposite corner and stood there, sucking it all in as if her life still depended on it. Only there was nothing significant about that corner, except to her. Well, nothing that mattered.

A giant billboard over the drugstore dominated the intersection. There weren't many billboards in San Diego, and never any that large. It depicted a man's face, framed by the inscription, "The man, the music, the word." Just that, nothing else, except for a funny little symbol that looked like a couple of stylized letters, a *t* and an *s*. She wondered what it meant. It couldn't have been "tough shit," as she thought.

The face on the billboard captured her eyes. The man's fair hair was long and swept back off a commanding forehead. A mustache kissed his upper lip. With his eyes, he said that he knew your deepest secret, with his smile, that he understood. He radiated enough sensuality to power an orgy.

Why then, confronted by such magnetism, did her gut twist worse than the last time she tried a bargain energy bar? Why did she feel such a desperate need to flee from the place that she'd been determined to find just moments before?

So focused was Zoey on the revulsion she felt for that charismatic image, she never noticed the scuffing of footsteps until they came to a halt behind her.

" 'Because I could not stop for Death, He kindly stopped for me,' " a raspy voice quoted.

Zoey gasped.

"I thought I'd find you here."

Oh, God!

Seven

DAMN YOU, ZOEY. *How long did you think he'd stay in that waiting room?* She'd taken a lot of risks in her life, yet she never expected to lose, not even after yesterday. Did anyone?

She turned to face her destiny. Her stalker looked like a killer, all right. A biker-thug, a celebration in studs and leather. He'd stuck a toothpick in the corner of his mouth, which he twirled with smug dexterity.

"Do you really think violence answers anything?" Zoey asked primly, like someone's old aunt.

Twirl, twirl. "Depends on the question."

Her shrug admitted grudging defeat. "I don't intend to make this easy for you. You'll have to kill me here, in front of everyone passing by, not that it stopped you yesterday."

He spit out the toothpick. "Kill you? *Kill you?* Woman, I'm the guy who saved your life. Why would I want to kill you?"

Tilting her head thoughtfully to one side, Zoey considered his voice. It was grainy with a Southwestern twang, the kind that should be singing soulful blues ballads not failing to keep visitors to San Diego safe from attempted murder.

"Your voice sounded higher-pitched yesterday." But the quality was the same, no matter where urgency had pushed it on the register. This was that guy, Dale Terry, her savior.

"You heard?" he asked.

"You'd be surprised by what they keep up on in hell."

She widened the beam of her scrutiny, but he still looked like a mugger. It wasn't just the black jeans and unseasonable leather boots and jacket that created that impression. It was the equally dark hair worn like some fifties hood, complete with drooping forelock, and the scar that cut across one cheekbone. That scar took him out of the finals of drop-dead gorgeous and put him over the top in the category of outrageously sexy. He seemed to know it, too. Or did the scar simply transform his wicked smile into a superior smirk against his will?

She couldn't see his eyes. They were covered by dark glasses. The thick-framed, old-fashioned kind that would normally be considered geeky, but which some guys make cool with Attitude. Zoey always assumed people who wear glasses that impenetrable want to keep something hidden, hence her own iridium glasses, which she felt naked without.

The things she liked best about men were the ways they were different from women. The way they were hard where women were soft, rough where women were smooth. She liked 'em hairy, too. This guy filled his black T-shirt with just the right amount of masculine build to look great and work well, but not so much as to be a pointless muscle sausage, and his five o'clock shadow was ahead of schedule. Still, he wasn't pushing her buttons. But then, she'd long acknowledged that she liked men better in theory than fact.

Zoey cleared her throat. "Yes, I remember your refusal to let me— "

He jumped in quickly, asking, " 'Not go gentle into that good-night'?"

"What do you know? A cop who quotes poetry. Not just Emily Dickinson but Dylan Thomas."

His forelock jerked slightly and he seemed taken aback, maybe because she could show off, too. "Surprised?" he asked after a moment.

"Of course not," Zoey protested.

He pushed his glasses down his nose and peered over them. His eyes were blue and smart and threw her lie right back at her. While it always infuriated Zoey when people assumed that because she was a jock she had to be brain-dead, he seemed more amused than offended by her discounting of him.

In the silence that followed, Zoey's unacknowledged gratitude hung heavily between them. Dale waited. Finally, he made a rolling motion with his hand. But the thanks that should have gushed forth stuck in her throat. She hated feeling beholden. Debt always seemed like a tax on her independence, and never had she owed anyone as much as this man.

Come on, Zoey, bend a little. "I…I'm…that is…thank you."

That scar was like a string that tugged his smirk into a grin. He popped the glasses back up, closing Zoey's window on his world. "What do you know? She still has all of her teeth."

When Dale suggested having coffee together, Zoey agreed in an instant, even though it just added to what she owed him. She needed the oasis of safety his presence offered more than she wanted to admit. As hazy as things were, she didn't know who she could trust. But Dale had saved her life, which made him the one person beyond question.

He steered her toward the Starbucks across the street, though his eyes hung for a moment on the man on the billboard.

"Who is that?" Zoey asked.

"Are you saying you don't know?" Dale demanded.

His mouth hung open and he looked startled, as if he couldn't believe it. His expectation made Zoey uneasy. Then he didn't even answer her question. Well, how important could it be?

He stopped beside his car, parked around the corner from the coffee house. Some little Ford, in a goldish-beige—she wouldn't have predicted that. He took a white plastic bag from it, which he carried through the door to Starbucks. And he held that bag out to her once they were seated with their orders.

Zoey didn't acknowledge it. Instead, she swirled the strong, hot liquid around in her mouth, the way some people savor wine. She loved coffee, though usually she settled for just enjoying its smell; it was too dehydrating for an athlete. But today she needed that caffeine jolt. She took another swig, then stuffed fully half of one of the little baguettes she made him buy her into her mouth. Hospital kitchens aren't geared to feeding endurance athletes. But Zoey couldn't keep her nose out of anything for long, so after a moment the bag drew her attention.

With an awestruck look at the amount she continued to eat, Dale muttered, "In your unceremonious discharging of yourself, you left your personal effects behind. I swiped 'em for you."

Terrific—another thing for her to be grateful for. But she had wondered how she was going to recover her stuff. She pulled her training shoes from the bag and put them on right there. For a big woman, Zoey's anonymous clothing benefactor had tiny feet. She yanked her favorite red tri-suit from the bag and thought it looked fine, till she noticed they'd cut it off her.

"They slashed this. This was my lucky... That is, it was a perfectly good suit that's not even made anymore."

He snickered and absently picked at the crumb topping on his coffee cake. "You started to say it was lucky, didn't you? Do you believe in luck?"

"Course not, it's irrational." She knew that. "Wasn't lucky for me yesterday, was it?" Balling it up in her hands, she sank a three-pointer in a trashcan.

Dale pushed his uneaten cake aside and leaned his elbows on the green metal table. "Is everything there?"

Zoey held the bag upside-down and let the contents fall onto the table. Her hundred-dollar Oakley glasses with one scratched and one broken lens were there, as well as her laminated insurance card that she always carried even though she imagined she would never need it.

"Looks like it." She finished off that baguette and began chewing another.

The key on a shoestring, which she wore around her neck when she trained, was in the bag, as were the grungy socks she must have been wearing. Odd, she rarely wore socks when she ran, and never any that pulled up as high as these did on the leg.

She wondered why she'd worn them that day.

Dale leaned closer. "Sure it's all there?"

She couldn't really say, but she dismissed his question with a nod. Strangely enough, he gave one of his dark eyebrows a skeptical lift. What else did he expect her to carry when she ran?

He asked how she felt.

Zoey shrugged. That hurt, but what didn't? "Like I took a bike spill." Into a canyon. "Been there, done that."

"Ready to talk about it?" Dale asked. When she nodded, he said, "Okay, give it to me. And don't limit yourself to the accident. You never know what will be important."

She waited till she swallowed to say, "Sounds like you want my deepest, darkest secrets, while I'm at it. What makes Zoey Morgan tick?"

"Exactly." His dark blue eyes bore into her with a curious intensity.

"Shortz SportzWatchez, of course," she said, referring to one of her sponsors. "What are you drinking?" Zoey asked of his covered cardboard container. He looked like he should be belting back boilermakers between fights in some biker bar.

"Decaf latte with nonfat milk," he said.

"Wild man."

His grainy voice gave up a short laugh, but he refused to be diverted. "Can you talk about the accident, Zoey? Did you see anything at all?"

"Oh, I'm sure I saw everything. There's just one hitch."

Eagerly, he asked, "What's that?"

"I told you I remembered everything that happened *after* I was hit yesterday. I don't remember a thing that happened *before* it from the time I landed in San Diego last weekend."

Eight

BY LATE AFTERNOON, heavy traffic ruled the streets of downtown San Diego. While navigating through those conditions demanded Dale's attention, from behind the wheel of his car, he took a moment to cast a questioning look Zoey's way.

"I don't get it," he spat with unexpected venom. "If your mind is such a blank slate, how could you find your way home?"

"This isn't my home," Zoey said of the condo complex she'd directed him to drive to. "It's just where I'm staying until the Touchstone Classic."

She glanced at the sprawling ocher stucco complex surrounded by a high wrought iron fence, and for a moment, she questioned whether it was the right place, after all. The headache, the hunger, the confusion were threatening to overtake her again.

Dale pressed on. "But didn't you arrive here during your memory blackout period?" Suspicion tainted his scratchy voice.

Zoey could have told him something about the vagaries of memory, but then she'd have to explain how she knew them.

"Just drop me anywhere," she said, unbuckling her seatbelt.

He must not have heard her. He parked the car half in a legal space and half in a bus stop. Before she could make a crack about cops who pull rank, he leaped out and raced around to the passenger door to help her out. Ever independent, Zoey pulled herself from the small car without using the hand he extended, and marched ahead of him to the condo complex gate.

The complex was comprised of several three-story buildings that faced a central grassy area. While crossing the courtyard, since Dale carried the plastic bag he'd rescued from the hospital for her, Zoey asked for the key, which was still tied on a shoelace in the bag. Before he could produce it, however, the rust-colored door of her borrowed ground floor condo flew open, and a girl in her early twenties stood in the doorway.

It was a testament to their friendship that the girl only gave Dale her modified once-over, before directing her attention to Zoey. Of course, he drooled enough for both of them.

"You're—Cindy Orr," he stammered.

Now it was Zoey's turn for suspicion. Triathletes don't attract groupies. She usually needed to explain to people their sport entailed swimming, biking and running, not skiing and shooting. And people were always astounded that triathletes could make a living doing it. Of course, lots of people unfamiliar with the sport knew Cindy. She was triathlon's glamour girl, the one the magazines hired to model workout clothing when they didn't want anyone who actually looked like an athlete. While still lean, Cindy was more rounded and conventionally built than most female triathletes. It also didn't hurt that she had dynamite cheekbones untouched by freckling, despite the hours she spent in the sun, and the flawless white teeth of toothpaste ads. But Dale had also recognized Zoey yesterday, when he and the other cop stopped beside her and the paramedics.

With a coquettish dip of her slim knees, bare beneath her pink Lycra shorts and sports bra, Cindy waved them into the condo. Even as Zoey performed the introductions, Cindy telegraphed her intentions to Dale with a sexy toss of her hair. Cindy's glossy shoulder-length hair was a striking red-gold and always styled in one of those jobs that dipped down over one eye. Zoey could never have accomplished that with all the showers she took.

Dale responded with the goofy grin Cindy often produced in men, but it was shorter-lived than usual. He quickly switched his attention to the cozy one-bedroom condo that was keeping Zoey safe from the elements while in San Diego. Even if not safe from runaway cars.

"What is this place?" he asked.

Zoey fell onto one of the living room chairs, too weary to even change into her own clothes. "It belongs to the SportzWatchez company. They keep a few units for the athletes they sponsor to use when they're in town. Great, huh?"

Dale stuffed his hands in his pockets and shrugged. "Did they purposely decorate it to look like a suites hotel?"

He'd been staying in better places than she had until now. At the rear of the unit was a galley kitchen that was hidden from view, and next to it, a dining area filled with a round oak table and seating for four. In the living room, a sofa of navy-and-tan tweed faced a modern brown marble gas fireplace. Surrounding it were navy side chairs and tables in oak. Off to the side was a small oak desk.

Okay, so maybe the innocuous landscapes decorating the walls did look as if a machine had painted them, and maybe everything was a little too aggressively color-coordinated. But that place was light years better looking than that box Zoey rented back in Boulder, which was filled with little more than the basics and her good intentions.

Without warning, Cindy took Zoey's hand and yanked her from the chair. Worry clouded Cindy's warm green eyes. "Zoey, where have you been? And what happened to your face? Took a bad spill, huh, hon?" She gave her friend's cheek a gentle brush with her fingertips, but she rushed on without giving Zoey a chance to respond. "Both Bucky Jack and Rob have called you, and I haven't known what to tell them."

From where he stood, still gawking, Dale's dark head whipped around to them. "Bucky Jack, the astronaut? The Touchstone guy?"

Bucky Jack, the last American hero, many said. Even Dale's cool abandoned him as his blue eyes widened in unabashed admiration. But Zoey was too spent to answer any more than the essential inquires. She held her hands out in the stop position to indicate that she was letting his questions slide.

Zoey gave Cindy the Cliff Notes version of where she'd been

for the last day. Then she took a closer look at the place and noticed that Cindy had been camped out there for a while. She left a pillow and blanket from the bedroom on the couch, while the remains of much of the food Zoey had stockpiled littered every surface of the room. As well as the inevitable little scraps of paper.

Cindy was always jotting a line or two on pieces of paper and Post-it notes, which when she perched somewhere, fell around her like pastel dandruff. Zoey never known what it was Cindy wrote on those slips; reminders, probably. The TV in the oak wall unit next the fireplace was turned to the inevitable tabloid talk show, but she'd muted it.

"Oh, my God," Cindy said when Zoey completed her story. "But you're okay now?" Her eyes gave Zoey an anxious search.

"I'm fine," Zoey said emphatically. If she wasn't, it was her problem. She'd never leaned on anyone. This was no time to start.

Cindy gathered up her little notes and stuffed most of them into the elastic of her shorts. Apparently, the few remaining were messages she'd taken for Zoey. She offered to let her friend's callers know Zoey was still among the living. Instead, Zoey extended her hand for the messages, though she waved them away an instant later without looking at them. She asked Cindy to toss them on the desk, the only uncluttered spot in the room. Though Cindy hesitated, looking surprised at Zoey's uncharacteristically laid-back response, she did as Zoey asked.

The beeper Dale wore attached to his belt went off, and he asked where he could make a call. Zoey started to send him to the kitchen, but remembering that Cindy was there, she told him instead where to find the bedroom phone. A small storage room connected the living room to the bedroom, and that buffer offered him more privacy than he would have found in the kitchen. With Cindy around, at least.

Cindy watched till his tight black jeans disappeared through the bedroom door, then turned back to Zoey. "Ooh, he's cute," she said. "You're going to throw him back, right?"

"Consider him thrown," Zoey said with a laugh.

Cindy inched toward the bedroom door. Feeling a superior grin form on her face, Zoey snatched the remote from where it rested against the Ritz Bits box on the coffee table and de-muted the TV. Bursting into sound were the sluttish mother and daughter that filled the screen, who yanked each other's hair and screamed insults across the barefoot boy wonder they shared. The scene so hooked Cindy, she forgot about the conversation she could have been eavesdropping on in the bedroom.

With a laugh, Zoey said, "Cindy, someday your nosiness is going to be the death of you."

"Mine? At least I limit my snooping to immediate circle of acquaintances," Cindy insisted with mock outrage.

Whatever that meant. A wave of affection swept through Zoey, and she threw her arms around Cindy in a spontaneous hug. Apart from a flicker of surprise, probably at such an unreserved gesture coming from her, Zoey saw sadness in her friend's moss green eyes. But she sensed no hesitation in Cindy's return hug. Sometimes Zoey thought she should take the trouble to get to know the girl who sent out those flashes of depth, instead of just reacting to the Barbie Doll on the surface. But not today.

The sound of Dale's footsteps scuffing against the cinnamon wall-to-wall carpet approached. "That was Lou," he announced when he appeared. "He's on his way here with something you'll find interesting."

"Lou is Dale's partner," Zoey told Cindy.

Dale's deep blue eyes registered surprise again. As if he still didn't believe she heard everything yesterday. While he gave Cindy a more elaborate account of Zoey's time among the undead, she started straightening the room.

"Zoey, I intended to clean all that," Cindy insisted, though the only action she took was to tip her head for Dale.

"Doesn't matter," Zoey said. She looked at the trash in her hands and realized it really didn't. With a sigh, she tossed it back on the table.

Cindy's smooth forehead crinkled with concern. "Zoey, maybe

I should call Marty."

Marty. With no warning, Zoey's eyes began to sting. That sweet, gentle man was the only person who'd ever completely pierced her defenses. Part of her wanted nothing more than to hide in the safety of Marty's arms. But Marty admired her independence. She always feared she'd lose him if she became clingy. Or maybe that she'd lose herself, which would be worse. When Zoey's chin began to tremble, she turned away from Cindy and Dale and began cleaning the room in earnest. And she waited till she was sure her voice wouldn't betray her emotions before she spoke.

"Absolutely not, Cindy. I'm not his only client. He's cutting some important deals in Colorado Springs for his mountain bike racers, and they deserve his attention as much as I do."

"But, Zoey, he's— "

"He's what?" Zoey stuffed all the food wrappers into the wastebasket next to the desk.

Cindy hesitated, then shrugged.

Dale slipped into one of the navy side chairs and propped his black leather boots on the coffee table. "Who's Marty?"

"Martin Nolan Wright. He's Zoey's fiancé and agent, and my agent, too. He—" Cindy stopped and reached into a pile of cupcake wrappers on an end table for a video cassette buried beneath. "Wait. I could show you. That's why I came over here, Zoey. To bring you a copy of the video outtakes from the shooting we did at Vail."

"Shouldn't they have released that by now?" Zoey asked, but Cindy seemed to have forgotten about her.

Standing before Dale, Cindy cocked her trim hip. "Zoey and I shot a training video. Too bad I finished my taping, but I should be doing an ad soon. Maybe you could come by when I'm shooting sometime."

Zoey's focus began to blur as she watched Cindy pop a video cassette into the VCR under the television. She turned away to finish straightening. When Marty's infectious laughter filled the room, with her back to the TV, she could almost believe he was really there. Her throat tightened. She turned back to the screen just as Marty's lovable face, with his crooked nose and narrow hazel eyes, became distorted by the camera lens when he drew close to jeer at it. All at once, Zoey began to sway, and she understood what they mean in the movie business when they say, "Fade to black."

When Zoey came to, Dale was stuffing her head between her knees.

"You just had to sneak out of the hospital," he snapped.

Why did he care? Zoey wondered. *You'd think it was his life.* "I've seen the results of my CT scan. There's nothing wrong with me." To prove it, Zoey refused his help and pulled herself to her feet. "I'm just famished."

"How could you be? You ate about four baguettes."

Cindy and Zoey just shook their heads. People had no idea how much they had to eat every day. At the peak of her training, Zoey bet she took in seven thousand calories a day. Cindy dashed to the kitchen and returned with a stack of peanut butter and jelly sandwiches. Zoey felt a little better after wolfing them down, but she still didn't feel well, which was odd. Despite her hunger, it should have taken more than a day in intensive care to knock her out. The vapors weren't exactly her style.

She must have appeared sufficiently recovered, however, because Cindy concluded she was okay and left to share her experience with everyone they knew.

"Where's she headed?" Dale asked, as he watched the door close behind her.

"Home, I guess." Zoey picked at the crumbs on the plate.

"You mean she's not sharing this place with you?"

She shook her head. "No, why would she? She lives here, up in Encinitas."

He turned back to the door. "Then how did she get in?"

"Someone must have given her a key. Or maybe the complex manager let her in." Zoey shrugged. "Cindy always finds people who'll do things for her."

She leaned back, propping the pillow behind her head. Dale cleared away the last of Cindy's trash, and Zoey didn't stop him.

"Is Cindy any good?" he asked. "As a triathlete, I mean."

She sure had hooked him, Zoey thought with sour grace. Why should she care? It wasn't like she wanted men looking at her the way they looked at Cindy.

"She's got more raw talent than me, but she doesn't hunger for victories. Triathlon is play to Cindy. I'm not sure she knows yet what she wants to do with her life."

Dale studied Zoey with an enigmatic smirk that accentuated his cheek scar. "Doesn't that bother you? Saying she's better."

His full lips twisted skeptically when Zoey said it didn't. She envied a great deal about Cindy, but she'd never resent talent, if it was the real thing.

The buzzer for the main gate sounded, and Dale hit the release next to the door. He threw the door open and watched as someone crossed the courtyard, until their visitor filled the doorway. With his gray herringbone tweed jacket and blue button-down shirt, the man who passed through the door sure didn't look like he belonged with the Harley Davidson poster child.

"Going okay, Penny?" Dale asked.

"*Mas o menos*, Dale Evans."

An old joke, she could tell. But women's names? Pretty childish insults for grown men.

The second voice that Zoey had heard while semi-conscious yesterday introduced himself to her as Detective Peña.

Dale placed a hand on the detective's arm. "No, Lou—we're keeping it informal. She's Zoey and you're Lou."

Why? Not that she cared what she called them. How much contact would they have?

A private communication passed between the men, which ended with Lou's crisp nod. While the exact content of that exchange remained closed to outsiders, from the way they related, Zoey gathered the similarities they shared might outweigh their differences.

Neither of them looked like cops. With his short hair and ram-rod back, Lou looked more like a Marine, though the sweeping mechanism of his espresso-colored eyes, a reflex of those who've seen it all, put him squarely in the law enforcement category. Dale just looked like a criminal. Their smart aleck grins echoed each other, as did the Southwestern drawls, though Lou's was fainter. And they were both in good shape. But Lou wore a wedding ring, and Dale didn't.

Dale told Lou about Zoey's memory loss. They shared another silent conference, only this one wasn't as hard for her to read.

"Convenient," Lou concluded, as he paced before the couch.

Zoey sat up straighter. "What did you say?"

He pulled a plastic Ziplock bag from his pocket and held it out before her. "You see what's in there?"

"Looks like a knife." It was silver and though scratched now, it had once been elaborately etched.

He shook the bag before her eyes. "It's a switchblade. You know how they work, Zoey?"

"I watch TV," she admitted.

"From prints and reputation, we've identified this knife as belonging to Jorge 'the Blade' Ramirez. Friend of yours?"

She shook her head.

"*Bueno, chica.* He's a gang leader. A multi-murderer, known to have killed a number of his victims with this very knife. No drive-bys for this lad. He likes to be right in his victim's face." Lou shook his head. "He did spearhead a gang truce last year, and some said he was turning his life around, but rumor has it he's also the one who broke the truce."

Zoey slumped back against the couch, unconcerned. "Yeah? That's too bad. Why are you telling me?"

"When they wheeled you into the ER...? They found Ramirez's knife taped to your ankle."

Nine

LOU'S QUESTIONING OF Zoey began at that point and went on for hours.

"Right," Lou snapped as he paced before where she huddled on the couch. It was less a word than the sound of contempt. "You're going to have to do better than that, Zoey."

"How?" Zoey demanded. If this was how the police treated innocent victims in San Diego, what did they do to criminals?

Lou snorted. He kept throwing questions at her, while Dale, perched against the desk, limited his role to making grunts that reeked of skepticism. What had she done to deserve this?

Lou came to a stop and glared down at her. "Where did you get the knife, Zoey?"

Zoey threw her hands up in the air. "How many times do I have to tell you, Lou? *I don't know.* I don't remember."

Why was he doing this? Couldn't he see how learning about that knife had shattered her? It was one thing not to remember the event that caused the trauma to her head, but quite another to realize there were gaps totally unrelated to the accident. Experience had taught her why we keep secrets from ourselves. Zoey didn't even want to think about what this meant.

"Why don't you ask this Blade-character why I had it and he didn't?" she snapped.

Lou frowned. "Since there's an outstanding warrant on him, he hasn't been making his whereabouts known to us."

Touchy subject, she saw. Score one for the victim. "Skipped town, huh? Well, there you have it. He must have needed money and hocked it. Bet I saw it in a pawnshop." Were they just trying to find Ramirez? Maybe they thought she'd conspired with him over something. And how could she prove she hadn't?

Lou shook his head. "Ramirez would never part with it."

Lou's relentless questioning was driving her fatigue all the way to her bones. Zoey forced herself to stand, to face him. "Maybe you don't know Ramirez as well as you think. Or maybe I found the knife somewhere. Or took it away from him."

From their burst of laughter, she gathered they enjoyed her comic relief. But it didn't distract Lou for long. "Let's go back to the accident, Zoey. Still don't remember it? Funny that you didn't see fit to disclose that to Dale right off."

"Does Dale have some medical expertise I don't know about?" she fired back.

Lou rubbed his red-rimmed eyes, but hardened his jaw. "Okay, Zoey, let's take it from the top."

He kept at it. Repeating his questions, rephrasing them. Like that would catch her in a lie. He didn't stop until the sunbeams streaming through the wooden blinds at the windows were reduced to slivers and shadows had overtaken the room. Even then, his unnamed suspicions never waned.

But Lou finally gave up. Once he did, Dale tried to make nice by offering to call someone for her. Too little too late.

But Lou never wavered. The last thing he said to her was, "I'm gonna be watching you, *chica.*"

Ten

WHEN THEY LEFT Zoey's condo, Dale and Lou paused beside Dale's car. Dale brought his fist down on the gold-beige hood.

"Damn rental," he grumbled. "What I wouldn't give for my bike."

"It's not the car, Dale Evans," Lou said patiently. "Hey, why so glum, chum? You should be cheering. Not only did she live, against all odds, but you actually tracked her down when she slipped away."

The sun hovered so low now in the sky that Dale had to shield his eyes to look at Lou. "Do you believe her, Pen?"

"Like I said, it's real convenient that she lost her memory *now*." Lou snorted, before stopping to study Dale's face when he didn't join in on the cynical laughter. "Don't tell me you do?"

Dale gave a sheepish shrug. "She's not what I expected."

Lou's slow nod seemed to carry an understanding born of experience. "Give 'em a face, and they rarely are. Are you what she thinks you are?"

Dale's laugh was short and bitter.

"You gotta toughen-up, *amigo,*" Lou said.

True. But it was harder than he expected. The circles under Zoey's eyes had darkened to a dangerous level during Lou's questioning. And when he'd turned back at the door for one last look as she stretched on the floor, Dale thought she looked so lost. Like a little kid acting grown up to scare away the bogeyman.

He had surprised himself by saying, "Maybe you shouldn't be alone right now, Zoey. Isn't there someone who can stay with you? Cindy would come back." But even he, after the shortest of acquaintances, understood that while Zoey could be Cindy's rock, despite her worrying, Cindy could never be Zoey's. "Can we call someone for you? Your mother maybe, your father."

"There's…" Zoey's voice caught. "No one. Anyway, I'd really prefer to be alone."

He didn't doubt that there was no one. The admission had been torn from her. Yet it was made with a striking lack of self-pity. She thrust her little chin out with defiant strength, daring him to feel sorry for her. He did, but he kept it to himself. Though not so much that he let it lead him off-course.

He couldn't afford to worry about her. She'd made her choices. He had to think of Holly.

"Unless you want to pull back," Lou suggested. "It's not too late."

Remember Holly. "Yes, it is, Lou. Way too late."

Eleven

BY THE TIME her confused protectors left, a numbing weariness held Zoey in its grip. She nearly gave into the impulse to spend the night curled up on the couch, only dedication weighed too heavily on her. She was a professional athlete at a critical point in her career. She had to learn how far the accident had set her back.

Zoey dragged herself to the bedroom. Sturdy modern oak furnishings dominated this room even more than the others, since color was limited there to the black-and-sand geometric prints of the bedspread and drapes, and a black recliner. She stood next to the queen-sized bed and finally shed her stolen getaway clothes.

After folding those garments into a neat pile, she slipped into a pair of green nylon shorts and a T-shirt that she found tossed on the recliner, while she considered her options. An athlete can't realistically expect to live without pain. She'd competed hurt many times. But that only worked when the injury was relatively minor. If she trained hard while seriously hurt, not only would she destroy any chance she had in this race, she'd put herself out of action for a long future stretch as well.

Zoey went back to the living room, pausing only long enough to grab the key on the shoestring from the hospital bag, which Dale had left on the coffee table. But panic set in when she stepped from the condo. Not because of her fractured conditioning, but the mental fog that still shielded the truth. Was someone waiting out there for her? The possibility would have seemed laughable, had every inch of her body not hurt from her their last encounter.

Zoey hesitated on the doorstep, for just an instant, but that was long enough to shame her. She slammed the door shut behind her. Besides, she wouldn't be alone at this hour. The downtown exodus was in full swing. While that meant breathing the exhaust that filled the air, there was safety in the numbers of people on those crowded streets.

Zoey took a settling breath and walked down G Street toward Pacific Highway, planning to go out and back, turning before she hit the airport. Ideally, a triathlete reduces her training by a third each of the last three weeks preceding a race the length of the Classic. Zoey had begun cutting down last week—funny that she remembered that. It was really too soon to taper to the final work-out schedule, but it might not be critical if that proved to be all she could handle. Her strength coming into this period should sustain her to the race, assuming she healed sufficiently by then.

She started off with a slow jog, forgetting to breathe while she assessed her body. The scabs were like fine wires cutting across the surface of her skin. The bruises felt tender even to the brush of her nylon shorts. The muscles in motion were sore down to the bone, and she was embarrassingly exhausted—but she suffered few real pains. Yes! With a little juggling of her workout schedule, she'd still have a fighting chance in the race.

She celebrated by letting her mind drift off, carrying her awareness of the pain with it, as she settled into a comfortable pace. Her arms and legs moved in perfect syncopated harmony, while her lungs and heart kept time. She threw minor challenges down for herself and felt great that she met them, again and again. Even hurting, this was her natural state. Her body only really felt hers when in motion. If she couldn't do this, she wouldn't want to live.

As if she would get to choose. With the genuine concern for her conditioning swept aside, irrational fears flooded in again. That creepy feeling of being watched stole over her, starting with the muscles tightening across her shoulders.

Zoey remembered the knife—back in the condo. Lou had left it on the table, as if he'd forgotten it, though she doubted Lou Peña forgot much of anything. When she discovered it there, she assumed he hoped to trap her into using it. Instead, she wrapped it up and stuffed it into one of the bedroom drawers. Now she wished she hadn't acted so hastily. The knife's illegality wouldn't bother her anymore. If Lou was to be believed, it never had.

Zoey's breathing began to gallop. How can you keep yourself safe when you don't remember what you're running from? Frustration clenched her fingers into fists. She took a sudden turn, stopped beside a building, and peered around the corner. Feeling half a fool, half a survivalist, she held her breath and waited for her stalker to show his face.

But the only face she saw was that of some klutzy little boy kicking a soccer ball. Oh, there were other people in the distance. Suited women striding as fast in their trainers as race walkers, men swinging briefcases in their rush home, but none gave her a second look.

Still unsure, she watched the kid. He wasn't very good at soccer, missing his kicks more than he connected. And he didn't seem to take any joy in it. Grim determination made his lips as hard as the bones in his skinny little face. She kept trying to catch his eye, so she could send him a thumb's-up—encouragement to keep going. While Zoey never yearned to parent one, she harbored a real soft spot for kids, especially the ones who seemed to need somebody on their side. Only the boy never looked her way.

Why would he? Why would any sane person want to connect with some nutjob hiding in the shadow of a building? She'd learned what she needed about her conditioning—why was she still out there? Some days just cry out for euthanasia. For the record: when she headed back to the condo, the closest she came to danger was when she tripped on the kid's soccer ball when he accidentally sent it her way.

But that awful day just refused let go of her. Sleep came quicker than she expected when she stretched out on the quilted bedspread, still in her running clothes. Too bad it didn't arrive alone. A face appeared to Zoey in a dream. A gruesome countenance with eyes that tugged down at the corners, and with a brush over lips that mocked her with their gaping scorn. The ghoul pressed its face to her face, its body banged against hers. In her dream she put out a hand to push it away. The face felt cold and clammy, yet molded and hard.

Zoey awoke with a start, shivering in a pool of sweat.

God, no—it was happening again.

How many demons could she face and still survive?

Twelve

IN THE TIME it took Zoey to fall back to sleep after that unsettling dream the night before, she vowed to banish the nightmares from both her days and nights, and to take back her life. Instead of counting sheep, she sketched out a tentative training schedule. Light running and cycling only at first, with swimming added in a few days. If that worked, she'd beef it up for a few more days, before cutting back in the final stretch.

At the first hint of daybreak, Zoey put it to the test. She drove to Torrey Pines and chose a running route that began and ended at the top of a hill, with long up-and-down grades between them. Much tougher than what she'd tried the evening before. She intended to go out and back and just hoped she didn't end up walking most of it. Anxiety mushroomed within her while she slowly stretched her stiff, sore muscles, fear that the baseline she'd established the night before had been nothing more than wishful thinking. But the wounds stung less than she'd expected in this morning's shower, and her skin already looked a little less like an overripe banana. She could do this.

Technique is more critical running downhill than it might seem because the impact on each foot strike is greater than on level ground. Gallop down those suckers and you could be looking at a world of pain. Zoey adjusted her stride for the angle of descent and started out with a slow pace, concentrating on keeping it steady till she neared the bottom of the first hill. Then she inched up her speed before starting to climb.

Charging uphill had been her greatest love for as long as she could remember. What a rush. Zoey couldn't risk that speed today, yet she was moving at a respectable clip by the time the road began to climb in earnest. She forced her mind to stay with the program, no drifting off this time. She monitored it all, even technique that had become second nature. Lowered her arm swing, shortened her steps, bounced off her toes. It isn't efficient to bend into the grade, as many runners do. The ideal is to run with a nearly straight stance, as if you're climbing stairs. The trick is feeling like climbing those stairs, at high speed, for long stretches of time, is the most natural thing in the world. It was for her.

Her excitement began to build as she reached the turnaround, and she allowed her speed to move up a notch. She hadn't chosen a rolling out-and-back course by accident. While shorter, this type of route mirrored the run course in the Classic. In the final stretch of her training, she always tried to simulate race conditions.

Yet she hadn't chosen it for purely practical reasons, either. Out-and-back courses were her favorites. Zoey couldn't explain it, but such a sense of anticipation always came over her as she approach the turnaround point. Sure, it was just the expectation of victory. What else could happen in the middle of a race? But sometimes that sense of expectancy was so great, it felt like something awaited her there that would change her whole life. As if that could really happen.

Zoey felt that sense of expectation now and struggled to keep a lid on the speed, giving in to it only in last dash. When the hill crested, so did she. As she streaked through a finish line that she alone saw, her heart soared. She should never have doubted it. Her body was the one thing that had never let her down.

Thoroughly satisfied, she stretched, while filling her lungs with big rushes of air until her breathing returned to normal.

Deciding to reward herself with a treat, she hiked to the edge of the cliff that overlooked the ocean and sat with her feet dangling over the side. Risky perhaps, but after shaming herself by cowering in fear along the side of that building the night before, she knew she didn't want to live like that. Zoey kicked her feet in the air and drank in the misty morning view.

The air was still cool, but the sun already felt warm against her skin. It was too far for the ocean spray to reach her, but with each wave that crashed against the shore, she felt the past being washed away.

Zoey loved the healing power of mornings. Nights were hell for her even when she didn't have bad dreams. In sleep, she felt too vulnerable, and that presented a problem. The punishing extremes to which triathletes push their bodies demands a minimum of eight or nine hours sleep a night for repairs, with ten to twelve being even better. She sure didn't get it last night.

But there in the sun, in that fresh natural world, she finally succeeded in banishing the demons. The morning's cleansing gift put everything into perspective. Zoey saw it as it actually was, not with the fearful skew the accident gave it. With it all so easily explained, there was no cause for alarm.

Then someone stepped onto the trail behind her.

"I could kill you," he said.

"That's twice you let me get the jump on you, Zoey," Dale snapped. "What's the matter with you? If I wanted to, I could have killed you. You would never have even seen it coming."

His concern was touching. Wasn't he one of the guys who gave her the third degree the night before? But his regard for her life did seem genuine. Zoey felt herself grinning, as if seeing him delighted her or something. She gave him another chance.

Waving her finger at him, she said, "Ah, but I would have heard. I knew it was you. You scuff your feet."

He did even when he wasn't wearing his Ode to Leather. He had on tiger-printed Lycra shorts and running shoes today. His legs were as lean and tight as she imagined. Nicely hairy, too, the way she liked them. All the male pros she knew shaved theirs. She might accept the necessity for it—road rash heals faster on smooth skin—but never the aesthetics. Ironically, Marty shaved his out of some misplaced sense of solidarity.

Dale insisted on having the last word. "It'd be small comfort to you if your killer did, too. Scuffed his feet, I mean."

Zoey laughed. His toothpick was back. Kicking cigarettes must have been hell for him.

She shielded her eyes from the sun, wrinkling her nose when she looked up at him. "How long did you smoke?" she asked.

"Never smoked."

Go figure. She just couldn't get a handle on this guy.

She moved over to let him sit next to her. "How did you find me?"

He sat in the space she'd made for him. "I called Cindy. She told me this was your favorite spot in San Diego."

Zoey gave her head a swift shake. "Am I that predictable?"

"Not to me, you're not," Dale said with feeling. "Did you know your phone was disconnected?"

"Uh-huh." She pulled it out last night when her loneliness reached a record low. Avoiding Marty seemed easier than lying. Or caving. When Dale's bare leg pressed against hers, she inched away. "You really must have made Cindy's day. You're probably at least fifteenth on her must-have list of men." Instantly shamed, Zoey couldn't believe she said something so catty.

His scar deepened when he smirked. "Jealous?"

"I'm taken, remember?" she said.

"Oh, sure. Marty Right or something."

"That's Martin Nolan Wright."

"Kinda funny you don't want him here now, with all you're going through."

"What's funny is that I'm not going through anything at all. I won't have him dragged away from something important just because *you* think someone's trying to kill me."

Zoey figured her new take on the accident would shock Dale, and she'd seize the upper hand. Instead, he just looked at her as if she'd spoken in a foreign language.

"Look, Dale—we have only one woman's word that someone was trying to kill me. We've built this whole scare scenario on the basis of that." She clapped her hands together in a gesture of finality.

Dale picked up a couple of stones from the ground and tossed them one-by-one down to the beach. "Well, there was also the little matter of being declared dead and spending a day in intensive care."

"I didn't say I wasn't hit. Someone just lost control of his car, and now he's afraid to come forward."

"You're forgetting a big part of it." His blue eyes darkened as he searched her face. "You really can't remember, can you?" He ran a shaky hand through his black hair. "The least I could admit to is that it was a joke that got away from someone. Only not a very funny one."

A joke? Zoey waited, but he didn't give her the punch line.

While tossing a stone, he also threw another question at her. "What about the knife?"

"I'm in a strange city, need protection. Despite what Lou said, I'd still bet Ramirez pawned it."

Dale admitted the possibility with a grudging shrug.

He bought it—so why couldn't she? Though she wouldn't admit it to him, the knife troubled her. Why would she risk injuring her muscles by carry it so close to a major race?

Unless what happened with the car wasn't the first attempt on my life.

A tremor shook the foundation of the strength she'd so carefully rebuilt that morning. Not remembering things is like wandering blind, never knowing which step will send you tumbling into an abyss. All your natural defenses are disabled. Zoey closed her eyes, willed her memory to return until she felt weak from the strain. The fog just closed in tighter.

Flight suddenly felt safer than fighting shadows. She told Dale she had to get back to training and bolted away.

"Wait!" he shouted. "I thought we could run together."

Zoey turned back to him. "Don't you have to work?"

He hesitated, before saying, "I'm on a disability leave."

"Psycho, huh?" She laughed too loudly.

"For your information, I was shot." He looked away, as if he was embarrassed to admit it.

She checked him over, but didn't spot any holes. And he didn't elaborate. Given his discomfort, she figured it had to be in the ass. She stifled a smile.

He explained that both he and Lou were age-group triathletes, amateurs who competed against members of their own age category. She'd already guessed that; no one else would know so much about the sport.

"Come on. You shouldn't train alone. You know that."

Knowing he was right, knowing she needed him, her gut knotted. "I charge for coaching, Dale," she said, resisting it.

"Then it's a fair exchange—I charge for bodyguard work. Come on, Zoey, humor me."

Zoey cocked a hip and propped her fist on it, as she studied him. "You might not be so terrible to have around, assuming you can keep up." She suggested that perhaps he wasn't fit enough yet.

"Don't worry about that. I expect I could get cleared to go back to work tomorrow." He did a silly little stretch to prove it. "Hell, I rode around with Lou yesterday without pay. But since they're willing to let me have this time, I'm taking it. We don't always get much time off, you know?"

He rattled that out so fast, she figured the idea of his duplicity made him feel bad. But it was his conscience, not hers.

"I've already run today," she said. "I need to ride now. My new bike was delivered shortly before I went out to be struck dead by a car, and I still haven't given it a try."

He looked dismayed by her suggestions. But he had to ride if he was a triathlete. "Well, sure, we could ride some," he finally decided. "I'll get my bike and meet you at your place."

Dale insisted on following her van back to the condo, where he waited till she was inside. When he returned a short time later, she understood his reluctance to ride with her. His bike was of decent quality for someone at his level, but it wasn't a good choice for him. He got had.

"That bike is a little small for you. You ought to sell it to Lou. It'd fit him better."

"We can't all have state-of-the-art bikes like you." Dale whistled at hers.

"State-of-the-art a decade from now, you mean," she said as they walked their bikes through the courtyard. It even made the latest aero bikes look awkward and old-fashioned.

"But it looks familiar," Dale said. "Like I've seen it before."

"You may have. It's been on display in bike shops all over the area. I've been using a prototype of this for a while. My sponsor took all of my suggestions and specifications and made this for me. Isn't it fabulous? I can't believe how great it turned out."

While peddling up Fifth, she described its advanced features. Its featherweight combined with outstanding rigidity, its breakthrough gearing.

"Even the tires are new," she explained. "They aren't natural rubber, but a polymer that's tougher than Kevlar, yet lighter. And they're filled with a gel that's not only weighs less than air, it will seal off any small puncture they do get. Not absolutely flat-*proof* they tell me, but flat-resistant enough to seem so."

Zoey considered him pretty pushy when Dale directed her to turn on Laurel and head for Balboa Park. She knew her way around San Diego. The choice also surprised her. She could handle it, even in her present condition, but it was a steep hill. They moved at what should have been a good clip for Dale, but he not only kept up, he had enough wind to talk when we rode side-by-side.

"Do you enjoy the carnival atmosphere of race day, or do you like it quiet?" he asked.

Zoey turned her head his way. "Carnival?"

"Not in the pejorative sense. I meant the crowds, the venders—you know, the fun."

The crowds always seem pretty thin to Zoey. Triathlon hadn't picked up a spectator following in the US. Once she did a race in Germany, and the cheering on the bike course was so loud, she couldn't hear herself changing gears. But she understood what he meant.

"I need to internalize at the start," Zoey said. "But that carnival atmosphere reassures me that we have some future. Americans feed on that kind of thing. If only someone could create a media circus within the sport, we might be around forever."

Zoey noticed Dale suddenly slipped behind her. And just as they approached the park, where the road would finally level out. Though her body was getting weary, Zoey stood on the pedals and really hammered it, savoring the feeling of flexing and stretching the long muscles of her legs.

"Hey, lazybones," she shouted, "don't give up now."

Though she had to ache more than he did, Zoey couldn't resist sprinting forward, making it harder for him. The bike was a dream, even if it didn't ride as smoothly as she expected. It became rougher still when the road flattened out, but she didn't start to worry until it was too late. Without warning, she suddenly felt the clips releasing her shoes, as her body was hurled through the air.

Fortunately, she landed on soft ground, but even still, it added bruises to her bruises.

Dale came up next to her where she landed on the grass, and placed his bike down. "Zoey, what happened? Are you all right?"

"Forget about me—how's my bike?" Knowing she could reach it faster in bare feet than cycling shoes, she ripped the Velcro fasteners from her shoes and slipped out.

Dale beat her there. He whipped the rear tire off with more expertise than she would have expected from a guy who bought the wrong bike.

"So much for space age tires," she muttered.

"Well, I reckon they wouldn't even be able to handle this one in outer space," Dale said with a quizzical look. "These tires have been slashed."

Thirteen

AN UNEASY SENSE of *déjà vu* took hold of Zoey when the whole gang gathered again at the condo. After she was thrown from her bike, Dale tracked Lou down and asked him to meet them there. He arrived just as they did, and they all discovered that Cindy had already made herself at home and was busy scarfing down more of Zoey's food.

Now, an hour later, Dale stood at the wall unit, where he appeared totally engrossed in studying the spines of the *Reader's Digest* condensed novels the SportzWatchez company had provided for the reading pleasure of the condo's guests. While Cindy, wearing jeans and a coral T-shirt today, stared out the front window, munching on a carrot sticks. And Lou paced the same path in the carpet, only this time, he swung the damaged tire at his side.

He stopped before the tweed sofa where Zoey hovered and thrust the slashed part of the tire into her face. "The tire wasn't designed to hold up to this. Someone cut into this rubbery stuff, and after you put some weight on it, it burst. The gel tried to do its job. See where it bubbled up at the sides of the cut?" He turned to Dale to say, "This stuff's amazing, *amigo,* works just like blood, but it was too much to expect it to clot this wound."

"Colorful metaphor," Zoey muttered under her breath.

"Creepy," Cindy added, briefly frowning at Zoey before she turned back to the window.

Shaking the tire at her, Lou demanded, "Zoey, who wants you out of this race?"

Stiffening her facial muscles so as not to cry took all her concentration. The courage she'd felt earlier drained away. It was hard enough grabbing control of the reins of her life, but harder still to *keep* doing it.

Zoey retreated into the sofa, clutching a tan throw pillow tightly to her chest, along with her denial. "Why do you assume it was meant for me? That bike has been on display in shops from Los Angeles to the Mexican border. You mean to tell me there isn't one sicko in all that geography who wouldn't get off on this?"

Lou slumped into one of the navy side chairs. "It's too much of a coincidence to believe all the sickos just happened to be clustered around you. Someone's out to get you."

She pressed her face into the pillow. What could she have done to warrant this? The fog shielding her memory remained impenetrable. Anyone might be lurking in it.

Lou leaned forward and grasped her arm, making another angry demand that she spill her guts. She flinched at his touch. His hands were elegant, she noticed. Not feminine, just well-shaped, like those of male hand-models, with white half-moons capping pink well-trimmed nails.

Hands like…

The sight of that hand around her arm suddenly made her feel as it would if it were elsewhere on her body. She couldn't breathe.

No! It really was happening again. *Why now?*

When Lou released her arm with a disgusted sigh, she pressed her whole face into the pillow—she couldn't let them see any evidence of what those feelings did to her.

"You're not the most popular person in this sport just now," Lou said.

Her head snapped up. "How can you say that? Cindy, tell him."

"Well, lately…" Furious carrot crunching.

"Cindy!"

Cindy turned, pressing her butt against the wall below the window and gesturing with a carrot. "I'm sorry, Zoey, but there's been some talk recently. Maybe because you're a little remote. You are even with me."

Considering her distancing of Cindy the day before, Zoey couldn't deny that. Did everyone feel as out-of-step with other people? By the time Zoey had life nailed, she'd be ready to kick it.

"Drives my wife crazy that I'm such a pack rat," Lou said. "But sometimes it comes in handy."

He pulled a rolled-up magazine from the inside pocket of his navy blazer and tossed it on the table. An issue of *Sports Insider* from a couple of months back, a magazine that covered the lesser known sports with an approach that fell somewhere between *People* and the *National Enquirer*, stared up at them.

"Because of you, Patrick O'Hara received a year's suspension," Lou said. "And at a time when I doubt he's got many good years left."

Was that what these attacks were about? Had she caused it all herself with her big mouth? "For the record: O'Hara received that suspension because he put a performance enhancing drug into his body. His fault—not mine. I just pointed a finger." Zoey's tone softened with, "I wouldn't have talked to that guy if I'd known he was an *Insider* reporter. I've kicked myself a thousand times for it. But every word I said was true."

Dale squatted on the other side of the coffee table. "I'm curious, Zoey. Y'all don't compete against men. What was it to you?"

Did she really have to tell him why it was wrong to *cheat?*

"O'Hara's a desperate man, Zoey," Dale went on. "You of all people must understand that desperate people do desperate things."

Why me of all people? she wondered.

Lou stared at the magazine cover. "I didn't realize there was so much use of steroids and whatnot in the sport."

"The stories I could tell you…" Cindy muttered absently.

Zoey was never sure whether Cindy really knew the insider dirt she bragged about. If she did, why was Zoey the only one speaking out? Why was Cindy so secretive?

"You slandered anyone else lately, Zoey?" Lou asked.

"I try to limit it to one-a-day," Zoey said with a laugh. But her laughter faded when a face drifted into her mind. No, that was crazy.

Lou accurately read her face. "Spill it, *chica.*"

Zoey absently placed the pillow to her side, as she glanced at the ceiling. "There is someone who'd love to see me out of this race, and she's staying in this building. She's really the worst drug offender in the sport."

Lou's rigid body twitched with anticipation. "And you've said that to people?"

"Once or twice. Never reporters," Zoey rushed to add. It was their private concern. But they needed to fix it. "It's Alicia Salaz."

Lou's dark face brightened. "No kidding? Ali Salaz is in this building? Don't tell me her wins are drug-aided."

"Come on—look at her race times." Zoey shook the pillow for emphasis. "Not only have they gone down too much, too fast, she's become too lean and muscular."

"Maybe she's been over-training," Lou suggested.

Were all men that naïve when it came to women? Zoey looked to Cindy for some expert testimony, but Cindy had turned back to the window.

"I know I sound like a self-righteous prig saying this," Zoey said with a sigh. "But Alicia doesn't do things the hard way. Everything about her is phony. You know, her name is really Alicia *Daniels*. She just took her husband's name because it's glamorous to be considered Hispanic in some circles."

Lou stood and drifted back into his slow pacing. "Yeah? I guess I don't move in them."

Zoey rose and followed behind him. "Well, your father-in-law's probably not the philosopher-farmer."

Dale shook his legs, which had to be tight from squatting. "Oh, right. I'd heard her father-in-law was Enrique Salaz."

Enrique Salaz was the humble Mexican immigrant who had organized migrant farm workers, rising through the ranks of California society, until he was now being touted as a Congressional candidate.

"I think he's a pretty good guy," Lou said.

"I do, too." But she'd never thought his innate wisdom had rubbed off on his ambitious, Stanford-educated son, Rick. "Ali's own parents aren't that noble. Her mother's just some old-money WASP princess, and her old man heads up Daniels Pharmaceuticals. Is it such a stretch to think he might keep his daughter supplied with the latest in performance enhancing drugs and the stuff to mask them when she gets tested?"

Lou and Dale shared an uncomfortable glance. Had she gone too far again? Cindy continued to stare the front window, and her rigid posture looked anything but relaxed. Zoey wondered whether she'd ever learn when to shut up.

Dale stood before her. "Let me get something straight, Zoey. The condo unit Alicia Salaz is staying in here is that owned by the Shortz SportzWatchez Company, too?"

Zoey nodded.

"So they're also sponsoring her. Which other triathletes do they sponsor?" he asked.

Counting them off on her fingers, she said, "Miranda Griffin and Tony Bianco, of course." The unquestioned leaders in the sport. "And Dick West."

A sudden smile tugged Dale's scar. "No kidding? Neon Dickie?"

"Don't let the goofy look fool you. Dick's a great athlete," Zoey insisted.

Dickie West was one of the new guys in the sport, who quickly claimed a place with his brash, raw power, which he supplemented with attention-getting stunts. Zoey thought he was underestimating himself.

"And Alicia and me, of course. That's it," Zoey said.

"Okay, let me see if I've got it," Dale said, reasoning slowly. "SportzWatchez corralled the two old pros. But Griffin and Bianco aren't going to be around forever, so they have to snatch the up-and-comings before a competitor does. They've bet on Neon Dickie as the male frontrunner. But for the women—why are they sponsoring two of you?"

Zoey shrugged. Cindy's carrot crunching filled the silence.

"My guess would be they're hedging their bets," Dale continued. "You and Alicia are in a horse race. But since she specializes in longer events, and you're just turning to them, I'd say she's more of a threat to you than you are to her."

Zoey hated know-it-all amateurs.

Lou swung the tire in the air. "Okay, we're getting off-track here. Who else is on your hit list?"

Zoey shook her head. "No one."

Lou didn't seem to buy it. "Has to be someone. Zoey, people like you start wars."

Zoey burst out laughing. "There's no one else, Lou."

"What about the rest of your life? Anything there that would make someone mad enough to kill you?"

Zoey stomped her foot. "Will you listen to me, Lou? There's nothing else in my life. *Nothing!*"

The force of her denial seemed to convince them. Too bad it didn't do the same for everyone.

"Except the award." Cindy turned away from the window. "The award has made some people *really* mad."

If Zoey didn't know better, she would swear that was anger darkening Cindy's cheeks.

Fourteen

THE COZY GATHERING in Zoey's borrowed living room disintegrated from there.

"Let me see if I understand this, Zoey," Lou bellowed a short time later. "You do my job as your hobby."

Hands on her hips, Zoey stepped up to him. "Let me see if *I* understand it, Lou. You do *my* job as *your* hobby."

Momentary frustration flashed in his dark eyes. "Lots of people engage in amateur athletics—I never heard of a dilettante cop."

Zoey threw her hands up and walked away. "How many times do have to tell you: I'm not trying to be a cop." She'd explained that she volunteered several hours a week in the offices of Operation Innocence, a group of Boulder-based lawyers and who worked to overturn unjust convictions. Lou took it as a personal slap on the justice system. "People, cops included, do make mistakes." Cops especially, from what she'd seen lately.

Lou waved his hand in the air. "You got too many open boxes, Pandora. You'll just have to lay low for a while."

"Wait. You mean I have to stop training? No way." Zoey gave her head an emphatic shake.

Dale came up behind her and clamped his hands on her shoulders. "Pen, I can be with her sometimes," Dale said.

She pulled away. "Like hell. Today was just play, pal. You can't keep up with me."

"Aren't you afraid?" Dale asked.

More afraid than you could ever understand. But she couldn't surrender her life to shadows. She'd lose herself in them. "Look, I have to do well in this race. Sponsors want wins. You know I've taken some career gambles. If they don't pay off, I'm sunk."

Cindy strolled out of the kitchen, clutching a package of cookies. "Besides, there's the award." she added.

Cindy sure was hung up on that. "An additional personal reason why I have to win. Petty, but—yes."

"Oh, yeah—the award. What's that about?" Lou asked.

Cindy pulled a race flyer from the pocket of her faded blue jeans and offered it to them.

" 'The San Diego Touchstone Classic presents the First Annual Touchstone Made-a-Difference Award'," Dale read.

"Zoey's getting that for her work for Operation Innocence," Cindy explained.

"Why you? Why not some of those lawyers? They do the hard part," Lou demanded.

A question many had asked. From the defiant set to her full pink lips, Cindy seemed to be thinking it now. Zoey started to give her usual answer. "I am a high-profile person. Perhaps they thought the publicity—" Who was she kidding? "Look, I don't know why they picked me. But no one would *kill* me over it."

Dale kept reading the flyer. "Does any money come with it?"

"Some…well, a lot actually. To me, anyway. Ten thousand dollars. Marty and I talked about giving it back to the Foundation."

"Zoey, that's great," Cindy suddenly exclaimed. Her defiance vanished in a flash, and just as quickly, Zoey's friend with the laughing green eyes returned. "I'd do anything I could for those Touchstone kids. I mean, I'm so lucky to have my mom and dad, and when I think about those boys, no sacrifice is—" Abruptly, Cindy clamped her mouth shut.

Cindy sure was changeable lately. What was that about?

A light seemed to go on then in Dale's dark blue eyes. "You *do* know Bucky Jack? What's he really like?"

Zoey felt herself smiling along with him. "With Bucky, what you see is what you get. I don't think I've ever met a more authentic person."

"A great American," Dale said with a solemn nod.

A great American? Well, she supposed Bucky was. A maverick test pilot, an astronaut who single-handedly saved a mission. And now the director of a foundation that sponsored shelters from coast-to-coast for throwaway kids. Still, she'd expect that kind of comment from a straight-lace like Lou, not the biker-thug. Who was this guy?

Ever focused, Zoey returned the conversation to what mattered most to her. "So you can see why I have to win," she said. "I'm going to receive this honor during the race's awards ceremony."

"Yeah? So?" Lou asked. The men shared baffled glances.

After scraping the cream filling off a cookie with her sparkling white teeth, Cindy explained, "She doesn't want to be Miss Congeniality."

"Congeniality will never burden Zoey," Dale insisted.

Zoey accepted that with a good-natured chuckle. But shallow as it probably sounded, it wasn't a joke to her. Perceived standings in the sport sometimes mattered more to sponsors than actual rankings. "I can't accept an award, especially one nobody thinks I deserve, at a race where I don't first collect a trophy. I won't be seen as an also-ran." She whirled around on Lou. "If you'd find out who's doing this to me, there wouldn't be any question about my training."

"If you gave me something to work with, I might. Were you doing anything out here for Operation Innocence?"

Zoey shook her head. "Why would I? I told you, I'm just a lowly keyboarder."

Dale folded the flyer and put it into the pocket of his black jeans. "Were you pursuing anything on your own? Any other windmills?"

"Of course not." But causeless panic flooded her.

"Then why did you bring that leather portfolio from Boulder? Isn't that where you kept your Operation Innocence notes?" Cindy asked. "There's a file folder in it now."

Cindy obviously hadn't limited herself to eating Zoey's food. Cindy dashed to the bedroom now and returned with a zippered portfolio case. That was hers all right, Zoey thought, she just didn't know why she'd brought it to San Diego. Cindy pulled out a manila folder.

"There's nothing in here now but a greeting card," Cindy reported.

"A card?" Lou asked.

"Yeah, a lovey-dovey one from Marty," Cindy said.

She gave Zoey a sheepish look, embarrassed maybe to have opened something so personal. Then she actually turned back and read it. Zoey wondered when she lost complete control over her life.

"What else did you have in the folder, Zoey?" Lou asked.

So that old saying was true, Zoey discovered. Be careful what you wish for, you might just get it. After an agonizing struggle to reclaim even a fragment of the time she'd lost, Zoey suddenly remembered something about memory retrieval. How memories return without warning, and often packing a punch. She'd been down this road before. There was something familiar about the way her heart quickened. Zoey felt a door opening within her. Without thinking, she rushed to slam it shut. Too late.

Zoey turned to Lou and Dale. "I...don't know. Does the name...Willi Bogs mean anything to you?"

From the look of pure astonishment on Dale's face, which was echoed on Lou's, Zoey figured it meant a lot.

Fifteen

DALE TOOK ZOEY back to *the* corner, the one where she had almost left her life, and he directed her attention to the man on the billboard, whose face had both captivated and repelled her.

"Willi Bogs?" she asked.

Shoving a toothpick between his teeth, Dale muttered, "That's what they say."

Why did that picture make her feel so uneasy? Everything was still so fuzzy. And not fuzzy enough.

Frowning, Dale searched her eyes. "You really don't remember ever seeing this?"

"Just...after. With you. I told you I don't recall much about the time I've been here."

"If this isn't familiar to you, then you don't remember much from before you came, either. There are billboards like this where you live, too." Dale kicked a pebble on the sidewalk with his thick, black boot.

Zoey tossed her hand in the air. "You don't know Boulder. Commercialism—"

"Trust me, Zoey—unless you've been in a coma for months, you've seen them. And not just billboards, I'm talking about the whole danged Willi Bogs phenomenon. There hasn't been anything this big since Elvis left the theater for good."

Zoey was stunned. How could she have forgotten all of that?

"You're really serious, aren't you? About not remembering any of it. Shee-it," he said with a groan.

Why should he care? "Do you mean to tell me that everyone in the country—" Zoey began.

"The country, nothing—the world."

"They all know who Willi Bogs is?"

Dale hesitated, then said quietly, "*Was,* honey. They know who he was."

"You mean he's *dead?*"

Dale turned and started drifting off down Robinson. "When they find someone's skeletal remains at the bottom of a ravine, that's what they call it," he said over his shoulder in clipped tones.

Then Willi Bogs hadn't been driving the car that hit her. Zoey wondered why she feared he might have been.

She rushed to catch up to Dale. "But you said people are coming to San Diego because of him. Was this where he was born?" Once she drew level with him, she saw the answer on Dale's taut face before he could say it. "Oh. It's where he died."

"Appears he was just passing through, but San Diego was the last place Willi Bogs was seen alive."

Zoey slowed to a stop. The sidewalks were crowded, and bodies streamed around her like waves around a rock. But her leaden legs wouldn't move.

Zoey shouted to Dale, as walked away from her again. "So people are—what? Making a pilgrimage?"

"Zoey, you are slower than a hog ridin' sidesaddle." With a resigned sigh, Dale returned to her side. "Some, sure. Others, the paranoiacs, are here to prove Will was really murdered. The conspiracy theories have become a cottage industry, along the lines of Marilyn Monroe and JFK. The real space cadets and the kids are convinced he's still alive. Holing up someplace, I guess, with Elvis and Bigfoot."

"Is it true? Was he murdered?" she asked, surprised at the desperation in her voice.

Dale shrugged. "There's no evidence to suggest it." The five o'clock shadow forming on his face wiggled when he smirked at Zoey. "You were here on a Willi-watch, too, weren't you? Which of the loony camps did you fall into?"

"Forget about me, will you?" Zoey turned back at the billboard, though it was nearly out-of-sight from where they stood. "What about him? What did he have that took hold of so many people?"

Taking her arm, Dale said, "That you'll have to see for yourself."

While Dale dragged her through the outlying parts of the Hillcrest shopping district, she tried to put a date to the start of her memory gap. It shook her to realize the loss was more extensive than she thought, and more random. Her life was a house of cards—with gaps. How much longer would it stand? Would *she?*

Yet her conviction that she had come to San Diego when she did *because* of that Bogs-character felt even stronger. She'd had some kind of plan... How strange it was to know something, without knowing *how* she knew it.

Whenever possible, a triathlete arrives at the location of a long race two or three weeks early, though Zoey's circumstances hadn't always permitted that luxury. Who was she kidding? She was usually lucky when a race director found a family to put her up for a couple of days. Now, with the resources available, it was only natural that she'd want to come early to acclimate to the area when she could. Yet Zoey sensed that only lent plausibility to a need that overrode it. What could be more important than her race?

Dale suddenly stopped and looked around, perplexed.

"What are you looking for?" Zoey asked.

He answered absently, "A CD store, but a DVD rental place would do."

"There was a good store near where we were. From here the closest music store is on University, around Vermont, I think."

Dale hesitated.

Zoey snapped, "Right at the corner and over several blocks."

"I knew that!" Dale snapped "I was just trying to decide whether it was worth going back for the car."

But they walked on to the distant store, with Zoey leading the way. Which of them was the visitor?

At the store, Dale approached a bored teenaged clerk, with a sparse auburn goatee, whose homemade T-shirt read, "The Will-Man Rules." Dale's request that he show Zoey a Willi Bogs DVD, giving him to understand that she'd never seen one, roused the boy from his indifferent lethargy to a state of guarded distrust. He popped a disk into a DVD player on display, but stood a little apart from her, shooting her nervous peripheral glances. Zoey couldn't have said what the kid did after that—because of the face that suddenly came to life on the screen.

If Willi Bogs' had drawn her even from the static state of the billboard, in motion, he captivated her completely. There was such a peaceful quality about him. Not religious, but spiritual. He wasn't a High Priest who compelled you to deliver your perfect soul to him, but merely a man who offered to share his flawed one with you.

His musical style wasn't Country or Rock or Blues or even Folk, and it was all of them. He was The Troubadour. His voice was strong, throaty, even cracking at times, but with underlying melodic resonance that rang pure and true. His only musical accompaniment was the picking of his own acoustical guitar; anything more would have intruded.

The lyrics were equally haunting:

As I journey along that narrowing path,
Pushing forward, my gaze always high,
As my mind and my body move slower
To where the mountain meets the sky,
I reflect on the travels behind me,
But I never need to ask why.

Zoey later learned the first song she heard was called *Willi's*

Song, though it could just as easily have been hers.

> *I have no regrets about living*
> *All my life according to me.*
> *Not accepting the ways of religion*
> *Or government or family.*
> *Never losing sight of my being,*
> *Never accepting conformity.*

Zoey loved the words. If she'd had the gift, this might have been the way she'd describe her own life.

> *I've made all my own decisions*
> *About what is right and what is wrong.*
> *I've learned to play my own music,*
> *To compose and sing my own song.*
> *'Cause it isn't that life is too short,*
> *It's that death is far too long.*

Yet that mesmerizing man still repelled her. How could anyone hate a stranger this way? And he must have been a stranger. Even on an unconscious level, she couldn't anticipate his gestures or expressions.

On the video, Willi Bogs went into the next song with no greater break than a simple utterance of its name, which she didn't catch. Once again, it was his personal story, and Everyone's. It spoke of a young girl who had freely given him gifts of joy, whom he must now repay with his life. The girl's name was—

Oh, God, Zoey thought with a gasp. Willi looked right at her. The instant he did, her breathing took on a ragged, gasping quality. Crazy. She knew he was just looking into the camera. Hell, Willi wasn't even there with them anymore. But she felt...

"Turn it off!" she shouted.

Sixteen

DALE INSISTED ON buying her lunch, though they drove to the restaurant in La Jolla in silence. Zoey was surprised that he didn't press her for the reason for her outburst, but grateful. She didn't know herself.

Since it was late for lunch, they had no trouble snagging a table on the terrace of a little French bistro with a great view of the La Jolla cove. Zoey always considered that gentle inlet, with its clear aqua water swirling among magnificent craggy rocks, one of the most beautiful spots on earth. But the sight of it also pricked her conscience. Local triathletes use that peaceful inlet to practice open water swimming. Something she'd intended to do, which, even with memory gaps, she knew she hadn't. What had she been doing instead?

Despite her guilty conscience, the rhythm of the gentle waves eased the tension the morning had injected into her tight shoulders. The humid air, carried on the ocean breezes, felt heavy against her skin. So different from the drier climate she was used to. Yet today she found the sensuous touch of the moist air against her arms comforting.

A muscle-bound waiter, with a white butcher's apron tied below a green Gold's Gym T-shirt, came to take their order. Dale limited himself to the chef's salad. But as Zoey had little since the breakfast shake she had made that morning, she asked for French onion soup, a chopped salad, and chicken-and-mushroom crepes. No one had ever accused her of being a cheap date, she thought with a suppressed smile.

While she dove into the basket of crusty bread the waiter left on the table, Dale still clutched the bag he'd acquired in the music store. Great to know that while her soul shattered into fragments, he used the time to grab a few CDs. He also had some photocopies the clerk had given him.

Dale had asked the boy whether they had any clippings, whatever that meant.

"Yeah, I think we got some around somewhere," the kid had said. "Nobody's needed any in a long time." He shot Zoey one of those looks of unspecified accusation. "Where's she from? Mars?"

"Something like that," Dale had cheerfully agreed.

Zoey asked about those copies now, while Dale placed his package on the patio floor. "Gonna share those with the Martian? What are they, anyway?" she demanded.

Dale explained that when Willi Bogs first leaped into prominence, the stores would copy newspaper articles and press releases to offer to customers of his CDs and DVDs. Now they weren't needed for anyone except freaks like her. Once Dale's salad and her soup arrived, he placed the stack in front of her.

While she stuck her spoon into the melted cheese on her soup, Zoey's eyes skimmed the copies. The uppermost sheet described the discovery of Willi's body, slumped over the wheel, at the bottom of a canyon in rural San Diego County. There was no suggestion of foul play. Only days before the accident, a mechanic had told Willi that his old wreck had been leaking power steering fluid, but apparently, he decided to delay the repair. It was his bad luck the steering went out at that point on a hairpin turn.

Without any awareness of having consumed most of her soup, Zoey found her spoon resting on the onions at the bottom of the brown crockery bowl. She piled a huge helping of the soft onions on a big hunk of bread. "According to this article he wasn't exactly skeletal," she said, before stuffing it into her mouth.

She read the grim description of the condition of the body aloud. Dale's fork hovered unused in his hand, as his skin grew pale. She saw for the first time that he had another scar, a tiny one over one eyebrow, which she only noticed because the pale tissue stood out from the greenish tinge his face had taken on. Big, tough cop. Though she'd heard some were awfully lily-livered, but too macho to admit it.

Still, she read silently after that. There really wasn't any doubt of the body's identity. Its DNA matched a sample Willi had left in Texas. The appendix had also been removed, as Willi's had, and his family dentist confirmed the jaw structure and the alignment of his cavity-free teeth to be his.

The waiter took her soup bowl away and brought her salad. "Who doesn't have cavities?" she muttered before diving into it.

"My two younger brothers, twins, never had any. On the other hand, I have a twelve-year-old sister whose mouth looks like a silver mine. But that girl's got a powerful sweet tooth."

Zoey stared across the table. "You have a twelve-year-old sister? How old are you? How old is your mother?"

"I'm thirty-two, and Mama, I hope, is old enough to be out of the baby-business now." He crossed his fingers and looked to the sky, with a flickering grin. "But in her day, my mama was a real fertile woman. She just couldn't pick a good man to save her life."

"So—what? She just kept marrying losers and having babies?"

In addition to the chopped greens, Zoey's salad contained bits of turkey and cheese and roasted pine nuts in a basil vinaigrette dressing. While Dale just seemed to pick at his lunch, Zoey made short work of her second course.

"Something like that," he muttered around a small bite. "Not exactly your ideal mother maybe, but she can't help it if she's just a silly woman. She's actually kinda fun." His blue eyes sparkled with affection and forgiveness.

"Where are you in the line-up?" Zoey munched on a bounty of pine nuts she found hidden among the greens.

"I'm the oldest of six. Four boys and two girls."

"Ah." This time, Zoey flashed the smirk.

"Ah?" Dale asked stiffly.

"Yeah, I got the picture now." She giggled to herself.

"Got what? How old are you? Thirty or so?"

"Excuse me—that's twenty-eight. But I know I look older."

Dale frowned. "It's not that you *look* it, so much, you just seem older somehow. I bet you were never a kid?"

She waved her fork at him. "We weren't talking about me, my boy. I have you figured out now. You're the one who plays nurse-maid to the rest of the brood. Probably your mother, too."

Dale confirmed it with a nod.

Zoey laughed and finished off her salad, handing the dish to a passing busboy. "All this time I thought you were a bad boy and here you're a mama's boy."

He laughed good-naturedly and stabbed a sliver of cheese in his largely uneaten salad. "I think a mama's boy would be enjoy-ing it more." The laughter went out of his eyes as quickly as the air from a punctured balloon. "I'm just a guy who can never seem to do near enough for any of 'em."

While buttering another piece of bread, she asked, "So where are they all now? Here?"

"No, mostly they're back home, in Texas," Dale said.

"That's something. Space is freedom."

"Think so?" Dale stared out over the ocean.

The unblinking intensity of his gaze made her believe that all the ocean's space wouldn't set him free. She sure understood that one. Even with all the thousands of miles she'd run, she had never managed to leave her demons in her dust.

Her entrée arrived, but though the rich cheese sauce covering the crepes smelled enticing, it was still too hot to eat. While wait-ing for it to cool, she read more of those clippings. One addressed Willi's music and even quoted some of his haunting lyrics.

"Who wrote these songs?" Zoey asked, her voice sounding sharp to her own ears.

Dale jerked at her voice, as if he'd forgotten about her. "Will, they say. Willi Bogs."

She didn't believe it. But how could she know? She tested her sauce with a fork. When she found it had cooled sufficiently, she ate in silence.

The waiter cleared their plates and offered them dessert. Though she'd had plenty to eat, Zoey had been eating too little at a time when she should have been taking in more. Losing a few pounds could give her an advantage in a short race, but it would sap her endurance at the length race she faced. They both chose glazed apple tarts from the tray the waiter held before them.

But while Dale actually began eating his, a sudden thought drew Zoey back to those copies. She flipped through the sheets of paper, trying to make sense of the dates.

"I must have misunderstood something, Dale. Wasn't Willi Bogs a star before his death?" she asked.

Dale shook his head and touched his lips with the white linen napkin he took from his lap. "Complete unknown. Became an instant sensation with the release of *Willi's Song,* especially when people learned he was missing. Then he shot into the stratosphere when the body was found."

Zoey absently picked at an apple slice with her fork. "Who's releasing the recordings?" She remembered the logo on the billboard, the curling *t* and *s*, and a connection slipped into place. "The Touchstone Foundation?"

Dale nodded. "Will recorded and filmed twelve songs and DVDs for Touchstone before he died. They've been releasing one a month. The last one's due shortly."

Why did that nobody think even a charitable institution would want his ditties? Zoey wondered. She put down her fork and just held her head in her hands. Her brain was beginning to feel like a bad bruise. Desperate for a distraction, she asked Dale about what he bought in the music store.

"I had a lil' idea, but I'm not sure you're up to it."

"How much worse could it get?" she muttered.

With a shrug, he leaned over the bag that rested next to his chair on the floor. She heard the paper rustling. He popped back up with his purchase plastered to his face.

Her screams must have been heard in China.

Seventeen

AS DOUG TOMASO muscled his way through the hairpin mountain turns, he beamed with satisfaction. *Lucky again, Dougie boy,* he
thought to himself. Once more, though, that name deflated his
mood. Considering all the different lives he'd taken on, all the
names he'd used, why was that still the way he thought of himself? The name he preferred was "Zoey's killer," treating it like an
accomplished fact. She might still be among the living, but he
never considered her anything but a dead woman.

Her amnesia proved to be a lucky break for him. He just about
shit a brick when he heard she was still alive. After what she'd
learned, every instant that bitch drew breath endangered him
more. He hadn't come this far to lose everything now. Now,
thanks to her amnesia, he'd won a little time.

And because of that reprieve, Tomaso decided to take a different approach, rather than just finishing her off. How quick would
she be to bounce back if he whittled away at that strength she took
such pride in? Eroding it, till she was just a shell. Besides, after the
trouble she put him through, shouldn't the cat have a little fun
with the mouse, before he devoured it?

He took the precaution of bringing in outside talent for his war
of nerves. He didn't want to run the risk of his style of attack trig-
gering a return of her memory. Besides, shouldn't he share the fun
of taunting her with others? Righteous bitch. She really made you
want to play with her head.

Fortunately, he had the inside track on a select group of San
Diego's best thugs-in-training eager to prove themselves. Some of
them were almost as creative as he was. Cutting her bike tire—

what an inspired idea. Sure, she probably only scraped her knees, but she could have broken her neck. She had to know that, too. Yeah, she must have been running scared now.

Some people were lucky. He always had been. If good things didn't happen to him outright, they never needed more than a little tweaking to make them fall his way.

Who knew? Maybe one of these protégés would even get it right. Wouldn't it be a hoot if someone else actually did the dirty deed for him?

Eighteen

A WILLI BOGS mask. That was what Dale had bought in the music store and stuck on his face at lunch, scaring the hell out of Zoey. Alone in the condo now, the ghoulish thing still gave her the creeps.

No wonder. Apparently, the witness she'd overheard when the paramedics put her into the ambulance swore Willi Bogs himself had driven the car that hit her, but others who came forward later said the driver had been wearing this mask. That didn't narrow things any. According to Dale, though Halloween was still a season away, Willi Bogs masks were as plentiful as "June bugs on a summer night." Whatever that meant.

Lying on her back on the couch, she held the mask out in front of her. That was the face from her awful dream, all right. It even felt the same. Had she actually seen the driver of the car that hit her? The Hillcrest area alternated one-way streets. Running up Fifth, she was moving *with* the traffic, not facing it.

The things you can bury in your mind no longer amazed her, knowing what she'd buried there once before.

Was that mask, and its awful association, the reason she didn't buy into Willi Bogs' sainthood? With another skimming of the clippings, she learned why he had been on the road where he met his death. He'd been living in Los Angeles, but stopped off in San Diego on the way to Houston, where a sister with leukemia waited for a bone marrow transplant. From a large family, in which only one child was reported dead, it seemed Willi was the only matching donor. No wonder they had specimens readily available to compare to the body. Donating bone marrow, pretty saintly.

His sister was said to be the girl in *Fair Exchange,* the second song he sang in the DVD, whose title Zoey only learned from the clippings. The song made it sound like an *un*fair exchange, like he was trading his life for hers. It was only bone marrow—he'd grow more. Now that Zoey understood, Willi seemed more of a loser to her than ever. What about the sister? Did she find another donor or had she run out of time?

Zoey wondered whether she might she have stumbled onto something really negative about Willi, before she lost her memory. And if she had been on a...what was it that Dale called it? A Willi-watch? She wasn't some nutcase who chased squirrelly urban legends to the ends of the earth. But Willi's name came to her in connection with that empty file folder in her portfolio.

Still clutching the mask, she looked to the small oak desk, where Cindy had left her leather portfolio. Zoey didn't put any stock in the misplaced card it held. Appearances to the contrary, order didn't come naturally to her. Her career demanded discipline, and she always took things over the top. Yet sometimes she just left things any old place.

A troubling thought crept into her mind. Might she have taken on the insane crusade of proving Willi Bogs had been a murder victim to show herself worthy of the award that Operation Innocence was planning to give her? How embarrassing.

Why was she making so much of it? A re-creation of Willi Bogs' face had been worn by the person who tried to kill her. Why wouldn't she hate it?

Reality had finally stripped away the last of Zoey's denial. Someone really was trying to kill her. *Kill her.* How was that possible? She could still only barely take it in. Who could hate her that much?

She flung the mask over her shoulder so it would fall on the floor somewhere out of her sight. Then Zoey grasped one of the tan throw pillows to her chest and rocked back-and-forth, back-and-forth, to soothe herself into oblivion. But the healing trance didn't come this time. Truth, that hideous devil, wouldn't let go of her. What hurt wasn't knowing that she was alone out there on the firing line. Her personal drummer had always played an uncommon beat. It was that for the first time, being alone didn't feel safer. She acknowledged to herself how lonely she felt, and maybe, she always had.

Zoey tossed the throw pillow aside and slipped off the couch, to the floor before the oak coffee table. She glanced at the cordless phone from the kitchen that Cindy had left there. The last thing she needed now was more truth, more pain. Still, her fingertips tapped out a number against the table that she knew by heart, even if she'd never actually dial it.

What would you say, Mommy, if you knew someone was trying to kill the child you carried for nine months under your heart?

Maybe her mother would even remember her for once, and maybe she'd care more than Zoey thought. But it wouldn't change anything.

And Daddy, we all knew how angry you would get when your needs weren't met. How could my life compare with that?

They brought her into this world for only one reason—to serve their needs, conflicted as they were—and she failed them both. That was her secret shame. One of them.

When Zoey felt a burning in her eyes, she pounded her fist against the tabletop. How could it still hurt so much? Pathetic. *No one likes a victim, Zoey. You take the cards you were dealt and keep your mouth shut.*

God, she longed to take a bath. All athletes bathe a lot, but not like her. She knew her skin was going to look like bad leather someday, but she couldn't help it. She never could. She was the only little kid she knew who rushed home from school to take a bath. And if she had to miss the one in the morning, she would feel filthy all day in school. Worst of all, she feared the other kids would find out. Somehow the silly habit felt like a secret shame she had to guard with her life.

She caught sight of the TV remote and felt another impulse

that drew her before she could name it. She pressed the button to start the disk that was still in the DVD player, the one Cindy had brought with the outtakes of their video.

As a snowball fight between Marty and her, somewhere on a Colorado ski trail, took shape on the screen, the sound of their laughter came alive in this room. She remembered that day so well, having pressed it like a treasured flower in her battered memory book. Tenderness tore at her heart. That day had begun badly. They were only shooting the part of the video that dealt with staying in shape in the off-season, in this case with skiing. But though she'd taped interviews and promotions before, this time the taping unnerved her. She felt so stiff and self-conscious, she couldn't do anything right. Until Marty began taking pratfalls off-camera to make her laugh. That snowball fight loosened her up enough to ski the way she did when there wasn't a camera watching.

When Marty's face filled the screen, Zoey hit the pause button. She crept along the floor until she knelt before the TV, so close she could have touched him, if he'd really been there. The still picture captured Marty at his most typical, laughing. He wasn't gorgeous like Dale. Good thing, too—she'd never trusted attractive men. His short, fair hair was thinning, and stuck out at odd spots on his head, which he was always smoothing down. His nose looked crooked enough to have been broken at some time without being properly set; his hazel eyes were too narrow. And forget about the build—his chest was nearly concave. But Marty had the greatest laugh. It just rolled out from somewhere within him and carried everyone else along with it. Even at his most somber, she always thought she saw a laugh hidden in Marty's eyes.

As if it had a mind of its own, her arm drifted toward the screen. Zoey pulled it back before it touched that cold, hard surface. Her throat hurt from warring emotions. The longing to have him there was great, but she knew if he were, she'd only push him away. Closeness stifled her in the best of times. She hoped he never sensed that. But that wasn't her only reason for not wanting him here.

She remembered that glorious day of taping had ended painfully, though not for them. An avalanche occurred elsewhere on the mountain that took two lives. Well, an avalanche was building here in San Diego, too. All sorts of unstable forces were being set in motion, which weren't any less dangerous than the snow that had buried those two people. Marty wouldn't want to be buried for eternity with her if her past came tumbling down on them. He wouldn't love her if he really knew her.

Footsteps overhead startled her back to the present. Lou and Dale, she'd guess. They went to talk to her friends in the sport to learn which of them wanted her dead. Though it was warm in the condo, goose pimples formed on Zoey's arms.

She snapped the TV off and raced to the bathroom. She turned the faucet above the tub on full blast, and stripped and climbed in as it filled. She had bought a new loofah— she'd rub herself raw.

Too bad all the things she wanted to wipe away were on the other side of her skin.

Nineteen

NEON DICKIE WEST lived up to his name, Dale thought, when he and Lou arrived at Dick West's Shortz SportzWatchez condo, on the floor above Zoey's. The source of his nickname, "Neon," wasn't hard to figure. Dickie's bushy head, dyed in bright streaks of red, blue, green, and really hot pink, looked like a variegated Bozo wig; the blonde tail that trailed down his back just added to the impression, like a stray clump escaping from the cap.

But Neon Dickie was not a clown. He was as big as a bull and twice as strong. You'd expect to find a kid that size playing college football, Dale thought. Maybe even pro ball—he must have been a little past college age now. Instead, he was lean and hard as a stone, in a sport that didn't attract the media spotlight he seemed to crave.

But maybe it wasn't so surprising at that. When Dale looked at Dickie's gray-gold eyes, the words "wolf eyes" sprang to mind. It was just the shading that gave that impression, but it made Dale think that, despite the sprinkling of freckles across the nose of his square all-American face, Dickie had found his rightful place among people who didn't favor teams.

Seated across from each other on a pair of sofas, matches for the navy-and-tan one in Zoey's unit, Dickie cracked his thick knuckles and waited for Lou to finish his explanation of why they had come. Dickie hadn't stopped fidgeting since they were seated. Was his body simply an inadequate container for the power it generated, or was he nervous?

Lou reached over an empty Doritos bag for the can of Coke Dickie had placed before him on the wide oak coffee table, which was covered with fast food containers. Before taking a sip, Lou said, "You don't seem too surprised."

Dickie continued to crack his heavy knuckles. "I'm not," he said, without expression.

Eyeing him over the top of the soda can, Lou asked, "Because you expected something like this to happen to Zoey?"

"No, because Cindy Orr has a big mouth. Everyone in triathlon knows that Zoey's having some trouble. Maybe you ought to talk to Cindy. She probably knows more about it than you."

Dickie suppressed a snicker, but those wolf eyes gleamed with triumph. Score one for the big dumb kid, Dale thought. Maybe not so dumb at that.

Lou's unemotional face looked unfazed. "Zoey isn't just having some trouble—someone is trying to kill her."

Dickie's skin became so pale, his freckles seemed to jump out from it. "Sure?"

Lou nodded with more certainty than Dale knew he felt. "You don't seem to care too much. If it was me, and I heard—"

Dickie exploded, stabbing in the air before Lou with his large index finger. "Now you don't know that! You wanna see how much I care? You find the guy that's doing this, and give him to me. I'll do to him what you can't."

"I'll remember that," Lou promised without making any commitment.

Assuaged, Dickie nodded. He grabbed a quart bottle of some orange sports drink from the table and took a swig from the mouth of the bottle. He gave his lips a swift wipe with the back of his hand.

Lou glanced around. "Great setup you got here. It's bigger than Zoey's place."

It was a two-story unit, but they couldn't see enough to judge its decor. Discarded workout clothes and an incredible collection of beer cans and junk food wrappers covered every available surface. Like a dorm room, Dale thought. Dickie hadn't developed the discipline Zoey brought to her life.

"Is Marty your agent, too?" Lou asked.

"He offered, but—" Bluster burst from Dickie again with, "I don't need anyone's help. The sponsors, they come to me. Everyone wants Neon Dickie." After a pause, he added grudgingly, "But Marty's doing okay for Zoey. At least he's getting her to listen to reason."

Lou raised his dark eyebrows. "Yeah? How so?"

Dickie looked down at the one spot on the coffee table not covered with debris, but by the current issue of *Triathlon* magazine with Zoey's cover photo. Watching his face, Dale understood why Dickie might not want Marty managing his career.

Dickie gestured to the magazine with his big hands. "Well, like this. You know how it works? Guys get covers because they win important races. Girls…uh…women get 'em for being pretty or built." His gray-gold eyes ricocheted between Lou and Dale. "Hey, I didn't make the rules. Zoey always said she'd never take it on those terms. But there she is, actually wearing a little makeup and smiling like she likes it, skin glistening with that stuff they spray that looks like sweat." He sighed deeply. "What's the difference between looking sexy and this?" He gestured to his head. "You use whatever it takes to get to the head of the class."

From the arm of the sofa he sat, Dale asked, "Does that include drugs?"

The wolf eyes narrowed, though Dickie's manner became that of a lap dog. "I'm kinda naïve when it comes to drugs. I'd like to think no one in the sport uses them, but Zoey says they do. She knows more about that stuff than I do."

Lou leaned over the table and said quietly, as if it were a secret, "And she names names."

"Yeah," Dickie admitted.

Lou shook his head. "Not smart."

Stabbing the air again, Dickie insisted, "Zoey's got more courage than ten guys rolled together. She says what she thinks, and I respect that."

Lou said, "But not everyone does. Sometimes even friends—"

Dickie held out his hands to stop him. "Look, you oughta understand something. Zoey doesn't have any friends. Not really."

"Because she says unpopular things?" Lou asked.

"Nah, because she just don't allow it. Look, there are people Zoey likes and people who like her, some even—" Dick hesitated, then rushed on. "But it's like there's always a piece missing from the puzzle that would finish the friendship, you know? Well, Zoey holds that piece and won't put it in."

"What about Marty?" Dale asked.

Dickie cracked his knuckles three times in succession before speaking. "Marty looks like he's got it all, but...well, I'd bet Zoey's hiding it from him, too."

Not dumb at all, Dale thought.

Zoey's bath wasn't working its usual magic. Probably because she couldn't wrestle her focus away from the action upstairs. If she'd gauged the sound of footsteps right, they'd left Dickie's place and were with Alicia now. Did they believe her? Most people did. Even those who doubted her usually considered Zoey's remarks sour grapes. Not true at all, though she had to admit no one raised her ire like Alicia Salaz.

Somehow, Zoey never seemed to be in step with everyone else. But what could she do? She cared about what happened to her sport.

Zoey hadn't started out as a jock. Sometimes it seemed to her as if everyone's lives were determined by how they were categorized on the first day of school. In that regimented world, she was classified as one of the smart ones, and that should have ruled out athletics. But she broke their damn mold.

While in middle school, she saw a sign calling for track team tryouts. Zoey still couldn't say why she showed up. She had never even liked PE, though only because she hated changing in front of others in the locker room. She didn't even remember deciding to go, she just found herself in the field.

But that was the story of her life. Every time she felt herself pulled down a path that made no sense for her, it proved to be the right one. Whenever she made a choice after deliberation, she was always sorry. So much for the power of intellect.

Zoey didn't know what happened to her that day. Maybe all the rage she kept bottled up inside ignited into a fire that propelled her across the field. The coach's eyes glowed when she looked at Zoey after that, and Zoey felt differently about herself. She found a pride and confidence on that field that she never felt in the classroom, for all her accomplishments.

Her father wouldn't hear of her joining the team. He didn't want "his little girl" developing muscles. She forged his name to the parental consent form. He left later that year, and she'd always liked to think her choice played some small role in his departure. Her mother still carried her outrage, even into that private mental hell she now inhabited.

Zoey didn't care. She found a place where whims couldn't rule, where they didn't keep shifting the finish line, the way the academic world did. In sports, there were no essay questions. Zoey threw an angry glance at the bathroom ceiling. Though lately, they were beginning to see crib sheets.

If Zoey was right about Alicia Salaz, if Ali would go to those lengths to create a false standing in the sport—how far would she go to protect it?

The comfort Zoey usually derived from a long soak suddenly abandoned her, leaving her feeling like a sitting duck.

She *had* to get out of there.

While Dale knew he'd never be able to think of Dick West as anything other than Neon Dickie, he had a harder time associating Alicia Daniels with the name Salaz. She looked too much the definitive WASP to fit the Latino name.

She was a big, rawboned woman, who had reduced her body's fat to the lowest possible level while still sustaining life. Though she lacked Zoey's natural beauty and Cindy's glamour, she had something that more than made up for them, which lent her a style all her own. A presence that commanded attention. Though maybe, Dale thought, it was merely the bred-in awareness that she would never finish out-of-the-money.

She didn't look like one of the women on the society pages. Even if the muscles stretched over her thoroughbred bones weren't too hard for that, the expression in her cool blue eyes was too direct. But Dale would bet she'd developed her taste for competition at the horse shows the nobility favors for its young.

Her background thoroughly infused her. Dale had already watched her manner flicker from imperious disdain to regal charm as if on a switch. She seemed like a woman who was used to getting her way, one way or the other.

Rick Salaz's charm was more effusive, but then the road he'd followed hadn't been nearly as well paved. With his warm brown liquid eyes, flashing dimples and rugged jaw, he was better looking than his wife. But they seemed a good match. The few rough edges Rick retained balanced Ali's overly-polished ones.

Dale didn't consider their marriage a dynastic arrangement, as Zoey implied. They communicated too well with looks and gestures, and he thought he saw love in some of those looks, or at the very least, lust.

They obviously worked as a team. Rick had graduated at the top of his class at Stanford Law School. He must have had his pick of offers. Yet in deciding to manage Ali's career, he hitched his cart to his wife's star. The only surprise was that those two high flyers had chosen to bury themselves in a relatively small sport. But maybe not so surprising at that. With his drive and her ability, they were destined to stand out. And Dale guessed neither of them had ever been comfortable with second place.

"Muy triste," Rick said in response to Lou's explanation why they were there, shaking his head with philosophical resignation. Very sad.

Real smooth, Dale thought. Using the background they shared

to bond with Lou. Lou went along, as he always did, Dale noticed. Whatever it took to loosen them up. Lou never had any illusions that it meant anything, and from the look of him, neither did Rick. A game.

Their condo was a two-story one like Dickie's, with furnishings that also matched the other two. But their temporary home was even neater than Zoey's. And it had been personalized with framed photos of Alicia's triumphs, which rested on every table.

Rick absently reached out to the oak end table at his side and adjusted the placement a photo displayed in a plastic cube. "I tell you, Luis, Zoey's really out of control. It doesn't surprise me that someone is striking out at her, however inappropriately."

The marble facing on this unit's fireplace was a paler brown than Zoey's, but was otherwise the same. Lou stood before it, and as he spoke, traced the grout line with his finger. "Not you, is it, *amigo?*"

The quick look that passed between the couple triggered a round of laughter.

"Hardly. Our car insurance is high enough without running people down in the street." Rick beamed indulgently at his wife. "Alicia doesn't limit her speeding to races."

"You've heard what she says about your wife?" Lou asked.

With a shrug, Rick said, "Of course. Triathlon is a small sport. I'll admit it, I've considered taking legal action against Zoey. She's too free with her mouth. But Marty assured me he would reason with her. Maybe she's beyond reason now."

From where he sat on the sofa next to Rick, Dale asked, "You gonna sue her?"

Rick shook his head. "Alicia won't let me. She's too kindhearted for her own good."

Dale thought "kindhearted" wouldn't have been a description of Alicia Salaz that leaped to his mind, but he didn't really know her.

From the couch opposite the one her husband and Dale occupied, Alicia shrugged. "Her talk is just the rabble of the second-rater. Zoey is a tremendous athlete, but there's something missing from her that I have in abundance."

Dale believed that. He didn't imagine there were many of Zoey's obvious pockets of insecurities in either Ali or Rick.

Rick wandered over to the window and slouched against the frame. "Ali's too generous. Just because she worked her ass off during the off-season and is now benefiting from that training is no reason why she should be subjected to accusations. I'm not as forgiving. I won't lie to you, I think it would be a hoot if something happened to Zoey." Rick suddenly looked at the gold Rolex wrapped around his wrist. "Jeez, I forgot the time, and I have an appointment in Encinitas. Luis, can I walk you and Dale out?"

They had no excuse to stay. Rick took Lou's arm and led him toward the door. Dale hung back long enough to swing by the window Rick had been standing before. It looked out on the complex's parking lot. With Lou and Rick engaged in a conversation at the door, Dale wandered back to the sofa where Alicia had remained. She interested him more for the anger she seemed to bring out in Zoey, than for herself. He felt certain Zoey was wrong about the source of Alicia's success.

But he didn't say that. "Alicia, just between you and me, is Zoey right about you?" he asked softly. "Have you been getting a little help with your training?"

Ali stood and looked down her aristocratic nose at him, amused and distant. He thought she had every right to be angry with his suggestion. But when she spoke, she really shocked the peasant with her answer.

She asked him, "What are you, some kind of boy scout?"

Twenty

OUT IN THE condo complex parking lot, when Zoey opened the door of the loaner silver minivan she'd been using during her time in San Diego, the appealing scent of new car smell tickled her nostrils. A car dealership sponsor had provided some of the athletes with brand new vans, which had been outfitted to meet their equipment needs. She settled herself now behind the wheel, cranked the engine, and just took off.

Drifting through streets, it was as if the van had a mind of its own. Why shouldn't it? It was nothing to her, stupid loaner. A minivan, for chrissakes, as boring as Dale's car. She missed her rugged green Jeep Wrangler. She missed her home. Let's face it, she missed the time when she didn't feel like a target.

Maybe it was crazy to leave the safety of the condo, but that place was making her stir-crazy. She had to get away from it, if only for a while. Zoey did check the rearview mirror occasionally, but she discovered it wasn't as easy to tell if someone was following you as on TV. Lots of cars travel long distances together. Were they all threats? She played tag for a while with a little guy on a motorcycle who never once tried to kill her.

At least her tin cocoon provided distraction by parading her through some fascinating neighborhoods. She grabbed a few burgers from a fast food joint in a shopping center where every sign was written in Vietnamese. Zoey discovered you ain't lived till you experience a Big Mac-type concoction in which the special sauce is closer to sweet-and-sour.

There was a lot she didn't like about California, but she loved its diversity, even if it had caused tensions between the old-timers and newcomers. Change is always hard, but she thought the texture all those cultures added was worth it. Of course, she and her fellow Colorado residents resented theirs new immigrants just as much, but most of theirs were Californians. Zoey was nothing if not inconsistent.

Periodically, she noticed guys selling some kind of map at the side of the road. If this had been LA, she would have figured those were maps to the stars' homes. What was the equivalent in San Diego? When she slowed while passing one seller, she saw they offered directions to something called *His Last Days*. A religious tract? Then she got it: they were maps to the places Willi Bogs traveled during his final days in San Diego.

On impulse, she pulled over before the next map seller. For ten bucks, a bored guy in a yellow *guyabera* shirt handed her a grayish sheet of paper produced by a copier desperately in need of cleaning. At the top of the sheet was a map of San Diego, which had been reduced so small, it was hard to read. Heavy black dots, larger than the areas they marked, had been drawn on the map with a felt-tip marker. Listed below it were the makings of your very own Willi-watch. According to this list, Willi had made no stops other than at churches and homeless shelters.

What a crock. Zoey crumbled that expensive sheet of paper and threw it to the ground. As she climbed back in the minivan, she saw the guy pick it up and smooth the sheet out for resale.

Was she the only one who considered it a little creepy to deify a ghost? She gave her head a toss. *Better watch it, Zoey. First stop on the train to Paranoia is believing you're the only who knows the truth.*

But she was so sick of thinking about Willi Bogs. Willi Bogs and Dale Terry and everyone else who had come to inhabit the gaps in her life. Tired of not remembering, of never knowing which of the people who'd entered her life she could trust. Zoey shook the sheering wheel in frustration. She'd left the condo to vanish for a while, yet the questions *still* haunted her. Her foot came down harder on the accelerator.

A steady procession of small planes kept buzzing overhead.

She made a game of finding their landing place. And though she wound up in a couple of dead-ends during her first tries, it didn't take long to arrive at the entrance to a place called Montgomery Field.

Zoey had no idea that San Diego had any airport other than Lindbergh Field, its commercial airport. But Montgomery appeared to be strictly for the small private jobs. It was a big facility, though. They ought to switch them, she thought; landing in downtown San Diego was like an emotional toll visitors paid. Hairy! But it was safer than running through the streets. The funniest thought occurred to her: if Willi Bogs had flown to Houston instead of driving, would he still have become a star? So cynical.

She found a parking place just a grassy field away from the runway and stopped to watch. For the first time, she understood why people must learn to fly. She would never do it, mind you. As if she could afford it. But camped at the end of the runway, she longed for the freedom the people in those planes must feel. Imagine being able to fly off anywhere and never look back.

It wasn't that she didn't love her life, but even if someone weren't hunting her, the pressure would still have been intense because of the career choices she'd made.

There are basically four triathlon lengths, from the very shortest, called sprints, to the mid-sized international length, to the longer half and full Ironman events. Until now, she'd specialized in the shorter distances, though she'd never intended to stay at that length. Like everyone in the sport, she envisioned herself with the tape across her chest at Kona's Ironman. The shorter length was simply a natural progression from her track background.

Only something happened along the way. She found she was really good at short events. Maybe capable of being the best. And she loved speed so much, she craved it like a drug.

There were also other advantages to specializing in the shorter events. Sure, they were more popular with athletes, so the competition was stiffer—but since shorter events were easier on the body, she could race more of them. Nothing feeds the ego, or the purse, like regular wins.

But with the crowded sporting field in the US, triathlon hadn't captured a big following, and the shorter events were the least popular with the public. Naturally, sponsorship dollars followed public interest.

"Face it, Zoey," Marty once said. "You say 'triathlon' to John Q. Public and he thinks the Ironman. He might not even realize there are other Ironman-length events all over the world. Hawaii is it to him. If you want to make this your career, babe, you have to give some thought to longer events."

It required more than mere thought, it required tough choices. Sure, it's possible to *race* at every length, but not to simultaneously *train* for both speed and endurance. Endurance training has to dominate, but endurance workouts kill speed.

The longer events also take more out of the athlete's body. Preparation time is longer, as is recovery, which means the athlete can't schedule as many races. More eggs in fewer baskets. Zoey had always been fearless in her life's choices. Why else would she have chosen a sport that prided itself on having no limits? But she'd never before had anything to lose.

Marty didn't seem to feel like it'd be much of a loss. "How long do you want to scrape for every dime, Zoey?" he'd asked. "Working part-time, scrounging for coaching work, financing your career on your credit card?"

That was the way it had gone for a long time. She'd charge a couple of airline tickets to events at the start of the season. If she placed high enough in those races, she'd win enough to pay off those charges and have a little extra for luxuries like basic living. If she didn't, she had to work full-time in the off-season to pay the charges off.

"Think about our future, Zoey," Marty had said.

She did think about it. That was why she socked away every cent she could save from the living allowance he gave her and hid that money in a secret savings account. She would surprise him with it when she had enough. But as long as she could stay afloat, money had never meant that much to her. She'd seen what too much could do to people.

Then Marty played his trump card, without even knowing it. "If you were in the sport for fame, Zoey, there wouldn't be any question in your mind. The only household names in triathlon are the athletes who win in Hawaii. But I know that doesn't matter to you, honey."

He didn't know her at all. To look at her, no one would guess how much she lived for the roar of the crowd that greeted her when she finish a race, small as it was. But God help her, she craved that recognition. So she made the choice to enter longer races, which she might have made anyway, someday, for better reasons.

Her income rose quickly. Zoey wouldn't deny that it made life easier. But maybe that would have happened anyway. Marty underestimated his powers of persuasion; the man could sell snow cones on a glacier.

Some part of her questioned the wisdom of chasing applause. Wasn't that just another way of shifting that finishing line, as they did in school? But there were holes within her, and somehow, she had to find a way to fill them.

Would she ever? Maybe, if she lived that long.

Twenty-one

AFTER LEAVING THE Salaz condo, Dale and Lou approached Lou's metallic blue Taurus, parked at the curb.

With a nod back toward the complex, Dale asked, "What do you think, Penny?"

"That there was enough ambition in that room to put a bum in the White House. A *real* bum. If the Rick and Alicia Salaz wanted to turn Zoey's life on its ear, they could do it without losing any sleep."

Dale agreed with a slow nod. "But wouldn't they do it better? I smelled a lot of efficiency in there, too."

Lou shrugged. "Maybe they're only looking to wage a war of nerves."

When Rick Salaz's maroon minivan, a match for Zoey's apart from color, sailed past them on the street, he tossed off a friendly wave. They returned the same.

"He sure left in a hurry," Lou said, watching the van. "Did something out that window catch his eye?"

Dale ran his fingers through his shiny blue-black hair. "Well, now, I don't know. A train, 'bout ten cars, a hog, and a garbage truck caught mine. Which one do you figure's important?" He absently kicked at the grass along the curb with his scuffed black boot. "Pen, what if we're wrong about this? It could be as simple as Zoey suggested. That maybe they want her out of the picture because of what she says about Alicia. You could even build a case against Dickie West."

Lou pulled the remote from his pocket and clicked it to unlock the car's doors. "How so? The fool's besotted by her."

"There's a lot of ambition in him, too. How much would he care for her if she learned that brute force of his wasn't natural and threatened to turn him in? They might have had a real blowout, only she can't remember it now."

"If you believe that amnesia crap."

Dale looked to the ground he kept kicking. "Yeah, if you do. But, Lou, it really could be that simple. The intrigue we imagine might not have anything to do with it."

Lou went around to the driver's door. "Is that what you been doing with your computer, Dale Evans—imagining things? Sure, the attacks on Zoey could be coming from the obvious parts of her life. And we're checking them out, if only to eliminate them. But you and I know how much she keeps hidden. And I'm betting *that's* where we'll find our answers."

"So have we eliminated anything?"

Lou shook his head. "Not yet. What do you say we go see Pat O'Hara and muddy the waters some more?"

They went together in Lou's car. Lou suggested to Dale that he pop in on Zoey when he came back for his car.

Dale stared out the window. "It doesn't have to be that contrived, you know. She doesn't seem to mind having me around."

With a cynical snort, Lou said, "If someone wanted me dead, I might not mind having the cavalry around, either, even if it meant curtailing some activities. When she tries to ditch you—that's when it'll get interesting."

They drove in silence, but Dale couldn't let it go. "There's one thing I just don't get, Penny. Why is Zoey so hung up on this steroid business? I mean, if she really was as honest as she appears...well, sure, then I'd understand it. But knowing what we know, I don't get it."

"Maybe she doesn't like when *other* people cheat." Lou glanced at Dale in the passenger seat. "You ever seen her race?"

While Dale admitted he hadn't, Lou hopped on the 5 Freeway, which he took to the 163. "A powerful competitor. I saw her in one race where she took a terrible spill from her bike. Some young buck was trying to pass her, and he just crashed right into her. You know how some of these age-group guys are, thinking they're better than the female pros."

Even driving through the restful setting of Balboa Park, ever the cop, Lou's eyes watched the traffic around them.

"What a mess—a tangle of legs and arms and bike parts sliding down the pavement. You should have seen her, *amigo*. Blood from her ankle to her hip. Worse than she looked after being hit by a car. Her derailleur got bent, and she was stuck in a high gear with the steepest part of the course ahead of her. She just jumped on that sucker and peddled with everything in her, and it must have taken everything. Tough course. She'd been in the lead at the time of the crash, but at least a half dozen women passed her while she was down."

Caught up in the story, Dale unconsciously reached into his pocket for a toothpick, which he slipped between his lips. "Most of the pros would have quit, figuring they should save it for another day."

Lou took an exit near Hotel Circle. "Not Zoey. She overtook two of the women on that decrepit bike, but she really poured it on during the run. Man, she was like a giant wound, but she kept running."

"Did she win?"

While navigating surface streets, Lou shook his head. "Not quite. But she was no more than ten seconds behind the leader. I've never seen anyone come from behind like that. The crowd went nuts. I don't think anyone even noticed who won. Ali Salaz should be looking over her shoulder. On her worst day, Zoey's got more heart than Ali will ever have." Lou sighed. "I tell you, *amigo*, if I'd had any illusions left, the things you've told me about that girl would have shattered them."

They found Pat O'Hara, suspended triathlete, hawking Volvos in a dealership along a sprawling auto row near Hotel Circle, all of which shared the same ownership. He was a shaggy, sun-bleached blonde, whose thirties were now just a memory.

All smiles, he rushed to greet Lou and Dale before they'd even taken a few steps onto the lot. "Hey, guys. Which of these babies do you want to make yours? We're dealing."

Since they weren't that close to any of the "babies," the pitch was overeager to say the least. Dale hadn't known how right he'd been when he told Zoey that O'Hara was a desperate man.

Lou flashed his shield.

O'Hara's bonhomie evaporated. "What do you want?"

"To talk about the attacks on Zoey Morgan."

O'Hara's thick features reddened, but he showed no surprise. "Attacks, huh? Couldn't happen to a better bitch. Tell me someone succeeded."

O'Hara must have remembered he was supposed to present a friendlier face at the dealership. He tossed a nervous glance over his shoulder and suggested they talk in his cubicle. He led them to a tiny three-sided cube, lined in a knobby gray tweed fabric. Two guest chairs in a darker gray faced a small white Lucite desk. The desktop was empty apart from a few files and the latest issue of *Triathlon*.

Zoey's cover was really making the rounds, Dale noticed. Only O'Hara hadn't treated his copy as reverently as Dickie West. Dale felt himself cringing at the sight of the broom handle that O'Hara had drawn on it, which appeared to be shoved up Zoey's vagina, and the doodled knife stuck in her heart.

Once the oversized O'Hara took his chair behind the desk, the space felt too small for the three of them. Though O'Hara's face was red and blotchy, with sweat beading on his upper lip, Dale presumed it to be more from anger than fear. He didn't claim to have an alibi for the time she was hit, and even admitted to having seen Zoey's bike in a store.

"I tell ya, I'm your best suspect," O'Hara conceded. "Nobody could want her out of the way more than me. But I didn't do it. She already wrecked my life enough. Why should I go to jail for her? Righteous bitch."

"She wrecked your life?" Lou asked. "How did she do that? Didn't you test positive for—"

"Lies!" O'Hara exploded. "That test was rigged. I'm challenging it, too. As soon as I can find a shyster with some balls."

Dale didn't think the test had been wrong. They'd scarcely recognized O'Hara. No longer the lean, mean fighting machine of tri-zine fame, he was now the anabolic poster boy. His strong, lean thighs had become tree trunks. And in his sleeveless T-shirt, they could see acne pitting his shoulders, a classic sign of steroid abuse. Dale couldn't imagine why a triathlete would use steroids—the added weight was a burden—though he heard they aided recovery time. It looked like O'Hara simply hadn't known when to quit.

O'Hara stared at Zoey's picture with more malice than Dale ever remembered feeling for anyone. "To think someone who looks like her—could *be* someone like her."

Amen, Dale thought. Not only was she a beautiful woman, she looked like such an honest one.

A sound escaped from O'Hara; it might have been a sob.

"They're ruining the sport. These stupid little chippies with their business managers and custom-made bikes." O'Hara looked up, his murky eyes appealing to Lou. "You know what it was like for us in the glory days?"

Lou shook his head.

O'Hara clasped his hands and shook the resulting mass in front of their faces. "Man, we were one. We'd fly into a place for a race, you know, and we'd be together all the time. Training together, hanging out. All of us pros. Then after the race, we'd party all night till it was time to go." He sighed. "But then they turned it into a business. It's just not the same anymore."

"Nothing ever is," Lou said softly.

O'Hara might not have heard him. He went back to staring at Zoey's picture. "Did you ever notice there are people who travel such a smooth road through life they don't notice how bumpy it is for the rest of us? How can you help but hate them?"

Lou looked at the showroom. "How do they treat you here?"

O'Hara's head popped up, startled. "At the dealership? Great. I mean, if this was what I wanted, I couldn't imagine a better place. They haven't even tried to turn me into a suit."

In San Diego's relaxed climate, casual clothes on their salesmen might be just good business, Dale thought. Though since the dealership offered so many makes of cars, he thought they might have found a better fit for O'Hara than selling conservative family cars.

"And the perks are awesome," O'Hara went on. "They gave me a loaner car on my first day, even pay for my gas."

Lou slowly removed a notebook from his jacket pocket. "So I guess that means your old car is—where? At home?"

"My...?" O'Hara's eyes flickered away.

"Your Mercedes."

"Mercedes? You're confusing me with someone in a whole other tax bracket," O'Hara insisted with hearty bluster.

Lou flipped through the pages of his notebook. "Didn't you win a Mercedes sports car in a race in Germany about ten years ago?"

O'Hara abruptly pushed him chair away from the desk, to the extent the small cubicle allowed. "That car's long gone. Sold it once when I ran a little short."

"Funny, the DMV has no record of it being sold," Lou said.

"Look again. It's there," O'Hara said.

"I will." Lou made a note in the notebook. "By the way, refresh my memory. What was the color again? White, wasn't it?"

O'Hara hesitated. "I don't remember."

The sound of laughter erupted from a nearby executive office. A tall slender man emerged, shouting farewells. Though the carefree expression on his well-tanned face was conveyed through decades of lines, his walk was a loping, boyish gait. Dale, who sat next to the cubicle's opening, watched him.

"That's—that's Bucky Jack," Dale sputtered.

O'Hara leaned around to look. "Sure is. He's a good friend of this dealership. The family that owns it has been a Touchstone Foundation sponsor for years."

"No can do," Bucky shouted in response to some unheard request. "Got to get my machine tuned-up."

"If they're such good friends, why doesn't he just have his tune-up done here?" Lou asked.

O'Hara giggled. "Don't think we service that model."

Lou and Dale exchanged a look in search of the joke. Dale finally realized that Bucky must have been talking about his plane, not a car.

"Bucky's a good man," O'Hara insisted. "He's the one who got this job for me. He asked the boss to take me on when I got the shaft in triathlon."

"Do you know him that well?" Dale asked.

"Don't know him at all. Rick Salaz asked him for me." O'Hara laughed. "Rick said Zoey Morgan's enemies had to stick together."

Twenty-two

ZOEY SAT AT the end of the runway, letting the steady hum of the takeoffs and landings mesmerize her. Until a car screeched to a halt behind hers, blocking her only escape. Her heart lurched. Only then she recognized the driver. Despite the toll that jolt of adrenaline took from her, she couldn't stop smiling. Bucky Jack's engaging grin, when he stepped from the car behind her, reflected the one she felt forming on her own face.

She'd never understood how Woodrow Byron Johnston became known as Bucky Jack, but like everyone else, she could never think of him any other way. Born to Wyoming ranchers, while Bucky looked the quintessential cowboy, with his steely sapphire eyes set in a leathery line-etched face, his rightful place had never been the back of a horse, but the cockpit of a plane. The aging fly-boy had to be sixty-something now, but the most fearless test pilot in the history of aviation and NASA's most irreverent maverick, was eternally young in spirit.

Bucky could have exploited his moonwalk for personal gain, as so many of them did. Instead, he formed the Touchstone Foundation, which built homes for troubled boys from coast-to-coast, and beat corporations senseless for contributions. Along the way, someone sued because girls were excluded.

"Well, shoot, Your Honor," Bucky had said to the judge. "We never meant to keep 'em out. What's an old bachelor like Bucky know about little girls? But I reckon they need the Touchstone Houses as much as the little guys do, so we'll make them welcome."

Zoey supposed the Touchstone Houses did have places for

girls now, but she didn't know for sure. Either way, Bucky must have had a lot more kids to care for these days, since he'd really been turning up the heat on the fundraising. Too bad so many of the kids turned out twisted, but Touchstone got them too late. Survival is a fragile thing and always temporary. Zoey had first-hand knowledge of that.

Bucky came around to the front his car. "Zoey Morgan, you come here and give me a big wet one," he shouted and spread his arms wide.

Bucky was also an outrageous flirt. Zoey so hated predatory men, that she generally felt an irresistible urge to flatten guys who said things like that. But somehow, she never took Bucky's remarks seriously.

Zoey joined him next to his convertible, where she clasped his hands and held them at arms-length. Bucky might be harmless, but she wasn't letting anyone get away with what he tried.

"Girl, do you have to work at looking so fine, or is this how you look first thing in the morning?" he shouted.

"Bucky, you'll die wondering," Zoey promised.

He threw his head back and laughed richly. "Honey, your honesty just kills me. You tell your Marty he's a lucky guy."

A man, wiping his hands on an oily rag, emerged from a corrugated metal hanger nearby, and gestured for Bucky to join him. Bucky held up one finger to Zoey as a shorthand statement that he'd be back in a second and jogged over to the guy.

She leaned against Bucky's car, but moved away when she noticed how dusty it was. The battered old LeBaron, with its dents and oxidized brown paint, had seen better days. For all his efforts, Bucky didn't take much for himself. Though it probably belonged to the Foundation, which had better uses for its money. Come to think of it, she wasn't even sure where Bucky was based. Somewhere back East—Pennsylvania, maybe, or Delaware. Or maybe he floated among the Touchstone Houses using whatever cars and rooms happened to be available.

She noticed a worn leather case in the backseat, like a passport wallet only many times its size. She loved the feel of old leather. While she wouldn't normally reach into someone's car to examine his possessions, it didn't seem as intrusive with a convertible. The case had multiple compartments with transparent pockets for sections of maps or charts or something. She wasn't sure what land masses they represented.

Bucky dashed back to the car so fast, he was a shade breathless when he arrived. "Zoey, got a few minutes to grab a beer with the old Buck?"

Was he kidding? That airport had given her the first peace she'd known since she came to that damn town. She might never leave.

Bucky suggested a restaurant in the little strip mall at the entrance to Montgomery Field. Though it was only a minuscule block away, he had already snagged a table and a brew before she arrived. Bucky's beer consumption was as legendary as his heroism, but he never seemed the worse for it. Well, except for that map of fine red lines scoring his wrinkled cheeks. His hands were as steady as granite. She signaled the waitress and asked for a Coke and a club sandwich with a double helping of fries.

After a big pull of beer, Bucky brought the frosty mug down hard on the scarred green Formica tabletop. "So, Zoey, how's San Diego been treating you?"

With a shake of her head, she admitted, "Not so great." She told him some of what had been happening.

"Hooey! Run down by a car. How are you now?"

"It takes more than getting personal with a street to get to me." Truth was, the worst of the aches were little more than muscle memories now. She would be back on her original training plan sooner than she thought. She healed fast. Outside.

"Well, they wouldn't have released you from the hospital if you weren't okay."

The less said about that, the better.

Bucky took another big drink, then held up his nearly empty mug to indicate to the waitress that he wanted another. "And you don't remember any of it?"

A plump waitress straining the seams of her worn jeans deposited Zoey's plate before her and brought Bucky another beer. Zoey tore a big bite from the sandwich. While she chewed, she shook her head to show how little memory she had.

Bucky took a drink and wiped his foam mustache with the back of his hand. "The police must know something."

"Truthfully, Bucky, the detectives on it don't seem to know anything." It occurred to her that Dale probably wasn't assigned to the case if he was on disability. So why was he always sticking his nose into what didn't concern him if he wanted to scam some time off? "What can they do? They weren't there."

Bucky took another deep pull of beer. "But not to remember something that frightening. You must feel so lost."

Zoey tossed off an indifferent shrug. "Actually, it's pretty peaceful." He was just being nice. Why should she burden him with how terrifying it felt to live in blinders? "What's weird is that I also can't remember some things from before."

"Zoey, did it ever occur to you that maybe you're just slipping into Old-Timers Disease a little early? Seriously, girl, what can't you remember?"

She took a sip of Coke. "This guy, Willi Bogs, who recorded those songs for you—I can't remember ever having heard of him."

Bucky guffawed and slapped the tabletop. "I can't believe that. Why, when I saw you in Boulder, you told me you were a fan. I even gave you his latest CD."

What a change of heart. "Then I guess it'll be there when I go home." Munching on a French fry, she said, "You know, Bucky, coming upon it fresh has raised some questions in my mind."

With a quick grin that acknowledged his guilt, Bucky stole a few fries from her plate, which he nibbled between gulps of beer. "Like what, honey?"

"Like who paid for the recordings, and why this complete unknown thought his songs would be valuable to you?"

"Your first question was answered often enough in the papers,

Zoey. You oughta get hold of some of them clippings they have in the stores. A wealthy old man up in LA saw promise in the boy and offered to launch his career. Last good thing the poor soul did before he died in a car crash."

When Bucky helped himself to a couple more fries, she put her plate between them.

"But it really touched Willi," Bucky went on. "Because someone was kind enough to do something good for him, he wanted to share that with others who needed it. You see, Willi knew he would have a great future, and he didn't mind delaying raking in those big bucks till my boys were set up, too." He gave his head a sad shake. "Such a loss. When he died, I figured the money should go to the family, but they were all for carrying out Willi's last wishes. Good folks."

Disbelief must have taken shape on her face.

He shook a fry at her. "Now don't you go looking so cynical, girl. Lots of people offer to do things for us. Sometimes they work, sometimes they don't. That don't matter, the thought counts more'n anything. Why look at you, offering to turn back the little stipend on your award. Now that's pretty generous for someone who ain't rolling in it. Really good for us, too, since it's the race director who's actually putting up that money."

Had she told him she would donate her award money? She thought she would make the grand gesture on the dais. This Swiss cheese head was really going to prove to be the death of her.

Bucky drained his beer and announced that he had to go. He didn't fight her too hard when Zoey insisted on buying. But when he stood to leave, she thought of something she still needed to know.

Zoey took hold of Bucky's hand to stop him from leaving. "Bucky, wait. Some people...I mean, I just wondered how I came to win the award. How...?"

Bucky smiled at her with mild exasperation. "You really can't remember anything, can you, honey? Like I already told you, I just went around the country, talking to all the people folks had nominated—" His sapphire eyes bore deeply into hers. "And I gave it to you, girl, because I thought you needed it most."

Zoey's cheeks instantly burned. She felt so transparent, she wondered how much she ever hid from anyone.

Bucky didn't seem to notice. After grabbing an autograph-seeking little boy into a bear hug, and shouting a remark to the waitress that made her blush, he was off.

Zoey nursed another Coke while she tried to resign herself with going back to the condo. But defiance set in. Why should she? Long as the van had gas, she was free.

She returned to her parking spot and took off again. Now and then she felt a longing to look over her shoulder, especially when an intrusive sound broke into her reverie. But she probably felt more relaxed than she had in days.

She came upon one of San Diego's natural parks, Tecolate Canyon. She seemed to remember there was a parking lot and rec building at the base, but being nowhere near them, she left her car in a strip mall lot and just picked up a trail. She started meandering through the park, halfway tempted to stay there until the police arrested her for vagrancy.

The canyon was deep at that point. She climbed part way up the canyon wall and sat leaning against a tree. Everything was so green and comforting. Even the surrounding city sights and sounds couldn't destroy the peace she felt. A car backfired somewhere; didn't matter.

A fly or something buzzed past her ear. She swatted at it aimlessly, her serenity undisturbed.

Until she heard another car backfire. Her heart thudded to a stop. A second buzz whizzed past, and struck the dirt, sending a little cloud of dust into the air.

Zoey hit the ground and slid along it till she reached a large enough bush to hide her. A third explosion cracked the air. A fourth.

Someone was shooting at her!

Twenty-three

EVEN AFTER ZOEY retreated to the safety of the condo, someone continued to fire shots at her, although these were salvos of a different kind. They wouldn't have taken her life, but they were just as unexpected and hurt like hell.

Dale squared off before her in the center of the living room. "Sure you don't have some idea who was firing on you?" After he asked that question a hundred times or so, his scars seemed to tug his face into a permanently skeptical squint.

"No," Zoey roared at him. "What will it take for you to believe me? I *don't* know who is doing this to me."

Zoey thought it was as if they were riding a roller coaster. Best buddies one minute, mortal enemies the next—which impression was real?

Dale's tone softened. "Come on, Zoey. You have to know more than you're telling us."

Her jaw dropped. "What are you saying? Someone has tried to kill me not just once but *three* times. I'm the victim, dammit!"

"For what reason? You're part of the picture, aren't you? Dear Lord, woman, why don't you let somebody in there for once?"

Her breath caught in her throat, as she found herself with no snappy comeback. She wanted to let someone all the way into her life, more than he could imagine. But people had always let her down. Now she was in quicksand, and she didn't know how to reach out.

Not that she'd find any hands extended here.

As if he could read her thoughts, Dale abruptly thrust his fingers into the pockets of his tight black jeans. "This game is getting old, Zoey. Why don't you cash in your chips—while you still can?"

Crossing her arms over her chest, she said, "If you have something to say, just say it. Quit dancing around."

Dale glared back at her. "Fine. If you're lying, you're dying—that direct enough for you?"

Zoey's head throbbed with dull pain that was building in intensity. How could she prove she hadn't done anything wrong if they wouldn't give their suspicions a name? If they wouldn't put it on the table so they could all deal with it, they could just fuck themselves. She told him so.

Dale seemed to grasp that he went too far. He ran his fingers through the black hair drooping over his forehead and approached to within inches of her. "The answer is in you, Zoey. If you find yourself on a path you don't recognize, there are people here for you who can help you find your way back."

She'd trade a year of her life to believe that. She allowed herself to wander lost in his deep blue eyes, whose expression fell a little short of outright accusation, but never reached anywhere near trust. *Why couldn't you have believed in me, been my friend?* Pointless question. She gave her head a slow, sad shake.

They wandered off to opposite sides of the room, Zoey at the desk and Dale before the wall unit, like boxers returning to their corners, where they stewed in angry silence. After a while, Dale awkwardly offered to make her some tea, or run her a bath.

Never raising her eyes from the golden oak surface of the desk, she snapped, "Just tell me how your interviews went."

Leaping at the chance of a truce, he covered the distance between them at a trot. "If you ask me, Pat O'Hara could easily slip down the road to Psychoville, and he's no friend of yours." He related some of the exchange.

Zoey snorted in disbelief. "He said I've had it easy? Did he look like he'd know how to spell *ironic*? What about Rick and Alicia?"

Dale leaned on the arm of the couch and gave his head a pensive shake. "I don't much think I'd want them as enemies, but I figure they'd find better ways of getting someone."

Zoey wished she could believe that.

She heard the sound of the doorknob turning and looked up in time to see Lou push the door open. "Ever think about locking this door?" he asked.

"Sure, that'll stop him," she said. "See anything?"

The part of Tecolate Canyon where she found herself under attack was rimmed by homes and apartment complexes. She'd scurried from one bush to another, inching up the canyon wall, only to find herself facing a fence at the top. Rather than come out of hiding to scale it, she slithered along the perimeter until she found a hole in one fence that she could squeeze through. She didn't stand until she rapped on a window, begging the woman beyond it to call 911 and to page Dale.

Why the hell did Dale carry a beeper anyway? Zoey thought during the worst of her frustration, rather than the cell phone that was attached to every inconsiderate asshole out there today? Probably for the same reason she didn't have one—because he wanted to be accessible, but not *too* much so. She didn't even have a cell phone, and she couldn't even manage to keep a landline phone consistently connected, so who was she to talk?

Despite his technological handicap, Dale had arrived in record time, followed shortly by Lou. Half of the cavalry took her home, while the other half went off to search the place where she figured her attacker had been.

"Lou, did you find the shooter?" Zoey asked again.

Lou exchanged a slow glance with Dale, then approached the desk, where he loomed over her. He gave the brown stubble appearing on his chin a slow, absent rub. "Funny that you knew right where to send me, Zoey."

"I visualize well." Her voice stammered, from the shock she knew, but it sounded defensive, even to her.

"*Very* well." Lou's tone had grown sharper.

Zoey, like many athletes, used visualization as a training tool.

She also had a good feel for the logic of space. Once she brought up the image of the park, it wasn't hard to direct Lou to the area where she thought the shooter must have been.

He pulled a few shell casings from his pocket, which he extended to her on his open palm. "We found these right about where you said they'd be."

She sensed if he didn't find anything—a good bet in that thick growth—he would have said she made it up.

"Lucky for you he didn't know what he was doing. Or maybe he wasn't seriously trying to hit you. Which do you think it was, Zoey?"

Her fingers tightened around the pen on the desk. "It felt pretty serious with my face in the dirt."

"It was a handgun, *chica*. From that distance, it would have been a fluke if he hit you."

He expected her to defend herself. *Her,* not the shooter.

The telephone rang. The sound made Zoey jump. Who had reconnected that thing?

Dale offered to get it and dashed into the bedroom. He burst back into the room just moments later. "That was Cindy," he announced. "She wants us to turn on the TV."

Dale snatched the remote from where it rested on the coffee table and gave it a swift click. Lou joined him before the TV, and Zoey slowly came up behind them.

The smooth baby face of a young male reporter, obviously jazzed by his scoop but faking solemnity by drawing his thick eyebrows together, filled the screen. "That concludes the press conference of Randall Ames, Commander of the San Diego chapter of the United Christian Confederation. To recap, Ames has vowed to shut down the annual San Diego Classic Triathlon, citing its threat to family values. Now back to you in the studio, Jill."

For a stunned moment, nobody moved. Then Lou sank into a chair in exhaustion, Dale groaned, and Zoey laughed like she would never stop.

Twenty-four

SINCE ZOEY FIRST arrived in San Diego, hordes of people had seemed intent on stripping her of her memory, her sanity, and maybe even her life. Now her sport. But finally, she felt she had a chance to fight back.

Last night, after being shot at by a stranger and emotionally mauled by the men whose job it was to defend her, she wanted nothing more than to crawl into a bath and stay for a week. Only she saw that ridiculous news story about the man threatening to stop the Classic. She settled for a quick shower and glued herself to the tube until they replayed the press conference, which wasn't until the late news.

Just what she needed, she thought, something else to torture her sleep. She hadn't had a nightmare since the awful one of the Willi Bogs mask. But she'd slept every night as if in a drugged stupor and awoke feeling poorly rested and always aware that something about Willi—the mask, some song lyrics, the face on the billboards—had floated through troubled dreams. Her synapses were still so fried.

Yet this morning, she awoke feeling more the hunter than the hunted. She hadn't felt so good since that day she sat on the edge of the cliff, kicking her legs in the air and laughing at death, before the continuing assaults wore her down. Now she could see one of the enemies in her sights—and she intended to take aim.

Zoey longed to skip her first workout, but she had scheduled her last interval session for that morning. Not only couldn't she inch a speed workout any closer to the race, she needed that test of her recovery to plan the remainder of her training. She still felt a little uneasy leaving the condo alone, but fortunately, the track proved to be crowded. To save a little time afterwards, she went straight from the track to the office of the race director, Gus Robbins, known to everyone in the sport as Rob.

Outsiders might find race management complicated, but the way it functioned was really very simple. Income is produced through sponsor contributions, which the sponsors regard as a form of advertisement, and the entry fees the amateur athletes pay. Sometimes race directors justify inflating the latter with the understanding that a portion will be donated to some charity, which delivers additional publicity.

From that coffer, the race director pays for municipal permits and the salaries of the off-duty cops who handle crowd control, the purses and appearance fees paid to the winning professional athletes, the donation to the charity, and all other expenses, including his own salary. Since most race directors put on a series of races, naturally they hope, by the end of the season, to add to their own net worth. Zoey couldn't say she ever noticed any desire for the last part in Rob, but she had to admit his family lived awfully well.

Just because race management is a simple concept, doesn't mean all race directors are as easy to grasp as their setups. Zoey had never understood why someone with a cool first name like Gus wanted people to call him Rob, but that was merely the most innocuous of the many questions Gus Robbins raised. He had burst into the sport a number of years ago as a complete unknown. The pros showed up at a pre-race meeting, only to discover the prior race director had sold his company to a stranger. If they hadn't been at the witching hour and all deals guaranteed to be honored, pros would have defected in droves. But they were all pleasantly surprised by a well-run race.

Of course, a very-pregnant Lacey Robbins had been at Rob's side during that event, following up on every detail. She left the business with the birth of that baby and hadn't returned except for occasionally pitching in on race day. Rob had struggled after Lacey's retirement, until he hired his current assistant, Gretchen Tyler, whom Zoey had to admit made an adequate replacement. But it was a grudging admission.

Zoey stopped off now at the offices Rob rented in the plant of a workout clothing manufacturer, who was a big sponsor in the sport. While she cooled her heels in his outer office, with its pale peach walls and thick amber carpeting, she was reminded again of how much she disliked Gretchen. Zoey tried to lose herself in her thoughts, while she nervously paced the small office. But every time she looked up, no matter where she stood, she'd find Gretchen staring at her. It was like being trapped with one of those paintings whose eyes seem to follow you. Creepy.

Remember the warnings teachers used to give, that kids who made funny faces would find their faces frozen in those positions? Well, Zoey always thought Gretchen's face had frozen while complimenting herself on her own superiority. Her plump cheeks only exaggerated the smug set to her perpetually pursed lips. And though she was shorter than average, she always tilted her head back so she could look down her nose at everyone. Fortunately, she drenched herself in a heavy rose perfume, an early warning system that made Gretchen easy to dodge.

To be fair, Zoey thought, Gretchen possessed qualities worthy of pride. Not her pear-shaped body and dimpled thighs, nor her neon red hair, a shade unknown in the natural world. She was, however, a financial whiz and excellent with details, areas where Rob tended to drop the ball, but which successful race management depended on.

But Zoey considered her more trouble than she was worth. Gretchen reveled in stirring up conflicts, and she had a thing for men in committed relationships. According to Cindy, she'd had an affair with the married accountant she worked for before Rob. Then she immediately set her sights on Rob when she came to work for him, though Lacey set her straight. Now, judging by the venom Gretchen sent her way, Zoey guessed Gretchen's latest target to be Marty.

Gretchen patted her puffy hairspray-stiffened hairdo. "So sad for you, Zoey dear, that you have to go through your recovery from the accident all alone. But Marty does have to concentrate on what matters, doesn't he?"

Zoey refused to bite. "Gretchen, I ran my life perfectly well before I found Marty, so I think I can handle it now."

"How wonderful. Then you'll be fine when he leaves."

You wish. But she had enough of Gretchen. When Rob buzzed Gretchen to tell her to send Zoey in, she was through the door of his office before the buzzer ended. Zoey might have complained about Gretchen if the stakes were less critical.

Instead, she said, "Tell me Ames is joking, Rob." She'd hoped to hear Rob's silly laugh and to be reassured that this wouldn't be another obstacle in her, and every other pro's, path.

Grim-faced, he answered, "No joke, Zoey. This guy really wants to shut us down."

With his features in repose, Gus Robbins was movie star handsome. Thick lashes ringed his dark Mediterranean eyes, and his granite jaw contrasted interestingly with his full, soft lips. Of course, he didn't always look so awesome. A slightly crooked grin distracted from the effect, and a high-pitched laugh that all but the most generous would describe as "girlish" almost shattered it. But Zoey liked him better for them.

She slipped into a black leather guest chair before his huge rosewood desk. "How serious is it?"

He shrugged. "I think I derailed the bastard's train for now, but who knows? He's been trying to get our permit pulled. The city assures me that is not going to happen, and I believe it. But the sponsors are another story—they can't handle the bad press, and I can't afford to lose any of them."

"Don't you have some contingency money?"

With a lift of his dark brows, Rob looked like she made a bad joke. But he should have had emergency money this early in the season.

Rob sighed in disgust. "I just don't know what this Ames

character is out to prove. So women wear skimpy clothing. What does he expect them to compete in? Bustles? With all the Jesus-freaks we have in this sport, he's fighting his own kind."

Shifting into a high-pitched voice, Rob did a dead-on imitation of one female pro who, in her victory speeches, always insisted Jesus wanted her to win.

He broke off, embarrassed. "Not that I'm making fun of anyone's religion, you understand."

She got it. Rob was Jewish; he thought he might have offended her. Zoey shrugged. That woman just confirmed what Zoey always thought—if God existed, He played favorites.

She rested her hand on his desk. "Is there anything I can do?"

His silly grin flickered. "Got any money?"

She choked.

"Just kidding, Zoey. Nah, I'm just panicking for nothing. It'll work out. Things always do, no matter how I seem to screw them up. I'm just lucky, I guess. One of these days, I'll accept my good karma and quit worrying."

"Must be nice to—" A wisp of something seeping from his desk drawer caught her eye. "Rob, is something burning in your desk?"

He flushed and dismissed it as nothing.

"Gus Robbins, are you *smoking?"*

He shrugged sheepishly and took an ashtray with a lit cigarette from the drawer.

"I can't believe I'm seeing this."

"Zoey, you're such a saint." He took a deep drag. "I keep it down to a few. The truth is, I always sneaked one now and then. Even when I was competing."

Rob occasionally dropped references to some past time when he competed, but she'd never heard of him in this sport before they found him on their doorstep.

He waved the cigarette at her as an extension of his finger. "Don't tell Lacey," he cautioned.

She fanned the air. "Oh, Lacey knows."

His dark eyes widened. "She told you that?"

"No, it stands to reason. How could she live with a smoker and not know it?"

From the vantage point the ten years he had on her, Rob flaunted his superiority. "Believe me, Zoey, reason doesn't play a big role in marriage. There are always things you choose not to know."

"Yeah? Like what?"

"Well, like... Okay, here's one: Lacey snores. Wouldn't think it to look at her, would you? But she snores like a buzz saw. Since she'd deny it, I just don't tell her. But half the time she wakes up and finds me sleeping in my son's bed. She never says anything, mind you, so she must know. We both simply choose not to acknowledge it."

Their game seemed harmless enough to Zoey, but the idea that she would soon be a player made her uneasy. She'd lived with so many kinds of lies. If unspoken compacts were part of marriage, did she really need it? Or was she just looking for an out?

Twenty-five

AFTER TALKING WITH Rob, Zoey felt so pumped and ready to take on Randall Ames, the guardian of Family Values, that she considered going straight to his office. But arriving in her workout clothes would have been adolescent. Satisfying as hell maybe, but she knew in-your-face attacks rarely win people over.

Besides, she had scheduled a ride, and she needed to get that in early enough in the day to allow her body to rest that afternoon. A local bike shop had sent over a bike for her to use until her cycling sponsor could replace the slashed tires. She kept the ride short, but she really hammered it, and it felt great. *Look out, world, Zoey Morgan's on her way back.*

If you want to be an athlete, you have to get used to sweat; Zoey rarely noticed it anymore. But while stripping off her smelly cycling jersey, she was struck again by how stupid Ames's beliefs were. When she finished a race, reeking of the most offensive of bodily fluids, unbridled lust was rarely a problem. And she remembered when athletics were considered wholesome.

She found the offices of the San Diego chapter of the United Christian Confederation over a liquor store in a rundown building near downtown San Diego. She had to step over a man, passed out in the liquor store doorway, who was obviously determined to stay close to the source. Couldn't Ames find enough to keep him busy in his own neighborhood?

Not much about the UCC's outer office surprised her. Given the area, she expected the furniture to be strictly garage sale, and the lumpy mud-colored couch didn't disappoint her. The place also cried out for an earnest receptionist hunting-and-pecking begging letters on an old Selectric typewriter, though the bright yellow letterhead provided an original touch. The receptionist herself, wearing dowdy mustard dress that made her complexion sallow, was right off the rack. Yet Zoey noticed the woman wasn't completely devoid of vanity. A large, ruby-encrusted cross covered her chest, and cheap earrings with Volkswagen insignias, the kind you see at car washes, dangled from her ears. Talismans.

The only real surprise in the office—was that Dale was there. Bad pennies had nothing on him.

Scarcely looking up when Zoey entered, he didn't seem as interested in beating her with a rubber hose today. Instead, he appeared to be reserving all his anger for Ames. She didn't understand why he would care, but he kept grumbling how Ames was "messing up everything."

Shifting to a less uncomfortable part of that awful couch, Zoey asked, "Have you spoken with him yet?"

"Briefly," Dale said with a tight nod.

"Does he seem the type to go the distance?"

After an angry shake that shook his drooping forelock further down his forehead, Dale erupted with, "You think you can peg everyone into a convenient slot, don't you, Zoey? You can't figure out whether I'm a bad boy or a mama's boy, when I could easily be both. Why do you do that?"

The stinging force of his attack made Zoey unusually candid. "So I always know where they're coming from."

"Woman, not everyone is out to get you," Dale went on. "Dear Lord, do you trust anyone?"

"I trust you," she lied. "Do you trust me?"

After that, they waited in silence.

The inner sanctum, with a chipped wooden desk that Zoey thought she remembered one of her elementary teachers as having used, and mismatched guest chairs in gold and puke green, looked as seedy as the reception room. But Randy Ames wasn't quite as predictable as his office. While he had looked more force-ful on TV, away from the cameras, he was a slight man with the energy of a hummingbird, whose thin neck poked through a gap-ping collar. *A perfect runner's bod, only then he'd have to wear sinner's garb.* Zoey wanted to dismiss him as a lightweight, but the fire of righteous zeal did burn in his pale blue eyes.

On the other hand, he couldn't stop staring at her breasts.

That was saying something. When your body fat gets down into that ten percent range, there's not much left of what makes breasts worth ogling. If Zoey ever let her weight rise to conven-tional levels, she'd have to beat men off with a stick. Reason enough not to. As anger mushroomed in her, she struggled to re-member there was more at stake than her petty wish to hurt this man.

Once Ames's eyes managed to find her face, he smiled kindly. "Miss Morgan, I'm not your enemy. You may not understand it now, but if I have my way, your life will be better for it."

She rested her clenched fist on the front of his wobbly walnut desk. "From where I stand, Mr. Ames, you're trying to take away my livelihood."

" 'Give not thy strength unto women.' Proverbs 31. It's a way of life that's all wrong for your womanly nature."

"I suppose it's irrelevant that it's what I *like* to do?"

"'She that liveth in pleasure is dead while she liveth.' Timothy 1:5."

They continued to bat that ball back-and-forth for a while, but it was impossible to argue with him. He presented his views in ordinary speech, yet when she countered them, he retreated into Biblical quotations. Like a boxer who danced around the ring rather than exchanging punches.

Ames gestured at her in a way that made Zoey think he was mentally copping a feel. "Look at the way you dress in your races. I can't imagine a more fitting advertisement for a brothel than the way you move through our streets. You're breaking down the fi-ber of the American family."

"Form follows function," Dale said softly, from the chair at her side.

Ames looked at him in surprise, as if he'd forgotten Dale was there. She sure was irresistible. Ames's eyes strayed back to her chest. Yup, her baggy jeans and extra-large race T-shirt were such a turn-on. Zoey's stomach tightened. She shouldn't have come. That pathetic little man had the power to make her feel vulnerable.

Zoey brought her fist down heavily on his desk. "You see sin everywhere because that's what you *want* to see."

While sitting back in his creaking walnut chair, with his hands folded over his sunken chest, Ames concluded that someone must have led her into her dreadful life because she was too pure to have found it on her own. Showed what he knew.

Dale inched the puke green chair a bit closer, forcing Ames to focus on him. When Dale related the series of attacks on her, Ames pulled out his calendar without hesitation. He produced an alibi for the time of the accident and the shooting. But that didn't mean anything. Judging by the frump in the outer office, there were minions to carry out his wishes.

Ames gave his wispy blonde hair a regretful shake. "I'm sorry to hear of Miss Morgan being victimized, but you people have no one to blame but yourselves. By making the world an unstable place, the forces you've released are now wrecking havoc onto you."

She'd had enough of people blaming her for the things that were done to her. Zoey made for the door, but turned back to Ames. "I've got a quote for you—predates yours, ancient Rome. 'Who will watch the watchers?' Think about it, you hypocrite."

But he wouldn't. Wasn't that the advantage of being one of the watchers? She told Dale she'd wait for him in the hall. She felt safer in a place that reeked of urine and vomit than she did in that man's office.

Dale joined her before long. Leaning against a pale, dirt-streaked wall, he asked, "Does he strike you as sincere?"

Now who was trying to peg someone? "Sincerely opportunistic maybe, but desperate. With Operation Rescue covering abortions and the Christian Coalition in tight with the Republican Party, there's not enough sin left for him to be choosy. Some of the sheep are bound to follow him, but most people will find this campaign ludicrous."

"Doesn't mean he can't create problems for us," Dale muttered absently. His face tightened. "And I saw the way he looked at you. It also doesn't mean he can't be dangerous."

As if Zoey needed to be told. That Ames would go to any lengths to promote his crusade was clear to her. She pitied the person who happened to get caught in his crosshairs—especially if she found herself there.

Twenty-six

ALL KINDS OF sounds produced in the indoor pool on the UCSD campus echoed through the water as Zoey swam laps, but she was too upset to focus on any of them. Though she'd become a strong swimmer, she had never developed the amphibious grace of those athletes who came to the sport from a swimming background rather than running, as she had. And that night—forget about it. Despite having visualized herself gliding through the water with the grace of a seal, frustration had turned her muscles to stone.

What could she expect after that session with Ames? She was starting to feel as if she were navigating a twisted tunnel to hell. Each time she thought she'd found the way out, she had merely turned another corner that drew her deeper within it. All the empowerment she'd felt that morning had now drained away.

Dale had argued against her going anywhere alone after having dodged those bullets yesterday. Funny. If she'd staged the whole thing, what did she have to worry about? But Zoey wasn't crazy. She'd driven to the pool along a busy route and arranged to meet Cindy and Dickie West there. Actually, she and Dick were supposed to go together, but he begged off at the last minute. Naturally, she arrived safely only to find neither of them had made it.

Dick's absence surprised her. Despite his appearance, he was usually reliable. Cindy's nonappearance made more sense, considering how oddly she'd been acting been lately.

"I'll be there," Cindy had insisted on the phone before Zoey left. "I just might be a little late. There's someone I have to meet."

When she learned Cindy was meeting a man at a bar near her

house, Zoey didn't expect her to show up at all. "You're never going to leave a date," Zoey had told her.

"It's not a date," Cindy rushed to assure her. "I would never date this guy. I just need to get clear on something."

When Zoey asked who Cindy was meeting, the girl insisted it was someone Zoey didn't know, but she stammered so dreadfully, Zoey knew she had to be lying. Zoey's bet had been Rick Salaz. It would be like Cindy to try to mediate tensions. Cindy promised to tell her all about it after their swim. Now Zoey just figured the non-date had turned into a real one. That was the Cindy she knew. She would still love the mystery man to be Rick, but Zoey knew that wasn't likely. Alicia kept him on a short lead.

Zoey flailed down the lane again with all the finesse of a horse. She'd held off on swimming until the cuts from the accident had time to heal. Bathing was tough enough without chlorine. But Zoey found now that she had lost way more ground than she expected.

If the swim had been the lone item on the agenda, she wouldn't have cared if neither of her bodyguards made it to the pool; there were plenty of people around. But the strain had pushed her to the breaking point. When Cindy suggested they check out a little blues club downtown later that night, Zoey jumped at the chance. She needed that distraction tonight, and she *really* needed the drinks.

Concern for her friends began to outweigh all her own troubling thoughts. Zoey stopped at the end of that lap and tore her goggles off so she could see the clock. Dickie ran in just then, so fast she feared he'd slip on the wet deck.

"I didn't think you were coming," she shouted as he rushed past. "What kept you?"

He didn't answer. Dickie suffered from ear infections if he didn't wear earplugs in the water. He stuffed them into his ears and yanked his cap over his bushy colored hair fast, but not so fast he hadn't heard her question.

"I'll cut my workout short," he said, shouting because now he really couldn't hear, and jumped in before he finished adjusting his goggles.

He didn't want to tell her where he'd been. What other secrets did her friends have?

Cindy still hadn't arrived when Zoey finished her swim. Her non-date must have been heating up as much as the Jacuzzi Zoey slipped into. But everyone was acting weird lately. She'd swear Dick had been avoiding her until she coaxed him into joining them tonight. Dickie didn't live in either San Diego or Boulder, he lived in Miami. Since they only saw each other at races, they tried to train together when they could. Now he ditched her whenever possible and acted embarrassed when they were together. He was still swimming now, but she'd bet anything he'd stay in the pool until after she left the Jacuzzi, rather than join her there.

How had Zoey become such a pariah?

And how much longer could she pretend she didn't care?

Zoey must have drifted off in the warm water, because suddenly, some half-perceived threat caused her to start. But it was only Dickie, towering over her on the side.

"Sorry, Zoey, I thought you saw me. Cindy's still not here?"

"Not yet."

He slipped into the spa, but he rested his thick neck on the edge so his eyes faced the ceiling. Her guess about his avoiding her wasn't far off.

"I've been thinking, Zoey. Why don't we go back to our places to see if she left either of us a message."

Zoey considered that a good idea. During the drive, she never let Dickie's taillights out of her sight. Yet she began to feel vulnerable alone in the car, so she punched the radio on and searched for something soothing.

The automatic scan stopped on a station. "How many Willi

Bogs does it take to screw in a light bulb?" a DJ asked.

She waited, wanting to know.

"There's only one Willi. He holds the light bulb, and his songs move the world."

The radio played a song she hadn't heard yet, a love song called *Together:*

We've walked a long way
Together.
We've stumbled, been bruised,
Discouraged, confused.
We've walked a long way
Together.

We've charted our course
Together.
We've crossed rivers and streams,
Climbed mountains and dreams.
We've charted our course
Together.

As with Willi's other songs, this verse produced a schizophrenic reaction in her. While the words attracted her intellect, her emotions reared up in outrage.

We've shared our whole lives
Together.
We've worked and we've played,
Our passion won't fade.
We've shared out whole lives
Together.

No, this was different, she realized, as her gut twisted with every word. Far worse than it had for the other songs.

And now here we are
Together.
I would not change a thing
About this gold ring.
I'm glad that we're here
Together.

Strange, though, the last stanza didn't upset her as much as the others. She was really splitting hairs now. That had to be how insanity started.

She followed Dick's lights to the condo, but parted at the parking lot entrance. They'd decided they would take her van, so she left it at the curb. She made her way up the dimly lighted path through the courtyard, clutching the small flashlight she kept on her key ring, but stopped when she saw a shadow outside her door. She paused and flashed the light at the person's head.

"Get that light out of my eyes," a grainy voice with a Texas drawl shouted.

"Dale? What are you doing here?"

He stepped under a courtyard light. "Can…we go inside?"

"Sure." What was the matter with him?

"Did you get this door re-keyed or something?" he asked.

She nodded. How did he know? She unlocked the door and threw it open for him. But he hovered behind her, like an awkward guest. Once in the bright room, she saw that his beard, always dark, stood out more dramatically from his pale skin tonight.

Fear rose in her as she dumped her gear bag on the coffee table. "What is it? What…?"

Dale appeared at her elbow. "Zoey, maybe you should sit."

Zoey whirled around to him. "What's wrong?"

"There's no easy way—"

"Just spill it, dammit," she snapped.

He sighed. "I'm sorry, Zoey. It's Cindy—she's dead."

Twenty-seven

GRIEF FLOORED ZOEY instantly. Denial never stood a chance.

Dale put his arms around her. "Zoey, let me help you sit."

She was an athlete, she never needed help, she thought, even as she felt herself grasping his arm. Once she sank into the sofa, she clutched the tan throw pillow to her, like she was holding onto something. Someone.

Dale sprinted to the kitchen and came back carrying a couple of juice glasses filled with amber liquid. "Drink some brandy, Zoey. It'll do you good."

"I don't like brandy," she muttered as she clutched the glass. "I bought it for Marty."

Still, lacking the will to resist, she took a sip. The warmth spread through her like a vapor; she hadn't realized she felt so cold. Dale chugged back half of his.

"Then who's been putting it away?" he asked, his voice thick. "The bottle's half empty."

Why were they discussing inanities and avoiding what mattered? Zoey willed herself to take control…but didn't.

"I don't know. Cindy doesn't—" Her breath caught. "Cindy…doesn't like brandy, either." She couldn't switch to past tense.

They downed the rest of their anesthetic in silence.

Finally, she asked, "How?"

Dale slipped next to her on the tweed couch. "She was hit by a car just a block or so away from her house."

Zoey suddenly understood what people mean when they say someone walked on their grave. "Wait! She was meeting someone at her neighborhood bar."

"We know. He never showed. She took a call during the evening, but no one even saw her leave." Dale hesitated. "I don't suppose you know who she was meeting?"

Zoey slowly shook her head. "She wouldn't say. But he must have been her killer. He called to lure her out so she'd be an easier target. What about the bartender? Couldn't he tell you something?"

"The place was jammed. He can't even say whether the caller was a man or a woman. The only thing he remembers is that Cindy seemed unusually somber tonight, like she dreaded this meeting." Dale cleared his throat. "We think it was the same car that hit you, but we won't know for sure till the lab tests come back."

"What do you mean? What tests?" Zoey asked.

"The guy who hit you bumped into another car getting away. The white paint that flaked off has been identified as belonging to a Mercedes of the same vintage."

So the good guys actually won one occasionally. Afraid to hope, Zoey snapped instead, "I thought Mercedes drivers only cut people dead at parties." Yeah, that control was taking hold now. Felt natural, felt awful.

Dale looked at her and sadly shook his head. "For a minute there, I actually thought you might be human, but the armor's back in place now. Zoey, what made you like this?"

She jumped unsteadily to her feet. "What do you care? Who died and made you Sigmund Freud?" What she meant to sound droll, came out harsh. She had no power to change anything now.

The bedroom phone rang. "Let the machine get it," she said.

"It could be important." Dale went to answer it. He wasn't gone long. "That was Dickie West."

"Oh, we were supposed to— did you tell him?"

"Not over the phone. He's coming down."

Dale must have seen from her face that she didn't want to see anyone, even Dick, and he offered her a reprieve. "I noticed the message light was lit on the answering machine. Why don't you check it?"

Zoey seized the chance to escape, though when she did, she just slumped on the bed, ignoring the message. From the other room, she heard a knock on the door, followed by the murmur of voices. Even muffled, Dick's cry sounded like that of a wounded bull. But she remembered how late he had been arriving at the pool. How hard would it be to fake that reaction? No, what was she thinking? Dickie wouldn't hurt Cindy.

The bedroom was dark. Its only illuminations were the living room light streaming through the doorway and the blinking orange message light on the answering machine. Grief comes in waves, and another bout threatened to overcome her. Anger, she had found, was the only antidote to despair—if Dale wanted to interpret that as hardness, she couldn't help it. But even anger wasn't a strong enough weapon right now. Since the message offered a distraction, she hit the play button.

"Hey, Zoey, it's me—Cindy."

A cry escaped from Zoey's throat at the sound of that effervescent voice preserved on the tape.

"What do you know? She actually has the machine on for once. I feel so lucky," Cindy had joked. "Listen, honey, I'm gonna have to take a pass on the pool workout, darn it. This guy's running late, and I really have to see him."

Cindy had sighed then, though it dissolved in a blur of background voices. She had called from the bar.

"What do you say I meet you guys at the club? And maybe we could ditch Dickie before it gets real late, Zoey. I need to talk to you about someone who is…well, proving to be untrustworthy. But, more about that later, dude." Her voice shifted back to what had been the livelier part of her register. "Ooh, guess what? I saw Dickie with a woman who looks a lot like someone we know. Short blonde hair, brown eyes, really pretty—sound familiar? But old, Zoey. She must be thirty-five. Wanna tease him? Anyway—gotta go. Be well, stay fit. Love, Cindy."

Her closing devastated Zoey. Cindy had never gotten the hang of leaving messages. She treated them like letters, complete with greetings and salutations. It had always exasperated Zoey that Cindy couldn't leave a message like everyone else, and the way she spoke volumes and jumped from subject to subject. Now Zoey wished she could grasp whatever produced that quirkiness and keep it for the rest of her life.

The finality of death was the hardest to grasp. The idea that the person no longer existed. That you would never get another chance to tell her how much she meant to you, especially since you didn't know it yourself until after she was gone.

Zoey felt so ashamed. She had convinced herself Cindy was no more than a summer camp kind of friend. Someone to share a few laughs with when they happened to be together, to be forgotten when we were not. Zoey never looked below the surface, even though she knew there was more to her friend than she acknowledged. Zoey had clung rigidly to her sense of superiority within the relationship, obviously needing to believe she was the more accomplished athlete and the brighter person. What a joke. While Zoey knew infinitely more about the uglier aspects of life, but Cindy had known how to live. And who would ever again care enough to show her how?

Wracking sobs consumed Zoey. For Cindy, for herself. She felt so alone that she never even sensed another presence until Dale sat next to her on the bed. From habit, she tried to pull back, but too much had happened. She came into his arms and cried as she never had before.

Dale held her tightly, yet his touch was gentle when he stroked her hair. He didn't tell her that everything would be all right, the way people do. They both knew it wouldn't.

She kept her face pressed to his chest, even after the tears were spent, oblivious to sensation. Until the bedroom grew darker. Someone must have been blocking the doorway. Before she could lift her face to see who it was, a voice hit her.

"Zoey, what in hell is going on here?" Marty demanded.

Twenty-eight

AFTER MARTY SPOKE, everything happened at once. Marty threw on the overhead light, Dale's pager buzzed, and Zoey jumped away from him as if she'd been caught in the act. Which was crazy—she didn't even like Dale.

The chaos went unchecked. Dale remained on the bed, looking up at Marty with such interest, but no sign of the awkwardness Zoey felt, that he apparently forgot to turn off his beeper. With that noise wailing, she flitted about the room turning on more lights. Marty remained in the doorway, still gripping his suitcase, raving to beat the band. But his face didn't look as loving as when she'd frozen it on that videotape.

"What the hell were you thinking, Zoey?" Marty asked in a hoarse voice.

A rhetorical question, she presumed. She saw none of the usual twinkling in Marty's eyes, but his hooded lids had narrowed to such slits, she could only just make out his hazel irises.

"I know you need to internalize as you head toward a race, so I'm used to you're not calling. But your focus hasn't been so concentrated this time that you couldn't make an exception."

She shouldn't have turned on all those lights. It felt as if a thousand spotlights were aimed at her.

"I started hearing rumors about some injury you suffered." Marty's crooked nose twisted as if it had caught the odor of something particularly repugnant. "But when I tried to call you, this number was never working. I've had it checked by so many operators, they're talking about taking back my phone privileges."

His black duffel couldn't have weighed much, Zoey noticed.

Marty wasn't a strong man, yet he lifted it effortlessly again-and-again as he flapped his arms like an injured bird.

"So I called Rick and Ali. They actually kept their phone connected—imagine that. Rick said you'd slipped in front of a sports car, but weren't hurt. But then Dick West told me somebody was trying to kill you. *Kill* you! Zoey, what in hell have you been doing?"

She hesitated, but rather than defend herself, she turned on Dale, shouting, "Will you shut off that damn siren?"

Seemingly stunned, Dale did. Turning back to Marty, she saw him frowning at Dale.

"Oh," Marty said.

Marty's response sounded less a word than the air exhaled when someone is hit below the belt. He looked around, as if he only just noticed the nature of the room in which he'd found them.

"Oh," Marty repeated.

This time, the word sounded more like a whimper. She rushed in with an introduction.

Marty's confusion faded. "Detective Terry, huh? Glad to meet you," he said. Apparently, her introduction also provided an explanation. When Marty extended his hand to Dale, he seemed to be stifling a smile, probably at what he'd been thinking.

Dale insisted Marty call him by his first name.

"Glad the police are taking this seriously, Dale, because I know this one won't." Marty indicated her with a toss of his head.

"Oh, I think she's taking the threat seriously now." Dale glanced at her. "And the target isn't only Zoey anymore."

Zoey told Marty about Cindy.

Marty slumped next to Dale on the bed and buried his face in his hands. "Poor little Cindy. You know, Zoey, when I first heard you were hurt, I thought about asking Cindy to stay with you, but I figured she'd drive you batty. If I had asked her, maybe she'd still be here."

Shame suffused Zoey because that probably would have been

her reaction. *If only,* the most futile words in the language. She swallowed hard.

When Marty insisted on hearing the long version, Zoey felt uneasy. Was she the only one who noticed they were still in the bedroom? But she told him everything that happened from the time she was hit, taking pains to describe the extent of her memory loss in the hope of forestalling questions she couldn't answer. When she came up for air, Dale reminded her that he had to make a call. Eager to escape that room anyway, she led Marty out to the living room.

Alone with Marty now, she felt more strain than when a third person had been there to buffer it. She busied herself with fluffing the sofa pillows, while Marty stood and glared at her.

"That could have been you in the morgue. It should have been, but for a lucky break," he said.

His face looked frazzled, as it would from traveling, and his receding dirty-blonde hair stuck out in spots around his head. But his T-shirt, with its the cartoon image of a gleeful mountain biker poised before a suicidal descent, looked fresh.

Marty hurled his duffel to the floor with far more force than necessary. "What were you thinking, Zoey? Even if you were nothing more to me than another client, I should have been here. But I thought we had more going for us than just a business relationship. Sometimes, I'm not sure if I know you at all."

No kidding. "How were things going with your mountain bikers? Were you able to put together some good deals for them?" Zoey asked.

He shook his head. "That doesn't matter to me anymore."

Hyperbole, she hoped. She would try to get him to go back to Colorado soon. Marty slipped onto the sofa and closed his eyes. When he opened them, she noticed his hazel eyes were glazed, but hard.

He tossed his head toward the bedroom. "Is he...?"

"No! How can you ask?"

Warmth crept back into his hooded eyes. When he smiled, the

skin crinkled attractively along his crooked nose. He leaned forward, and she thought he was going to come to her, but he simply took her hand and tenderly kissed her fingertips.

She felt so creepy, undeserving maybe, or guilty.

He laughed, that Marty-laugh everyone loved, and smoothed down his cowlicks, a signal that everything was back to normal. "I don't suppose you have any brandy in this dump?"

She still felt so awkward, she decided she really must be nuts. "Of course, I do, Marty." She rattled off his favorite foods, which she'd also bought, and hoped they were still there.

"Just the brandy, babe." He ended with the corny click he sometimes made with his mouth to punctuate sentences.

While she'd always found that silly clicking to be oddly endearing, it irritated her now as she slipped off to the kitchen. The tiny Pullman kitchen was a study in gold: gold Formica counters, matching appliances—even the brown-gold vinyl flooring in a design made to look like ceramic tiles. Dale had left the brandy bottle on the counter next to the sink. He was right, someone had been drinking it; the bottle was more than half empty. The idea should have frightened her, but now the effort of wondering who proved to be too much bother. Grief builds rage to the detonation point in one instant and saps all energy the next.

She noticed the wall phone was still lying disconnected on the counter. She popped it into the jack and lifted the receiver to make sure it worked. Rather than the dial tone she expected, she heard a wan woman's voice and a bit of her conversation.

"…should have the results later tonight," the woman said.

"Holly, you know I'm—" Dale started.

Zoey must have made some sound that let them know she was there, because Dale broke off.

"Sorry," Zoey said. "I was just checking to see if the phone worked."

"A likely story," the woman, Holly, said with a laugh. Her voice sounded weary, but there was a warm, melodic quality to it.

"Hang up, Zoey," Dale demanded brusquely.

Stung, she did. She wasn't being nosy, but what could he have to say that was so critical, it couldn't be overheard?

Zoey brought their drinks back to the living room: a glass of brandy for Marty, a bottle of beer and a glass for her—nothing for Dale. Unfortunately, Dale didn't notice the slight when he finally emerged from the bedroom. He relayed Lou's request that they come to the Sheriff's Station. Cindy had been hit outside the city's limits. Another police jurisdiction, another complication.

Zoey recalled the words that woman had used, "...should have the results tonight." She must have been a technician from the police lab. They didn't run regular medical tests at night except for emergencies.

They went together in Zoey's minivan, which was larger than either Dale's car or the car Marty rented. Ironically, Marty ended up renting with the same gold-beige Ford Focus that Dale drove. When Zoey saw them parked together at the curb, she said, "Look —they breed." No one seemed appreciate the joke.

Marty snatched the keys from her and slipped into the driver's seat. Preferring to be out of the loop, she offered the front passenger seat to Dale. Too bad he was one of those people who twist around to include the backseat passenger in the conversation. Though Marty did manage to keep him occupied. Shock hadn't dimmed Marty's mind as much as hers. He questioned Dale about things that hadn't occurred to her.

"Something puzzles me, Dale," Marty said. "How did they identify Cindy so quickly? I thought I heard you say she didn't have a purse."

Zoey didn't remember that, but she would have guessed it. Cindy traveled light; holding stuff was what she thought pockets were for.

"We found a note with a time and the name of the bar on her." Dale admitted that only grudgingly.

"Like she'd made a note to herself about her meeting? I still don't get it," Marty said. "How did that tell the deputies who she was?"

Dale hesitated. "My name and number were also on it. I made the identification."

Though Marty rattled on about how Dale had saved those of who had cared about Cindy hours of worry, Zoey was stunned. She could see that note in her mind: a time, a place, a name. What was wrong with Marty, chattering on so effortlessly? Was she the only one who realized the man Cindy went to meet—must have been Dale?

The thought hit her with a wallop. How could she have been more upset by the idea of Dale's guilt than she was considering Dickie for the role? She really didn't like Dale. What was there to like? He was smug, he was arrogant. But was he a killer? No, she couldn't believe it. Could anyone fake caring that well?

There were other reasons why Cindy might have written Dale's name on her note. While Cindy's pursuit of him had been less aggressive than usual, Zoey had sensed some interest there. Maybe Cindy intended to invite him to join them later. Zoey felt a familiar exasperation with Cindy for not being clearer.

When they approached the Sheriff's Station, Zoey saw news crews setting up out front, in the clearing across the street. That media attention couldn't have been for Cindy. She might rate a few lines in tomorrow's sports section, but triathlon wasn't important enough for more.

Dale directed Marty to drive around to the rear of the station, where Lou met them at the door and said he'd bring them to the cop in charge.

Lou led them to a big man leaning over the gray metal desk in the squad room's bullpen. The man, who wore a form-fitting denim work shirt and tight jeans, looked up swiftly, introducing himself only with a brusque "Mackenzie." Zoey wasn't even sure whether that was guy's first or last name, but she bet on the latter since she pegged him as having been called "deputy" from birth.

Mackenzie fit her image of a cop. He flaunted his brawny body with an arrogance that belittled Dale's. His arms bulged enough to push his shirt's short rolled-up sleeves into his armpits, and his neck was so thick it dwarfed his head, especially since he kept his hair quite short. Mackenzie sported the requisite brush mustache, and while he certainly wasn't wearing the aviator glasses cops always seem to favor indoors, Zoey just knew he owned them.

Lou and Mackenzie took Marty off to call Cindy's parents, while ordering Dale and her to wait. She followed Dale when he wandered to a coffee pot on a little wooden stand, next to the door that led to the station's front desk. In silence, Dale poured himself some coffee that was so burned, Zoey could smell its acrid order from a few feet away.

After a few absent sips, Dale drifted into speech. "Cindy was a good kid. She thought the world of you."

"You knew her that well?" Hadn't they just met?

Dale shrugged. "We talked a few times." His voice sounded defensive. He stuck a toothpick in his mouth and bit down hard. "Marty's not what I expected. How old is he?"

"Thirty-three. Why?"

His shrug looked more like a involuntary twitch. "Just wondered. He looks older, closer to forty or so."

"Wiry people do."

Dale agreed with an absent nod. "Does he smoke? I thought I caught a whiff of it on his clothes."

Zoey reached into a box of wooden sticks for stirring coffee and took one. Without giving it a thought, she proceeded to break it into little pieces. "I certainly didn't. He's been traveling, he must have spent time in a smoking section somewhere," she insisted. "Marty isn't a competitive athlete, but no one in the athletic world smokes."

She should have qualified that statement. Especially since the one exception she'd encountered to it, suddenly appeared on the other side of the station's front desk. Gus Robbins.

Rob spotted Zoey through the doorway and shouted her name. When she motioned for the cop at the desk to let him through, Rob raced over and pulled her into a hug. She didn't smell any smoke on him, either. Maybe she just wasn't sensitive to it.

"Did you get my message?" Zoey asked. She'd called his home, but not wanting to leave such bad news on voicemail, she asked him to call her in the morning.

Distracted, he shook his head. "I haven't had a chance to check my phone. Lacey's away, and I was out all evening, but I came home to find a reporter camped out on my doorstep."

"Because of Cindy? What an honor. I mean, you know how little attention the major sports outlets pay to us."

He just continued to shake his head. "This guy doesn't cover sports. And it isn't triathlon that interests him."

"Then why…?"

Rob's only answer was an enigmatic lifting of his thick dark eyebrows before he announced that he needed to find the men's room. But as he left, he added, "Why don't you take a look outside."

Twenty-nine

ONE DOWN, TOMASO thought, one to go. He flexed his arms and shadowboxed his own twisted grin in the mirror over the dirty white sink. Bam, bam, bam. Tomaso by a knockout.

Cindy was no loss. She'd outlived her usefulness anyway. Besides, it was her own fault. She just had to make waves. He'd banked on her being able to keep her mouth shut for a while, yet in the end, her loyalty to Zoey proved stronger than what they had shared. He wouldn't underestimate the loyalty people would feel for Zoey again. Go figure. Did anyone actually sense some warmth in that righteous block of muscle? Maybe it was her earnest dedication that hooked them, that fair-minded work ethic that Zoey radiated like a gas.

She was just like his old man. Tomaso laughed at a connection that would outrage them both, though for different reasons. But it was true. The old man was always going on about the rules of the game. Was he really that clueless? People considered him an animal. Did he think he could become respectable just by talking the talk? The old fool had always maintained laws were just for keeping the suckers in line; so why did he insist on a strict, if bizarre, code of conduct from his own people, too? Why would corners exist if not for cutting?

Nothing had ever given Tomaso as much satisfaction as knowing he'd gotten the old man in deep shit with his "associates" when he bailed. Course, the hot seat hadn't lasted long enough. He hadn't clipped them for enough to do much harm. He intended to cut a lot deeper this time, really make 'em take notice.

Course, he'd be long gone by then. Not that he had any doubts that he could outwit them if they found him—he wasn't the screw-up the old man always said he was. But why take the chance? Still, he would give anything to see the old man's face when he learned the one who set him up—was his own son.

Tomaso craved that look like a drug. That one moment when the full impact of his betrayal crystallized, and they grasped the price they would pay for it. God, it was great!

Cindy had cheated him there. She never knew what hit her. Stupid little sap was so confident that life was good, she didn't even turn around when he drove the car at her. Tomaso giggled. Well, there must have been a moment when she realized she'd blown it. Even if he hadn't gotten to see it, just knowing how she must have felt gave him a lift.

You had to consider the scope of the target, anyway. Doing Cindy had been like killing a fawn. Fun, but not like taking out a tiger.

Now Zoey had already paid off in spades in the coin of satisfaction, and she wasn't even dead yet. The expression in her eyes in the instant before she leaped from the car's path when he'd come at her had been choice. Yum, yum. Good thing he picked that up when he did. He knew now that he'd lost the element of surprise, all he'd get from Zoey now was steely anger.

So he was back to that—the loss of surprise. Doubt stabbed at him. What if he couldn't pull it off at all? If he failed?

But why was he worried? He was wearing her down. Besides, didn't he have a backup plan? Leaving a living Zoey holding the bag wasn't as good as seeing her dead, but there was something to be said for it.

Tomaso thought about Zoey's expression if that happened. Raging against the injustice of being jailed for his crimes would gradually give way to despair, to insanity, which would fade into mental death, while her softening, aging body would live on.

He flexed and pummeled his unseen opponent again. Yeah, that could be pretty satisfying, too.

Thirty

ZOEY FELT HER shoulders tighten in instant dread when Rob sent her off to look outside the Sheriff's Station. Part of her wanted to run as fast as she could in the opposite direction. She didn't know what awaited her there—but she couldn't take anymore. But she went anyway, because she couldn't afford not to know what form the next blow would take.

A cluster of deputies had gathered just outside the front door, blocking her view. While muscling her way through, the noise assaulted her first. A huge cry of approval went up from somewhere nearby—the roar of a crowd. Where had that come from? There had been a few news trucks out there when they arrived, but no thundering masses.

She reached the front of the pack, only to face another attack on her senses, this time in the form of blinding light aimed straight at her eyes. When her eyes adjusted, she saw that light had come from one of several giant high-wattage spotlights. Someone was throwing enough incandescence at the night sky to upstage the sun. Had Willi Bogs risen from the dead and hosted an impromptu concert? That was the level of excitement she felt coming from out there.

Not Willi, she discovered when she spotted the figure at the center of this circus, but someone she disliked as much. Randy Ames. He'd set up a stage in the park across the street, to which the faithful had flocked. The lighting he'd used was first-rate, but he'd gone a little cheap on the sound system, so he had to shout. Yet it worked to his advantage. The raspy quality the shouting gave his voice lent such a note of sincerity. Punctuating each of his remarks were the cheers of his uncritical audience.

"I want to return to a simpler time," Ames cried.

From the looks of things, he could do that at home. Standing off to one side, out of the limelight, were a washed-out little woman and two forgettable children whose vacant stares suggested they'd been lobotomized. Maybe it was just past their bedtime.

Ames's voice rose again. "To a time when the family was the backbone of this country."

Family. One of those buzzwords that was supposed to produce instant warm fuzzies. Only there were all kinds of families.

"A time when the man was the unquestioned head of his household, and the woman the heart. When fathers worked and mothers greeted them at the end of the day with a hot dinner on the table, wearing a shirtwaist dress and pearls."

This guy just needed to catch up on old TV reruns, Zoey thought.

She slipped back to the squad room to look for Rob and spotted him with Dale. Well, not so much *with* Dale, as *pinned* by him. Rob cowered like a mouse with a cat looming over him. She shook her head. She had to be reading the body language wrong.

Zoey squeezed through the deputies again in time to hear the last half of one of Ames's homilies.

"...instead of racing through the streets in skimpy threads that would shame a prostitute."

One of the cops rapped her on the shoulder. "Don't you feel terrible? Shamin' hookers?"

She frowned at him. "Can't you do something about this?"

One of his stone-faced buddies answered instead. "We are doing something. We're monitoring it."

That would make her sleep better at night.

"He's not breaking any laws," the first cop told her. "He has a permit for this rally."

"He does? When would he have applied for it?" she asked.

He shrugged. "Yesterday, maybe. Or the day before."

Yesterday? *Before* Cindy was killed? Why had he chosen to hold it *here*? Wasn't that too much of a coincidence?

She stared into the crowd, but it was getting harder to see. Moist air was drifting in from the ocean. The mist shimmering in the spotlight beams gave the scene an eerie, otherworldly effect. That it didn't look real also made it feel safe. Without pausing to question her decision, she stepped into the street and meandered through the growing crowd.

Another cheer went up. What kind of person wolfs down candy-coated poison with such relish? The commonalties among those gathered there weren't as obvious as she expected. She saw the young woman from Ames's outer office with an older woman, from whom she'd obviously acquired her doughy features and her taste in clothes. They were both enraptured by him. There were also homeless people in the crowd, probably because they had nowhere else to go. And people whose eyes gleamed too brightly over sad, fixed smiles—the lost ones, desperate for answers, willing to follow anyone who promised to deliver them. And some strange bedfellows: in that crowd of mostly fundamentalist Christians was even a small cluster of women in traditional Muslim garb. A harsh reminder that there were places on earth where Ames's arguments wouldn't be so laughable, where being seen in performance wear was a stoning offense. Zoey even saw a skillful pair of pickpockets working the crowd—that should leave the lost ones thoroughly bereft.

When she'd seen enough, she turned back toward the station, but a large man blocked her way. Blinded by a searchlight, she had to shield her eyes to make out who it was. Pat O'Hara, the man who blamed her for his suspension from the sport. Restless agitation radiated from his massive body. He set his legs apart and shifted from one foot to the other, like he wanted to be sure of blocking whichever way she tried to detour around him.

The scared little girl who lived in Zoey froze, and she felt… well, that peculiar dread she always felt when confronted by aggressive men. That feeling would devastate Zoey, if she let it.

While she never managed to get rid of that little girl inside her, she had learned how to contain her. She was Zoey's private hell—she never let that girl show.

The woman that Zoey had almost become stared at O'Hara in angry defiance. He formed a gun with his fingers and fired it at her. Zoey held her ground until he'd had enough of the game and went off to threaten someone else. But she didn't kid herself. She'd seen something demented in his eyes. If O'Hara wanted her dead, he'd risk anything to do it.

Only she was alive—and it was Cindy who was dead. Did O'Hara have any reason to hate Cindy as much?

Thirty-one

DARKNESS—THAT AWFUL phony, Dale thought, his aimless stare lost in the unlit room around him. How could it posture as something to hide in, while offering no protection from unwanted thoughts?

Of course, light or dark, there was no escaping unwelcome messages delivered by phone. He heard the dial tone return to the receiver still clutched in his hand. What was he doing? Did he think he could temper the finality of the report he'd received if he didn't end that call? He groped at the bedside table until he successfully hung up.

Son, you're gettin' pretty cowardly, Dale told himself. Time was running out. He'd have to move things along, if he was still going to pull it off.

He'd only been dozing anyway before the call came, his mind stepping gingerly around a touchy conscience. Now he wouldn't even try to sleep. He stared at the room's only illumination, the lighted laptop computer screen. Ever vigilant, his ally in the world of information. He'd hoped it would be enough of a tool to reach his goal, but he'd also been prepared to use some people if he had to. He just hadn't counted on getting entangled with them.

He'd been expecting a different Zoey Morgan. A pretty face masking a Machiavellian mind. He didn't know that face would light up with delight when he bought her something as insignificant as a cookie. He'd expected her to be a woman of rigid dignity, and she sure was that; he didn't know she could discard her precious dignity in a flash and laugh at herself with abandon. And he certainly hadn't expected that tight little body to trigger feelings that were best left unacknowledged. Who would have thought someone so exasperating could get under your skin?

If Zoey had been the woman of his expectations—he would be on schedule now. If Cindy hadn't been so trusting…he might have been able to sleep tonight.

With a sigh, Dale planted his feet on the floor. He groped at the wall for the switch that operated the overhead light. The sudden glare made what he saw around him worse. The first sight of his temporary home-sweet-home was never good. His eyes traveled the length of the long, narrow room, moving between the warring factions. From the high-tech hardware, which was perched on an ugly round table that dripped ornate grape cluster carvings, to the new bike hanging from ceiling hooks above the sofa bed, which not only became an uncomfortable bed when pulled out, but an eyesore folded up. Hokey old man's taste providing shelter for an ungrateful young man.

There was a knock at the door. So he wasn't the only insomniac.

Lou popped his head in. "Saw your light, *amigo.* Thought you could use some company."

Dale's eyes flickered to the large window that overlooked the backyard. With the blinds pulled up, it became a massive reflective surface on his side, but a beacon on the other. Not only ungrateful, inconsiderate.

Lou waved away Dale's apology and motioned for him to sit down when Dale rose to lower the blinds. "Nothing bothers Carolyn and the kids when they hit the pillows, and I wasn't sleeping anyway."

Dale sank back onto the bed with a sigh. "Did you get that stuff I left for you?"

"Yeah. I'll take care of it." Lou took a chair at the ornate table. "How did the boyfriend strike you?"

"Like a wheeler-dealer wannabe." Dale shook his head. "No, that's not fair. He seemed real sharp, asked tough questions."

Lou shrugged. "Makes sense that she wouldn't want him here

now."

Dale nodded, as he absently traced a pattern on the rumpled sage green sheet. "Penny, what if she really has forgotten what she was involved in?"

Lou rolled his dark eyes. "You're asking me to believe a lot, Dale Evens. But *if* she has—she'll pick up right where she left off when her memory comes back."

Dale gave a slow, sad nod. "I can't help feeling I'm trading a life for a life."

"What could you do differently, *amigo?*"

Dale shrugged. "Nothing that would matter, I expect. But it kills me, Lou, to think that Zoey Morgan will use her magnificent talent running circles around the prison exercise yard."

"And if you stop now?"

"Same thing—only one more person will die."

Thirty-two

ZOEY SPOTTED THE hand floating toward her an instant before it grasped her breast. The longest instant of her life. Well, one of them—she'd been there before. The hand was the same as always. An elegant male hand, just peaking out of the conventional crisp blue pajama sleeve, which would, in no more than an instant, perform an unspeakable violation of her.

Panic took hold. Her hseart rate rose till it threatened to explode. Bile burned a path to her mouth. Yet she could take no action beyond watching that hand press down on her with a horrified sense of disbelief.

At the last moment, she bolted. And when she jerked in her dream, she awoke.

Another nightmare. Zoey's runaway heartbeat still pounded in her ears. With a sob, she fell back against the pillow to let recovery wash through her. Reminding herself it wasn't real never did a thing to calm her shattered nerves.

Something touched her arm. She gasped and pulled away. But it was only Marty moving in his sleep. The shadowy room closed in on her. She'd always hated the dark, but never with such intensity as after one of those awful dreams. Twenty-eight years old and still afraid of the bogeyman. She rose and went to the living room, where she turned on all the lights.

Zoey stopped in the kitchen to grab a beer, before curling up on the couch. She took a long pull of the cold liquor, straight from the bottle, and willed the alcohol to dull the sharp edge of fear. That nightmare was one from a familiar repertoire of recurring dreams. She hadn't had it in a long time, but it was always with her, hiding in the haziest part of her consciousness. Somehow the dreams seemed to know when she was most vulnerable, and that was when they hit.

How much longer could she go on like this? Her throat hurt from the tension, her eyes burned with fatigue, and anxiety and confusion were constant companions. Her days were spent panicking about someone she couldn't remember, her nights were haunted by something she couldn't forget. Somehow, it had to stop, she had to *make* it stop. She couldn't bear it anymore.

Zoey drained the last third of her beer in one swallow and put the bottle on the coffee table alongside the beer bottle she'd left there earlier. Feeling a little sleepy now, she stretched out on the couch.

She was just drifting off, when a frightening thought blocked her path to oblivion. She forced her heavy eyelids open. Just as she suspected, the two empty beer bottles were on the table where she had left them. But they were alone now.

Someone had stolen their drinking glasses.

Thirty-three

THAT AWFUL NIGHTMARE nearly destroyed Zoey, yet she came through the night clinging to the hope that she would rid herself of all the toxic emotions it had generated—with one of the great traditions in the San Diego area, the Wednesday morning ride.

Every Wednesday at eight, triathletes and cyclists gathered for a group ride that headed up the Coast Highway through Camp Pendleton, north of Oceanside, and back. Often with a hundred or more cyclists, it was an awesome event.

The turnout when Zoey arrived at the gathering point was greater than usual that morning. The upcoming race was one reason. For most of them, this would be their last long ride. While triathlons were almost always held on Saturday or Sunday, when most people could attend, the Classic was held on the Fourth of July. Just eight days away.

Yet the crowd was quieter than usual today. Probably for the other reason for the increased attendance. The ride's favorite cheerleader wasn't with them and never would be again.

They shared a moment of silence for Cindy before the start. No speeches beyond dedicating the ride to her. A memorial service had been scheduled for the next day, and many of them would attend that as well. But if the others were like Zoey, this was where they would say their goodbyes.

The sky was gray, the air cool and damp—perfect cycling weather. But it also proved to be a fitting match to the grim mood of the crowd, which was devoid of the usual camaraderie.

Zoey had expected everyone to be somber. What she hadn't expected was the way that feeling would spill over onto the other riders' attitudes toward her. Admittedly, they expressed their hostility subtly. But taken together, those sidelong expressions of scorn added up to one conclusion: some of those people blamed her for what happened to Cindy. Zoey kept picking up snatches of conversation like "...started with her" and "must know more than she's letting on." She wished she could say it didn't hurt.

A few people rallied to her defense with their unspoken support. One was Dick West. He didn't say much beyond, "Yo, Zoey," when he tucked in alongside her, but his presence sent a message. Strange though, Dickie always dominated the lead male pack, and she hadn't seen him drop back. He must have come after the start and spotted her while working his way forward.

He couldn't stay there long, not without wrecking his own workout. She wasn't even in the pack with most of the elite women. With as little sleep as she'd been getting, she didn't intend to push. But she appreciated Dickie's endorsement, especially considering how he'd been avoiding her.

She remembered Cindy's comment about seeing him with some woman. Could it be that simple? That Dickie, her perennial suitor, felt guilty about his interest in another woman?

Despite the "You wanna take on Zoey, you gotta come through me" demeanor, Dickie was still uncommunicative. But he had to be grief-stricken, too. Still, Zoey was glad when Dale called to them as he moved up through the pack behind them, and Dickie yielded his spot. She felt her mood brightening with Dale's arrival, though only because it meant someone had arrived who might even talk to her.

"Hey, new bike," Zoey said.

He flashed a grin below his dark geeky sunglasses. "Yeah, you like?"

"It's great," she admitted honestly.

Dale had made a better bike choice this time with his pricey mountain bike. A good looking one, too. The bright silver logo on the crossbar stood out in bold relief against the paint job of his new wheels. Blue Jay-blue, like his eyes.

He gave his silver helmet a shake. "This ride sure is some-thing, isn't it? I don't think I've ever seen this many riders outside of a race."

"You're kidding? You mean you've never done it before? I thought all the local triathletes did it occasionally, even if it meant calling in sick."

"That's not so easy in my line." He went on quickly, adding, "It's not as if I hadn't heard of it, I just couldn't make it before to-day."

"Sure, Dale." What was he trying to prove?

They fell into a pattern of alternating bouts of chatter with pe-riods of companionable silence. Dale rode well. At the pace she intended to maintain today, he could probably keep up, assuming he could go the distance.

A friend from Boulder, Rita Fiske, a tall brunette whose un-usually slim face always made her look ravenous, slipped along Zoey's other side.

"Hey, Zoey, you look great, considering what you've been through," Rita said. "But you always look gorgeous, even though you never try, dammit."

Zoey's bruises were fading, and they weren't as noticeable in this crowd, anyway, where spills weren't that uncommon.

Rita's black helmet nodded in Dale's direction. "Who's the tal-ent?" she asked, honoring Dale with a smile.

That smile, Rita's best feature, reduced the "talent" to bab-bling. Zoey introduced them, but didn't bring Dale into the con-versation. Let him work out his own social life. Besides, Rita was married to one of Marty's mountain bikers. Zoey asked how her husband was doing.

Rita pursed her thin lips thoughtfully. "It's been disappoint-ing. He had such high hopes for snagging some new sponsors in Colorado Springs. You should consider sharing Marty."

The jabs sure smarted today. Zoey hadn't called Marty to San Diego, he came on his own. She could understand Rita's anger if she'd called Marty right after her accident. But he'd been in Colorado Springs long enough to make some good deals for Rita's husband, if any of the sponsors wanted him. Zoey didn't stop her when Rita decided to ride with someone else.

Once Rita moved on, Dale said, "I thought Marty would be here with you today."

"Why did you think that? He'd never be able to keep up with me." The jury was still out on Dale.

Dale asked how they met.

"I'd been coaching girls' track in a private high school in Denver. Great in the off-season, but with the summer approaching, I needed something part-time and flexible. I didn't have many sponsors then. I'd have loved to coach age-groupers, but it's not easy establishing a clientele, and some of those guys don't have the loyalty of whores."

Dale laughed.

"Anyway, a bunch of weekend warriors worked out at this school's track, including Marty. We fell into a conversation one day, and I shared my predicament. Within hours, he convinced a bunch of those people to hire me as their coach. Soon he was advising me on races and sponsors, and I couldn't imagine how I ever got along without him."

"And you just fell in love with him along the way?"

"Right." Zoey felt the chinstrap of her helmet tighten with her grimace. Talking about her feelings made her uncomfortable.

"So you met him in Denver, but he must be from...what? New York?" Dale asked casually.

"New York? Where'd you get that? Why do you care, anyway?"

"Just curious. I thought I detected Northeast sounds in his speech."

Dale's attempt to convey a New York accent—Texas style—cracked Zoey up. "Don't ever try working as an actor," she said. "You'll starve. You'd never convince anyone you're anything but what you actually are."

"Think so?"

When Dale started puffing on a climb, Zoey considered whether to ditch him. But Rick Salaz made the decision for her. Rick came barreling from behind like a runaway train. Hadn't anyone started the ride on time that morning? Zoey wondered. Alicia reigned, as usual, just behind the leaders with the second-tier men. Zoey couldn't say what triggered the warning. Maybe that nasty look on Rick's face. But something in her peripheral glance told her he wanted to do her harm.

With Dale on her left, she was protected on the street side. Rick took a wide swing to the right as he came around her, then cut in sharply on a path designed to clip her front tire. Since Zoey had seen it coming, she slowed, creating enough clearance for him to pass. What was wrong with that idiot? Didn't he realize he'd be setting up a bike crash that would take out a lot more people than just her? Judging by the skills of those around her, she had the best chance of coming through it okay.

"Sorry about that, Mr. Terry," Rick shouted from several bike lengths ahead.

Dale cursed, but Zoey had a less-futile response in mind.

"I'll take care of this," she said, and took off.

In good cat-logic, she let the mouse think he could outrun her. Just when Rick reached what she judged to be his maximum cruising speed, she tucked in behind him.

Drafting is illegal in most triathlons, though some in the international community continued to tout it, to the extent of sponsoring drafting-legal races. Like most American triathletes, Zoey didn't think it had any place a sport that designed test individual limits. In training rides, however, drafting was acceptable as long as all the riders took a turn out front.

Zoey didn't. She hitched her caboose to Rick's engine and let The Little Train That Couldn't try to pull it. He did everything he possible to lose her. Sped up, slowed down, made swift changes. But Zoey was with him all the way. She wished she could have seen his face—it had to be as dark as a thundercloud. When she sensed he was slowing, not out of strategy, but from strain, she left him in her dust.

On to Ali. The huge field had spread by then, breaking into smaller clusters, making it easy to weave forward. She knew exactly where to find her rival. Alicia never competed in close proximity to other women if she could help it. Zoey always took that as a subtle message to fans and other athletes alike that Alicia was in a class by herself. *We'll see about that.*

Zoey placed herself off Alicia's shoulder. Not close enough to draft—Zoey wouldn't take anything from her—but enough for Ali's pack to spread around them both. Zoey stuck with her. When Alicia poured it on, so did she; when Alicia coasted, Zoey did the same. After three power bursts, Zoey decided she had enough of the game. She hammered it until she'd established herself well ahead of Alicia.

Ali obviously couldn't stand trailing Zoey. She passed Zoey and turned it up. Zoey let her keep the lead long enough to think she owned it, then overtook her. They played that game for the rest of the ride.

Zoey hadn't intended to work that hard, but it felt right. She even felt in-synch with Alicia, as they alternated for the lead. Too weird. Of course, Zoey made sure she finished in front. Alicia's hard-boned face looked pinched with anger when she sailed through the turnaround behind Zoey. A race victory couldn't have tasted sweeter.

After completing her ride, Zoey stretched on the sidewalk, while sipping a recovery drink, and waited for Dale. Her enjoyment must have been apparent because he reacted to it instantly.

"Zoey, I guess you didn't grin like that when you were riding, or you'd have bugs in your teeth." Given the cheerful expression on his face, he should have collected a few bugs himself, Zoey thought.

Zoey had left her minivan in an Encinitas strip mall lot. So had the Rick and Alicia, who parked several spaces away. They had beaten her back to their cars and were already loading their gear when Zoey and Dale approached hers. Rick never looked in her direction, but Alicia came toward her. She clutched a half-eaten bagel in her hand, so tightly her knuckles were white. She stopped about five yards away and stared.

"Good ride," she said. Grudgingly.

Zoey didn't return the compliment, though it was true. She knew Alicia wouldn't want it from her, someone she didn't consider her equal. Zoey just nodded, her gift to Ali. It must have been the right choice, judging by the couple of head bobs Alicia produced before turning away.

While only half-listening to Dale's chatter about the ride, Zoey opened the side door of the van and started fitting the bike into the rack the dealer had installed. Only she noticed the minivan seemed lopsided. Zoey walked around the other side.

Someone had slashed one of her tires.

Thirty-four

ZOEY RUSHED INTO the condo and headed straight to the bedroom. Marty must have been there—she heard him slam the phone down.

"Who are you mad at?" she asked, coming up behind him.

He whirled around. "Zoey!"

"That's my name."

"I was starting to worry. What kept you?"

She hesitated, not wanting to add to his worries. He didn't have to know she and Dale had changed the tire and dropped the damaged one off at the dealership. But the lie took too long kicking in. Before she knew it, she'd spilled the truth.

Marty shook his head. "What does he hope to gain with these tactics?" He looked deeply into her eyes. "How you holding up, babe?"

"I don't intend to surrender in a war of nerves." Fighting words. What a joke. How much longer could she endure being continually yanked like a yo-yo?

But Marty obviously believed her. His narrow eyes widened. "By God, you really think you're invincible, don't you?" Marty gave her a shaky, enigmatic smile.

Let him think so. Not wanting to deal with Marty's concerns any more than her own, Zoey diverted the conversation by asking who he'd hung up on.

He glared at the phone. "Oh...Tom Pearson. You know, the guy producing the training video. He wants to step up production to get it on the shelves sooner that we planned. I'm supposed to help him cut it."

"So? What's the problem?" She went to the dresser and pulled some garments from various drawers.

Marty came up behind her and put his hands on her shoulders. "He's trying to capitalize on the sympathy for Cindy while it's still strong. It makes me feel as exploitive as Ames."

Zoey whirled around on him. "Oh, Ames—were you able to learn anything about his demonstration permit?"

"It looks like the paperwork didn't go in until after...you know...Cindy died."

"Are you sure, Marty? It was the middle of the night. Why would he have chosen to hold it precisely where the activity would heat up only after Cindy's death?"

Marty gave a little click with his tongue. "What can I say, hon? Either Ames has someone in his pocket who fixed the permit fast, or who faked the paperwork. We'll never know."

Zoey gave him a grudging shrug. "Thanks for trying."

She went into the bathroom and turned on the shower. She'd started to pull her riding jersey over her head when Marty came in. she tugged the jersey down.

"Listen, Marty, I understand why you feel like you're exploiting Cindy," Zoey said over the blast of water. "But she was proud of that video. She wouldn't care why people were buying it, just that they were."

"I guess. And her folks could use the money." He smoothed his hair down. "But you know what it means, don't you? I'll have to spend so much time on it, I won't be around to protect you. You shouldn't be alone now, Zoey. This morning proves that."

She made light of it. "Oh, I'm not good enough to die young." She told him about the workout schedule some of the athletes had set up, letting him think she intended to participate, without giving herself time to question her deception.

"If you're sure," Marty said with obvious reluctance. "Now don't you go asking about the DVD in the stores. I don't want to build up demand until I know we can get it out." He smiled at her through the steam billowing out of the shower. "You taking baths with your clothes on now?" He gestured to what she still wore.

"Need I remind you that you interrupted me?" She meant that to sound playful, but it came out strained. Lying was getting to her.

Marty smiled absently. "Zoey, would you mind turning the water off? We need to talk."

She followed him back to the bedroom and sat on the edge of the bed. He took her hand.

"Honey, we've both been awfully busy lately. Sometimes it seems like we hardly spend any time together. If it hadn't been for the danger you've been facing, I'd still be in Colorado."

"That can't be helped, Marty. Our careers—"

"Maybe it can. What do you say to going away together after the Classic? You may not have noticed it yet, kid, but we've been drifting apart lately."

He seemed pretty stationary to her—she was the only drifter. What was she doing to him?

"Marty, I have a race in Boulder mid-month?"

"A sprint, you could win it in your sleep. What do you say, Zoey? You'll need some recovery time after the Classic anyway. Maybe we could keep your loaner car and just drive somewhere for a few days. Come on, it'll be good for us." He took a quick look at his watch. "Oh, shit. I have to meet Pearson. Zoey…?"

She promised to think about the vacation and walked Marty to the door.

"Train only with the group from now on," he said. "Or tell your friend, Dale, to keep an eye on you—but tell him to keep it strictly business."

"It *is* strictly business with him," Zoey insisted.

Marty snorted. "Right. Zoey, now-and-then, you oughta look in the mirror. What man wouldn't want someone who looked like you?" Marty grabbed her arms and pulled her to him. "I need you, babe. Don't run from me." He pressed his lips hard against hers. Then he slipped out with a reminder to lock the deadbolt.

Zoey exhaled hard and involuntarily brought her fingers to

brush her lips. Her breathing raced. What was happening to her?

No time to think about it. She stripped on the way to the bathroom and, under the shower, scrubbed as if she'd been stained by dirt. She spent so long under the hot, steaming water, she was running late by the time she toweled off.

Zoey threw on her jeans, zippering them as she headed to the closet for shoes, when a thought occurred to her. Not a thought really, more of a sense of urgency that spread through her. She slowly approached the dresser and pulled open the second drawer. Hesitating for a moment, she finally slipped her hand beneath her underwear for the object wrapped in a towel.

The knife. Jorge Ramirez's blade, if Lou could be believed. How strange that it felt natural in her hand. She practiced flipping it open a few times, only she didn't seem to need the practice. She took it to the bathroom and looked for the first-aid kit she always brought on her travels.

The new roll of adhesive tape, which she bought before leaving Boulder, had already been opened. She tugged up the leg of her jeans and began taping the knife above her ankle. A wave of *deja vu* stole over her. Lou hadn't lied—she *had* done this before. She knew instinctively where to place it so she could pull it off quickly, as if she'd already worked it out.

Remembering the time, she rushed back to the bedroom for her big canvas tote bag. As she reached for it, she caught sight of something peeking out under the nightstand. It was a brochure for some mountain retreat out past Ramona, a rural community northeast of town. Was this what Marty had in mind for their vacation? He must have dropped it when he used the phone.

But when had they printed that thing? The colors had faded, and the pictures looked like they'd been taken forty years before, judging by the clothes the models wore. Maybe Marty was trying to be economical. How funny—she was usually the frugal one. People always said that couples sometimes changed places in long, healthy relationships. Maybe they had a future together, after all. Despite her.

If only she could get out from under this dark cloud, she might even have a good time. She could call ahead and have champagne waiting in their cabin. Yeah, she liked that idea. Zoey tucked the brochure into her underwear drawer for safekeeping.

Thirty-five

ZOEY HAD PROMISED Cindy's mom that she would help pack her daughter's things. But dread began to consume her during the drive to Cindy's house. If other people blamed Zoey for Cindy's death, would her mother hold her responsible, too? Zoey's vision of the road ahead began to blur, until she blinked it clear.

Charley Orr was already there when Zoey arrived, sitting in a rented Mercury Sable parked before the house, dabbing her eyes with a soppy tissue. Even today, with her face tear-stained, it was easy to see where Cindy had gotten her striking looks. Though her body carried more padding than Cindy's had, Charley had the same traffic-stopping power, even if she was the mother of grown children. Zoey always figured Charley also had to be the source of Cindy's sense of style. While the cost of her clothing generally reflected her status as a proper Seattle matron, Charley always seemed to put things together with unexpected panache.

Not much panache today, with her jeans and T-shirt, and especially not in the way she slowly stepped from the teal Sable. Charley and Zoey just came into each other's arms, dispensing with the platitudes.

Zoey muttered an apology for being late into Charley's soft red hair. "Charley, I feel terrible about making you wait."

"You didn't, honey. I came early, but I didn't want to be alone in there after…" Charley pulled away and shook her head in answer to Zoey's unspoken question, instructing Zoey to walk up the path to the front door with a nod of her head.

"Do you have the key?" Zoey asked, confused..

"You won't need it," Charley said with thinly suppressed anger.

Unsure of what that meant, Zoey rushed up the flagstone path to the heavy cedar door. She found it unlocked and a few inches ajar. She gave the hand-carved door a tap to push it open. Total chaos and destruction stared back at her through the doorway. Someone had trashed the place.

Zoey's grief mushroomed along with her anger. She'd always envied Cindy that little A-frame house with its cedar siding and shake roof shingles. Zoey used to tell her it was the one thing she'd leave Boulder for if Cindy would let her have it, though Zoey always thought the house would be more at home in the mountains where she lived than at the beach. She considered Cindy's décor, with its ruffles and lace, too cutesy for the design, but was awed by her completion of it. Cindy was one of those people who devoted herself to finding just the right touch to finish a room. The house Zoey rented back in Boulder was just an empty shell.

Zoey had heard about people who defaced the homes of the dead purely for the twisted fun of it. But didn't they usually wait till the funeral when they could be certain it would be empty?

On closer inspection, she wasn't as sure this was the result of pointless vandalism, after all. While the plants were overturned, the vases broken and the drawers emptied, she saw no sign of the sick excesses she'd read about. No slashed cushions, no ugly writing on the walls.

Zoey heard Charley's slow steps on the path behind her. "We'll never finish packing this place today," Charley muttered sadly. "I'll come back next month. No matter. I don't think I could bear for anyone else to live here yet anyway."

Zoey glanced over her shoulder. "Won't the landlord want to rent it?"

"I assumed you knew, Zoey—John and I own it. Well, you know how little some of you girls make. We didn't want our baby to do without nice things because she had to pay rent."

Why did Marty believe these people needed the money the training DVD would produce? And why did it always hurt Zoey when she heard about the extravagant gifts other people received from their parents? They were just *things*. She did okay without them.

Zoey wandered over the scratched wooden doorstep, pausing before the old-fashioned roll-top desk in the corner. The contents of its drawers had been dumped on the floor, and the stuff from the little cubbyholes was scattered everywhere. What she saw just confirmed her belief that this wasn't the work of malicious kids. Someone had been looking for something.

Charley groaned at the sight of the desk and began to paw through the torn, empty file folders scattered around it. "He took her poetry. She wrote it longhand, so she didn't even have copies of most of it."

Zoey stared at her, shocked. "Cindy wrote poetry?"

Charley nodded absently. "She was always scribbling her little verses, mostly on scraps of paper."

"I remember her scraps, of course, but she never said anything about writing."

"I know, honey. Cindy was afraid her friends would laugh, or think her writing wasn't any good. But some of her poems were quite moving. I always told her she should try to get them published."

"Do you think she did? The magazines would have copies."

Charley dismissed the idea with a futile shrug. "She'd become secretive about it. Lately, she never read it to me over the phone anymore, the way she used to. I thought maybe some of her poems might have been accepted for publication, and she was planning to surprise me. Now..."

Now they were gone forever. "How you must hate me," Zoey blurted, without thinking.

Charley's green eyes widened. "Hate you? Zoey, why?"

"This is my fault. All of it—the defiling of Cindy's home, her death." *Where had that come from?* "If only I could have remembered my accident, maybe I could have..." If only she had *tried* to remember. *Really* tried.

"Is that what you're thinking? That Cindy was killed because she knew something about you?" Charley tossed pink-and-green flowered cushions back on the ruffled couch and patted the surface, gesturing for Zoey to join her there. "Zoey, how do you know it isn't the reverse? That someone didn't try to get rid of you before you could talk some sense into Cindy?"

Zoey slipped next to her on the sofa. "What are you saying?"

"Zoey, dear, taking everything I've learned about Cindy's death—with this," she stabbed her finger at the desk, "I can't help but think my little girl had been foolish enough to get involved with a married man."

Thirty-six

ZOEY SPENT ANOTHER restless night chasing sleep on the condo couch. If she didn't get a handle on this insomnia soon, she was going to get sick and wreck her whole season. But try telling that to her head.

Charley's belief that Cindy's married lover had killed her kept rattling around in Zoey's mind. Had Cindy been the primary target all along? She'd always been goofy about men and too trusting of everyone for her own good. But if Cindy's relationship was at the root of the puzzle, why had Zoey been attacked? Was the man someone Zoey knew? Knowing her own aggressive honesty, Zoey wondered whether, before she lost her memory, she might have threatened to tell the man's wife.

Zoey finally gave up on sleep and just stared at the night sky through the window, until dawn safely overtook it.

The phone rang shortly after six. Zoey had been in the kitchen blending a breakfast drink, so she grabbed it on the first ring. It was Dale, asking whether she wanted to run with him. She hesitated. There was something she wanted to do today, something she only engaged in on rare occasions, but which she'd been yearning for lately. While she'd never shared it with anyone, on impulse, she asked Dale if he was up for a surprise. She hung up before she had a chance to change her mind.

She met him out front and, as they ran, she took him on a circuitous route that ended on one of the sleazier blocks of Fifth not far from the Gaslamp Quarter. The Gaslamp Quarter was a semi-slum near downtown that San Diego had substantially revitalized, though upscale yuppy restaurants could still be found beside flophouses. Dale wasn't suspicious until they reached their destination, when he hesitated mulishly on the sidewalk before the building. He must have guessed they weren't going to find any yuppies in there.

He squinted at the sign above the door. "You're kidding, right? When you said gym, I thought…" Dale shot another look at that sign that read, "Sam's Fighter Training Center," as if he expected it to change. "Isn't this a place where they train *boxers?* I've never seen one of these places, except in movies."

"Then it's time we complete your education," Zoey said with a laugh, reveling that she'd gotten the jump on him for once. She led him through the door.

The smell of sweat and blood and battered dreams pelted her nostrils the instant the door closed behind them. The large room was shadowy. Dirt defused the light coming through the windows, placed just below the high ceiling, like tattered lace. But the mirrors lining the walls below the windows were bright and streak-free. And the equipment, while worn, was well maintained. There was such a feeling of streamlined efficiency about the place. Form had never followed function more directly.

Several boxers were working out on the bags, while a couple others sparred in a ring. Some glanced indifferently at Zoey and Dale. Recognition flashed on the manager's aging chocolate-colored face. He gave her a nod and ambled over. Zoey pulled some bills from her the small pocket on the inside of her stretch shorts and insisted on paying the day charge for Dale.

"My treat," she said.

"Some treat," she heard him mutter.

"Come on, Dale, you can't really be a stranger to the pugilistic arts. How'd you get those scars?"

He lagged a step behind when she crossed the floor. "That was in a vacant lot soccer game. I was the goalie and—" He paused for a fond smile. "And some little squirt kicked me in the face. Not on purpose, mind you. I expect his foot just slipped that first time. Now the second time—he was going in for the kill."

"I take it he scored."

"He did *not*," Dale insisted.

"All-right!"

He was still gawking when she taped his hands. "I'm surprised they let women in here," he said.

Zoey was surprised they let wusses like him in. "You're really out of it, aren't you? Women box now. And boxing aerobics was a trend a while back. All sorts of places sprang up. Women's gyms, executive gyms—those are place for white males who never run into things like glass ceilings and don't want to work out with anyone who does. This is the real thing."

"I can see that," he muttered.

By following Dale's eyes around the place, she unexpectedly wandered into uncomfortable territory. Their faces were the only white ones among all the black and brown. It troubled Zoey that while she continued to be drawn to these places, she had to condemn a sport in which members of the underclass was encouraged to pummel each other into unconsciousness for the amusement of others. Still, she knew that wouldn't stop her from coming back.

"Is that when you discovered it, when it was in?" Dale asked, flexing his taped fists.

"That's me, always got my finger on the pulse of popular culture."

Dale laughed.

After starting Dale on jump-roping sets, Zoey thought about the first time she found herself in a boxing gym. She had gotten lost in a seedy neighborhood in Denver and stopped in a gym to ask for directions. While waiting for the manager to finish a phone conversation, she watched a man pummeling the heavy bag. When the manger finally turned to her, instead of asking for directions, she asked if he could teach her to do that. Once again, she found herself on a path that made no sense in the context of her life, but which felt right.

After a short while, the jumping winded Dale. "This is harder than it looks," he said, puffing.

She'd made the same discovery. But while she found boxing workouts to be surprisingly good cross training, she never told anyone about them. Until now. Look who she started with. As she showed him some moves, she watched the concentration on his face in the sparkling mirror. Biker-thug, mama's boy, enigma. Which was it? Why did she care? After she left San Diego, she'd never see him again. She resolutely refused to acknowledge the sadness that idea made her feel.

Dale gave out after the shadowboxing lesson. He took a stool by the side of the ring, where he watched two guys sparing. Leaving her free to lose herself in the bags. She loved the speed bag. It took her a while to pick up the technique, but once she did, she began to feel as she did during her best races. Like a finely tuned machine.

But she *needed* the heavy bag. There was something primal in the way it drew her. Sure, she worked on technique. If she didn't control the speed with which it came back at her, it would take out her shoulder. But she knew it was more about *hitting* something. She pounded the bag until she couldn't hold her arms up anymore. She felt exhausted then, but fit—ready, even if she couldn't have said what for.

After leaving the gym, she figured they'd run back to the condo, only Dale pleaded fatigue.

"What do you say we walk down by the harbor?" he asked.

Just beyond the Convention Center was a marina filled with pleasure crafts, lined by a row of high-rise tourist hotels and a picturesque park.

"Walk? Elite triathletes don't walk. You can't enter walks in the training log." But with a laugh, she agreed to make an exception for him.

"These paths are great, aren't they? Have you been running here, Zoey?"

She shook her head. "Strictly for amateurs."

"Hey, I run here."

"So? You *are* an amateur—one who doesn't wear a heart rate monitor like he should," she said with mock severity, though she skipped wearing her own more than not.

"How did you know?"

"If you did, you'd know they work erratically in this area. I figure it's the interference all from the Navy's ships." The Navy casts a big shadow in San Diego, and its ships were often anchored in the harbor. "One time I was wearing my monitor during a run out on Harbor Drive, and it just stopped. I thought I had—" Zoey gasped.

"Sobering thought."

Right. Talk about killing moods. "I've seen enough here. Why don't we cut through one of these hotel lobbies?" she asked, indicating the buildings lining the path.

Dale didn't budge. "Zoey, I'm dying for some frozen yogurt. Come down to Seaport Village with me." Seaport Village was a tourist shopping center some distance ahead of them. "Indulge me," he said.

Since he'd humored her outing, she shrugged her agreement. But they didn't recapture the jovial mood they'd shared earlier.

Dale pointed at the boats in the marina. "Do you ever dream about having a boat?"

She kicked a stone on the path. "I'm from a landlocked state, remember?" Gazing at the marina, she experienced none of the pull she'd felt watching small planes take off. She looked away from the harbor toward the town, but Dale keep tugging her attention back.

"Will you look at the size of some of these? Don't you wish you could afford one?"

"Not really."

"Ah, come on. Everyone wants that kind of money. It's just a matter of what they'll do to get it."

Suit yourself. He tugged her to the heavy decorative chain that functioned as a rail and began pointing at various boats.

"Let's look at some of the names. Aren't they a hoot? There's the Misty Lou out of Chicago, the Nancy Fancy, the—"

"Why is it here if it's out of Chicago, whatever that means?" she asked. "Sounds like a stud book."

"Don't know," Dale said with abrupt dismissal. "Look, there's one that's not named for a woman." He pulled her farther along the railing. "Can you see the one I mean? The huge one at the end of the pier. It's called—"

She stopped. "The Toy Boy," she whispered.

He jumped at her. "That's right. The Toy Boy out of Philadelphia. Do you know it?"

"Why should I?" Her voice sounded guttural.

"You knew the name."

"I read it," she insisted. "The same as you."

But she hadn't. She knew that gleaming white yacht on sight. Just its appearance, nothing more. Except that the association wasn't a good one.

She turned away. "I gotta go, Dale. You're on your own with that yogurt. I need to change for the service."

Yanking her arm from the hand that still gripped it, she turned in the opposite direction and started running—from that yacht and the unpleasant feeling it gave her.

"Zoey—wait," Dale called.

But mostly from the man she felt certain knew that memory better than she did, and tried to force her to face it.

Thirty-seven

AS ZOEY RUSHED away from the harbor, back toward the condo, time and distance made her doubt her suspicions. How could Dale, a disabled cop she met by chance, know more about her experiences than she did? *Get a grip, Zoey.*

But she didn't question what that yacht evoked in her. That fragment of a memory returned as they always did, first as a feeling that stole over her, tainting her mood. An ambush, by her own mind.

But what association could Zoey have had with a yacht? She told Dale the truth, her experiences with water was limited to swimming and drinking. She couldn't remember ever having been on a boat, not to mention a yacht.

Marty was on the phone again when Zoey returned to the condo. After waving in his direction, she grabbed a dress bag from the closet and carried it to the bathroom to shower and change. Before jumping into the shower, she peeled away the plastic bag that had covered the dress, and she eyed the garment warily. She still wasn't sure about it, but Charley had insisted.

When they began packing Cindy's house the day before, Charley suggested that they start in the bedroom. Zoey dropped a box on the closet floor and just started yanking garments off hangers.

But Charley stopped her. "Not so fast, Zoey. We'll need to sort through these things. I know Cindy's sisters will want some. But I also want you to help yourself."

"I couldn't," Zoey insisted in all honesty. Cindy's most conservative things were light-years more flamboyant than anything she'd ever worn.

Charley gave her chin-length reddish bob an emphatic shake.

"Nonsense. Cindy would have wanted you to have them. Did you know she'd itched to help you shop?"

Zoey had sensed that and always managed to avoid it.

"Let's see." Charley pulled out a rust dress in a knobby silk. "Here you go. Wear this for the Classic's award ceremony."

In shorter triathlon events, which hold their awards ceremony immediately following the race, getting gussied up means trading a sweaty singlet for the race T-shirt. But longer races, like the Classic, sometimes dispense awards at banquets. Zoey hadn't planned on dressing, though. When society refused to support athletic performance in women, she believed, it was hard enough to be taken seriously as a professional athlete without engaging in appeasement. Besides, it was hell stuffing broken, bloodied toenails into girlie shoes.

But she remembered this dress. Cindy had bought it to wear to the Ironman banquet, before an old injury flared up that forced her to cancel. Maybe Zoey would wear it to the Classic Awards ceremony, after all. For Cindy.

Charley pulled something else from the closet. All Zoey saw was a flash of greens and golds, like autumn leaves. Charley twirled her around before the mirror and placed the dress before Zoey.

"Perfect for your coloring," Charley announced. "Wear this one tomorrow."

"Tomorrow? But it's…"

"I know what it is," Charley said softly. "My baby would never forgive me if I let you go in black."

Now, Zoey glared at the dress in the mirror while buttoning it. Charley was right about it looking good on her. The tight bodice showed off her bust and narrow waist, and the puffy skirt made her buff legs look slight.

Zoey wondered whether she had time to change.

She stuffed her hands into the little pockets on the skirt. Typically, she felt one of Cindy's little scraps of paper in there. When she pulled it from the pocket, she found something written in

Cindy's handwriting. "I would not change a thing about this gold ring," it read. Gold ring? Had Cindy gotten—married?

"Zoey, what's taking so long?" Marty shouted.

She stuffed the paper back into the pocket and dashed into the bedroom. Marty didn't comment on the dress, as he hustled her out the door, so maybe it wasn't as inappropriate as she thought.

The memorial service was held in a chapel in La Jolla. Quite a few people had arrived before them. Some of the athletes wore work-out clothing, though most had assumed the traditional look.

"Hasn't she been to a funeral before?" someone behind her whispered.

Marty turned that way. "Zoey, was she talking about you?"

Zoey told him he could bet on it.

"Why? You don't look any different from anyone else. Look at her." He pointed at a woman in a charcoal print dress.

Zoey started to laugh. But she saw he was serious. Was Marty colorblind? She never guessed, though there were clues, which she had simply taken as an eccentric color sense. Marty spotted the minister and rushed off before Zoey could kid him about it.

Even after they opened the chapel doors, most everyone continued to mill around the chapel's vestibule. Music began drifting out. Willi Bogs' *Together.* Had Cindy been a fan? How sad that Zoey didn't know. She moved away from the door and the irritating sound of that song.

She saw Alicia head into the church, trailed by the ever-present Rick. Would a less-demanding woman have appealed to him? She tried to make it fit, but honesty reared its ugly head. She couldn't see Rick Salaz as Cindy's married man.

She spotted Dale meandering around the fringe of the crowd. He didn't seem to know many people in triathlon, and it was a close-knit community, though maybe he wasn't any more social than she was. He'd slicked his hair back today and donned a navy suit and a somber expression. He looked so shockingly handsome, he took her breath away as effectively as a belt of vodka. She turned away before he spotted her.

She bumped into a woman in a black knit dress. Miranda Griffin, five-time Ironman winner and the unquestioned queen of the sport. Zoey had never raced against her. Miranda only competed in the Ironman and a few Ironman-length events a year. She never raced in the Classic. In her simple black dress, she looked more like a young society matron than the fiercest competitor Zoey ever seen. She remembered that Miranda's husband was some corporate executive, so Zoey wasn't far off about one aspect of her life.

Miranda grasped Zoey hands and held them out so she could inspect the dress. "Zoey, you were the only one who had the courage to get it exactly right."

Zoey felt like a hypocrite.

Fortunately, Miranda switched to a more comfortable topic. "I hear you had quite a showing in yesterday's ride. I wish I could have made it."

Now Miranda was being hypocritical. She trained alone.

"I'm looking forward to taking you on in Hawaii one of these years, Zoey." Miranda smiled when she said it, as if she considered Zoey an interesting challenge, not a serious threat. Zoey vowed to change that.

When Miranda moved away, Rob and Zoey spotted each other on opposite sides of the crowd and made their way toward the middle. She'd forgotten how brooding he looked when humor didn't soften his features; today's dark circles under his eyes increased that impression.

"My, God, Zoey—I still can't believe it." Rob gave his head a helpless shake.

She nodded in agreement. "Where's Lacey?"

Rob turned and motioned for her to follow him. She thought he was leading her to his wife. Instead, he just drew outside the chapel door, where he promptly lit a cigarette.

"Lacey's...away just now. I haven't told her about Cindy." He must have sensed Zoey's disapproval because he rushed to add, "Lacey's being here wouldn't bring Cindy back."

Is that why we honor the dead? To bring them back? Zoey looked at her friend, but a veil of smoke hampered her scrutiny. She hated what she was thinking—that Rob had been Cindy's lover. Was that why he didn't tell his wife about her death?

The sound of sirens tore Zoey's attention away from Rob. Police cars came into view, one after another. Brakes squeaking, they jerked to a halt, surrounding the chapel.

Thirty-eight

CHAOS. THE POLICE came to impose order on them, but what they released instead was chaos. And panic. And when the bomb squad arrived—desperation.

But first, police officers armed with bullhorns herded the mourners out of the chapel and gathered them together on the rich grassy lawn. One cop with a rifle attempted to guard the crowd, his eyes continually circling the rooftops around them. Zoey would have laughed, since none of the surrounding structures were higher than one-story, but for the cop's grim expression.

Police cars fanned around the chapel, blocking the street. Lou arrived after the first rush of patrol cars, followed quickly by Mackenzie, even though that wasn't his jurisdiction.

Cindy's shattered parents were allowed to leave. Charley asked Marty to drive them back to their hotel. And after a brief whispered conference with a beefy man with a shaved head, whom Zoey took to be Lou's superior, they let Rob wander off up the block, where his cell phone signal went through when he placed a call. But they squeezed the rest of the mourners into a tight mass of humanity, where fear cultivated like fungus in a Petri dish.

The procession of cars and vans continued, but the next round of vehicles carried the press. Though they were forced to park at the end of the block, the men and women of the media, armed with their microphones and cameras, strained at the tape the police had strung, calling to the mourners, shouting to the cops, demanding answers.

Dale left for a quick exchange with Lou, then returned to the group on the lawn. Zoey wormed her way through the crowd to join him.

"Dale, what's going on?"

"Why ask me?" he barked with savage force. "You're the one who wished for a media circus, Zoey. Are you happy with it now?"

How could he ask?

It took more than an hour for Rob to line up a function room in a nearby hotel. In small groups, they were finally permitted to return to their cars. But they were ordered to wait in them until everyone was ready, when they rode in a caravan to the hotel under a police escort.

The gathering that followed had been billed as a pro meeting, such as the ones race directors hold before their events. But Rob was apparently the only one who believed he could contain it to the professional athletes. Or that the small room he'd rented would suffice. Everyone who had known and loved Cindy, from her elite triathlete friends, to her grocer and bartender, pushed into that inadequate room until the bodies poured out the door and snaked down the hall. The meeting was held up again when the hotel insisted they shift to another space, and Rob argued with the function manager about the price. And with each delay, the pressure mounted.

It had neared the detonation point by the time the large bald man, introduced to them now as Lieutenant Phillip Taylor of the SDPD, climbed onto the riser that had been set up at the front of the room and took the mike. Holding a sheet of paper before him, he dispensed with preliminaries.

"This correspondence was sent to our headquarters and all the area media outlets this morning from someone who calls himself 'Reckoning.' " Lieutenant Taylor paused to hold up a Ziplock bag containing a typed sheet of canary-colored paper, the original presumably, then read from a copy. " 'Free the Prophet, Willi Bogs, from his enslavement by the self-serving athletic and pseudo-charitable establishments that twist his truths to serve their ends—

or the infidel, Cindy Orr, won't be the last to die. For every day The Prophet remains in captivity, another athlete will be sacrificed on his altar.' " Taylor cleared his throat. " 'Reckoning' added this postscript: 'Unless they all die together today.' "

Silence gripped that room, until a shrill voice at the rear cried, "I warned you, didn't I?"

Everyone twisted around in time to watch Randy Ames climb onto a folding chair. The frump secretary hovered by his side, still glowing with awe of the Great Geek.

Ames didn't look especially thrilled by the victory he claimed. His lean face was pinched and shiny with sweat. "Didn't I say that you were releasing forces you couldn't control?" he screamed.

Ames himself proved to be the force that shattered Lieutenant Taylor's control. Chaos triumphed again as everyone shouted at once. Some rushed for the door, pushing aside anyone who got in their way; a fight broke out. The press burst through the barrier the police had established and swarmed over them like locusts. Taylor's repeated demands for silence were lost in the storm of noise. Hysteria ruled with abandon.

Except within Zoey. A curious sense of relief stole over her, despite the new threat. This reign of terror wasn't about her, after all. She felt vindicated. No one could blame it on her anymore. No one. Except maybe…Zoey herself.

Thirty-nine

IT STILL CAME down to Zoey, Dale reminded himself. She was at the heart of it, the ultimate cause, the primary benefactor.

He leaned over the men's room sink and splashed water on his face. He didn't even wipe it off, he just stared into the mirror, with the water dripping down, soaking into the fabric of his only available suit.

This latest wrinkle was a nightmare.

Lou didn't agree. "Don't know what you're griping about, Dale Evans," Lou had said earlier. "If this joker follows through on his threat, it's gonna be hell on the athletes. Won't catch me working out till we pick him up. But it's a break for you, *amigo*. It focuses the attention right where you need it."

Dale didn't know about that. The nuts and grandstanders were stirring it up so much, would anyone recognize the truth when it finally surfaced?

He was also running out of time. The athletes weren't the only ones who'd be lucky if they survived till the race. Well, he had to take the hand he was dealt and play the best damn game he could—knowing the life he was staking wasn't his.

Dale yanked a paper towel from the dispenser. The water hadn't cooled him down at all. And it didn't do a thing to relieve the ever-present knot in his gut and the questions that produced it: When the truth did come out—as it must—what would happen to Zoey? And why did he care?

Forty

IT HAD NOTHING to do with me. Zoey kept repeating that to herself, and it calmed her like a mantra. Cindy's murder had nothing to do with her. Anyone could see that.

After the meeting, Marty had dropped her off at the condo, taking only enough time for bathroom and snack breaks before returning to the hotel to meet with Rob and the police. They were going to set up training guidelines and a schedule the athletes could follow. Before Marty left, he ordered her not to leave the condo, and she hadn't. Yet.

But neither had she been alone. The phone never stopped ringing. Mostly the point of the calls was to engage in mutual hand wringing. "Isn't it awful?" and "What are we going to do?" were typical refrains, along with a few, "He isn't going to stop me!" which you'd expect from triathletes. Zoey's only question was why they all wanted to share their angst with her. Finally, she realized those calls were unspoken apologies from people who had held her responsible for Cindy's death. While she'd have respected them more had they been more direct, she still felt grateful for the impulse.

Yet for the first time she questioned the unnamed hostility that had been coming her way for some time. Okay, so she blabbed to the press about Pat O'Hara's dirty little steroid secret. But triathlon was the sport of mavericks, where directness and honesty were valued. She certainly wasn't the only one who felt as she did about O'Hara's transgression. Could she be wrong about the source of the friction between her and her community? What else could have been at the root of it?

The phone kept ringing. As gratifying as vindication was Zoey couldn't keep taking those calls—she needed to think. She disconnected the phone again.

But the thoughts filling the silence that followed weren't so comforting. If Zoey believed her friends should have been more forthright, she knew she had to hold herself to the same standard. While Cindy's death wasn't entirely her fault, she wasn't blameless, either. Locked away in her mind were memories that might have made a difference, which might again.

She kept telling herself she was trying to remember, but she finally faced that lie. She hated looking into the murky corners of her mind that she kept shuttered from view. Everything that ever came out of those places had devastated her. But she should have known by now that the price of giving in to fear was higher than the price of pain.

She'd lived a large part of her life cowering before her fears. No question, giving in to it then had saved her—but it had also robbed her of what she needed to face herself. After years of heedlessly throwing herself at every challenge that came her way, she still hadn't gotten back what that frightened time had taken away. She couldn't afford to lose any more of her self-respect now.

She tapped the reserve of strength that had gotten her through when everything in her cried out to quit—and she pledged it in the name of truth. Big, tough words—but she meant them. She would learn what was behind the door that shielded the forbidden part of her mind—or she would die trying.

Zoey Morgan was gonna kick some ass.

Forty-one

RECKONING? TOMASO THOUGHT. *Who* the hell was Reckoning?

Could it be one of his protégés, writing his own scenario? Nah, they were psychos, but this was too weird even for them. Besides, they knew enough not to cross him. It had to be some crazy independent, working on his own.

Tomaso dried his face. He had to calm down, to assess how much damage this nutcase could do to him. He didn't care if someone else wanted to take credit for killing Cindy, but the fruitcake was also focusing attention on an area best left in the dark.

This serial screwball's manifesto could work to his advantage in one sense, though. Now they would blame Zoey's death on this Reckoning-character when they nabbed him. Especially if he picked off a few more athletes first. The cops would never question that Zoey and Cindy were just part of the series.

But the timing was critical. If anyone looked too long and hard at the administration of this race—Tomaso was in deep shit.

He'd just have to hurry things along.

Forty-two

HIDDEN MEMORY IS *a feral creature,* Zoey knew. You can't just say you're going to remember something you've locked away and have it happen. You need to trick the truth into showing itself. Feed it clues, coax it into the open. That yacht had produced such strong feelings in Zoey, it had to be the place to start. She couldn't see how it related to Cindy, but this was a puzzle. As long as she kept putting pieces in place, even if they didn't seem individually relevant, eventually a picture would emerge.

With someone hunting them all now, leaving the condo without camouflage amounted to wearing a target. No problem. Previous occupants of the place had left all sorts of things behind. Zoey remembered seeing a San Diego souvenir T-shirt, still in the package, as well as a tote bag and baseball cap. There was even a little makeup in the bathroom.

She put a belt around the oversized T-shirt and bloused it stylishly the way Cindy often had. The hat covered her hair, and a large pair of sunglasses that Charley had given her further obscured her features. She had already painted her face to what she considered a ludicrous degree, but it fit the persona she affected: a tourist with an attitude—don't mess with her. The knife went into the pocket of her jeans.

Trepidation didn't kick in until she had to cross her first street. Streets were where athletes became targets. Maintaining the tourist's jaunty walk became harder. *Hang in there, Zoey. Victories only count if you have to fight for them.*

She recaptured her tourist's demeanor, even if she couldn't shake the feeling of being watched. Paranoia seemed normal, under the circumstances, though she spotted no consistency to the people around her beyond a group of noisy little boys roughhousing on the sidewalk behind her. As an added precaution, Zoey cut through Seaport Village, using the crowds as cover.

The initial sighting of the gleaming white yacht called Toy Boy made Zoey cringe. The gates to the slips were locked, but she'd discovered long ago that's it's easy to gain entry to some places just by acting like you belong. Zoey timed her approach to coincide with a group's departure and glided through.

But when she drew closer to the yacht, her sense of familiarity diminished. She went back to the boardwalk and found a bench, where she could study it from a distance. Yes, that was how she knew it.

Someone tapped her on the shoulder.

Zoey jerked at that touch, but the intruder was just a man wearing a T-shirt from the San Diego Zoo who wanted her to take a picture of him with his wife.

Picture…? she thought as she took his camera into her hands. Of course. She'd seen the Toy Boy in a photograph. But where? Handing back the tourist's camera as fast as she could, Zoey fought the urge to force the memory and returned to the bench to wait. The image seeped in slowly, like a solvent that stripped away her mind's protective seal.

A key. Somehow…it involved a key. Zoey pulled a set of keys from the tourist tote bag she carried. No, those were for her San Diego stay, keys to her loaner car, her loaner home.

She hurried back to the condo, heedless of her safety. She had to know. Where had she put her keys from Boulder? She found them in her purse. A key to the house, to her car and Marty's car. She felt nothing about any of them—they weren't the right keys.

Her mind drifted… As if guided by instinct, she went to the closet where she had stuffed her empty suitcases. She didn't hesitate over which suitcase to try. Something drew her right to it. She slipped her hand into the fabric pouch along one side. Her fingertips touched something metal. *The* key, the right one this time—she felt certain of that. She held it in the palm of her hand. That unconscious guidance didn't fill the blanks in so easily this time. It was just a small, brass key. Really shiny. She rubbed her fingers along the teeth, which felt a trifle rough. A copy, only recently made.

What did it open? A locker, a briefcase? No, they weren't right. Frustrated, Zoey chewed at her lower lip. She recalled a key like this from her distant past. That key had opened a post office box.

A post office box! A grainy image, like a bootleg film, formed in her mind. She could almost picture her hand opening the box— she could see it shaking. The feelings of that time returned as well. Agitation, a fear of getting caught. She had snatched the envelope out of the box and scurried away, intending to open the envelope someplace where she wouldn't feel so conspicuous. There was no letter in the envelope, she sensed, just the photographs of the yacht and the surrounding marina. No return address, either—just a postmark, from some town in Pennsylvania.

Pennsylvania? Where was she getting this? The yacht was from Philadelphia—was that knowledge coloring her memory? She squeezed her eyes shut and tried to sharpen the focus. It vanished completely. Fortunately, there was also a little voice inside that let her know when her course was true. She eased the pressure and let the voice come through.

Philadelphia—it *was* Philadelphia. Photographs of a boat in San Diego were mailed from Philadelphia to a Boulder post office box. And she saw them, she was sure of that now.

If only she were half as certain of what any of it meant.

Forty-three

ONLY MINUTES AFTER feeling so sure about that post office box and its contents, doubts began to cloud some of Zoey's conclusions. It was as if she was on a permanent roller coaster. She still felt strongly that a post office box existed, but how could she say that it was in Boulder? With her time in San Diego so murky, she could just as easily have seen those pictures there.

Still standing in the condo bedroom, she held the key up before her eyes. Besides the warmth the metal retained from being clutched in her hand, there was nothing distinctive about it. No box number, no code to suggest its location. Trying to hunt down that box from all the postal branches in the San Diego area, would make the search for a needle in a haystack look like a sure thing. She slipped the key onto the ring with the other keys from her temporary life in San Diego and tried to let that end of it go.

She closed her eyes and coaxed the image of that envelope to return. Something began to take shape. The address was handwritten, she sensed, in a bold, black marker wielded by a fussy hand. It was…

Gone. Just as effectively as a piece of broken film.

She would have to try another approach. Zoey put another image into her mind, consciously this time. The old Will-man. Willi Bogs was an infection that had festered below her skin from the start. It was time she lanced it.

It occurred to her that if she had discovered anything about him, she knew where she might have recorded it. In her training log. Her log wasn't merely a record of the mileage she'd covered, but also a journal, in which she recorded not simply how far she went in a workout, but how she felt doing it. She also tended to note everything happening in her life at the time, on the assumption that it all had an impact on her health and fitness.

With everything so chaotic lately, she couldn't remember seeing her log since the accident. She had just been scratching her training mileage on a pad she found near the bedroom phone. Yet she must have made entries before that car caused her life to detour. Her log had always a regular part of her routine, even when she traveled.

It took a few tries before she could find where she put it, but she finally came across it in the small living room desk. She turned the book over in her hands, touching the blue tweed surface. Zoey flipped through it for what she might have written after coming to San Diego.

Only she couldn't find anything. She looked again, but there were no entries for those dates. Really unlike her.

She closed the journal and just stared at the front cover, as if she expected some truth to pop from it. In the face of its stubborn silence, she turned it around and demanded as much from the back. She kept turning it, hoping for some answer. She didn't find it until she became desperate enough to study the binding. There seemed to be a gap of several pages. She opened the log so widely, the spine should have popped. Yet it didn't—because it had already been broken when someone took a razor and neatly cut out those entries.

The book slipped from her hands. All doubt vanished. She must have learned something important during that dark time she had lost in the accident. And someone didn't want her to get it back.

But who? Until she changed the lock, that condo attracted more traffic than a bus station. Much as she hated to admit it, even Cindy could have done it. Zoey had picked up her condo key from Rob's office, but it was anyone's guess where Cindy had she gotten hers.

Zoey remembered she had only started this journal about seven or eight weeks ago. She'd raced twice in Malibu during that time. If Willi Bogs had interested her that long ago, she might have looked into his life in Los Angles while she was there. She held her breath as she approached those earlier entries. When she first spotted Willi's name, she exhaled in a grateful rush.

More than an hour and several readings later, still trying to make sense of it, Zoey slowly turned the last of the pages until she reached the missing section. Deep in thought, her fingers idly moved across the next blank page. Zoey gasped when she realized what she felt. She did everything all out. She swam, biked, and ran hard—but Zoey also wrote hard; she really pressed on her pen.

Where in this place had she seen a pencil? The kitchen. Taking a moment to tuck the log back into the desk drawer, she was on her way to the kitchen, when the doorbell rang.

She really didn't want to see anyone now. She crept toward the door and pressed her eye to the peephole. Dale stood alone on the step. This business was really taking its toll on him. His beard stood out dramatically from his fair skin, and the smudges below his eyes had become tattoos. Despite her determination to stay on the trail, she threw the door open for him.

The sides of his mouth pulled down at the sight of her. "You look chipper." He made it sound like an accusation.

"You don't," she said with cheerful honesty. Still, she softened her nastiness to the extent of offering him a beer.

While grabbing a beer for him and a soft drink and cookies for herself in the kitchen, she remembered to hunt down a pencil in a kitchen drawer, and stuffed it into her pocket.

"What's wrong, Dale?" she asked when she returned. "Oh, God—no. He didn't—"

"No, Reckoning—jeez, couldn't he come up with something more clever than that? No, he hasn't attacked any other triathletes…yet. But how can you ask what's wrong? A serial killer is stalking every weekend athlete, Ames is having a field day, the media's going nuts. It's like they opened the gates of the San Diego Zoo and let the animals out to take over the city." He downed a big gulp of beer. "They've released the last Willi Bogs recording today, ahead of schedule. The pandemonium will be uncontainable now."

"It's funny that you should mention Willi Bogs," Zoey said. She told him what she discovered in her log. "Let me tell you, Dale, Willi wasn't an altar boy."

"Oh?"

"No way. He used to hang out on Hollywood Boulevard with the teenage hookers and runaways. When Willi was broke he would deal drugs to the kids, when he was flush, he would give them away. It seemed important that they like him. He slept with fourteen-year-old girls. He might have been a terrific singer, Dale, but he wasn't the pied piper you see in the DVDs. He was a weak, sleazy man."

Dale's blue eyes developed a steely glint. "Really? And what's your source for this tripe? Hookers and hustlers?"

Did he need a bandage for that exposed nerve? "I don't know my sources. I've told you only what I read in my journal, I don't remember any of it. But have you ever seen how sleazy Hollywood Boulevard is? Why would anyone hang out there if they didn't have to?" She drifted across the room.

Dale followed her. "I can think of a lot of reasons why a good man would frequent a neighborhood of runaways. Those kids need help. What do you suggest we do, just lock them up and throw away the key?" he snapped. "I can think of one very good reason why Will would keep going back there."

Instead of telling her what that reason could be, Dale just drained his beer and smacked the bottle down hard on an end table, saying he had to go. Why had he come?

Zoey didn't have time to care. Before the door clicked shut behind him, she was back at the desk, digging out her journal once again. She turned to the first blank page after the missing section. She pulled the pencil from her pocket. Using the side of the pencil point, she rubbed the graphite lightly over the whole page. Apparently, she hadn't pressed evenly when she wrote on the missing page. She could only just make out the word "Willi," but the words "Pacific Beach" were not only distinct, they were underlined.

Pacific Beach? Anxiety tightened her chest.

She went back to the kitchen for another cookie, which she absently munched while wandering around. But when she noticed she was leaving a trail of crumbs, she decided to put the time to better use by straightening the condo as she mulled things over. She had canceled the cleaning service Shortz SportzWatchez provided when she changed the locks.

She went back to the kitchen for a dish towel she could use as a dust cloth and a paper bag to empty the wastebaskets. Busy work. None of the baskets had more than a tissue or two in them, except for the one next to Marty's side of the bed. That was stuffed burger wrappers, gasoline credit card receipts, as well as two copies of supermarket tabloids. How such a classy guy could have such atrocious taste in reading material, she'd never understand.

Her cowardice returned when she came across her leather portfolio. It was still where Cindy had left it on the desk, and dusty now. She hesitated while cleaning it. Could Cindy have missed something the day she had it? Zoey made herself open it.

Funny, it looked even emptier now. Where was that card, the one from Marty? She searched through everything, the folder and all the portfolio's compartments.

The card was gone.

Forty-four

PACIFIC BEACH, SAN Diego's funky seaside neighborhood, was raucous. Crowds poured from doorways and filled the sidewalks, boom boxes blasted. It was summer and the livin' was easy. Except for Zoey.

The place gave her the creeps, though that feeling could have been just a residue of guilt. She told Marty she was going swimming with Dickie. Marty would have fought her about going to Pacific Beach alone, so she had to tell him something. But that didn't make the lie any easier to live with. She was being unfair to him, but she didn't know what else she could do. When denial and flight failed her, the only weapon left in Zoey's arsenal was fighting alone.

A skater zeroed in on her. By hopping to the side, Zoey avoided having her feet crushed, only to step on someone else's shoes. She'd be safer in the street. She stepped off the curb—and instantly heard the approach of a roaring engine. She didn't even look at it until she'd jumped from its path. But it wasn't the dreaded white Mercedes that Dale said had hit both her and Cindy, just a motorcycle being ridden by a little kid. The driver didn't look more than twelve. They say when new drivers start looking too young to you, you know you're getting old. Only twenty-eight, and she already felt over-the-hill.

She made her way to the boardwalk. It was more crowded, naturally, but the skaters there didn't seem to be taking such deliberate aim. Zoey kept finding herself searching the crowd, without knowing what she was looking for. Her nerves felt so edgy, her skin crawled.

She felt Willi's presence, but why wouldn't she? His latest

song poured from every open window. What was wrong with her? Why was she so determined to label the man who produced those magnificent lyrics as a sleazy lowlife?

Willi would have felt at home there in Pacific Beach, Zoey thought. Kids crowded the streets, so many of them on the fringe, most already lost. The little girls peddling their prepubescent wares were out in force. Some already pros, while others hadn't taken that final step into the abyss, but weren't far away.

Zoey passed an alley without giving it a thought, until she'd walked several yards beyond it. She stopped and turned, causing several people to bump into her. Bucking the human current, she made her way back to the opening of the alley.

Dark. Not a place she'd enter willingly, yet Zoey felt certain she had at sometime. Another flashback kicked in, a sensation this time. She suddenly felt as if the knife were in her hand, instead of in her pocket where she knew she'd put it before leaving the condo. This must have been where had come into her possession. But how? Was that where she bought it from Jorge Ramirez?

Fumbling absently at the set of keys she'd pinned to the elastic waist of the black knit pants she wore tonight, Zoey found the small flashlight attached to the key ring, and she pointed it into the alley. Apart from enough trash on the ground to top-off a landfill, and stains on the stucco that indicated many men had used that alley as a bathroom, there was nothing significant about it. She pushed at the memory, but it dissolved. Though it left her with a sense of empowerment. She felt stronger as a result of whatever happened there.

As her preoccupation faded, Zoey's awareness that she was still gaping into that dark alley returned. As did the sensation that she was being watched. Yet when she glanced around, the only real attention she drew was from some hostile looking kid, and then only in passing. Maybe he needed to pee. She walked on.

Zoey passed the open door of a club that sent out waves that assaulted various senses, the stench of stale beer, and the sound of atrocious singing. The stand-up sign on the sidewalk said, "Willi

Bogs Impersonator Night."

And she yearned to be a household name.

Zoey felt familiar with the area, but her sense of *deja vu* was shadowy at best, except for that alley. Though maybe there was also something in the deliberate way she felt her eyes searching the distance. What was she looking for?

After a while, her sense of familiarity drifted away. She took a turn and went back to Mission Boulevard where she'd parked the minivan. Halfway there, she spotted Bucky Jack on a corner, surrounded by a group of little boys and one teenager. The teenager seemed to be scanning the crowds.

Zoey's first thought when Bucky spotted her was whether he would spill to Marty that he'd seen her. Poor liars always worry about things that will never happen. The only association Marty and Bucky shared was her award. Once the arrangements were made, neither Marty nor Zoey had any reason to see Bucky. Though she did keep running into him.

He waved at her. "Zoey, you sweet thing, come over here and catch up with ol' Bucky."

She didn't need to get that close to know ol' Bucky was a sheet or ten to the wind. When he planted a sloppy kiss on her cheek, his breath almost knocked her out. And she thought he could hold it.

"Zoey, say hi to Nick." With a toss of his head, Bucky indicated a tawny-skinned teenager of mixed racial heritage, with wary gray eyes in a long ferret face. "Nicky and me, we thought we'd take some o' the little guys out on the town."

While the little ones came in a variety of sizes and colors, they shared the same haunted look. If all the Touchstone Foundation did for them couldn't wipe those expressions off their faces, a night of fun wouldn't make a dent. She put her arm around the small boy standing next to her, and the poor thing clutched her leg. The shoulders beneath the tattered shirt felt so frail. Her heart just ached for them.

"Jeez, Zoey, the last time I saw you, you were telling me about getting hit by a car, and now it seems there's a killer on the loose. I sure feel bad about your little friend, Cindy. That was one fine-looking woman."

Contempt flickered across Nick's dusky face. At his age, he probably considered Bucky too old to appreciate a young woman like Cindy. Zoey wasn't that crazy about what Bucky considered Cindy's most important attribute, either. But that was Bucky. She could see genuine regret for her death in his watery blue eyes.

"You remember any more about what happened to you, girl?"

She shook her head. Even if she wanted to share her flashbacks, it wouldn't be with someone who wouldn't remember the conversation in the morning. Bucky's being drunk bothered her. Was he their only driver?

She tentatively broached that subject. "I have plenty of room in my van, Bucky. I could drop the boys off for you at the Touchstone House."

Bucky's head swiveled around. "Well, where's your car at?"

Nick rattled a set of keys in the pocket of his tattered, faded jeans. "I've got it covered. Still gotta round up a couple of 'em, anyway." His voice sounded a little sharp, but he offered Zoey a flickering smile.

He didn't look old enough to drive, not to mention being the designated adult. Why is it the kids always get stuck shouldering the responsibility? She knew what that was like. She felt lousy about the ferret-thought; the boy couldn't help the shape of his face. She made her goodbyes, promising to see Bucky again at the race, and headed off toward her car.

She had to park the minivan beneath a burned-out street lamp. Not ideal, but the best she could do. She didn't notice anything wrong until the smell hit her nose. She directed her flashlight first at the grass strip along the curb, then at the car.

It took her breath away. Someone had written the word *bitch* on the side of the van in dog shit.

Fumbling with the remote door opener, Zoey scrambled into the van. Even after she pressed her hands against the steering wheel, they wouldn't stop shaking. Despite her precautions, *he'd* found her. She pounded the wheel until her fists hurt. Yet her frustration remained unspent.

She lurched into traffic. Inching along the crowded narrow street, she couldn't say if she was followed. But once traffic opened up, she tried every maneuver she ever read in hardboiled PI novels. Last second spurts through red lights, sudden left turns before oncoming traffic. Considering how jealously she guarded her own right to run on the roads, it was like she was out to collect bumper trophies tonight. Too bad it would never be the right one. Worse still, after all those dizzying turns, she couldn't say for sure whether she'd lost him. Her stalker was clearly better at this than she was.

Her assailant's expertise began to bother her. Zoey thought about the types of offenses he'd perpetrated. Cindy's murder and her attempted one were pretty straightforward. No games. But the other actions taken against her, such as slashing her bike tire and especially the dog crap, just felt spiteful. And after declaring war on the whole sport of triathlon, it still felt as if she was being singled out for his nastiness.

But what did she know? Not even where she was now; she had gotten lost.

Fortunately, she'd discovered a local map in the glove compartment. She studied it now when she stopped at lights. Despite all the time she'd been driving, she didn't think she'd gone that far. Too many turns. She sensed she was somewhere near the Sports Arena, maybe the Loma Portal section, or Roseville.

She'd raced through those areas occasionally, but had never paid much attention to the scenery. Wasn't that the story of her life? The area seemed solidly upper-middle class, but without the distinction of the glitzy new convention center area where she was staying or chi-chi La Jolla or even funky Pacific Beach. And what an incredible number of stores. On Rosecrans, the main street, there was a shopping center on every corner.

She pulled into a gas station and used the time while she pumped gas for further surveillance. No one showed any interest in her. She noticed the station had a small car wash. One of the simple ones, in which soapy water was pumped through a brush that the driver wielded. Too bad it was closed. She took a chance and told the lone attendant about the disgusting calling card someone had left her. The nice guy took pity on her and turned the equipment on.

The dog crap had dried, naturally, solidifying beyond her level of elbow grease. She soaped it well and let it soften. While waiting, she remembered she'd told Marty she was going swimming. She pulled off the baseball cap she wore in a useless attempt at disguise and ran a handful of suds through her short hair.

Her life made less sense to her every day.

After leaving the gas station, Zoey cruised Rosecrans in search of a supermarket. Despite her fears, she was famished again. Zoey thought she'd pick up a few sandwiches at the market's deli. But after just marveling over the proliferation of shopping centers, now she couldn't find any. Some Naval installation hogged one side of the street and there was nothing but houses on the other. She made a U-turn and pulled into the first large shopping center she came across. While stepping from the van, she spotted Dale driving past.

Funny, she never thought to ask where he lived. This seemed more like Lou's kind of neighborhood. Zoey couldn't say where he was headed, beyond the other side of the sprawling shopping center. Trailing behind him on foot, she lost sight of his little Focus for a moment. But pedestrians and speed bumps slowed him, and she spotted him again after he had parked and as he was approaching the stores. Zoey nearly called out to him, only then she saw where he was headed. To a mail center.

A private mail center—she'd forgotten about those when she

found that key in her luggage. Their presence probably increased the number of mailboxes in the area by tenfold. Not that she expected to find the box that fit her key by just trying them all.

Dale hadn't noticed her yet, though she wasn't far away. Still, she hesitated about alerting him to her presence. She didn't suspect Dale, did she? No, that was crazy. She hadn't even met him until after the accident. How could she have *his* key?

But with all the gaps in her head, how could she be sure of anything? She remembered that bit of conversation she'd overheard on her phone, the one with the woman, Holly. She couldn't remember now why she concluded she must be with the police. Could she have been his wife? Could Dale have been Cindy's married lover? They both acted as if they'd never met when they came together at her condo. But maybe what she'd taken to be Dale's star-stuck greeting to Cindy was just shock.

Once Dale entered the mail place, Zoey crept to the door and watched to see where his box was located. He had been right about her, she wasn't very trusting. She hated that part of herself. Still, she knew she'd come back and try her key in his box. She *had* to know who was on her side, and especially, who wasn't.

Forty-five

DAYS CRAWLED BY. Zoey didn't see Dale during that time. Nor had she tried her key in his mailbox—part of her wanted to know whether *that* was the box where she had found the yacht's photo, while another part resisted. And neither she, nor the police, turned up anything to relieve the unrelenting pressure on her community. Nerves chafed like a marathoner's thighs.

But the sport of triathlon had made the big time. The bottom-crawlers from the major TV networks staked their tents in San Diego in the hopes that the one who called himself Reckoning would reward them with some particularly gruesome footage to grab the ratings. Success, as usual, was a two-edged sword.

The fallout that hit Classic was predictable. The more sensible competitors dropped out, while others flocked to it in record numbers. Pros included, Zoey was sorry to say. For her, there was no question of leaving—it was her fight. For once in her life, she refused to permit herself the option of flight.

Rob called an unprecedented number of race meetings, supposedly to keep the competitors informed. Too bad he hadn't arranged for someone to do the same for him—Rob always seemed so vacuous at those meetings, Zoey thought he looked like he'd wandered into the wrong room. And forget about his other races. The Classic might have been his flagship event, but it was only one of a series spread throughout the season. Rob showed so little interest in those, you would have thought he intended to quit the business after this race. He was either a man in denial—or he knew something that Zoey didn't.

And through all of it, Zoey continued to live her secret life of lifting rocks, desperately hoping she wouldn't find her nearest and dearest under them.

Fortunately, she had the time for it. This close to the race, she had tapered her training to its lowest level. Sure, she should have used the hours she freed up to rest her body, but she rationalized that she couldn't relax until she learned the truth. And she stubbornly refused to acknowledge how the strain was wearing her down.

Zoey returned to the marina to take another crack at the Toy Boy, but she found it had left. She panicked when she saw it was gone. She couldn't let any of the pieces wander off before she put the puzzle together. She spotted a portly man wearing a hokey navy blazer, with gold braid, and a yacht captain's cap. Zoey stopped him before he stepped through the gate into one of the slips and asked him about the Toy Boy.

The man removed the cap and scratched absently at the inky black comb-over pressed against his time-spotted scalp. "The Toy Boy? I heard it went up to Oceanside for some repairs."

"Where in Oceanside?" she demanded. But he didn't know. "Did you see it go out?"

"Not me, I was down below gettin' some bubbly for her date. You ain't a cop, are ya? I mean, I don't exactly ask them for an ID, if you get my drift."

Considering that it was delivered like an elbow in the ribs, how could she help but get it?

"My girl saw it, though. She said it had been piloted by a guy who reminded her of Heathcliff, whatever that means. Hey, isn't Heathcliff that cat in the comic strip?"

This aging Lothario made Zoey sick. She hated men who reduced women to an age they thought they could buy.

"Heathcliff? It's a rap artist," Zoey answered with a straight face. "Not your kind of music."

The guy stuffed the captain's hat back onto his head. "What do you mean? Sure, it is. I knew that, I just forgot."

The idea of his wasting a day hunting for the CD cheered her.

Until he started rubbing her arm.

"How about you, honey? You wanna go for a little spin? Bet I could show you things you never seen before." The old leach wiggled bushy black eyebrows that looked like caterpillars in the throes of death.

"No doubt you could, hotshot," Zoey said, removing his hand forcibly from her arm. "But then you'd need to take your meals through a straw."

Great, Zoey, burn a source. But it did feel good.

After striking out at the marina, she finally returned to the shopping center where she'd seen Dale. The question of whether to test her key in his box was tearing her apart. By the time she gave into it, however, someone had hung a sign on the door of the mail center indicating it would be closed for several days due to a death in the family. Box-holders could still enter with their door keys, as they did at night. But the store was closed to all others.

Zoey rapped on the front door anyway. Someone had to come in and sort the mail. She drove around the back, where she pressed her ear to the rear door. Quiet. There was nobody in there now.

Continuing to strike out sapped Zoey's momentum like a slow tire leak. She escaped to the minivan and drove without direction. Somehow, she wound up at Cindy's house.

She let herself in with the key Charley had given her. With stacks of boxes, both the packed ones and the empties, filling much of the living room, and the air having taken on a stale quality since the house was closed up, Zoey couldn't feel Cindy's presence there anymore. Her fists knotted at her sides. Someone was going to pay for what he did to her.

Whoever had trashed the house must have left some clue behind. She and Charley had just been too upset to find it. Zoey tackled the desk again. Charley had just stuffed the dumped contents back into the drawers. Zoey grabbed a carton now and systematically worked her way down from the top. None of Cindy's poetry remained. Not much of anything of value, actually. Nothing that shed any light on the man in Cindy's life.

The bottom drawer was the only one the intruder hadn't dumped during his search, though they'd found it yanked out and pawed through. It had stuck a little, and Charley had forced it closed. Now it wouldn't budge at all.

Zoey removed the upper drawers and shined her little key-ring flashlight into it. One of Cindy's little slips of paper had gotten stuck in the drawer runner. Zoey gently worked it free and pulled the piece of paper out to see what Cindy had written on it. Dale's name and an address were scrawled on the top. Zoey would have to check the map to see whether it was near the shopping center where she saw him. Below that, Cindy had written Rob's name and telephone number.

Rob and Dale, a friend and an ally. Both beyond suspicion, right? Too bad both also fit the shorthand description the literate date of that slob at the harbor had given to Zoey.

Forty-six

ZOEY SAT BACK on her heels, still before Cindy's desk, staring at the note she'd freed from the runner. There wasn't any reason why Cindy shouldn't have had Dale's address. Zoey didn't, but she never made it her business to dredge things out of people the way Cindy had. Naturally, Cindy had Rob's name and number; the pros all had dealings with him. The curious aspect was their appearing together. Cindy organized her life with those little scraps. That she had coupled those names connected them in some way.

As Zoey drove back to San Diego from Cindy's house, her weary body cried out for a nap. But as compulsive as she was, she knew she wouldn't rest until she made some sense of the joining of Rob's name and Dale's. Had there been something Cindy had wanted to share with the both of them? As far apart as their worlds were, what could it be?

Zoey decided to tackle Rob first. Dale would be tougher—he still puzzled her. Circumstance was all that had brought Dale and Zoey together. When they weren't locking horns, the relationship they shared seemed deeper than it normally would after such a short acquaintance. But what did she really know about him? She drifted back to that semiconscious state after the accident when the paramedics wanted to leave her for dead, but Dale made them press on. He had recognized her. Sure, he was in the sport and had some interest in the leaders, but so was Lou and he hadn't known who Zoey was until Dale told him. Who recognizes someone passed out in the street that they've only seen in pictures?

She also remembered Dale's desperation. Whether she lived or died had mattered to him in some personal way. He even hung around the hospital while she was unconscious, when his department had merely asked to be called. Had she known him before? Or was he just some stranger who decided she would unknowingly play a role in his life?

When she approached Rob's office from a perpendicular street, Zoey noticed him crossing the parking lot at a fast clip. She thought about trying to catch him. Only there was something furtive about the way Rob kept glancing over his shoulder while he made his way to his car. Even as Zoey told herself her unnamed suspicions were crazy, she waited. When his Volvo wagon drove into the street, she let a few cars pass, then tucked in behind.

Wherever he was headed, he was pressed for time. His car alternated between lurching and sudden braking. She also thought she heard his horn a few times. Not exactly the attitude of a laid-back lucky guy. He seemed to be heading toward the Hotel Circle area. He wasn't having an affair, was he? *Another* affair?

Zoey sighed in relief when his car screeched to a halt at a Volvo dealership. This place was owned by the same dealer that had provided the athletes' loaner minivans. She and Dale had dropped her damaged tire off just a couple of lots down.

It was also where—according to the employees—Zoey had put in a personal appearance just the day before that car ran her down. How odd that she couldn't remember something so innocuous. She hadn't forgotten any of the times the Shortz SportzWatchez company dragged her out for their dog-and-pony shows. Why would one sponsor's appearance be remembered and another resolutely forgotten?

Rob had either come to the Volvo dealership for some reason connected to the race, or to have his own Volvo serviced. Yet he didn't head for the service entrance, and he threw off a salesman's approach on his way into the showroom.

But when he returned just minutes later, he wasn't alone— Patrick O'Hara trailed behind him. A race director and a banned athlete. *Oh, Rob—no.*

Rob's walk back to his car was so brisk, O'Hara had to struggle to catch up. A sad story for a man who was once a competitive athlete. Apparently, O'Hara didn't like being left behind, either. He grabbed Rob's arm and spun him around.

One look at Rob's darkened face must have told him that wasn't smart because O'Hara suddenly dropped his hand and his shoulders rounded submissively. But the action worked, Rob didn't run away anymore. They argued for a couple of minutes, then Rob appeared to acquiesce. But Rob's dark, handsome face looked tight with embarrassment as he turned back toward his car. For O'Hara—or himself?

Rob drove just as erratically after leaving the dealership. Zoey discovered she possessed some proficiency in following. Though she still cheered when Rob finally exchanged the streets for the freeway. It was much easier to follow someone on a wide, multi-lane expressway. As if by instinct, she tucked herself into his blind spot and waited for him to make some move. She couldn't help but wonder whether she'd ever done this before.

Rob cut over to the right lane. She let a few cars collect behind him and joined the parade up the Ardath Road exit and over the freeway. It looked like he was headed for La Jolla, but not down-town district, judging by the turns he made. Climbing into the hills, she lost her sense of direction. All she knew was that that was a residential area, with progressively narrower, less-traveled streets. Once their vehicles were the only ones on the road, she had to give him a big lead. When he took another turn, he was too far away for her to read the street sign, but she tried to count the number of the short blocks she would need to pass. Yet when she made what she thought was the right turn, Rob's car was gone.

How was that possible? He'd only been out of sight for a few minutes. Zoey knew she was tired, but she wasn't that confused. How could he have disappeared?

She pulled over to the curb and yanked a pair of maps from her glove compartment. Wouldn't you know? The place where Rob had lost her was north of the area covered by her San Diego map and south of what appeared on the North County one. Great—no-man's-land. But he couldn't have gotten far. She'd just drive around the neighborhood until she spotted his car, Zoey decided. Fortunately, the hillside area offered an ocean view; as long as she kept that in sight, she'd keep some sense of direction.

Of course, the city planners and builders couldn't have twisted those streets any more if they'd tried. All she could say for certain after a long search—were the streets Rob's car *wasn't* parked on. So where was it? Beyond some low-profile medical clinic at the end of one street, there was nothing there but private homes. Where could he have gone?

If she had to give up on Rob, Zoey vowed she would not let the other fish get away. She raced back to the dealership to have a talk with O'Hara. What could he do to her in a public place?

Her fears betrayed her as she drew closer, as something began to quake deep inside of her. She didn't know whether to feel relief or disappointment when she saw O'Hara behind the wheel of a new mustard-colored Volvo approaching from the other direction.

No time for either emotion. She made a quick U-turn. Since she was the last person he'd expect to see behind him, she didn't have to be as careful trailing him. Unfortunately, he didn't make it any easier for her than Rob had. O'Hara stuck strictly to surface streets and unfamiliar ones at that.

Zoey found San Diego hard enough to navigate when she wasn't trying to tail someone. She didn't know the city's history, but she suspected all those sections sprang up separately, and they only thought about connecting them later—when it was too late to set up a sensible grid. Streets stopped and started, names changed without warning. There were sections so isolated, she'd never found access, Yet people seemed to live and work in them quite comfortably. Maybe they dropped them in by helicopter.

O'Hara seemed to be leading her to one of those industrial neighborhoods she always noticed from the 5 Freeway. Could it be a trap? Zoey didn't think he'd spotted her. Just as she had read anxiety in Rob's driving style, she considered O'Hara relentless behind the wheel. Something was drawing him there.

When O'Hara coasted to a stop, Zoey braked to put more distance between them. The big lug threw most of his drug-induced power into slamming his car door shut after he parked. His destination, as well as the object of his ire, seemed to be a self-storage facility on the other side of the road. O'Hara started across the street just as a car approached. The bully stepped into its path and shot the driver an ugly look, forcing the woman behind the wheel to screech to a halt while he ambled across.

Surrounding the storage yard was a high fence and an electric gate. Judging by the way O'Hara kicked the electronic key reader, he didn't hold one of the badges necessary to gain entry. He yanked at the gate a few times. He didn't seem too bright, but his use of steroids told her that. He finally scaled the chain-link fence.

Zoey slipped from her minivan and followed him across the street. The owners of the facility had tastefully landscaped a small patch of ground next to the entrance, but they'd allowed it to become overgrown. Better for her. She crept between two sprawling bushes and pressed her face to the fence.

Though they had those self-storage places all over the country, Zoey had never paid any attention to them. The lockers appeared to come in two sizes, small ones that were accessed by ordinary doors and garages with roll-up doors. O'Hara stood with his back to her before the third garage along the near row. He yanked on that door as well, but it was locked. He looked around and finally noticed a small ventilation screen near the ground. Dropping into a pushup position, he stared through the screen.

Only seconds later, O'Hara jumped to his feet. He ran to the fence and tried to scale it so fast, his feet kept slipping. No ambling this time—he couldn't get away fast enough.

Zoey waited until he'd driven off before leaving the bushes and scaling the fence. Not being so macho, she didn't need to make it a pushup, so she just bent down before the screen. Since the garage was dark, she couldn't see very well, even when she directed her tiny flashlight through the screen. But it looked like the only object in the storage room was a car. A *white* car.

Now why did that surprise her?

Forty-seven

WAS IT REALLY *the* car? The white Mercedes that took her friend's life, and injured Zoey and stole her memory? All Zoey could make out was the bottom of a white rear fender, but it was shaped like an older Mercedes. The mere possibility knocked the wind out of her.

Who owned it? Was O'Hara stupid enough to run her down in his own car using nothing more than a Willi Bogs mask for camouflage? He had known where to look for that car, even if he didn't have the key to the facility. Was this whole reign of terror nothing more than a personal vendetta? It wasn't hard for Zoey to imagine his coming after her after the way he acted at Ames's rally. But what about Cindy? She had never hurt him. Though it wasn't such a stretch to see O'Hara declaring war on the sport that rejected him.

It would have all fit, if only Zoey could shake her conviction that O'Hara had been horrified by finding that car there.

Zoey *had* to question Rob. He still hadn't returned by the time she arrived at his building, so she parked on the perpendicular street. He didn't keep her waiting long. After careening through his driveway, he dove into a space and cut the engine, leaving the Volvo's rear end angled into the next parking spot. He wiped his brow with the back of his hand as he crossed the parking lot, and threw a quick look at his watch before grabbing the door. Seeing him from that distance, she had to admit he made a better Heathcliff than Dale. He had that Gypsy coloring—while apart from his five o'clock shadow, Dale looked more like Casper the Friendly Ghost. Well, Casper on acid.

By continuing to wait in the van, Zoey wasn't sure whether she was giving Rob time to get settled or just stalling. Neither seemed a good idea. She walked the short block to his office, passing close to where he had left his car.

She noticed his right front bumper was crumpled. Judging by the way Rob parked, it was a wonder the whole car wasn't dented. But she had to look at it. A streak of blue paint rubbed onto the surface stood out dramatically against the leaf green bumper, as did the flecks of white paint in the crumpled zone.

She sprang away from the bumper as if it had been on fire. What was she thinking? She and Cindy had both been hit by a white Mercedes. Finding white paint on Rob's car meant nothing. What was it that she thought he did? Crashed into the Mercedes?

Zoey's head kept spinning. She glanced at the door to Rob's building. Doubting her friend had depressed her so, it pushed her exhaustion all the way to the bone. She couldn't see him now—she didn't trust herself, as tired as she was. If she slipped and said what she was thinking, she'd never be able to take it back.

More than anything, she longed to return to the condo and get some sleep. No, more than anything she wanted to forget everything she saw today. But that was the awful thing about memory. Just as you can't remember on command, you can't forget that way, either.

Craving a distraction during the drive back to the condo, Zoey flipped on the radio and caught a subdued Bucky Jack vowing to halt the release of the last Willi Bogs song.

God, no. Had something else happened? So desperate was Zoey to shut it all out now, she could have slept behind the wheel. To stay awake, she scanned the radio AM band. But she didn't hit a single report before she pulled into the condo parking area.

When she went into the unit, she found Marty hovering near

the kitchen. Before she could address him, Lou, of all people, came walking out from it. For once Lou's shoulders didn't look so rigidly erect, but rounded with fatigue. The war of nerves was taking its toll on him, too. Or something was.

"Thanks for the use of your phone, Marty. I—"

The sight of Zoey immediately claimed Lou's attention. Marty then followed the direction of Lou's stare—right to her.

"Where have you been?" they demanded at the same time.

"Never mind. I just heard Bucky Jack promise to halt the distribution of the latest Willi Bogs release. What's up?" Zoey asked.

"Our friend hit again this afternoon," Lou announced shortly. "The victim isn't a triathlete, he's an orthopedic surgeon who was just out testing his new bike in his own neighborhood. He's not dead, either, but he's gonna need some help from his colleagues in the months to come."

She stopped by the sofa and absently lifted one of the throw pillows to her chest. "Where...?"

"La Jolla, only 'bout a block from the poor slob's house."

Lou went on to describe the area where she had lost Rob earlier today. The accident must have happened not long after.

Marty came up behind Lou. "Same car?" he asked. Tension had turned Marty's lean face to stone.

"The results are inconclusive. I tell ya, one good thing about this business is that our reports are coming back *pronto*. The city can't afford this negative publicity. But who cares if they're wrong?"

Zoey clutched the pillow tighter. "How do you know the report is wrong?" she asked, her voice pinched.

Lou shrugged. "Same color and vintage, but different make. The white paint registered as coming from an old VW beetle. Similar code number maybe, and the clerk just read it wrong."

"No, it was a different car," she said without thinking.

Lou's dark eyes widened. "Zoey, what do you know?" he asked, his voice as hard as stone.

Half expecting Lou to reach for his gun, Zoey forced a laugh.

"Don't you have to read me my rights?"

Lou drew close and waved a warning finger in her face. "You watch too much TV, *chica*. The law says we only have to give 'em their rights when we question them in custody. You want that to apply to you, Zoey?"

With a shrug, Zoey gave both Marty and Lou an abridged account of her afternoon, concentrating on O'Hara, leaving out all reference to Rob. Lou promised to check the storage locker. She longed to ask him whether the paint flecks they were testing could have been the ones lodged in the crumpled zone of Rob's car. Instead, she listened to a lecture in stereo.

"Why couldn't you just stay out of it? Why did you have to get involved?" Marty asked.

"I told her to leave it to the pros," Lou said, pacing in agitation. "Zoey, you don't know what you're doing, and you're going to get yourself killed."

She slumped against the arm of the sofa. "Lou, what color was the bike?"

He stopped short. "What?"

"The bike, the surgeon's new bike. What color was it?"

"Of all the..." Lou threw his arms out in exasperation even as she could see in his eyes that his mind was sifting through the hodgepodge of facts he kept filed there. "Blue. I think it was blue."

Forty-eight

TOMASO STEWED IN angry silence. Years of planning, months in execution—and now everything was in jeopardy because some jackass couldn't keep his bumper from between the wrong bike spokes.

It also increased the pressure on the cops. If ordinary citizens were in danger now, the public wouldn't rest until the police discovered who was behind it. Would they still buy the scenario he'd set up? Decisions, decisions.

Tomaso caught himself drumming his fingers against the counter, and he identified the strange emotion he felt overtaking him. Agitation. He always figured himself immune to those mundane afflictions. But then, he'd always been in charge. Now some lousy bit player had slipped out of the background to overtake the lead.

Normally, he loved living on the edge. He liked seeing how long he could juggle the various parts, before letting it all come crashing down on some poor slob. But it was getting too chancy to let it go on much longer. He'd already set the forces in motion. Now he just needed to accelerate them, making sure they crashed at just the right time.

In the meantime, he'd have to do something about this restlessness.

Forty-nine

ZOEY FIGURED SHE was in for another lecture when Lou left. Instead, Marty just cupped her chin in his hand.

"If I were to lose you now, babe," he said with feeling, "I think I'd just pack it in." His feeble tongue click just intensified the vulnerability she saw in his hazel eyes.

That was when she spotted the flowers. A bunch of daisies, still in the florist tissue wrap, had been tossed on the couch. Marty had never brought her flowers before. Well, Zoey always insisted they were a waste of money. She scooped the bunch of daisies now and buried her face in them.

"Like 'em, Zoey? I was going to put them in water, but then Lou came and I forgot."

Lou must have been there for a while. They were pretty wilted. Who cared? She couldn't have loved those droopy daisies more if it they were long-stemmed roses. She even thought they smelled like roses, or the room did. Perhaps they'd been clustered together at the florist.

She arranged them in a milk glass vase she found in the kitchen and brought them to the bedroom, while Marty made some calls from the kitchen phone.

Zoey was still felt so exhausted, the bed drew her like an oasis. She only barely had enough energy left to exchange her street clothes for her usual bed garb, an oversized race T-shirt and underpants. She remembered pulling the covers down and pressing her head against the pillow, but after that, she recalled nothing beyond the seamless black fog that enveloped her.

Until—*it* began. It came as it always had. The snake, as she thought of it. Slithering up her leg and creeping over the top of her pants, before groping with savage force.

She felt a hand circle round her throat. Her eyes flew open. Not a snake, after all—it was Marty. It wasn't the same at all. It only felt like it.

Marty stroked her neck, while murmuring softly against her throat. "It's been so long, Zoey. I need you now."

His hand strayed to her breast. As if it had a will of its own, her own hand moved to strike his away. She overrode it, but only by harnessing every bit of her will.

"Please, Zoey. These threats have kept us apart too long."

It wasn't the threats—it was what was happening to her. It wasn't fair to him. She answered not with words, but by throwing her arms around him and pulling him tighter to her. She could endure it, however it affected her.

His tongue slid into her mouth. It felt as vile as a rag. Yet she produced a convincingly pleasurable moan. The beat within her went on. Accelerating, but not fast enough. When would it end? She grasped at him as if she wanted more.

She couldn't let Marty see that making love had become as agonizing for her as rape. Her mind, and the knowledge that it wasn't the same at all, had no power now over her body. It had nothing to do with him—she loved him. This was just what the memories did to her. Not the ones that were hidden, but the ones that wouldn't *stay* hidden.

Marty was the first person who tried to see the world through her eyes, the first ever on her side. How could she not love him with all her heart?

When he came, the bile rose as far as her throat.

Thankfully, he was too sleepy afterwards to talk; she could never have faked that. Yet it wasn't until she heard the soft snores at her side that she let the tears flow. Tears of anger, of frustration. And even then, she stilled the sobs. To protect Marty, she could never let him see what this did to her.

But she couldn't go through it again until she managed to bury the past. More deeply this time.

Fifty

LOU AND DALE shared beers across a marble table in a shadowy bar not far from where Dale kept a mailbox.

Dale slid his frosty mug back-and-forth over the smooth surface between his hands. He felt so restless, he couldn't sit still. "Zoey really found the car he used?"

Lou shrugged. "Don't know. Someone's from Kelly's unit is checking on it now. Looks pretty good."

Dale lifted his mug, but instead of drinking, his eyes merely met Lou's over the rim of the mug. "Do you believe her?"

Lou slammed his mug against the tabletop. "*Amigo,* what are the odds? We had a guy on O'Hara until this Reckoning-shit stretched us too thin, and we couldn't tie O'Hara to squat. Meanwhile, Zoey just *happens* on it?"

"You'd think she'd lie better, wouldn't you, Penny?" Dale tapped his boot against the floor, faster than the beat of the music being played softly in the background.

"Yeah, you would." Lou's black eyes registered surprise. "I told you, didn't I, Dale Evans? I said when she didn't want you around anymore, not to let her out of your sight because she'd be ready to make her move. She can't wait much more. She's almost out of time now."

"So are we, Pen. So are we."

Fifty-one

DENIAL AND FLIGHT—Zoey's ever-ready tools. As a child, when things became unbearable, she just zoned out—a form of both denial and flight. There were years she only barely lived. Now that the cause felt the same, the effect just fell into place. So there she was, stuck in a crisis that cried out for the sharpest focus she could muster, yet she had checked out.

She felt like such a zombie sitting in Carlsbad coffee shop, which she'd gone into, that all she could do was stare out the window. She even had to remind herself to keep chewing the bite of the sandwich that had turned to sawdust in her mouth because even that had ceased to be automatic. She was still alert enough to count no less than four Ford Focus cars in that same goldish-beige tone driving by—they really were breeding. But if one of those drivers had aimed his bumper at her, she would have been powerless to save her own skin.

Well, she did have some shred of self-preservation left. Enough to know she was not going to let some temporary sexual aberration destroy the best thing that ever happened to her. Somehow, her past had transformed an act of love into something vile to her. She had to spare Marty from knowing that. She set out to do that earlier that morning.

She'd been in the bedroom when Marty returned to the condo.

"Zoey, you home?" he'd called. "Man, that Pearson's driving me crazy. It'll be a miracle if we get the DVDs on the stands on schedule."

Her stomach tightened when she heard him approach the bedroom. Zoey hurried to finish what she'd begun.

"Now I've got problems back in Colorado. That Sunday

magazine spread I set up for you is—" Marty stopped in the bedroom doorway. His narrowed eyes jerked from her duffel on the bed to the clothes clutched in her hand. "Zoey, why are you packing? Are you going somewhere?"

"It has nothing to do with you, Marty," she blurted.

"Why would it?"

"I meant…" She turned away and continued stuffing clothing into the bag.

"Oh, I get it—you're bailing. I can't say I blame you, but couldn't you have discussed it with me?"

"I'm not pulling out of the race. How can you think that? I'm not a quitter. But I have to go someplace where I can finish my training in peace. All I need is a few days. Then I'll just rest in the condo until race day. Even if the police don't have it cleared up by then, they should be able to protect us on the course. You know they can't now."

Marty sat on the bed next to her dark green duffel bag. "Where will you go?"

Zoey zippered the bag closed. "No one will look for me in Orange County. Hey, why don't you go home and get that Sunday magazine business settled in person? You could use a break, too." The circles under Marty's eyes darkened more with each long day he put in.

"Not gonna get rid of me that easily." His crooked grin flickered, then faded. Marty rose and gently stoked her cheek. "I'll always be there for you, Zoey, even when you don't think you need me."

She watched desire spread across his face, and she panicked. She couldn't stop her quickening breath from sending the wrong signal.

Fortunately, the phone rang. It was one of his other clients, who just arrived in town for the race. Judging by Marty's side of the conversation, the client had come reluctantly, and he needed to convince her she made the right choice. Zoey used that chance to slip out.

Now, despite Zoey's earlier need to get away, something held her back. Orange County was only an hour or so away. Why had she lurched across the freeway to that Carlsbad exit so she could hole up in a restaurant with food she had no desire to eat?

If any more questions entered her life, she'd never live long enough to answer them.

Zoey asked the teenaged waitress to pack up her sandwich to go, and she headed out. She hopped back onto the 5 North. She had considered driving up the coast. More scenic, certainly, but the freeway was faster. So if speed was her objective, why did she hover in the right lane?

Zoey spotted the sign announcing the exit for Route 78, a highway that headed east from Oceanside. An impulse surfaced, and she acted on it before common sense could override it. She took that exit and kissed her sensible jaunt good-by. Only then did she pull from her duffel bag, on the passenger seat beside her, the brochure Marty had dropped in the bedroom, and admit to herself what her intention had been all along.

When the road began to climb, she lowered the windows and savored the fresh air. It was cooler than it had been in the inland valley she'd just come through, like the coast, but with a different quality. Mountain air, not sea air. If she tried really hard, she could almost imagine she was back home, far away from everything that had happened in San Diego. Though when she felt the first stirring of homesickness, she clamped a lid on it. If she allowed that to take hold, she wouldn't stop driving till she hit Colorado.

Of course, if she had been in Boulder rather than Southern California, she'd have worried about those heavy gray clouds hovering over the mountains in the distance. But it never rained in California in the summer.

With some uneasiness, she turned where a detour sign indicated. The detour didn't bother her; it was clearly because of roadwork. What troubled her was that the detour wasn't the only variation from the map on the back of the brochure. Some of the landmarks weren't even there any longer.

With such a dated map, she kept her eyes peeled for the turn-off and still missed it the first time. She might have driven half-way to Arizona if she hadn't come across some kids on horseback who sent her back. She still wouldn't have seen it if she hadn't known what to expect. But the kids accurately described the wooden sign designed to swing between two posts, whose hinge had broken on one side, so it hung at an odd angle from the other. She could still make out the words, "Ridgewood Camp'n Cabins," but the paint had faded even more than the ink on the brochure.

Gullies and ruts pitted the dirt road that led up the hill. Zoey wished again for her Jeep; the minivan wasn't built for that terrain. But the road smoothed out after a while and even became paved near the end, though that surface was rapidly returning to its natural state.

She pulled her car alongside a largish building, more like a big house than a commercial structure, which probably served as the office and restaurant. The place was so quiet, the sound she made slamming the van door seemed to echo for miles.

The questions Zoey should have answered before she took that route finally kicked in. Why had she driven there? Did she really think she could fix the problems between Marty and her by coming alone to the place he had chosen for their vacation spot?

But she was there now, might as well check it out. She went up the steps and tried the door. Locked. She looked through the window into a large room filled with long tables surrounded by folding chairs, all coated with a layer of dust.

Behind the main building, cabins connected by a narrow road dotted their way up the hill. She approached the nearest one. Its door was unlocked.

Zoey had discounted the word *camp* in that Ridgewood Camp'n Cabins, but they weren't kidding. This really was a camp for kids. The main room was bare to its raw wood walls and blackened brick fireplace. But filling the other rooms were built-in bunk beds. The only things missing were the kids. Still, they might be expected. Despite the stripped mattresses and the look of abandonment, a pile of clean bedding was stacked on a folding chair in one room. And in the communal bathroom Zoey saw a couple of bars of soap and a bottle of shampoo. Someone was obviously expected to take up residence.

She also found four gasoline cans lined up in one room, along with a coil of heavy rope and some tools and hardware supplies. Maybe the owner was just planning to make repairs.

Zoey guessed this wasn't what Marty had in mind for them, after all. What an idiot she could be sometimes. That brochure must have been in the condo all along, stuck behind the furniture, and it must have come loose during cleaning.

Zoey walked back to the minivan feeling like a first-class fool. Though she also noticed that she felt more relaxed than she had in a while. She hesitated about leaving that beautiful, natural place.

What the hell? If she went on to Orange County now, she wouldn't find a room until late. She'd already completed her cycling and swimming workouts this morning. But when was she planning to run?

She decided to treat herself to a trail run. She started out on the dirt road, running past cabin after empty cabin. Well, maybe not entirely empty—the trashcan outside one of the last cabins overflowed with fast food containers. Ah, civilization—even squatters couldn't live without it.

When the road came to an end, Zoey picked up a trail. It was narrow and overgrown. This place had been empty too long—not enough pounding from little feet to maintain the trails. But it was mostly wide enough for her. Besides, the first taste of freedom she'd felt in too long was worth a little inconvenience.

At the foot of a steep grade, she charged up. The view from the top was breathtaking, even if the heavy dark clouds were overhead now. She sucked in a big, healing breath as she looked out over a huge wooded canyon and range-upon-range in the distance. Off to the right she noticed an even higher mesa that looked like someone had chopped off the top of a mountain to make it. That would be her next stop, Zoey decided, only the clouds parted then and the sun filtered through the leaves to press a pattern of warm and cool lace against her skin. She hesitated long enough to fill her lungs again with a quick, hard breath. The altitude there was more like she was used to, and the dry air felt more natural to her than the moist at sea level.

Zoey froze when she heard the rustling of dried leaves behind her. There couldn't be a soul for miles. Just an animal, she assured herself.

The two legged kind, unfortunately.

"Found you," a voice said.

Fifty-two

ZOEY STOMPED HER foot against the rural trail's hard-packed ground. "Dale! How can you keep sneaking up on me?"

He took his dark glasses off and squinted at her. "It's easy. By now you should know that. I didn't even scuff my feet this time, after you warned me."

"I meant, how can—" Fear's rush had flummoxed her. "What the hell are you doing here?"

"Seems to me I agreed to be your bodyguard in exchange for a little coaching. You did your part." His well-built shoulders tossed off a disarming shrug.

Zoey kicked a stone on the trail. "So you *followed* me? That was your car I saw from the coffee shop in Carlsbad? Why didn't you come in, instead of waiting until now to scare me to death?"

He hesitated. "I didn't want to intrude on your privacy, Zoey."

"What the hell do you think you're doing now?" she shouted in exasperation.

Without warning, she charged him, palms out. She knocked Dale down with such force, he rolled several yards before plowing into a tree trunk. He had tried to brace himself an instant before she hit him, but he wasn't prepared for her.

Nor she for him, apparently. She hadn't expected what she would feel when her hands pressed against his strong chest. Without warning, a butterfly, newly born in her stomach, tested its wings. Her breath caught in her throat. What was she doing?

Before she could answer herself, she thrust out a helping hand to Dale to help pull him to his feet. He eyed it with suspicion before deciding he could risk it.

She rushed into speech, as if she'd never knocked him down. "Wanna come with me? I was going to check out that mesa over there?"

Zoey took off without waiting, but she kept her pace slow enough that he was able to catch up and stay with her, despite the black jeans and biker boots he wore. Still, she was a trifle breathless when she arrived on the big flat field. Zoey Morgan, an elite athlete, breathless from a little jog.

"Isn't this weird? It looks like somebody cut the top of the mountain and plucked out all the trees." Why was she babbling?

Dale gave her a wary look, as if assessing how they were going to play it. "They probably did."

"No! Why would someone destroy this beautiful area?"

He gave her another enigmatic look, before slowly pulling a toothpick from his pocket and sticking it in his mouth. "Chalk it up to safety. They get a lot of fires out here. And this used to be a camp for kids. In case of fire, you always head for high ground."

How long had he lived there in San Diego? Not long enough to refer to the area like a native.

They studied each other in stealth, until their gazes collided and ricocheted away. Zoey's common sense finally returned to her. She told Dale she was now going back to the van to continue on her way, repeating the rationale she gave Marty.

"Orange County? So how'd you end up here? What happened, Zoey, you take a wrong turn?" Dale asked.

"Just a detour. I'd heard about this area and just wanted to see it." She slapped her palms together in a gesture of finality.

Dale twirled the toothpick. "This area or this *place?*"

"What's the difference?"

He watched her. "Just wondered."

Dale turned away and Zoey thought she saw his shoulders sag. When he spoke, it was without looking at her. "If you're really going to Orange County, you'd better leave now. As it is, you're going to catch some traffic."

He walked off the way they had come, without waiting to see

if Zoey would follow. She did, keeping a little distance between them until she realized she was watching him move, and knew why. She caught up with him just as the first drops fell.

"It's raining." She lifted her face to the drops. "It doesn't rain here in the summer."

"Tell that to the clouds," Dale shouted into a rapidly building deluge.

The skies opened up. Rain sheeted down. Though the trees offered some protection, the overgrown trails worked against them now. By the time they reached the dirt road that wove around the camp, they were streaked with mud and soaked to the skin.

Zoey motioned for Dale to follow her to the cabin she'd found unlocked. A burst of lightening briefly illuminated the cottage's main room, allowing them a moment to orient themselves, before the darkness closed in again with a threatening rumble.

Zoey groped her way to the room where she'd seen the bedding and selected the heaviest of the washed-out blankets from the stack. By the time she returned to the main room, her eyes had adjusted to the darkness, and she could make out Dale crouched before the fireplace. He had stacked some wood in the firebox and was about to put a match to it.

"Cross your fingers," he said. "I found a pile of wood, but there were only a few matches left in the matchbook on the mantle, and there's no kindling or paper."

The logs burst into flames. Old wood.

Dale knelt close to the fireplace and stretched his hands to the fire. Zoey thought she saw him shiver in the firelight. The temperature must have dropped twenty degrees in five minutes. She hugged the blankets to her, while she struggled to banish the thoughts that would neither form completely in her mind, or leave.

How many attempts on her life would it take before she got smart? Before she stopped denying that her life was in danger. Some unknown person was gunning for her—yet she allowed herself to be trapped with a man she didn't know and couldn't entirely trust. A man who, oddly enough, didn't seem to trust her.

Her breath caught in her throat. She was conscious of the smells around her: the mildew in that old cabin, the scorched logs, the scent of musk. She opened one of the dusty, threadbare blankets and leaned over Dale as she draped it around him. Her cheek brushed against his; his beard felt rough against her skin. Her arms lingered, when she wrapped the blanket around him, just a bit too long.

Fifty-three

THERE'S A MOMENT between men and women when it's all decided with the eyes. In that abandoned cabin, Dale and Zoey made their pact in the glow of the firelight, and the overture began.

Dale swept Zoey into his arms. He held her at a distance for a solemn moment, while Zoey watched tenderness overcome confusion in his rich blue eyes. There was such a wildly romantic feel about the encounter. Trapped in the middle of nowhere, alone together in the glow of the fire, it felt so much like an old black-and-white movie that Zoey could almost forget the real world. And another man who had every right to expect better of her.

Dale's first kiss befit that netherworld. It was soft, tender. Not tentative, but almost reverent. He caressed her face and neck, expressing with his touch that he considered her precious. And for that moment, she felt it.

Their tongues reached into each other's mouths, slowly, as if they had all the time in the world. Their bodies curved against each other. The lingering pace contributed to Zoey's sense that this was happening in another world. A safer one.

She noticed the signs of Dale's increasing arousal, yet she didn't recognize it as dangerous. Until the rhythm changed. Dale's hand probably hadn't actually yanked her T-shirt and groped at her breast, it just felt that way to Zoey. In that moment the walls of their haven collapsed and the real world flooded in. No governor regulated her reaction this time, as it had with Marty.

"No!" she roared, and jerked away.

The sound of the hammering rain filled the silence that followed, along with volumes of unspoken recriminations. All wrong. Humiliation flooded the part of Zoey that passion had vacated. Dale just looked at her, his face drawn and pale, his dark eyes open too wide.

"No," she whispered, giving the word a different meaning this time.

In shame, Zoey turned away. The sob that escaped from her sounded louder than the rain.

"I'm sorry," Dale said, his voice hoarse. "I thought..."

She owed him an explanation, but what could she say? That she had used him to test herself? That was all this could have been. She loved Marty, she reminded herself.

"Did Marty do this to you?" Dale asked.

Zoey shook her head.

"Then who?" he demanded.

She couldn't hold it back. "My father."

Dale only response was a sharp intake of breath.

She laughed bitterly. "Someone gets his rocks off for a few minutes, and you spend your whole life paying for it."

Too bad it wasn't just a few minutes, instead of night after night for years. Such horribly invasive assaults that after a while, she learned to just let her body lie there, while her mind drifted away to someplace with less pain. Until the shame overtook her, until she realized that whatever he did to her, if she refused him, would be better than life on those terms. She should have stood up to his threats years before.

"That must be why you take all those showers," Dale muttered softly, more to himself.

The remark struck Zoey dumb. Why hadn't she understood that?

"Zoey, come here," Dale said.

She couldn't face him. She'd always felt like a rag that someone had used to whack-off, but never more than at that moment.

Dale knelt beside her. He took her into his arms again, and it was beyond her power to resist. His touch was careful, but more like she was simply fragile, rather than soiled.

"Let it go," he whispered into her hair.

Wracking sobs overtook her. It occurred to her that Dale was the only person ever to have comforted her when she cried, first after Cindy died, and now.

Only when calm returned to her did Dale leave her side. He quickly tossed another couple of logs on the fire, then zipped from the room. He returned dragging a mattress, with some bedding under his arm, which he arranged before the fire.

Dale took her hand and tugged her to the mattress. Speaking softly, he encouraged her to stretch out beside him. She had no strength left to resist.

"Tell me," Dale said.

She told it sporadically, tossing out isolated pieces that came together to form a picture of a house built with lies and betrayals. A journey that began with the first time she was startled awake as a toddler, to that night at the beginning of her teens when she found the courage to kick him away.

"Did your mama know?" He gently whisked her wet hair off her face.

Though the storm still roared outside, a leak had sprung in the old roof. Zoey could hear heavy drops smacking against the floor somewhere in the cabin.

"I think she did, though we never addressed it. But I always sensed she blamed me. For taking him from her and for not being enough to hold him. I blamed herself, too, even though I always knew he signed on for her money and left when it dried up."

Zoey felt Dale stiffen beside her. In the quiet that followed, the drops slipping through the hole in the roof became louder.

"Your mother had money?" he asked at last.

"Still does, she just can't touch it anymore. My grandfather was a humble Irish immigrant bumming his way across the country, when he came upon the Colorado mines. He lived long enough to see the ecologists hang him in effigy as one of the most egregious strip miners in the country. He died loaded. Of course, with three wives and a mess of kids, it got spread a little thinner."

"But your mother still had some." The sound of urgency entered his voice. When a log cracked in the fireplace, Zoey felt his body jerk on the thin mattress.

"More than enough to buy the husband she wanted. But she became crazier and crazier over the years. Eventually, the trustees took control. That's when *he* left."

"But she still has some?" Now Zoey heard disbelief. Why wouldn't he let it go?

"Enough. I handle her finances now. I've set it up so they'll keep her comfortable for the rest of her life in that place where she lives, and then they'll get whatever's left once she's gone."

The sound of disbelief grew stronger in Dale's voice. "Zoey, are you out of your mind? That money could go to you."

"I'd rather eat garbage from a Dumpster," she said simply. She would. Why was it so hard for him to believe it?

They were silent again, as the rain continued to drum against the roof. Finally, Dale asked, "How did you survive it? You know, what your daddy did to you? How does anyone?"

On the mattress, Zoey shrugged. "Mostly, you put it away in a strongbox in the darkest, deepest part of my mind. And if you never look at that strongbox, sometimes you can pretend it was just a bad dream, not something that really happened. You always know, of course. Deep down. But you make a pact with yourself to never, never acknowledge what's in the strongbox."

"We all play games with ourselves," Dale said.

"Yeah." Zoey was quiet for a while. "The trouble with the game is that the pressure keeps building in that strongbox. When it gets too great, the lid blows, slapping the truth right in your face." She signed softly. "After that it's harder to go back to let's-pretend-you're-like-everyone-else."

Zoey pressed her head against the mattress and wished she could pretend it never happened, pretend she wasn't as she was, even now.

"But it's funny," she went on after a moment. "Even when the knowledge of what happened is safely locked away in that strongbox, even when you never think about it, what you've lived through still shapes the person you are. It still alters your behavior, even if you never admit to yourself that it happened." That was why aggressive men had always frightened her. Zoey remembered that night at Ames's rally, and how Pat O'Brien had scared her so. Would she ever be free of it?

"Zoey, I'm so sorry," Dale said.

She never wanted anyone's pity. She could lift her own body weight in a gym, but pity—the weight of that would break her.

"You've been…like this since you were little?" he asked.

A window in the cabin rattled with a sudden gust of wind. The sound made her feel cold, even though the fire was giving off plenty of heat. She wrapped her arms across her chest.

The shame of her dysfunction still suffused Zoey. But for the first time in her life, talking about it made her feel better. "Sex has always been…well, complicated for me. Sometimes there's no better celebration. Like when I've won a race and feel great about myself. But the past is always there, casting a shadow over the present. There have always been things that would trigger my fears, even when I didn't know why. Things that would force that strongbox to burst open. And then it feels as awful as it did the first time, when I was young." She sighed. "Why is it happening now? What's the connection? I can't explain it. But ever since that car hit me, I haven't been able to stand being touched anymore. I couldn't tell you what's triggered those old feelings if my life depended on it."

Part of her knew that she'd almost be willing to give her life for that answer. To know why this was happening now. But mostly, she admitted to herself, if she knew, she'd put the answer away in that strongbox and never look at it again.

Zoey yawned. "That's enough for tonight," Dale said. "Go to sleep." He draped his arm over hers. Strangely enough, she didn't jerk away.

"I can't stay here." She tried to rise.

"You'll be safe, Zoey, I promise you."

She wouldn't be able to sleep, she knew. Not there, like that. Not with his arm around her waist. Zoey yawned again and sunk back into the mattress. That was the last thing she remembered before drifting off.

When Zoey opened her eyes again, she was alone, with only the sun streaming through the window for company. She felt better rested than she had in longer than she could remember. Someone had left a container of orange juice and a couple of fresh pastries on the floor beside the mattress. Their cars must not have washed away last night. Dale had obviously made a run to town. Where was he now?

When he hadn't come back by the time she finished breakfast, Zoey wandered out of the cabin to where she'd left the minivan down by the main lodge. Though the ground was still muddy, and the potholes in the road filled with murky rainwater, the sky was a vibrant blue, the air so clear it might have been coated by crystal. For the first time in so long, it felt good to be alive.

Dale leaned against his car, staring out into the distance, in what would have been a casual pose were his arms not tightly locked over his chest. He looked at Zoey—then quickly glanced away.

He cleared his throat. "I just wanted to wait around to make sure you were okay. And to tell you something."

Dale's grainy voice sounded brusque. The way his eyes kept scurrying away from Zoey felt like a knife sliding into her heart.

"Forget everything I ever said to you, Zoey. You're right to be distrustful. Everybody's working an angle, and they'll all screw you if they can. Even me." His blue eyes, as deep a blue as the summer sky overhead, clouded over when they met hers. "Especially me." He leaped into his car, tossing over his shoulder, "You watch your back now, hear?"

Fifty-four

ZOEY COULDN'T SAY how long she stood in that spot staring after Dale when he drove off. Long enough for the mud flats his tires separated to seal together again, though not enough for the sting from that slap in the face to stop smarting.

What an idiot she had been to risk destroying everything she shared with Marty. But she'd learned her lesson. If Marty still wanted her, she was his for life. She'd always held something back from him, she admitted. Who was she kidding? She held back with everyone. Until last night—and look what that got her. But Marty deserved better.

His love for her had deepened lately, too. At one time, he wouldn't have objected to her training alone. He wouldn't have been indifferent to the threat, he would just have assumed she could take care of herself. The change now obviously meant he couldn't bear to lose her. Instead of finding his protectiveness oppressive, she should have felt treasured.

The sex was a problem, but she'd overcome it. Zoey had conquered every other obstacle that had come her way—she refused to allow an irrational reaction to destroy her. Though that would be the one thing she'd have to hold back from Marty. She couldn't take the chance he'd look at her the way Dale had.

Zoey suddenly felt so full of love for Marty, she couldn't wait to get back. She wouldn't go on to Orange County as she planned, she'd return to San Diego, to the life Marty and she could now share. Training would still be a problem, but she'd only need short workouts for a day or two more. She'd train with—

Hell—she was about to say *Dale*. Scratch that. How had that bastard worked his way into her life so fast? Well, she'd work out with other people. Or even with Marty, if she could wrestle him away from that DVD editing. Or even alone—she felt too full of hope to worry about a homicidal maniac.

She drove away from that camp as fast as the muddy roads allowed. She stopped at the first gas station she came across to see whether there was a more direct route back to San Diego. There was, but it still took too long.

More than an hour later, she burst through the door of the condo, just as Marty was preparing to leave. He waved at her with a half-eaten energy bar. "This is a surprise. How was Orange County?"

"Hot." Not exactly a lie—it probably was hot. It still went down like a lie.

But for once, she didn't run from intimacy. She took his callused hand in hers and brought his hand to her mouth for a light kiss. Then she ripped a big bite from his PowerBar.

"Is that why you came back?" he asked, stuffing the last of it into his mouth.

She wove her arms around his waist and rested her head on his shoulder. "No, I came back because I missed you."

Her guilt mushroomed. But that was true now, even if it hadn't been last night. She released Marty and lowered her eyes, away from his. She spotted a small square of white paper on the carpet just inside the door.

"What's that?" she asked.

"What's what?" Marty asked absently. He patted his pockets. "Oh, shit, I forgot—" He rushed to the bedroom.

She picked it up while he was gone, but didn't have time to look at it before he returned.

He hurried back from the bedroom, his skinny legs moving at half a ramble, half a jog. "Zoey, I have to go." In passing, he smeared a quick kiss across her cheek. "God, I'm so sick of that guy, Pearson, I'm almost sorry I started it this stupid DVD."

Zoey followed him to the door. "We'll make up for it after the race. Where was it you wanted to go?"

"What?" He looked around, as if he'd misplaced something else.

"After the race, Marty—you wanted us to go away together."

"Oh. Somewhere up the coast. Malibu or Santa Barbara. How's that sound?" He looked at his watch and gave her a final click with his tongue. "Let me know later, huh, babe?"

She felt her face heating up. Fortunately, it occurred just as he stepped out the door, so he couldn't have seen that vivid blushing announcement of her stupidity before he left.

Zoey noticed she still held the folded piece of paper she'd found on the floor. It was addressed to her—from Pat O'Hara. That was interesting.

He was in big trouble, he wrote in his oversized printing. No kidding. He apologized for everything he'd ever said about her. Profoundly yet—that's how he wrote it: "I apologize profoundly." He said they were in it together—whatever *it* was—so she was the only one who would believe him and who could help him. And he begged her to meet him. Ironically, he said he was hiding out in the country, and his suggested meeting spot was in the place she just returned from, along the road between the towns of Ramona and Julian. Below the note on that sheet, he'd even included a hand-drawn map.

It had to be a setup. Guys like O'Hara didn't suddenly start owning up to their mistakes. But why would he send her out there? If he was the one running athletes down, his track record of knocking them off in town was pretty good. Wouldn't it be easier to catch her unaware than to give her the chance to alert the posse?

If he was guilty. She remembered how he looked when she saw him at the self-storage yard. She couldn't shake the feeling that finding his car there had rattled him. This could be her chance to put the whole madness behind her. If she didn't take it, and another person was hurt or worse, she'd never forgive herself.

But she'd be crazy to try it alone. She looked at the phone, knowing she couldn't let personal pride stand in her way. She dialed information for the SDPD's headquarters, where she knew Lou worked. The cop who answered told her Lou was off, but he offered to take a message. While she debated whether to leave one, she cast her pride further aside and asked the cop another question.

His answer floored her.

Fifty-five

WHILE DRIVING, ZOEY glanced again at the address Cindy had written for Dale on the slip of paper that had gotten stuck in her desk. It was in the same Loma Portal neighborhood where Zoey had spotted Dale once before. She slowed the minivan now, and studied the house numbers painted on the curb. The house that matched that address proved to be a lovely old Spanish-styled house. Nice neighborhood, too, if you could overlook a couple of things. Instead of placing the streetlights at the curb, as they were in the rest of the city, in this area lights were arranged in the middle of the streets. Zoey thought something like that would keep you from coming home tipsy. The other detraction was that it was the home of an absolutely treacherous bastard.

She parked across the street and watched the house for a while. If she wanted to meet O'Hara, she had to leave soon. But she hadn't decided yet what she wanted to do about that note.

A taupe SUV pulled into the driveway, and a small woman jumped out. She opened the tailgate and reached into the back for a couple of grocery bags that seemed too big for her, as she shouted for a couple of little girls in the backseat to hurry. Zoey gave them all a moment to get into the house, then she swiftly approached the door before she could change her mind.

Zoey got a better look at the woman when she opened the door. She'd already noticed the woman was delicately built, but now she saw that short, honey-brown hair capped that woman's well-shaped head, and huge laughing brown eyes dominated her pretty, heart-shaped face.

"Hi," the small woman said with a polite smile that revealed a pair of deep dimples. "Can I help you?"

Where to begin? "I'm Zoey Morgan."

"Oh, sure. I recognize you from the magazine. Come on in." She gestured Zoey into a house that she instantly envied, an eclectic mix of Southwest and Scandinavian designs, put together with style and personality. If Zoey could have had Cindy's house, this was how she'd want it to look.

The woman led her toward the back to the house. "I'm just putting away groceries. Why don't you keep me company?"

The woman was as warm as her eyes had promised, and she seemed to possess the energy of a hummingbird. She looked to the ceiling and the sound of children's voices coming from the upper floor, and smiled with affectionate tolerance.

Zoey followed her to an updated kitchen whose pale modern cabinets had that sleek IKEA-look about them, which contrasted nicely with the hand-painted Mexican tiles that might have been the old house's original issue.

"Are you Holly?" Zoey asked. Her voice sounded sharp.

"Holly?" The woman yanked a plastic bag filled with fresh broccoli crowns from the brown bag and paused, frowning. "Oh, you're thinking of Dale. No, I'm Carolyn Peña, Lou's wife."

Zoey felt a wave of affection for Carolyn that she had never experienced for her husband. "Carolyn, I love what you've done with your house."

The broccoli disappeared into a side-by-side refrigerator. "It was a challenge, let me tell you. This house belonged to my parents. We bought it from my dad after my mom died. I loved them dearly, but they had dreadful taste." She hesitated before plunging into the grocery bag for another item and gave Zoey a speculative look. "Zoey, if you're ever around here during the school year, it'd be great if you could talk to my class about what you do."

Carolyn obviously knew a lot about her if she knew Zoey didn't live in San Diego.

"I teach seventh grade, and it pains me to see how many of the girls still limit themselves. I like to show them the possibilities that are open to them today." Carolyn gave Zoey that look again. "You might be able to use it as a…community project."

What an odd way to put it. "I'd love to," Zoey said. "I'll make it a point to be here." She meant that. Anything to save another kid.

Carolyn pulled a head of lettuce from the bag and returned to the fridge. "Great. Well, you'd probably like to see Dale, and I'm holding you up."

"He's here?"

She turned back to Zoey before the unopened refrigerator. "I thought you knew. He's in the apartment over our garage. We built it for my dad after we took over this place, but it's been vacant since he died." With a look through the kitchen window, Carolyn shook the lettuce in the direction of a detached garage at the rear of the yard.

Before she could change her mind, Zoey stormed out the backdoor and up a set of redwood stairs attached to the garage. She threw open the screen door at the top. Dale and Lou sat on mismatched overstuffed chairs in a studio apartment crowded with heavy furnishings. Dale jumped to his feet.

"You're not a cop!" Zoey shouted. "You lying son of a bitch — *you're not a cop.*"

Stunned silence followed. They must have figured anyone stupid enough to buy Dale lies would never see through them, Zoey thought. She couldn't let him think he'd hurt her. She *wouldn't.* She pounded the doorframe several times in anger. But she couldn't lie to herself any longer—that man had devastated her.

"How could you lie to me?" she screamed.

"I didn't exactly lie, Zoey," Dale said, choosing his words with exaggerated care. "You jumped to the conclusion that I was Lou's partner, and I didn't correct the assumption."

Zoey crossed her arms tightly over her chest. "You told me you were on disability. Were you even shot?"

Dale gave his dark head a reluctant shake.

"Maybe I could rectify that," she said, feeling a vicious grin form on her face.

Lou rose and started toward her, murmuring some vague defense of Dale.

But Dale cut him off. "She's right, Pen. I went too far filling in the gaps." He slumped forward in his chair, clutching his hands between his knees.

"Why?" Zoey demanded.

No one answered. Carolyn opened the door behind Zoey and stood in the doorway. Her big eyes still dominated her face, but there was no laughter in them now.

Zoey took another step into the room. "So what do you really do, Dale-the-liar?"

With a sigh, Dale looked at her. "I'm a claims investigator for an insurance company."

"So...you're investigating an insurance claim?"

He shook his head. "Not exactly. A death...but it's personal."

"Whose?" Zoey turned to both Carolyn and Lou, but they looked away.

"Willi Bogs," Dale said.

"Willi...? I don't understand."

"He was my brother."

Fifty-six

THEY ALL REMAINED rooted to the same spots in Dale's borrowed apartment. Zoey stared at Dale, but she didn't notice much family resemblance, apart from their Texas accents, between the carefully choreographed face in the DVD and the painfully embarrassed one before her.

She cocked her hip against an ornate wooden dining table. "Your brother? But you told me—" She remembered what he'd said: that his mother had produced a number of children by different husbands. It fit. Maybe that much wasn't a lie. "Why are you doing this?"

Still seated in that padded print chair, Dale absently slipped a finger through a frayed area on the knee of his worn jeans. "It has to do with Holly, my sister. She—"

"Oh, Holly's your *sister*," Zoey said.

"Right. And she has leukemia. Will was supposed to donate bone marrow when he…died." Dale absently worked at that fraying until he'd formed a hole in his jeans. "Holly was in remission at the time, but it didn't last. She needs that transplant now, or she's not going to make it."

"Donating bone marrow would have been the most decent thing your brother ever did. Figures he'd squirm out of it," Zoey snapped.

Dale's face colored angrily. She remembered how defensive he became the last time she criticized Willi. She couldn't resist twisting the knife some more.

"So…what, Dale? You don't think Willi's dead? Is everyone in your family such a hopeless dreamer?"

"I know *someone* is dead," he said sharply. "Will had an identical twin. If you read those clippings I got for you, you would have known about Will's twin, Tom. We hadn't heard from Tom since he ran away in his teens. Mama always insisted he had to be dead, wouldn't even hear about the possibility that he might be alive and not let his family know." He reached into his blue work shirt pocket for one of his toothpicks and stuffed it, with brutal force, between his teeth. "But Tommy had a job before he left home, so he had a Social Security card. After Will's body turned up, I started searching databanks, and I discovered someone has been making contributions to that account intermittently all these years. But the contributions stopped at the time of Will's death. What are the odds they *both* died, and only one body surfaced? One of them must be alive, and either one would work for Holly. I have to find whichever it is before her time runs out."

Zoey spoke softly, more to herself. "You told me you had twin brothers with no cavities, like the body. What about the appendix? Hadn't that body had its appendix removed?"

Dale rose and excitedly approached her, his hands gesturing actively before him. "That's right. Tom hadn't had his appendix out by the time he left, but Will hadn't yet, either. It didn't go bad until a couple of years later. And let me tell you, living with twins is weird. What happens to one of them, usually happens to the other."

Once he drew to within a few feet of her, it seemed to occur to him that proximity might not be advisable. He made an abrupt and awkward turn and paced back toward the pulled out sofa bed.

"You see, it could still be either of them," Dale said. "Why wouldn't Tom have reported to his job, same as always? But why would Will walk away from a career that was all he ever wanted?"

Zoey's head was spinning. But when she sorted through the story, she found there were still gaps.

"Why me?" she asked. "Why did you latch onto me and lie your ass off?"

Dale hesitated.

Lou turned to him. *"Amigo,* just tell—"

Dale stopped Lou with a stern look. "I had my reasons."

"Being a slug obviously runs in your family." Zoey whirled around on Lou and jabbed her finger in his direction. "And you're no better, Lou. You lectured me about leaving the investigation to the pros, and you let him in on it."

Lou spread his hands in a defensive gesture. "I know how it looks, Zoey, but you're wrong. Dale isn't a cop, but he's as good an investigator as I've ever seen." Lou gestured to the electronic hardware filing the table she stood beside. "He's better with these computers than anyone we have in the department."

As if on cue, Dale's fax machine began receiving a document. When it spit the sheet out, Lou reached for it, but Zoey grabbed it first. It was from someone in the San Diego Police Department informing Dale of the results of a fingerprint check. The prints belonged to a man called Douglas Tomaso, the son of a reputed New York mob kingpin. Tomaso was believed to have died while fleeing with some of the mob's cash, when the boat he'd been using to make his escape exploded. Lou made another grab for the fax, but Zoey stuffed it into the pocket of her khaki, where she'd also stored O'Hara's note.

"How nice. The San Diego Police Department now reports to Dale. But why shouldn't it, Lou? You let everyone think—*everyone,* not just me—that Dale was on the case with you. Is that kosher?"

Lou propped his clenched fists on his hips. "You know it's not. Hell, Zoey—you want to know the worst of it? *I* wasn't even assigned to your case. Hit-and-runs are handled by the Traffic Investigative Unit. I wasn't officially involved in until a task-force was set up with the sheriff's department after Cindy's memorial service."

"That's impossible. I never talked with anyone from the Traffic unit."

"Of course, you didn't. The detective in charge is a buddy of mine. Believe me, he has no shortage of cases. He agreed to let Dale and me do the legwork, and he put in the reports. But everyone on my squad knew what we were doing, even my sergeant."

She remembered the bald, beefy man who ran the Rob's pro meeting after the bomb threat at Cindy's memorial service. "How about Lieutenant Taylor? Was he in on your little shell game?"

Lou's helpless scowl was his only response. Carolyn came to stand alongside Zoey. Frustration, probably over the risks Lou had taken with his job, pinched her small face as she glared at her husband.

"Why would you do it, Lou?" she asked.

He scuffed one of his Nike trainers at the worn Persian carpet covering the tile floor. "My mother died when I was born, Zoey. I don't think my father ever got over losing her because he buried himself in his business after that. I had a lot of loving aunts to look after me, but their houses always seemed as fussy as mausoleums. Had a passel of cousins, too, but never any brothers or sisters except the ones I found in that sloppy house next door, which my aunts deplored. Holly Bogs is the closest thing I'll ever have to a sister."

Lou looked away, and Dale cleared his throat, in what Zoey found to be such a cloying rendition of male bonding that she wanted to gag. She should have guessed. The silly female names they used for each other could only be a boyhood ritual. She happened to notice Dale's scars and bet she could even guess whose little foot had created them.

Carolyn placed her cool, delicate fingertips on Zoey's arm. "What are you going to do, Zoey?"

Zoey knew what she'd like to do. But who was she kidding? Even if she could have given Lou the shaft, she couldn't do it to Carolyn and those kids.

"Despite what you think of me, I don't destroy people's careers. Not if I can help it. But you have to live with what you did, Lou. *You* sacrificed this investigation. You're still letting Dale set the priorities." Zoey pulled the crumpled fax from her pocket and shook it in Lou's face before tossing it on the floor.

Lou bent and picked up the ball of fax paper. "There is no investigation anymore, Zoey. It's solved. You did it—not a pro. You sent us to the garage. Happy, *chica?"*

She took a surprised step back. "You mean—O'Hara? You have O'Hara in custody?"

Lou stiffened his rigid shoulders. "We will soon enough. He skipped out with the car, but he left enough flaked paint on the floor, as well as tire marks. That was the car that hit you and killed Cindy."

Zoey momentarily considered sharing O'Hara's note, but that was too much. She might not wreck Lou's career, but she'd be damned if she'd help him earn a promotion.

"You're sure O'Hara was Reckoning?" she asked.

Lou gave his dark, close-cropped head a swift shake. "No, that was Randy Ames and his secretary. They were stupid enough to type the letters on their office typewriter and even used her ancient Volkswagen to hit that surgeon. Seems old Randy thought it would bring him and his cause a lot of attention, and since they were boffing each other's brains out, she agreed to help. She's singing up a storm now."

Why was it always okay for them? "So Ames really was an opportunist." Zoey directed her scorn at Dale. "There's a lot of that going around."

Dale started to say something, but Zoey held out her hand to stop him. "Forget it, Dale—you warned me. Better late than never, or so they say. Though somehow it didn't feel better from where she stood. Zoey turned to Carolyn. "If you still want me to talk to your class, I will."

"I do," Carolyn said, tossing her husband a defiant look.

Zoey moved past Carolyn and opened the screen door. Dale came up behind her.

"Zoey…" he began.

She slammed the door in his face.

Fifty-seven

SHE'D SHOW THEM, Zoey thought. *She'd* capture O'Hara. She could never depend on anyone but herself anyway.

Zoey pressed down harder on the accelerator, as the minivan sped away from San Diego. But her foot faltered when her own words came back to her. There she was, rushing off to meet a man the police believed to be a killer, like every air-headed heroine in all the damsel-in-distress books she'd read and hated. Only she wasn't as certain that O'Hara had killed anyone. He was a cheat. He might even hate her enough to kill her, but she couldn't see him doing it with a car. She would have expected him to be more direct.

Zoey glanced at the digital clock on the dashboard. Damn. She'd wasted so much time with those liars, Dale and Lou, that she had to hurry now. She tore up the 5 Freeway, though she would have sped even if she hadn't been late. Dale's betrayal hurt so badly that channeling it into racing anger was the only way she could keep herself from sinking into despair.

She didn't know what to believe anymore. There was a real woman named Holly because Zoey had heard her talking. She also knew Willi Bogs' sister had leukemia, since she'd read that in the clippings. But there were still lies to cull out from all Dale had told her.

They must have had a good laugh at her behind her back. And when she thought about how she almost sacrificed her relationship with Marty for that dirtbag, she felt sick.

She made good time getting to the meeting place, but she was still ten minutes late when she pulled into the vista point O'Hara described in his note. At least, she *thought* it was the right vista point; she'd mislaid his map. No sign of O'Hara, though. Zoey cut the engine and stepped from the minivan to stretch. She'd spent too much time behind the wheel lately, which wasn't good for her legs. But she left the door open, so she could get in there fast if she needed to.

The view of the canyon below her awed her. Brilliant leaves, in so many different shades of green, washed clean by the rain, fluttered in the breeze for as far as she could see. But the rain had left the ground awfully muddy in spots. Zoey walked around, easing out the kinks. But she kept away from the soppy edge and stayed well within range of the minivan's open door.

Twenty minutes. Had O'Hara gotten cold feet? Had she put herself through this torturous day for nothing? At least she learned the truth about Dale. She couldn't wait for it all to be over. Then she'd go her way and he'd go his, and she'd never have to think about him again. Except when she heard a Willi Bogs song. Or saw a knockout guy with a five o'clock shadow. Or remembered how safe she'd felt sleeping in his arms.

Who was she kidding?

It was so quiet. Outright silent, actually, apart from the occasional breeze rustling the trees. Which was why she didn't react the first time she thought she heard her name. It sounded as faint as the whistling wind.

She listened again. It seemed to be coming from the trees on the other side of the vista point. Could O'Hara be too afraid to show his face? With the wind kicking it, the air was turning cooler. Zoey slipped on the baggy cotton jacket with large pockets that she'd tossed in the car before leaving the condo. She put her right hand in the pocket now and felt the comforting weight of the switchblade knife. She inched toward the trees.

The sound of an approaching engine caused her to start. A white Mercedes—a small, old, sporty one in poor condition—rushed into the vista point. The driver didn't rely on just a mask for camouflage this time. All the windows, including the windshield, had all been darkened with film. O'Hara must have done the work himself; the edges were jagged and there were spots where air gapped between the film and the glass.

Zoey's panic subsided when she realized the car's trajectory was to her right. She caught a glimpse of the driver's silhouette through the dark windshield, and she stopped long enough to think about what she saw. Then the driver cut the wheels in her direction, just as he must have had on that San Diego street. The engine roared into a higher gear. It came right at her, cutting off her access to her van's own open door.

Christ, Zoey—nice job. Falling for the oldest trick in the catching-stupid-people book.

She realized her vehicle would protect her equally well if she could get behind its grill. The Mercedes driver had forced her to back up, but she wasn't far from the front of the minivan, which she could put between them. She leaped to the left, out of his path—and slipped in the mud.

Her scream echoed throughout the canyon when she went over the side.

Fifty-eight

"GIVE ME YOUR hand, and I'll pull you up," someone shouted down to where Zoey had landed after slipping over the side of the cliff.

Dale?

"Zoey, take one hand off the tree you're holding and stretch it up here."

It *was* Dale. Why was he always the one to save her life? Unless he was also the one who tried to take it. For one instant, the driver's silhouette through the dark film of the Mercedes' windshield had looked leaner than the bulky O'Hara. She kept both hands firmly gripped on the tree trunk from which she hung.

Zoey had figured she'd had it when she tumbled into the ravine. If she didn't go splat on the canyon floor, she was sure to hit one of the boulders studding the side of the hill. Amazingly, a spongy ledge broke her fall, and while it only slowed her descent, it put her in position to grab the trunk of a funny-looking tree that grew out from below a big boulder.

If she weren't in such great shape, she would never have been able to hold on that long. Even so, it was getting tough. She had started shouting for help right away, but even if someone could have heard her from the road, she would never have successfully competed with the overpowering sound effects the Mercedes produced after her fall. It had peeled away immediately. No more than a few minutes later, she heard a car go over the cliff with a screech, just around the bend. It exploded when it hit the bottom. Thereafter, for the longest time, she never even heard a car going past. Then one drove into the vista point so fast, she thought it was going to join her over the side. She'd put everything she had into shouting for help.

Wouldn't you know who'd answer?

"Give. Me. Your. Hand," Dale said, firing each word as if from a weapon.

She stretched her head back to look up at him. He had climbed down to a boulder just above her tree.

"What's the trouble, *amigo?"* Lou called from the top.

Why were they there?

More cars joined them in the turnoff. Innumerable doors slammed, urgent voices were lost in the breeze.

"Okay, Zoey, hang there forever," Dale shouted. "I don't care."

"You care." *Where had that come from?*

A helicopter swept into the canyon. He couldn't kill her in front of an audience, right? "Okay, hero," Zoey shouted. "Here you go."

She reached up, he reached down. Their hands didn't meet. *Oh, boy.*

She had considered swinging her legs up onto the tree trunk, which was roughly parallel to the ground, earlier, but she was afraid the movement would weaken its roots. Her hanging there was bad enough. Now she had no choice. She swung her legs back and threw them forward. They hooked around the trunk. With considerable effort, she pulled herself around until she was able to sit on the top of the trunk.

She felt the root loosen. "Dale, it's going!"

He slipped down to a lower ledge, not really wide enough for safety. Grabbing her forearms, he yanked her off the tree just as it broke.

He pulled her into his arms. If that ledge weren't so narrow, she'd have shoved him away—only she'd have fallen back into the ravine.

Breathless, she said, "You first," and with a toss of her head, indicated he should climb up to the vista point before her.

"No way. I'm not about to let you out of my sight again."

With his hand guiding her from below, she climbed onto the

boulder and up the hill. A stranger pulled her over the ledge.

Lou approached her in the vista point. "Smart of you to leave those bread crumbs, *chica.*" He waved O'Hara's note with its hand-drawn map. "You dropped this in Dale's place."

So that was where she left it. It must have come out of her pocket when she threw the fax.

Ignoring Dale, who had now been pulled up behind her, Zoey walked down the road with Lou to where that car had gone over. It was the Mercedes, just as she thought. The fire was out now, but much of the car had burned. She could see that the driver's side door was open, though. Detective Mackenzie appeared from somewhere and joined them there.

"The driver was thrown clear of the car when it crashed. They're bringing him up now," Mackenzie said.

"You're sure it's O'Hara?" she asked.

He pointed into the canyon. "See for yourself."

Attached by a line to the rising chopper was a basket carrying the still form of a man. The rescuers had covered him in blankets, but not so well she couldn't confirm his identity. That was O'Hara, all right. The fleeting impression she'd formed of a more slightly built driver had just been her imagination.

"He's pretty bad off. It doesn't look like he's gonna make it," Mackenzie explained.

She told them how she'd heard her name from the wooded area. They searched and found a remote-controlled tape recorder, with her whispered name recorded on an endless loop, though it had now been turned off. At least, that hadn't been her imagination.

Zoey shook her head. "Does it make sense to you that before O'Hara threw himself to his death, he took the trouble to remotely turn the tape off?" she asked them.

"Maybe that's why they call them *loco,* Zoey," Lou said. "What's your problem?"

She stuck her hands in her pockets and sauntered away. "Things don't add up. O'Hara is a mass of brute force. Isn't a tape awfully subtle for him?"

Lou walked behind her. "Worked, didn't it? Put you right where he wanted you. Why are you fighting this, Zoey?"

She shrugged. "Guess I just can't believe it's over."

Dale walked up to her. "Maybe that's because you know something we don't."

She stopped and glared at him. "I just can't get rid of you, can I?"

"Hey, you should be glad. How many times would you have been dead now, if it weren't for me?" Dale snapped.

Zoey kicked the muddy ground with the toe of her running shoe. "You have saved me, haven't you? I owe you something for that. Why don't I have Marty send you a check for your troubles? Then I'll never have to see you again." She brushed past him.

"It's not that simple, Zoey," Dale called after her.

It was for her. She walked back to the minivan and left. No one even tried to stop her.

Fifty-nine

NEWS TRAVELED FAST. By the time Zoey made it back to San Diego, friends were already calling to see whether it was true that the culprit had been caught. The relief frenzy picked up even more steam than the fear hysteria had.

The members of the national media must have been truly bummed. After flocking clear across the country, they found themselves reporting on the world's most ineffectual serial killer. However, they made the occasion rise to meet their expectations. They broke into that afternoon's regular programming with the announcement of O'Hara's attempt on Zoey's life and his subsequent accident. And of Ames's bid to turn one disturbed man's vendetta into a platform for his cause. They went on to provide continuous team coverage for the rest of the day. The local reporters sparkled so much, their reports more closely resembled a team audition.

The higher-ups in the United Christian Confederation quickly moved to dissociate themselves from Ames, who had been shooting through their ranks with meteoric speed only the day before. But they were stuck on a tightrope. While they had to condemn his zeal, they couldn't back away from his ridiculous campaign to eliminate performance wear and co-ed competition, since they'd already sunk a fortune into printing literature to support it.

Rumor held the DA's office was negotiating an immunity deal with the devoted secretary, despite allegations that she typed the threatening letters and even drove the car that hit that surgeon riding his bike. They wanted the bigger fish.

But it was doubtful her story would reach the stands before that of the little woman. Mrs. Ames announced her intention to file for divorce at a press conference called that very afternoon, in which she teased reporters with titillating sound bites regaling the bizarre sexual practices in which her husband had forced her to engage. A book deal was rumored.

It would have been too much to expect the media not to exploit Ames's downfall, but Zoey had to admit that not all the coverage had taken on the atmosphere of a circus. The tone became more serious when they reported on O'Hara, still unconscious but in the hospital prison ward, offering commentary that drew parallels between two men who would stop at nothing to fulfill their dreams, one of national prominence, the other of sailing first across a finish line, and who believed that no sacrifice of other people's lives would be too great to achieve them.

Bucky Jack climbed onto that bandwagon as well. He announced the resumption of the sales of Willi Bogs' recordings. Not that they'd been shut down that long. The distribution system seemed like a giant wheel, which wasn't easily stopped, though it started again effortlessly enough. Local radio stations announced Willi Bogs marathons that would continue through the Classic. Zoey felt sorry for every other recording artist; it was like no one else was recording music anymore. After a while, she stopped listening to all of it.

Of course, it was impossible not to feel relieved. And she wasn't alone in that. The euphoria proved to be so contagious, it was as if all of San Diego went on vacation. Many companies did shut down, and everyone seemed to take to the outdoors, now that they were free to in safety. You'd have thought all the other scourges of modern life—gangs and petty crimes, pollution and poverty, not to mention death and taxes—had ceased to exist.

Zoey didn't partake in the frivolity, she just used the time for healing. She went back to the condo and ate and slept, until she had to check in at the Classic's race expo.

She didn't do any more investigating. Lou was right—the case was over. Thoughts did float through Zoey's mind at times, questions about her peculiar obsession with Willi Bogs, but she pushed them right out again. Not avoidance this time, just not her problem.

She encouraged Marty to go back to Boulder. He insisted he should be in San Diego for the awards ceremony, but she convinced him it really didn't matter anymore. He didn't say it, but she thought he seemed relieved. He'd apparently been overtraining, around his video editing sessions, so he would be in shape to train with her, and only succeeded in injuring himself. When he left for the airport, though he stoically refused to admit it, he moved as if he was made of wood.

She promised him she'd fly back after the race, and they'd take their vacation from there. She wanted to leave San Diego so badly, she wished she could pack up and go with him now. But she had promises to keep, and miles to go…

Damn. Just thinking about poetry reminded her that Dale, the bastard, hadn't quoted any more poetry to her since the first time he nearly scared her to death. That memory would fade, too, she assured herself. In time.

The pre-race expo, featuring the wares of the sport's sponsors and various related vendors, was held in the smallest ballroom of the host hotel. A poor choice. With all the publicity, Rob sold half again as many booths than usual, but he squeezed them into a tighter space. Yet no one seemed to mind. If anything, the crowds added to the fun. Zoey stopped in at the booths of her sponsors, signed autographs, laughed, caught up with old friends, and did a fine impression of a being good sport—when the truth was, she just felt out of it.

She did come alive during the pro meeting, but only because she didn't like what she heard. Despite the unprecedented number of age-groupers registered, Rob decided to reduce the number of waves. Not a popular move with that crowd.

In triathlon, swimmers are released in set-apart waves at the start of the race, based on their category. Since swimmers can't always see when they're about to overtake someone else, the way cyclists or runners can, it's only smart to have fewer out there at one time. What was Rob thinking? Since each wave was given a different colored swimming cap, he might have saved a little money by buying a greater quantity of fewer colors, but the savings would only have been pennies.

He also cancelled the off-duty police officers he generally employed to enforce the course and replaced them with volunteers. Another bad move. When streets are closed, some people are invariably inconvenienced. Most drivers wait until the police allow them to cross, politely or not. But there are always some who'll just plow through a field of athletes if officers aren't around to dissuade them. Volunteers just don't carry the same punch.

Rob kept saying, "It's a new world order, folks—get used to it." Whatever that meant. Zoey thought if it were it not for his track record, he would not have quieted that bunch. As it was, all his credibility was on the line.

When twilight fell, the evening before the race, Zoey went out to perform her usual pre-race routine of tracing the course. She walked down the beach at Mission Bay to follow with her eyes the route between the buoys already in place. She ran up the beach to the transition area to gauge the consistency of the sand. She found the place where she would rack her bike, and studied and planned her transitions. Then she rode her bike through both the bike and the run courses.

The volunteers were out in force all over the course, trying to complete the impossible on time, as they always did. She knew they would work until late into the night, long after she went to sleep, and would be out there before her tomorrow. She always made it a point to express her thanks, but it never seemed enough. She just hoped they enjoyed their part of the operation as much as she did.

Zoey didn't actually save her favorite part of the ritual for last, it belonged there. But she was glad it did. After hanging her bike on one of the racks in the transition area, she walked back through the finish until she was about a hundred or so yards before it.

The big "Finish" banner had already been strung across the road. Just the sight of it gave her a tingles. But it looked a little bare all by itself. A wide arch of red, white and blue balloons had always framed the Classic's finish line. Zoey spotted Gretchen buzzing through the transition area with her nose stuck to her clipboard and asked her when the balloons would be arriving.

"No balloons this year, Zoey. We aren't made of money, you know," Gretchen said with a sniff.

Zoey didn't know why not, they hadn't released much of it.

"We owe it to those kids not to be frivolous, after all," Gretchen added, before bustling away.

Of course. Rob was saving money for the Touchstone Foundation. Zoey remembered the night she put her arm around that boy's thin little shoulders. She could do without the balloons, though she would miss them.

Their absence wouldn't deny her the thrill of victory when she accomplished it, however, and they wouldn't deny her this special moment now. She paused to center herself, then ran up the homestretch and across the finish line. She did it again and again. So she could capture what it felt like—she'd remember that when she visualized herself winning the race later tonight. Before you can accomplish something you have to really *know* it can be done, she believed.

On her last time through, Zoey threw her arms into the air as she crossed that line. Simulating the triumph, really reaching out and grabbing it. She pumped herself up so much, she was flying.

She just wished the inexplicable, nagging feeling, which came over her when she left the course—that that this would be the last time she'd see that finish line—wasn't pulling her back down.

Sixty

RACE DAY AT last. The emotional clouds of the prior evening, which had cast such a shadow of doubt over Zoey, drifted away during the night. With the morning light, she felt bright and clear and tingling with hope.

She awoke at three, even before the alarm went off. An ungodly hour, admittedly, but she needed to be in her rhythm by the start of a race. At times, Zoey also needed to settle a jittery stomach, but not that day. She ate an outrageous number of peanut butter-and-jelly sandwiches—her pre-race favorite—and drank gallons of water, while she reviewed her preparations. But she was ready, and she knew it.

A vague sense of unease did slip over her as she wheeled her bike through the parking area to the transition. A fear that she felt *too* good, that something would happen to change that. What an idea. How can anything be *too* good?

Zoey's whole life had been an unrelenting quest for happiness, yet it rarely occurred to her that happiness isn't a state of perpetual contentment, but a disconnected series of joyous times like this one, which she should cherish without question when they came and let go of when they moved on.

When she finally allowed her good mood to swell to the max, it gave a glow to everything. She found fun in stuff that had become routine. Shifting her heavy gear bag onto her other shoulder, she wheeled her bike up to the body markers. In triathlon, a racer's number is written with indelible markers on the thigh and upper arm, and the race category on the back of the calves. What a kick Zoey used to get out of that. Early in her career, she never scrubbed the numbers off immediately after a race so people would see them and ask what they meant. Now she felt that excitement again.

She inched up the leg of her tri-suit for the marker. She wore was a duplicate of her best tri-suit, which had been laid to rest by the emergency room staff after she'd been hit by O'Hara's car. She'd hounded her clothing sponsor for a replacement, but that red Lycra garment, with its skin-hugging, one-piece efficiency and well-placed cycling pockets on the back, wasn't made anymore. The sponsorship coordinator sounded testy when he reminded her the point of their sponsoring her was that she push their current lines. But his assistant took pity on Zoey, and she and found an old model in a batch bound for an outlet store.

It embarrassed Zoey to admit it, but she'd won so often in that suit, she considered it lucky. Not that she believed in luck, necessarily, but when something worked, she hated to upset the cart. The alternative was believing it had all been her doing—tough in those times when her confidence abandoned her. Today she felt so jazzed, she knew she could comfortably have worn the halter-top and shorts her sponsor suggested, despite their uninitiated state. But she had another silly reason for wanting to keep her midriff covered, so the one-piece made more sense. She didn't need luck today, however. She was ready for what she was meant to do.

While the sport promotes its participants as the most well rounded of athletes, it takes more than mere conditioning to sustain yourself through a half-Ironman. To claim a victory, your mind must also be prepared—and your soul must demand it.

Zoey racked her bike in the transition area and began the familiar process of setting up her area. She clipped her cycling shoes to the pedals and opened them enough to slip on while riding. She spread out her towel, filled her foot bath with water, and arranged her racing flats just so. She also placed her helmet on her bike's extended aero bars. Races are won and lost in seconds. When a triathlete enters the transition area, it's essential that everything be exactly where she expects it.

The process of arranging her transition area also produced another benefit for Zoey. Human beings find comfort in ritual. If Zoey looked around, she knew she'd see all the other athletes, elites and amateurs, finding solace in their private routines as well.

She glanced down her rack and saw Alicia setting up her station, with Rick right at her elbow. How could she stand all that hovering? They gave her brief identical glares. Apparently, their tacit truce from the Wednesday ride had ended. For all Zoey knew, they were furious O'Hara had flubbed the job they'd encouraged him to do. The idea didn't bother Zoey in the least today, she felt that invincible.

Before slipping on her wetsuit, she needed to make a trip to the portable johns. The sanitary aspects were the worst part of the sport for her, the bathing queen of the Western world. Just when she got used to the honey buckets, she turned pro and found pit stops were a luxury she could no longer afford. Learning to pee on a bike had to be the hardest thing she ever did. Some women triathletes can't. They just hold it until the pain becomes unbearable and they have to get off the bike, whatever time is lost. Zoey had never met a man who couldn't do it with ease. Equal, but different.

With that pit stop accomplished, she headed back to the transition area by way of the vendors' booths set up in the mini expo in the parking lot. She spotted the redheaded and freckled Tom Pearson manning a booth featuring the DVD Zoey had made with Cindy.

"Hey, Tom, I see you completed the editing and got it produced in time to sell here," she said.

Pearson guffawed. "Well, duh!"

"Excuse me?" Zoey stammered.

He viciously thrust back at the buyer before him a few bills in change, while continuing to glare down his freckled nose at Zoey. "You missed two appearances, Your Highness. So did Cindy, but she's dead."

Whatever the hell that meant. Marty was right, the guy was

callous. Zoey didn't have the chance to tell him so, however, because he was too busy taking in money. Those DVDs were flying off the shelves.

She hoped the interest wasn't purely ghoulish, but she feared it was. Many of the buyers justified their purchases to her by claiming to have heard great things about it. When would they have heard that if it had only released been that day? Though one woman asked Zoey to autograph hers, and the package looked like it had seen some use. Had there been any advance copies around before the release? She hadn't heard about them.

Zoey returned to the transition area and tugged her wetsuit on. Wetsuits are approved when the water's cool, as it always is in California. But they're a mixed blessing. While they offer additional buoyancy that benefits the swimmer, they require time to remove. It's a level playing field for most triathletes. But Zoey noticed some of the newbies had decided to avoid the expense or the bother. If they stayed with the sport, they'd learn.

Wetsuits also chafe some people, who have to use silicon spray to prevent rashes. While that had never been Zoey's problem, she found if the suit wasn't perfectly adjusted, she couldn't swim well. She bent over now to stretch it into place and felt a nasty pain in her middle. She contented herself with squatting to ease it into position.

This event had always attracted more spectators than usual since it was part of a daylong Fourth of July celebration, but this year broke the record. *Nothing like negative publicity to draw a crowd,* Zoey thought cynically. Though the added spectators did raise the excitement level, whatever their reasons for being there.

Then—after five hours of preparation—it was time. Zoey walked down the beach to the spot where the female pros gathered to wait for their wave to go off. As she did, she felt her eyes searching the crowd, till she acknowledged which spectator she was looking for. *Stop it, Zoey!*

She switched to looking for Rob. And she hoped to see Lacey with him, as usual—she wanted to put her fears for their marriage to rest. But she never saw either of them. One of Rob's longtime volunteers was acting as the starter today. Rob must have been elsewhere on the course handling a last minute problem. She didn't even see Gretchen throwing her vast weight around this morning. Who was running the show?

A familiar tingle caught in Zoey's chest when she stepped onto the sand. Like an actor must feel in the wings before making his entrance. With all of the competitors bunched together on the beach waiting for the first wave to go off, the excitement became electric. Zoey could feel the current in the air.

The first wave, the male pros, started off, allowing the elite women to gather in the water. Some of the girls used that seven-minute gap to catch up with friends they only saw at races. Zoey was part of the crowd that internalized. She forced everything down inside until it intensified enough to explode.

She spotted her sometime training partner from Boulder, Gloria Watson. Gloria was one of the few African-American pros in the sport. Gloria used her difference to her advantage. Because she stood out from the largely white field of competitors, the crowd noticed her and cheered her on, especially when she was the first woman out of the water, which she often was. Though she was only twenty-four, Gloria had been swimming competitively since she could walk.

They exchanged tight nods, while adjusting their goggles. Come to think of it, Gloria's stiff reaction might not have been the result of concentration, Zoey realized. Gloria had left a number of messages for Zoey on the condo's answering machine, asking for assurance that it was safe to come out there, but Zoey hadn't answered any of them. What had felt like self-containment at the time, now just seemed lousy. The bridges that needed repair stretched endlessly before her.

The starter's gun erupted and the field leaped in. Anyone new to triathlon is in for a shock at the start of the swim. Think funnel: as a wide group of swimmers squeeze down to the narrowest possible field to get around those buoys in the shortest time. It could get hairy.

Mission Bay was gentler than an open ocean swim, however, another reason for that race's popularity. Despite the jostling for position, Zoey made good time. But the swim portion was never her strongest leg. Alicia was the first out of the water, as expected. She was a big woman, and a gorilla would envy her reach. Gloria followed closely on her heels, and Zoey tucked in behind them. As if in unison, they yanked down the rear zipper pulls of their wet-suits, while they raced out of the water and up the beach, and peeled them as low as they could before they reached the transition area.

Zoey didn't worry about her third place start of the next leg; she knew she'd make it up. Her transition to the bike was so smooth, she beat Gloria to the street and was only a blink of an eye behind Ali. Though the sport was designed to be a test of a well-rounded athlete, she considered the running leg to be the most important, followed by cycling, with swimming coming up the rear. Zoey was a good swimmer, an excellent cyclist and a great runner. She was made for it.

The swim course was U-shaped, the bike a loop, with the run course a straight out-and-back, her favorite. Zoey overtook Alicia on the first part of the bike portion and quickly stretched her front place standing. She'd learned her lessons well during that Wednesday ride. Zoey's lead increased on the second leg. Some days, you have to disown your pain to make it through. Today, if it came, even pain wouldn't faze her. She felt that unstoppable.

Zoey spotted the Daniels-Salaz contingent on lawn chairs set up along the side of the road up ahead. Their faces tight with concern, they looked past Zoey for Alicia to see how much distance she had on their girl.

Incredible—the whole crew showed up for most of Alicia's races. Her father was some high-powered CEO, her father-in-law not only carried the concerns of California's migrant workers, he was beginning that long walk to Congress. Yet they were out there for her race-after-race. Zoey saw Alicia's mother and mother-in-law, their light and dark heads bent together. Their backgrounds were worlds apart, their politics incompatible, yet they came together over their love for their children and their support for their racer.

Alicia really was gluttonous, Zoey thought. *Two mothers—when some of us never really had one. Is that why I hate her?* The blow that thought struck echoed clear through Zoey. Did she really *hate* Alicia?

Zoey sustained her momentum, but something in her faltered. That she would have cloaked a personal resentment in an ethical crusade took a swipe at her self-image. Did feeling like nobody's child really hurt her that much? Was that why, unlike some of her friends, she never experienced a conflict between the short life of a competitive athlete and a finite biological clock? Maybe she just couldn't see herself as a mother until she felt like a daughter. And that was never going to happen.

The truth hit home. Zoey ached for what Alicia had. She felt, rather than heard, her sigh. The hardest thing in this world has to be letting go of what of what can never be. And right now, Zoey couldn't manage it. Instead, she tucked her head down and pumped even harder, still hungry for the victory that was open to her. The one that nobody would be there to share.

Sixty-one

ZOEY SHOVED THE bad feelings aside. No time for them now.

Banking the bike at a sharp angle, she slowed no more than necessary as she came into the transition area. She absently reached for her helmet strap, but remembered in time to wait. Pros have been disqualified for opening that clasp a few yards too soon. The governing official posted at that turn, a stout man in a navy suit that gave off the slightest whiff of *eau de camphor,* had spotted her lapse. He wagged a finger at her, a smile of disappointment twisting his fleshy lips. *Some of you guys love pulling the wings off of those of us who can fly.*

She yanked at the Velcro fasteners on her cycling shoes and pulled her feet out. Before the bike had slowed to a stop, she leaped off and ran barefooted with the bike to the rack. Then she immediately sat on the ground, where she slipped on her racing shoes and slid them closed with the black plastic lace locks she always used.

Transitions are hard, as newcomers who believe it's enough to excel at three disciplines soon discover. They're always surprised by how tough it is to catch your breath running up the beach, but shocked when they try the bike-to-run transition. That's why serious triathletes practice transitions. Straightening a back that's been bent over aero bars for miles and bringing together legs bowed by a bike saddle—not just to run, but run hard—demands, beyond practice and skill, great determination. Zoey's was unmatched. When she hit the street, Ali still hadn't entered the transition, and none of the other women were even in sight.

Zoey loved an out-and-back run course. While the shape didn't alter the distance, she liked seeing what lay ahead stretched out before her. Despite the fatigue everyone felt at that stage, she was always stronger after the turnaround, and the sense of anticipation ignited her so she could bring it on home.

Zoey's drive was exceptional even for her today, though she couldn't recapture the glow she'd felt earlier. But she tried not to take her mood swings too seriously. She wasn't new to this sport. Long distances can play havoc with the psyche. Some athletes just become bored and have trouble maintaining their focus. But emotional upheavals aren't uncommon, either. Nor physical changes. In Hawaii, some people almost fall asleep while running. Though Zoey had never experienced an emotional spread like the swing from her nearly manic joy at the start to the depths she now approached. But the stress she'd suffered lately had to share some of the responsibility.

Zoey filled her lungs with a big burst of air before tackling a hill. Normally, she got off on hills, but the course's ups-and-downs had begun to smack too strongly of Hillcrest, the neighborhood where O'Hara had run her down. While the areas weren't that much alike, she found herself noting similarities. Like the side of the building just ahead and the intersection she was approaching.

What was she thinking? The situations weren't remotely alike. She'd been alone that day, not surrounded by male runners as she was now. There hadn't been an aid station at the corner, either, nor a cluster of volunteers. If there had, O'Hara wouldn't have dared to hit her.

A volunteer in the intersection held up his hand to stop a car and a bike approaching from the cross street. The bike slipped past him. Zoey had told Rob a volunteer didn't carry much weight. But it was the car that held her interest. It was an old white jalopy. Talk about *deja vu.* The driver had one of those small crystal balls swinging from the rearview mirror.

A crystal ball? Could it tell her future?

No, as it turned out, only her past.

Something happened when the sunlight ricocheted off that faceted crystal right into her eyes. The flare hit her like a bolt of lightening. And it opened the strongbox in her mind where she kept what was too hard to face.

Images tumbled through, pictures of what had happened at a corner that looked like that one. Stunned and wounded, Zoey reeled away from them, stumbling across the street in slow motion. But the images refused to release her. Her feet sputtered to a stop. She fell to her knees, gagging.

She vaguely noticed a woman from the aid station coming toward her, her face concerned. Zoey couldn't react to her.

"Don't touch her!" someone shouted from behind Zoey. Alicia Salaz.

"She's hurt," the volunteer insisted.

"Don't touch her!" Alicia repeated. "You'll get her D'Qed." Disqualified. "Zoey, do you want help?"

Ali's demand for an answer snapped Zoey from her stupor to the extent to responding. "No, I'm all right."

Though it was still beyond her to move, Zoey felt herself coming back to life. She knew where she was. Alicia passed her, though moving slower now than she had been going to have overtaken Zoey.

"Get going," Zoey said. "Don't wreck your race."

Zoey pulled in a deep shaky breath. A professional performs no matter what—Zoey had always believed that. She staggered through a pretense of running. First, one foot, then the other. Each step required a conscious choice. Fermina Vargas, the Mexican triathlete who had recently begun training in San Diego, overtook her. Faster, faster—but Zoey's pace was still just a jog. When she heard the crowds crying out for Gloria who had to be gaining on her, Zoey began running in earnest, even if all the joy had vanished from it.

Something about the way the sunlight played with that crystal triggered a recollection of what had happened the morning she'd been run down and left for dead. And the truth eviscerated her. *Think about something else, Zoey.* Alicia. She couldn't be too much of a cheat and do what she did for Zoey. Zoey had posed a real threat to her. Even after seeing Zoey doubled over in the street, Alicia had to know Zoey could still win, if she rallied. If Ali had let the volunteer help her, Zoey would have been disqualified, and the threat she posed would have been removed. Her first outburst might have been spontaneous, but Alicia had time to think before the second. Could Zoey have been wrong about her? A good question, but a question for another day.

No more avoiding, Zoey. She had to be strong enough to face the unendurable now, if only to prove it to herself. With that commitment, her speed returned. Fermina was only a few yards ahead of her now. She could still pull it off.

Yet as she ran, Zoey couldn't help putting together the fragments that didn't seem to connect before. Cindy's little scraps of paper. A missing greeting card. Two piles of Mickey D and KFC containers.

She overtook Fermina. Some of the fight went out of the other woman's posture when Zoey did. It's said the one who wins on a given day isn't necessarily the best prepared, but the one who wants it most. No one could want it more than Zoey did. She spotted Alicia just ahead. It was still within her grasp.

She cranked up the steam. But another piece fell into place, a critical one. If Zoey read the scenario right, there was another life at stake. Would she still have time to put a stop to that sacrifice at the end of the race? There was no choice. The life in question wasn't worth losing her race for.

The turnaround point lay just ahead now. A bend to the right around a park, and down a parallel street, until the course cut back over to this one. Then straight in. And she was always stronger on the second half. In spite of every awful thing that had happened, the excitement she always felt at this point began building.

But where did she get off making judgments about which lives were worth saving? And what if no one believed her later? If it proved to be too late to save that life at the end of the race, she'd have to live with that for the rest of hers.

No! She couldn't give it all up. Not now, when it was almost within her grasp.

Look at it this way, Zoey, her little voice countered. *If you pull this off, you'll deserve the damn award.*

She still had to stifle a sigh when she hung a left at the corner, and left the course.

Sixty-two

GETTING TO HER destination required Zoey to hitch two rides and do a lot more running than she intended after completing most of a half-Ironman, but she made it there in good time. She walked the last stretch, unsure of what she'd find.

Spotting Dale crouched behind a dried bush, wearing his black T-shirt, jeans, and leather biker boots again, gave Zoey pause. Why didn't she expect that? She was obviously destined to have him around for the rest of her life. She crept closer.

Zoey quietly brought her lips to his ear and whispered, " 'Because I could not stop for Death, he kindly stopped for me.' "

Talk about poetic justice, literally. He spun around, clutching his chest. For once, Zoey managed to wipe that superior smirk off his face. Knocked his dark glasses off, too—they hung askew from one ear.

"Shee-it, Zoey. You 'bout scared me to death. What are you doing here?"

She crouched next to him. "I came to find out why you never quoted me any more poetry."

"How could I? I shot my whole wad that first time, trying to impress you." The smirk returned. "Did I?"

She felt herself grinning. Why was it so hard to remember she hated this guy?

He yanked his dark glasses off and studied her thoughtfully. "How'd the race go?"

She exhaled hard. "It got interrupted."

"By what?"

"By finally remembering my accident."

"Oh. I'm sorry, Zoey."

She stared straight ahead, into the bush, to avoid the sympathy she was sure she would see. "How did you know?" she asked, still refusing to look at him.

He took her chin in his fingers and turned her face his way. "I uncovered quite a lot about y'all."

"From illegal hacking?" she demanded, indignation channeling her pain.

Dale shrugged. "A chance remark you made got me to thinking, and I did a little more digging. Came up with a different picture." Now he took to staring into that bush. "You're okay, Zoey Morgan."

That was as close to an apology as she was likely to get, she figured. Might as well accept it. She still didn't know what he had suspected her of doing, nor why, but now she knew where to look for the reasons.

"You did okay, too," she admitted. "But you didn't get it exactly right. This isn't where we should be."

They had both turned up at Ridgewood Camp'n Cabins where they'd only recently spent a rainy night. Their camouflaging bush was off to the side of the road, just below the cabin they'd used that night.

Zoey pointed up the dirt road. "We should be higher up the hill, near that far cabin."

"That so?" Dale considered it and apparently decided she knew something he didn't. "How should we go?"

That was the sticking point. They'd make some noise cutting through the woods. The rain had knocked a lot of leaves and needles from the trees, which the low humidity that followed rendered them bone dry. The road would be faster, but it was risky— out in the open, they could be seen by anyone. She suggested they risk the road. Dale agreed with an emphatic nod.

They started up the narrow dirt road, trying to achieve a balance between speed and silence.

Bad choice.

Once they were level with the cabin they'd commandeered, its door swung open, and a man in a blue-gray camp shirt and faded jeans came out. She didn't know who was more surprised, her, Dale—or the man in that doorway.

But once that man's gun appeared, there wasn't much doubt which side liked it less.

Sixty-three

HE STOOD BEFORE them, the man with the gun. The one who had run her down with a car, not once but twice. Who had killed Cindy. The man to whom she had pledged her future.

Marty.

"Christ, Zoey," Marty snapped. "Is there anything you won't fuck up for me?"

Zoey found her voice. "Not if I can help it."

Marty's grin, which she'd always considered so boyishly engaging, taunted her now. When the memory of his running her down with O'Hara's car first struck back on the course, she was devastated. Now all she felt was anger. She wanted to knock his crooked nose right through to the other side of his head. But it didn't look like she was going to get that chance.

Apparently, he didn't think so, either. "Don't kid yourself, babe. You're no match for me. I could always handle you."

True enough. It pained Zoey that she didn't see much transformation in Marty. She'd always been aware of the laugh in his narrow, hooded eyes, she just hadn't known it was directed at her.

She remembered pontificating to Dale that even when someone refuses to acknowledge a painful memory, it still alters her behavior. Why didn't she see how it affected hers? She did everything she could to separate herself from this man. Those fearful dreams alone should have told her. Her mind saw the similarity between the father who had robbed her innocence and the man who had tried to take her life. She just wouldn't listen to them.

"Did you win The Classic, Zoey?" Marty's hazel eyes glowed as eagerly as ever.

"I quit before the end of the race."

He clicked his tongue. "Too bad. I was planning on taking what you won today, along with all your sponsor bonuses, when I left. But, hey—I'm not greedy." He giggled. "Why'd you drop out?"

"Because I suddenly flashed on an image of you trying to hit me with O'Hara's car."

He shrugged, causing his gun hand to jerk. "Shame you remembered that, Zoey. And just when I'd decided to let you live." He gave his head a *c'est la vie* tilt.

Dale's hands curved around her shoulders. "Don't let him kid you, Zoey. The only reason he stopped trying to kill you was because he couldn't pull it off. But he did intend to leave you holding the bag. Most of the proceeds from the Classic, including what should have gone to the Touchstone Foundation, have been funneled through your account. But all that money is gone now."

So that was why Dale suspected her. Figured. She hadn't thought it through yet, but money had to be Marty's motive. There were easier ways to leave your lover—than dead by the side of the road. Dale's reminding her of his presence there now, which she'd forgotten in her initial burst of anger, gave her an idea.

"You've outwitted everyone, Marty, so don't blow it now. You can't afford to kill Dale, not a cop. They don't leave a stone unturned when it's one of their own," she warned.

Marty threw his head back and laughed. The gun bobbed up-and-down with less than reassuring stability. "That's what I love about you, Zoey—you are so predictable. You distrust everyone, including the people who are out to help you, then you go and fall for the world's two biggest liars. He's not a cop, he's just another butinski, like you."

Zoey heard some annoyance in Marty's voice now. At least they'd created *some* problems for him.

"You knew that?" she asked.

His twisted grin returned with a vengeance. "And don't you want to know how? Come on, Zoey. Let's satisfy your curiosity before you die."

Marty motioned them up the hill to the cabin whose overflowing trashcan she'd spotted the last time she was there. Dale opened the door, but stalled in the doorway. With him blocking the way, she couldn't see what it was in that cabin that brought him to a halt. All she knew about the interior came to her through her sense of smell—she caught the faintest whiff of decaying garbage, combined with the overpowering scent of some sweet cologne. When she finally managed to slip around Dale, she became rooted to her spot as well. Despite her expectations, her jaw dropped.

There he was—the one and only, *living*—Willi Bogs.

Dale cleared his throat. "Hello, Will." His voice sounded rusty, like he hadn't used it in a long time.

Willi's mellow tones abandoned him, too. When he finally spoke, it came out in a squeaky rush. "Dale! Hey, man, what are you doing here?"

Dale removed his dark glasses. "As hard as I looked, I never really believed I'd find you, Will. Not if it meant you would let your sister die when you could stop it."

Willi's long, slender fingers, so perfect for playing the guitar, flailed spastically in the air before him when he aimlessly reached out toward Dale. "I didn't forget about Holly. But you don't understand, man."

"And I don't want to." Dale turned away from his brother.

Marty shoved Zoey from his path and slammed the door shut.

"Don't looked so shocked, Zoey. You spotted us together that night in Pacific Beach. I read your journal entry before I snipped those pages out. What were you doing there, anyway?"

"Looking for you." She remembered that now.

She'd overheard a telephone conversation Marty had back in Boulder. Apparently, his dead singer kept slipping away. No wonder rumors kept circulating that Willi was alive. Marty promised his caller he'd put a stop to it. Then he told Zoey he had to go to Colorado Springs. Instead, she traced him to San Diego. The day after she saw him together with Willi, he ran her down with

O'Hara's car.

While Marty began tossing newspapers off of a stack of mattresses piled to sofa-height on the scarred wooden floor, she took a look at the place. That cabin was larger than the one Dale and she had shared. Like theirs, no furnishings remained in the living area, and mattresses had been dragged in from the bunk rooms. But this place had also been outfitted with a mini refrigerator and a microwave, as well as an oversized boombox and a mess of CDs. All the comforts of home.

But what a pigsty Willi had made of that cabin. Despite having the means to do some cooking, it was obvious someone made frequent fast food runs for him. Several trashcans overflowed with take-out containers, and the leftovers were starting to rot. Dirty clothes covered whatever floor space was left. And stacks of tabloids, whose headlines screamed of the late, great Willi Bogs. Marty must have discarded the ones that didn't feature Willi back in the condo. Zoey remembered throwing them away.

This cabin had to be where Marty went every time he told Zoey he was going to work on the DVD editing. She realized now it must have been out for weeks. It cheered her a little to think of all the hoops Willi made Marty jump through.

As Marty cleared a place for them to sit, he asked, not quite as casually as he probably wanted it to appear, "What first put you onto me, Zoey?"

"It was the card," she said. "Pretty careless, Marty."

"Card?" He wrinkled his crooked nose.

"Yes, the card, dammit. You sent me a card expressing your great love." Her sarcasm probably gave him too much satisfaction, but she couldn't silence it. "Then you used the verse in the card for two stanzas of one of Willi's songs."

Recognition dawned on Marty's pasty face. It hadn't been important enough to remember. How did he keep from being sued by the card company? Zoey wondered. Marty had way more luck than he deserved. She'd give anything to short-circuit it.

Dale came up next to her. "So who wrote the rest of it? Him?"

he gestured at Marty.

"The same person who wrote all the songs I'd guess—Cindy." How she wished she could tell Charley. "What happened, Marty? You discovered Cindy wrote poetry, but she wasn't confident enough to believe she could write lyrics, so you gave her a start?"

The twitch of his bent nose told her she'd hit a bull's-eye. She remembered the look of surprise on Cindy's face when she read that card. She had to know Willi was alive—she must have been writing those lyrics throughout the year. Marty obviously convinced her the cause of helping the Touchstone kids justified keeping quiet. But even after she realized he'd fed her plagiarized lyrics, she gave him a chance to explain instead of coming directly to Zoey. Marty killed her before she could. Hell, Zoey thought, the prick even played the song he forced her to steal at her memorial service!

"The only part I don't know is who wrote the music," she said.

"That was Will," Dale said. "I recognized his style. He has that gift, but he isn't smart enough to string two words together."

Willi frowned at his brother's nasty remark, but he didn't challenge Dale. Zoey remembered the billboard: *The man, the music, the word.* The music maybe, not the words, and apparently, he wasn't even much of a man.

Still holding some of Willi's tabloids over the stuffed-to-capacity garbage can with his free hand, Marty finally just tossed them at the floor. "Well, now we're all caught up. Why don't you folks make yourselves comfortable? You're not going anywhere." He handed Willi his gun. "Here, Willi, watch them for me. I have to take a look around."

Like a villain in a bad TV show, Willi gestured with the gun for them to sit on the mattresses. He backed away from them and stood leaning against the far wall.

Taking a look at the rest of the large room, Zoey noticed there were also a couple of guitars. The signature acoustic, naturally, but also an electric with a big amp—that didn't fit the image.

Finally studying the legend himself, she saw more resemblance between Willi and Dale now than she had in the DVD. Willi's having shaved his mustache helped; the brothers shared the same shaped mouths. The dark roots growing in at the base of Willi's fair hair also intensified the resemblance.

But she saw less similarity between Willi in the flesh and the image in the music DVDs. This clown couldn't project depth for more than a few minutes before his features crumpled in anxiety. Zoey realized the dead star shtick had been devised to boost sales, but it also served another purpose. Willi couldn't keep the solemn dignity he projected on tape going for too long in real life. If the public really got to know him, they wouldn't like him much.

To think, she left a race she would have won to save this loser. But a thought occurred to her—she wondered whether Willi had any idea what Marty had to be planning for him.

Sixty-four

"DOUG?" WILLI SHOUTED from the cabin room where he kept Zoey and Dale at gunpoint, after hearing Zoey's theory about his forthcoming demise.

Doug? Of course—that was the name on the faxed fingerprint report Dale had received. Douglas Tomaso, the son of a suspected gangster, who had been fleeing with the mob's booty when his boat blew up. After which he became Marty Wright. So Mr. Tomaso had faked his death. Zoey couldn't decide whether another duplicity made her feel better or worse.

Marty, which was the only way she could think of him, ran into the room. "What's the matter?"

In a whine, Willi related Zoey's prediction for him.

Marty shot her a black look before turning to his toy star. "Now, Willi, can you think of one promise I've made you that I haven't kept?"

Willi couldn't. Too bad he didn't know a con man always gives something to win your trust. Marty re-spun the part of the web Zoey had torn to keep Willi firmly ensnared. The patter tripped out lightly, like a frequently told fairytale, touching on Willi's reappearance in the world and ending with the Grammy Awards and a Beverly Hills mansion. Marty smoothed his unruly hair as he spoke, an action Zoey now realized reflected his assurance that he'd firmly hooked the mark. His confidence wasn't misplaced.

"What about them?" Willi asked with a toss of his head at her and Dale, less indignant now. "I didn't sign on for no murder, and she said—"

Marty applied another patch. He assured Willi they were only going to keep Dale and Zoey out of action for a while. Judging by the glaze that came over Willi's blue eyes, a lighter shade than Dale's, he didn't even see the tear in the finished fabric.

Dale, who had been sitting next to Zoey on the mattress stack, lurched forward. "Will, use your head," he snapped. "He killed your own twin brother."

"That's not true! Tom just died. And we thought..." Willi looked to Marty for coaching. "We thought we might as well use his body to build up interest in me. The public loves dead idols. Marilyn Monroe, James Dean. But I'm gonna be the first one to come back."

Dale took one of his toothpicks from his pocket and stuck it between his teeth. Before he champed down on it, he said, "Open your eyes, Will. Tom must have wanted a piece—"

"You don't know that, Dale. You don't know nothing. Doug's given me everything. What did you ever do for me?" Willi asked in a martyred whine.

Zoey watched Dale's Adam's apple jerk, while he tried to swallow that one. For a moment there, Dale looked like a snake downing a cow. Beyond a sad shake of his head, however, he never bothered to respond to his brother. But Zoey bet she could answer it. Willi was such a taker, it wouldn't occur to him to notice what his brother did for him, much less give thanks. And Dale, that wild man, was too nice for his own good.

Willi had raised denial to a new level, Zoey thought. But who was she to talk? She'd made a childhood vow to avoid good-looking users like her father and took up instead with an average-looking one who was just like him under the packaging. And the worst part was, on some level, she always knew it. As she'd told Dale, just because you don't look at the strongbox, doesn't mean you don't know what you put on it.

Marty finished the web he'd spun for Willi on an upbeat, jovial note. "So if you want to keep these two tied up while you slip away to prepare for your triumphant return, Will-my-boy, bob on down to the other cabin for the rope and those padlocks. That chain, too. Come to think of it, why don't you bring up all my stuff? Just leave the rest outside."

Willi kept nodding his agreement as if his head was on a string. He handed off the gun to Marty and scurried out the door.

Zoey just looked up at Marty, who loomed over them, and asked, "Why, Marty?"

He didn't pretend not to understand. Actually, he beamed with satisfaction. He wanted to brag, she realized. She could have kicked herself for giving him that.

"To understand that, babe, you have to go back to one of my past lives. You see, I knew my former…associates had set up an… enterprise."

His gloating smile widened as he carefully picked his words. Why was he being coy with his secret *now*?

Marty began to stroll across the rough wood floor before them. "To everyone who saw it, this enterprise appeared to be a regular concern for making money, when it was actually set up solely for…processing funds."

Processing? Zoey thought. Did he mean *laundering*?

"Everyone thought the top guy was the man in charge, but he was just a figurehead. Slave labor, like me," Marty said with a bitter sniff. "But I figured that cherry was ripe for picking. And me, I do things in a big way. You know that about me, Zoey."

She did now.

"So I tried to find another angle to work into it. I noticed how charities can bring in the bucks when they give people something they want—and I mean a collector CD, not the satisfying feeling of helping the less fortunate. And how well sports fit that bill. So I looked around for a sport that was still undiscovered, and I found the most pristine person in that sport to vouch for me." Marty snickered at Zoey. "And then I showed my man, the figurehead, how we could bring in a pile of cash and see that it left with us."

The implications stunned Zoey silent.

Dale jumped in. "Didn't you leave something out? You also had to find Will and build him into a major star."

Marty tossed a glance at the door Willi had exited through.

"That was incidental. I needed someone. I could have done it with anyone."

Zoey finally found her voice. "You're describing Rob, aren't you? As the figurehead?"

Triumph lit Marty's very ordinary face.

"Is that true?" Dale asked. "How did your former *associates* keep him working at slave wages? His company pulls in a packet of money."

Marty's grin spread. "That's easy. You see, he likes little boys—way too much. And he wasn't discreet. They got pictures."

The last of Zoey's trust shattered inside of her. *God, no!* She couldn't have been so close with one of *them,* a child molester. Yet it made sense. Rob even told her his wife often found him in his son's bed in the morning. Sure, he said it was because Lacey snored. But they always have an excuse. Her father used to claim he needed to rub her back to help her sleep. An indifferent, verbally abusive father by day became caring at night? Zoey thought only her mother would buy that one, but maybe Lacey did, too.

Marty pointed at Zoey and burst out laughing. "Another one of your pillars tumbles into the gutter. Tough luck, Zoey." He ended with one of his signature clicks.

Zoey, how could you ever have found that habit endearing? That sound had brought down her whole world. She remembered now that she heard that click at the car dealership when she made an appearance there—while Marty was supposed to be in Colorado.

Marty's crooked nose twisted angrily. "You really are too much, you bitch. Don't pretend you're so crushed because this is exactly what you want. You look for the worst in everyone."

Maybe so, but she didn't want to find it. *I really didn't want to find it in you, Marty. I wanted you to be everything I thought you were so that someday, when I felt safe in your love, I might have opened my heart to the world.* Fat chance now, she knew. Who would have thought Mr. Wright could turn into Mr. So-Very-Wrong?

The door flew open and Willi stumbled in, winded. He carried the large coil of rope she'd seen in the lower cabin, along with a heavy metal chain and a few padlocks still in their hardware store packaging.

After demanding the keys to Dale's car, Marty yanked the toothpick from between Dale's teeth and tossed it to the floor. Then he directed his hostages into a storage area off the cabin's bathroom.

The room was probably the closest thing that rustic camp had to a dungeon. Apart from a hot water heater in one corner and a stack of old paint cans in another, the windowless room must have been empty before Marty tossed another mattress—this one covered by a dusty, urine-stained pale blue blanket—along one wall on the paint-encrusted cement floor. The stench of mildew and of chemicals breaking down in those paint cans stung Zoey's nose.

Marty ordered them to lie on the mattress facing each other. The smells didn't get better on that blanket. He had Willi bind their hands and feet. What do you know? Zoey thought. They discovered another unexpected talent the great Willi Bogs possessed—the boy could tie knots. A little too well, in fact. Zoey felt pressure begin to build in her hands and feet almost instantly.

Marty passed the gun to Willi and left the room. He zipped back moments later carrying a couple of leather guitar straps. He used those to tie them together, wrapping the lashes tightly around the two of them at different points on their bodies. Then he worked padlocks through the spaces at the end of the straps, normally used to attach them to guitars, joining the two sides together. Weaving the chain through both straps, Marty hooked it through an old cast-iron hook sticking out from one wall, and padlocked that, too. The whole arrangement took jury-rigging to a new level, but Zoey had no doubts it would hold them. For eternity. Another unexpected talent she discovered too late: Marty knew how to hurt people. Beads of sweat trickled from her armpits, and she had to remind herself it was cool in that awful room.

Marty tossed Dale's car keys to Willi. "There you go, my boy, your own transportation. You take the boat out at the time we arranged. Still remember everything I said? Sure you do." Another click followed.

Willi gave his brother one last look, but it didn't slow his departure.

Standing at the foot of the mattress, Marty pulled a cigarette from his dusty blue camp shirt pocket. "Don't have to sneak these now." He lit it and blew smoke at them. But even after lighting the cigarette, he held his disposable lighter in his hand and kept flicking it. "Dangerous gadgets, don't you think?"

Marty started to walk away, but she shouted to him. "It'll never work, you know—blaming me for your theft. You said you picked the most pristine person you could find in the sport. People know how honest I am. They won't buy my guilt, and they'll come looking for you."

Marty laughed. "You think small, babe. I've been spreading negative rumors about you for months. Every triathlete you know, every journalist who ever interviewed you, has heard something suspicious. They may not have heard the same rumors, but that'll just make them more likely to believe this when it comes out. With that much smoke, there's gotta be a fire."

So that was why people treated her like a pariah. For all her natural distrust, it never occurred to her that someone was undermining her.

Marty turned and walked away. But at the door, he stopped and looked back at them, his face unexpectedly serious. "Next time, Zoey, find yourself a better boy." He broke into a grin. "Only I guess, where you're going, they'll all have wings."

Marty flicked the lighter one last time and held it open while the flame grew. He laughed like a baboon gone mad. He reached for the light switch near the door, but stopped and smirked, apparently deciding it would be more agonizing if she and Dale had to watch each other buy the farm.

Marty closed the door behind him, turning a key in the lock, before he left them there to die.

Sixty-five

WITH THEIR FACES just inches apart, Zoey and Dale looked into each other's frightened eyes.

Zoey gulped hard. "What was Marty saying? That he intends to *burn* this place down?"

"Not a bad plan. When they find us, there won't be anything left of the rope," Dale said.

His breath felt warm on her face, and smelled minty. At least she discovered the secret to those toothpicks—he used them in lieu of breath mints.

Dale said, "It'll look like you and I shared a kinky little tryst in this hellhole, after you ripped-off the race's coffers."

And because Marty had tarnished her reputation in various ways, many would believe it. "Rob's role in the operation will come out, too, but he might already be gone. What about Marty? Won't he be the missing link?"

"I expect he's thought of that. Marty Wright will be dead in some way folks'll believe. Will won't be around to contradict anything," Dale surmised. "The question is how well this place will burn. It's dried out in the last few days, but it really took a dousing. And this old wood sucked up that rain. Without some kind of accelerant, I'm not sure how well it'll burn."

Accelerant? Zoey flashed on those cans of gasoline in the other cabin, and then the volatile paint right in this room. Dale must have shared her thought. She watched her own reaction mirrored on his pale face. Horror darkened his eyes, as sweat ran from his hair. Fear stiffened his features, tightening those troubled lines, until it looked like a appalling mask of pain. *He believes it's over, too!* She couldn't bear to think about it, or to let him.

"Guess this arrangement gives new meaning to the term *double-backed beast,* huh?" She gave her eyebrows a suggestive wiggle.

"Sure ain't the one I was shooting for."

But for once, Zoey couldn't sustain the denial. She pinched her eyelids closed. "How could I have been so stupid? I should have seen through him."

"You think you could understand a guy that twisted? Who died and made you Sigmund Freud?"

She remembered when she had thrown those words at him. They shared a moment of hysterical laughter, before it faded into a sober acceptance of reality.

"Zoey, I won't kid you. If we can get free, we might have one chance against the fire."

"Dale?"

"Yeah?"

"I taped the knife to my stomach."

Sixty-six

ESCAPE FROM THE horrible room seemed hopeless when even a tri-suit zipper presented a challenge.

The leather guitar straps, which Marty had wrapped around them, pulled so tightly their arms were pinned. By drawing hers a little closer, Zoey reduced the pressure across her shoulders, allowing Dale to ease his bound hands up to her throat. She took the top of her Lycra tri-suit in her teeth to hold it taut, and Dale grasped the tap of the zipper. Slowly, he managed to lower the zipper all the way to her middle.

The shape of the knife was barely discernible beneath the heavy packing tape she'd stretched across her waist. With their thumbnails, they each went to work on a side of the tape. Zoey's slipped often, as she lost feeling in her hands. Dale's wrists must not have been tied as tightly as hers, since he still possessed more dexterity. And she doubted Willi's devotion toward his brother.

Getting a trifle winded now, Dale groused, "Could you have used any more tape?"

"Had to flatten it, didn't I? You have no idea how hard it was to hide it."

The copy of her lucky tri-suit had a decorative fabric band in red, white and blue stripes around the middle, which thickened the waist area enough to camouflage the knife as long as she taped it very flat.

"Why did you think you'd need it?" Dale asked.

She lifted her eyebrows in lieu of a shrug. "I just had the strangest feeling it wasn't over."

"You have good instincts, Zoey. When they tested O'Hara, they found he was too drugged to have driven the car. He's hanging in there, by the way."

Obviously, Marty had driven the car. His slight build fit the shadowy image she saw through the windshield film. He must have leaped from the car on the way down. The way he landed, not overtraining, caused his soreness.

When Dale had loosened his end, he gripped the tape and angled his hands to the extent the rope allowed. Zoey gritted her teeth in anticipation, but she still grunted when he yanked it. She didn't know she had any stomach hair till she felt waxed.

Dale wasn't impressed with her stoicism. "Big tough triathlete and you can't take a little pain."

"Next time we'll try it on you."

Worse still, the operation only freed an inch or so. But three tears later, he'd opened a large enough section to reach in and wiggle the knife loose. They shared relieved smiles. Success was so relative.

They couldn't widen the gap between them, so Dale just had to flick the knife open. This time, Zoey managed to stifle her reaction when he nicked her. Dale rewarded her with a contrite grimace, before he began sawing at the rope binding her hands.

"How did you decide I wasn't one of the bad guys?" she asked.

"It wasn't one thing. You told me about your mother's money. If someone wanted to steal, wouldn't she start with the easiest place? I didn't want to believe it when you said you wouldn't take any, but it just rang true. Everything about you seemed *so* honest. I mean, you get a feel for people, for what side of the moral seesaw they occupy, don't you? Sometimes you just gotta go with what you feel. If it hadn't been for Holly, I would have taken a chance on you a lot sooner."

"I know, Dale. She only had that one chance. You couldn't get it wrong."

"Yeah," he said shortly.

Zoey cursed her big mouth. He had to be thinking he'd failed his sister, and she just made it worse. She struggled to distract him. "What else?"

"When you told me off that day when O'Hara went over the cliff, you said you'd have Marty write me a check. Why would you lie about that? Only Marty's not a signer on your account."

"He *is*. He's my business manager. He took care of everything."

"Sorry, Zoey, but your name's on every transaction. You made all the suspicious deposits and signed the orders to have money wired to Cayman Island accounts."

"I never—"

"I know. They weren't even *good* forgeries. But what were you thinking, Zoey? You don't have enough money for a business manager."

She didn't now. Zoey was just glad she opened that little savings account, which Marty didn't know about. If she ever made it out of there, it would be all she had left.

"Got it," Dale announced triumphantly, as she felt her hands break free.

They shared a brief moment of triumph until they realized they'd still have to cut at least one of the straps, before they could move. With her hands loose, Zoey was the logical one to take over. But even if pins-and-needles hadn't started prickling from within, her hands were slick with blood. Dale had slipped a few times with the knife. She'd never be able to hold onto it now. Dale started in on the strap, but it was harder for him to reach, and leather was tougher to cut than rope.

"What put you onto Marty?" she asked.

"Nothing at first, except his association with you. Only I couldn't establish any back trail on him. Martin Nolan Wright didn't exist until a couple of months before you met him. Then he finally showed up and I took a glass he'd used so Lou could run his prints."

She wondered how many other lives Marty had lived, and how many trusting women had made it all possible. The idea offered no comfort.

"How's the knife holding out?" Zoey asked.

"Getting dull. And the strap is thick and tough, and the padded backing just makes it harder."

Of course, it did. Nothing but the best for Willi Bogs. She had always loved good leather. Now, she knew if they made it out of there, she'd have to force herself to wear shoes.

"What about Rob?" she asked. "Any back trail on him?"

"Plenty. He's from Colorado, too. Did you know that?"

Zoey said she didn't.

"Yup. He worked as an athletic equipment salesman."

"He told me he was a competitive athlete," she said.

"Weekend marathoner. Pretty good, but not world class. He was up to his ears in debt. Even with both of them working, they couldn't stay afloat. And Rob was such a live one, he was always plunking money in one dubious scheme after another. Then one day, they folded their tents and popped up here. Now he's a flush race director and his wife doesn't have to work. Go figure."

"Any child molestation arrests or convictions?"

Dale shook his head.

Why would there be? You don't blackmail a person over something that's common knowledge. While Dale worked in silence, apart from his occasional grunt, Zoey mulled it over. Something, she found, didn't make sense.

"Dale? Remember how Marty said he looked around for an undiscovered sport? Why would he need to choose a base of operations when Rob's was already set up?"

"You're reading too much into it, Zoey. Guys like Marty lie so much they can't keep anything straight. He was just making himself sound important."

Sure, that was it. She took a deep breath, letting it go in a sigh. That was when she noticed something. "Dale, hurry."

"I'm working as fast as I can, Zoey."

"I smell smoke."

He stopped and sniffed. Without a word, he clenched his dark stubble-covered jaw and renewed his effort.

"Wait, I have an idea." Zoey rubbed her hands against the ratty blanket to dry them, then she grabbed the strap. "Let's stretch it."

Dale caught on immediately. They pulled at it, but the meager cut he'd made in the wide strap wasn't enough to give.

"We need a deeper slice," Dale said. He resumed his frantic effort, as the smoky smell became stronger.

"Let's try stretching it again," Dale suggested after a bit more time. He had nearly doubled his cut into the strap.

They yanked and pulled, again and again. At first it seemed hopeless, but after several tries, it felt looser across her shoulder.

Zoey alternated attempts to slip under the strap with pulling bouts. No chance, at first. But she stretched her body religiously, and, except for this awful time in San Diego, She never let a week pass without getting a good sports massage. If anyone could contort herself enough to slip under, she could. Finally, she made it.

She took the knife from Dale and freed her feet before cutting him loose.

Wisps of smoke drifted into the room. The fire was growing. They looked at the paint cans, then wordlessly divided the work. Dale applied himself to picking the door lock with the knife. She took the blanket and ripped it into several parts.

Dale moaned.

"What's the matter?" she asked.

"The tip of the knife snapped off."

No!

Dale flung the knife to the floor and threw himself at the door. It didn't budge. She released enough water from the hot water heater to soak those rags she'd torn from the blanket. They'd stuff one under the bottom of the door, and put the others over their heads. A feeble effort, but what choice did they have? Dale continued to ram the door. In the movies, the hero always shatters it. All Dale was going to break was his shoulder, Zoey thought. Real life sucked. Good thing she wouldn't have to deal with it much longer.

"Dale—stop," Zoey insisted.

"I can't, I—"

Zoey grabbed his arm and made him stop. She held him, looking into his dark blue eyes, until they admitted wordlessly what they both knew. They'd hit the wall. Big-time.

She wrapped her hands around his strong upper arms. "If you had just let me die that day in the street after Marty ran me down, you probably wouldn't be here right now. You must be so sorry you ever met me." A cry escaped from her throat.

Overcome himself, Dale gave his head a hard shake and pulled her to him. She buried her face in his chest, trying to use his coppery scent to block out the smell of smoke. She felt her eyes filling with tears, and she pressed her face harder against him so he didn't know. She looked down at the floor, where he had tossed the knife. Unexpected hope suddenly electrified her.

"Wait!" she shouted. "I have an idea."

She snatched the knife and stuck it between the edge of the door and the frame and tried to slip the lock. No dice on the first try, nor the second. The third wasn't much of a charm, either. But she kept at it. After several more attempts, Zoey thought she felt it move. She wasn't sure—till she was able to yank the door open.

Dale let out a whoop of joy. She was about to toss the knife aside—it was in bad shape now. But as she looked at it, the memory of how it had come into her possession floated back into her mind. She smiled fondly, as the recollection sharpened. Boy, would she love to tell Lou. Reason enough to stay alive.

Dale glanced at the ceiling, as if were listening to something overhead. She heard it, too. A plane, flying low. The engine noise was lost in a dousing reminiscent of the storm she and Dale had weathered in that camp.

"Water dropping planes," Dale shouted. "Let's go."

They rushed into the outer part of the cabin, desperately hoping Marty hadn't locked the outer door, too. He had, but the wood was so old, when Dale kicked it, he broke through it. *What a team we make.*

They covered their heads with the wet blanket strips and headed out. But smoke had blackened the sky and completely claimed the air around them. If they hadn't been there before, they would never have found their way beyond the cabin door, and it was still disorienting. The separate flares hadn't united into a solid firewall yet, but they were huge and growing. It wouldn't take long.

Zoey wanted to go *down* the mountain. There were people there, cars—help. But Dale insisted on heading up the hill.

"High ground, remember." Through the billowing smoke, she saw his hand extended. "Trust me, Zoey."

Zoey grasped Dale's hand and let him lead the way.

Sixty-seven

THE WATER-DROPPING planes were making inroads on the fire, but as the flames were doused, the smoke thickened. Zoey tightened the disgusting rag she wore around her face, but even after they reached the mesa, she couldn't stop coughing.

Dale yanked at her arm. "Zoey, look—there's a helicopter! It's got to be Lou! I told him where I was going, but I never thought he'd get there on time. He must have listened to his police scanner."

The chopper swung through the smoke for a landing. Lou sat in front, next to the pilot, with Mackenzie behind them. The door flew open and Lou jumped out. He herded them into the back of the helicopter and it took off immediately. As they rose, Zoey judged the distance they traveled from the fire by the changing color of the sky, from a deep, murky gray to bright blue.

Her lungs hurt from the smoke. Her ears hurt, too—she never knew how loud helicopters were inside. Mackenzie handed Dale his headphone, so he could talk with Lou without shouting. Zoey just stared back at the fire they'd been trapped within, wondering how many close calls one person gets.

Dale tapped her on the shoulder and shouted, "The Toy Boy left San Diego. Do you know where it went?"

"Oceanside," she shouted.

Dale relayed it to the pilot, and the chopper altered direction.

The Toy Boy. That must have been Rob's idea. What outrageous arrogance. Funny that she never noticed that quality in him. Well, that was the idea.

To be honest, she never sensed anything wrong about Marty, either. At first. Having molded himself into her ideal man, why would she? But nobody can successfully live a lie day-after-day. After a while, there are gaps in the act. When her suspicions began to sprout, Zoey took to eavesdropping on Marty. She followed him when he went to check his post office box once, she remembered now. And she made a copy of the box key. That was how she found the pictures of the Toy Boy, which Rob must have sent.

But Rob? He really had her fooled.

"Did Marty say what time the crew would take the Toy Boy out?" Dale asked.

She shook her head. Crew? Of course, a yacht that size would need a crew. Willi couldn't run it alone. One of them might be the mysterious "Heathcliff," the lecherous slob in the marina alluded to. No, what was wrong with her? That was Rob. She'd noticed how well he fit that description herself.

Still, appearances aside, she just couldn't buy it. Dale was right, you get a feel for which side of the right-wrong spectrum people occupy. Does anyone ever change that radically? Maybe occasionally, but not often.

She thought about one person who had changed quite dramatically, as she searched her mental strongbox for the memory of the night the knife came into her possession. She'd been following Marty and Willi in Pacific Beach, when a man pulled her into an alley and tried to mug her at knifepoint. So angry was Zoey at Marty's betrayal, she didn't even fear the guy she now knew to be the notorious Jorge "The Blade" Ramirez. All of her wrath at being victimized by Marty, channeled into her determination to prevent it from happening again. She punched Ramirez so hard, her knuckles bled.

The nimble Ramirez was a street fighter. She shouldn't have stood a chance against him. But her blow stunned him. By the time he recovered, something had happened in him.

"Getting creamed by women now," he said with a flash of white teeth. "Time to get out off the street. Maybe it's not too late for me."

But he'd paused at the opening of the alley and looked back at her.

"Don't let anyone ever lead you down the wrong path, sweetheart," Ramirez had said. "It's hell trying to get back." When his eyes stared off into the distance, or perhaps his own past, his lean, scarred face took on such a tragic expression of profound regret. Ramirez slowly closed the knife and handed it to Zoey.

With that, he walked out of the alley, and according to Lou, away from San Diego. Zoey glanced at Lou now, and thought she'd probably skip that gloating, after all. *Vaya con Dios, Jorge Ramirez. You saved my life.*

So perhaps people do change sometimes. Ramirez had. Or maybe he simply returned to the man he started out as and still wanted to be. Maybe always wanted to be.

Where did that leave Rob? Gus Robbins raised too many questions, but nothing in his life added up to this. She'd stake her life that he wasn't a child molester, and he wasn't a thief.

But why would Marty have lied? Out of perversity? Or to see how well the frame he'd constructed would fit? She saw how he could have set Rob up. Gretchen handled Rob's finances, and she would have been putty in Marty's hands. A new wave of anger came over Zoey when she remembered his reeking of Gretchen's awful rose-scented perfume and attempting to cover it with a cheap bunch of daisies.

But if Rob wasn't Marty's partner, who was? An image flashed into her mind. A word painted on the back of a boat, a city. Zoey was right: there *were* always gaps in the act.

"We're going the wrong way!" she shouted, before she could think it through.

All eyes but the pilot's turned warily to her.

"I mean, sure, we have to stop the yacht, but we can't go there." Zoey knew she was making no sense. She had to settle down, to plead what she thought to be true, or they'd never believe her. She took a deep breath and spoke with conviction. "Send the Coast Guard to stop the Toy Boy. It's going to blow with Willi on it. *That's* how Marty's going to kill him." She was right in believing no one changed that much, too. People *do* stick with what works.

Dale and Lou exchanged quick horrified glances.

"But Marty won't be there," she shouted. "We have to head him off at the airport." She held her breath. Would they believe her?

"Lindbergh?" Lou asked.

"No, the other one. Montgomery Field. And Marty's partner isn't Rob—it's Bucky Jack.

Sixty-eight

YEAH, IT HAD all fallen into place, Tomaso thought, while pacing on the tarmac. But why wouldn't it? None of them were any match for him.

Not that whiny sap, Willi, that was certain. He'd be blasted into a million pieces before the hour was out, with nothing left of the yacht except the paperwork that linked its lease to Zoey. Well, hopefully, a little evidence would remain to show that poor, innocent Marty Wright had also been on board, only to be destroyed by a bomb whose parts Zoey had ordered online. Tomaso laughed. God, he was brilliant.

Zoey and her nosy admirer must be crispy critters by now. Served her right, too, for making it so hard for him. The bitch had more lives than a cat. Surviving that trip over the side of the cliff was downright rude. Especially after he went to all the trouble of faking the note from O'Hara in case she came back early. And who would have thought she'd remember the greeting card? That was the trouble with women. They actually believed a guy meant everything he said.

Of course, where would he be if they didn't buy his lines? He wouldn't have had Gretchen Tyler risking her job for him. To think that she believed someone like him would give her a second look. Whoever said they were all the same in the dark didn't know jackshit. That doughy whale couldn't hold a candle to Zoey, for all her hang-ups. Gretchen was also way too clingy. Tomaso wasn't the least sorry that they'd find her draped over her oven door. And that note—it was such a hoot. How she'd become despondent when Gus Robbins broke it off with her to return to his wife. They'd never question the forgery—no bank ever had.

Tomaso didn't worry about O'Hara, either. Sure, he never figured on the guy surviving the crash, but he couldn't last much longer. The logistics on that crash had never been perfect, anyway, but Tomaso couldn't resist trying to take out two birds with one stone. He had planned to stop the car and place O'Hara behind the wheel before pushing it over the cliff, the way he had with the Willi's twin and the old man in LA who had provided the seed money for Willi's recordings, but it was too risky in daylight. He had to jump out after the car went over, hastily pulling O'Hara behind the wheel. Damn near broke his leg doing it, too. Who knew the big dead weight would follow him out?

O'Hara didn't know much, but he could point the cops in the right direction. Granted, he didn't know Marty Wright had put Rick Salaz up to getting him a job at that car dealership, but Rick would remember if anyone thought to ask. They could also learn the dealer had passed O'Hara's old heap to Marty Wright, if they asked the right questions. But why worry? O'Hara couldn't survive—not with all the drugs he put in his body.

Tomaso kicked a stone on the tarmac. Rob was the weak link in the chain, he had to admit. He never liked to leave his patsies around long enough to rap their gums. But the idea of sticking Rob only came to him late in the game when it looked like Rob's race was going to clean up from Ames's little stunt. Tomaso never wanted to pass up that kind of loot. Rob was a smooth one, but he wouldn't be able to talk his way out of this. Hell, even Zoey believed the story he'd created, and she was one of Rob's biggest supporters.

So it was over, Tomaso thought. Success—sweet, brilliant success.

Except for the perv. Tomaso threw an angry glance at Bucky, leaning into the engine of his plane, parked just off the runway. Why had he waited till now to make his pre-flight check?

But Tomaso didn't really fret about Bucky, either. The old Buck had been covering his tracks for a long time. Not a word had ever leaked out about him. Though how could it? Bucky's keepers protected their investment. They'd either pay off anyone who threatened to talk or eliminate them. There must have been a lot of little skeletons rattling in the old Buck's closet.

Still, Tomaso didn't like sharing. When the time was right, he'd leak word to Bucky's employers where to find him. Rule number one with those guys was that they didn't give second chances to anyone who ripped them off.

He'd let them know Doug Tomaso had masterminded it, too, though not where to find him. That would show the old man. If this operation wasn't perfect, nothing was. His father could see that now, and he'd have to admit his son wasn't a screw-up, after all—before he died.

Because rule number two covered scapegoats. When they couldn't nail the guy who cheated them, someone else had to pay. The old fart might have scraped through last time, but they wouldn't let him off this time, not after what little Dougie took today. When they finished the old man off, he'd be through with that Tomaso baggage once and for all.

Then no one alive would be a threat to him.

As if anyone was now.

Sixty-nine

LOU TOLD THE pilot they were changing directions. *They trusted me, no questions asked,* Zoey thought. Dale trusted her, even with his brother's life, and ultimately his sister's, hanging in the balance. So did Lou, a man who checked and rechecked everything. Disbelief still cast a long shadow over them, but they suspended it to the extent of doing what she asked. Zoey realized she had to get this close to death before anyone cared enough about her to do that. Maybe she had to get this close to *let* someone care.

Trust. It can ebb and flow like the tides, but as with the currents, there's always something enduring there. A con man must have to work a scam pretty fast. It's easy to sell people on something, but harder to *keep* them sold. Zoey bought into the idea of Rob's guilt because it fit the frame Marty had made. But the frame fell apart under scrutiny. She trusted Rob.

She also knew something about race management. A fair amount of money passes through an outfit like Rob's. But not the fortune Dale must have seen in Rob's bank records. And certainly not enough to serve as a vehicle for organized crime. The kind of money laundering scheme Marty described couldn't be done through race management on a large enough scale to matter.

But a national charity was another story. It had no ceiling. With Touchstone Houses from coast-to-coast and major corporate sponsorship, she wouldn't be surprised to learn the Foundation had been turning a tidy profit for its founders for years, beyond washing their dirty money, even before the Willi Bogs phenomenon sent it into the stratosphere.

They obviously weren't spending any more than they had to

on the kids. She doubted whether they even allotted the foster child stipends they must have been receiving from local jurisdictions, not to mention what they raked in above that. Why should the kids' clothes have been so worn, their bodies so thin?

It hurt Zoey to remember how that little guy clung to her leg. And she sent him back there! She had to make it right for those boys. Somehow. Now she understood now why Bucky's crude flirtations posed no threat to her. They weren't real, and at some level, she knew it.

She suddenly remembered how often throughout this ordeal, when she'd felt as if someone were following her, she'd spotted young boys in the area. Had Marty conscripted Touchstone kids for his dirty work? That explained why some of the attacks felt genuinely menacing, while others seemed more like childish harassment. That wasn't anywhere near as bad as the way Bucky had used them, yet it proved to be the last straw for Zoey. Her rage mushroomed.

Lou tapped her arm and pointed out Montgomery Field through the helicopter windshield. She flashed on that day she ran into Bucky there, and the way she absently pawed through the charts in his backseat. They were maps of South America, she realized now. Waves of acid rolled through her stomach. *Oh, God—I can't let them get away with this.* Time to pull all the stops, like she did before a race. Too bad there was no such thing as second place in this event.

Dale's pale face grew grave, as he listened to a message in his headphones. "Bucky Jack has requested clearance from the tower. They're stalling him."

Hurry, hurry. The chopper sailed over the fence and started down to the grass along the runway. Zoey spotted the small jet on the tarmac just off the runway. It was a sleek white craft with aqua trim. She didn't know enough about planes to say what kind it was, just that it was one of the ones whose hatch folds out to form a set of stairs when open. She couldn't have sworn that was Bucky at the controls; the cockpit window was too small. But that sure was Marty alongside the plane. He stood on the tarmac, ready to hop up those steps. Only he seemed to be taking a moment for one last look at the place where he had wreaked such destruction. What incredible arrogance.

The sight of the helicopter, or the sound of the approaching patrol car sirens, must have spooked Bucky. His plane began rolling, with the hatch still open. That took Marty by surprise. As the plane taxied faster and faster, Marty ran to catch it. *No!* She couldn't bear it if he got away.

Now or never, Zoey.

With the aircraft still a few yards off the ground, she threw the door open and jumped out. Already running when she hit the ground, she ducked under the circling blades, before she really opened it up.

The chopper must have landed behind her and its passengers disembarked. She heard Dale shout, "Let it go, Zoey. You can't make it."

You can't make it, Zoey—she'd heard that all her life. *You're not good enough, fast enough, smart enough, Zoey. You can't make it because we're changing the rules. Because we moved the finish line.*

Not this time.

Marty ran after the plane still racing down the runway. The plane lifted off the tarmac, but it listed badly to the side with that open hatch. It bounced down against the surface. But Bucky steadied it and kept rolling. The plane picked up more speed along the ground, as did Marty. Zoey topped it. She ran faster than she ever had. This was the Ironman, the Olympics, the race of her life. She filled her lungs to their capacity, and beyond. She felt when they tore, when her sides split. When her heart threatened to burst. She didn't stop.

Bucky tried another liftoff with no more success. The craft bounced more erratically when it hit the runway this time, slowing it. But Marty was gaining ground. Would he reach the plane? Would he be able to climb aboard and shut that hatch, allowing the plane to take off?

No! Zoey would make that finish line stop moving—or she would die trying. *Now.* She burned the last of her strength for one last burst. When Marty was nearly level with Bucky's plane, she threw herself into a sliding tackle, with no thought of what that would do to her body. She scraped her knees on the surface, since she still wore that stretched and sooty tri-suit. But before she slammed against the ground, she reached out for Marty's ankles. No moment had ever been as satisfying as when her fingers wrapped around them. She tightened her hold and yanked him—hard.

Zoey vaguely noticed the plane attempted another takeoff. She heard a loud crash shortly after. But she didn't spare a bit of attention to it. She was blinded to everything but Marty.

Winded and gasping for air, he lay on the runway, like a fish dying on a dock. She flipped him over, onto his back. Then she knelt over him to hold him there. She sent her fists flying into his face. She didn't give a thought to technique, but everything she learned about boxing came through. No shadowboxing, this time. She smashed his nose. Blood spurted everywhere. She hit him again, so hard she thought she might push that crooked nose right through his head, just like she'd wanted to.

She heard Dale shout from somewhere behind her. "That's enough, Zoey!"

It wasn't nearly enough. That was what people said when they thought you'd lost control. She hadn't lost it, she knew exactly what she was doing, watching Marty sputter helplessly while she reduced him to a bloody pulp.

"Next time, Marty, find yourself a better girl," she shouted, punctuating the line with one last blow. "Only, I guess, where you're going, they'll all have *dicks.*"

Weren't nobody putting that nose back together again.

Seventy

JUST AS NOBODY tells you that in real life, when the hero throws himself against a door, it doesn't shatter—they don't say when you bust up someone's face, your hand swells like a carnival balloon animal. Zoey spent two hours at the San Diego cop shop near Montgomery Field with her hand soaking in a bowl of ice water. But it was worth it. The people who said violence never solved anything needed to get out more, she decided.

Marty seemed unusually subdued when they brought him in. His shock that his scheme failed might have been to blame, though he could simply have been dazed from the blows Zoey dealt. He had enough sense not to talk without his lawyer. Too bad they didn't need a word from him to sort it out.

The Coast Guard reached the Toy Boy in time. Actually, there really wasn't any threat. They did find a bomb on board, but it wouldn't have gone off because it hadn't been wired right. The police surmised Marty tried to duplicate the bomb someone had once built for him in New York, where he blasted his father's boat. Only he unknowingly switched a couple of wires because he was colorblind, which Zoey never had a chance to tell him.

The bomb did perform one function. When Willi saw it, he sang like…well, like Willi Bogs. The police took his statement first, then with a police escort, they put him on a plane to Houston, where Holly waited at the hospital.

One thing after another just fell apart for Marty. A neighbor of Gretchen's smelled gas and coaxed the apartment manager to open her door. They found her draped over the open oven door. But since they discovered her rather quickly, she was well enough to be transferred to the hospital wing of the women's jail. Lou said she was squawking up a storm. Equally important, O'Hara's doctors were confident he would reach consciousness soon. It was anyone's guess how much he might contribute.

They brought Rob in for questioning, and Lacey came along with him. Zoey couldn't believe the change in Lacey, even if it was hard to put her finger on the cause of Lacey's transformation. It was like someone gave the statue a final polishing. With soft, dark curls cascading around her fair, heart-shaped face, she'd always been beautiful. Now she looked positively airbrushed.

Sometimes all you gotta do is ask, Zoey learned. When Lacey went in for surgery to correct her snoring problem, she had some minor cosmetic work done as well. Where did she go? A small private hospital in La Jolla—right where Zoey had lost Rob when she followed him. Zoey hoped she successfully hid that she considered Lacey's choice a little shallow. Probably her ambivalence about appearance, anyway.

Lou asked them an even better question—about the source of their money. They answered that just as freely. They won the lottery back home in Colorado and chucked it all to pursue their dream jobs, Lacey to stay home and have the baby they couldn't afford before, and Rob to spend too much money putting on races for others to compete in. Each to his own.

But Gretchen, under Marty's direction, had stripped the cupboard bare. When Rob discovered his company had gone broke, he thought it was because of his own bad management. Still determined to fulfill his promises, he and Lacey took a mortgage on their paid-up house. Lacey was coming out of retirement to see the money wasn't frittered away. Something many triathletes would cheer. Once all the dust settled, Zoey hoped some of the money Marty stole from their company came back to Rob and Lacey.

The police brought Bucky in shortly thereafter. Zoey was right about what she thought she heard while she'd been pummeling Marty—the plane did crash after that last takeoff attempt. Apparently, not even a pilot of Bucky's caliber could take off with the hatch open. The police brought him to the hospital after his apprehension, but Zoey had heard that, while the plane wasn't in great shape, Bucky got no more than some scraps and bruises.

Yet Bucky seemed to have shrunken during his time in the emergency room, as well as aged. When they led a handcuffed Bucky Jack up the hall where Zoey soaked her hand, he looked like a small, sad old man. But he still flashed her a smile when they dragged him past.

"Hey there, Zoey-girl. What did you do to your hand?"

She bristled at his approach, but she found herself answering in a neutral tone, "Beat the crap out of Marty."

Bucky laughed softly. "Well, he sure deserved that, didn't he, sweetheart?"

What was it with these con artists? Did he really think that nothing had changed, that she would continue to fall for his patter? She hated what Bucky did to those kids. Countless boys, year-after-year. She would never forgive him for it. Dale was right, she did peg people into narrow slots. No one is all black or all white, but you still have to know where to place those uncrossable lines in all the shades of gray. Bucky went light-years past it.

"Keep moving, Bucky," she said in a voice now too charged with emotion. "Or I'll give you some of the same."

The bleak realization that he would be treated differently from then on instantly striped the glow from the ol' Buck's blue eyes. He lowered his gaze to the floor when he continued moving past Zoey. One of the cops leading him gave her a nod of approval.

The days that followed saw just as much turmoil. After the way Marty had set her up to take the fall, Zoey had to stay in San Diego until she was cleared. Lou kept assuring her it would happen, though those wheels of justice did grind exceedingly slow. Worst of all, she was broke. That bastard, Marty, had cleaned her out to the extent of clipping what she had in her wallet before he tried to leave. The court even froze her secret account in Boulder.

And rats had nothing on her sponsors when it came to leaving her sinking ship. That was corporate America for you, Zoey discovered—the backbone of a wet noodle and the loyalty of a whore.

The Shortz SportzWatchez company asked her to vacate the condo immediately. It wasn't just the notoriety. Apparently, she'd also missed a couple of appearances for them that Marty neglected to mention. Carolyn Peña offered to double up her kids to make a place for her. But Dale knew she'd need more privacy. When he called Charley Orr to break the news to her, Charley not only offered Zoey Cindy's place, she sent Zoey money that she wouldn't even consider a loan. Eventually, though, Zoey returned to Boulder, only returning to San Diego for races.

Despite the consequences to herself, Zoey didn't regret a thing she did that day. Her actions went out in a rippling effect, touching more lives than she knew.

But still, she felt sick when she saw the race results. Fermina overtook Alicia in the last hundred yards. Zoey heard from everyone who saw the finish that the cheers broke the sound barrier. But Fermina won in a slower time than Zoey was on target to finish in, had she stayed in the race. Zoey groaned when she saw her name in the line-up. "Zoey Morgan," it read, "DNF." Did not finish.

So it goes. Some days you practically crawl that course, some days you almost soar. No promises, no guarantees, just the chance to go as far and as fast as your heart will take you. That's the way it is in triathlon, and life. Zoey knew that now.

Besides, her instant poverty had one redeeming feature—it meant she had to take every race she could, and she had to go out there to win. She carved her best season ever out of the personal defeats she'd experienced in San Diego. As she collected wins, more of her sponsors returned. Consistency isn't valued any higher in the corporate world than loyalty, apparently.

For once, Zoey didn't avoid remembering the awful things that had happened to her, she just channeled the pain through those long hours of training, and came out better for it on the other side. That race day in San Diego was the turnaround point of her life. And she was always stronger on the second half.

She learned she really excelled at every length event. How foolish she was to worry about it. She crowned her season at the Ironman. The conditions at Kona were even more brutal than usual, and that race prided itself on being hell: fifty mile-an-hour crosswinds, sweltering heat. Yet she still came in third. Now people who knew nothing about the sport often said, "You mean you didn't win?" But for a first-timer, third place was the ideal springboard for the following season. Miranda won again, but she looked at Zoey a lot more seriously than she had that day at the chapel. Zoey wore the dress Charley had given her to the awards banquet the next night, and she actually felt pretty good about looking good.

Ali had a bad race at the Ironman. Hawaii destroys the best. Though like the pro she was, she still pulled out a tenth place finish. Only she tested positive for opiates and was disqualified. Alicia was challenging the outcome, claiming the poppy seed bagels she munched before the race caused a false positive reading. Everyone in the sport knew how she craved any kind of bagel. Zoey was reserving judgment and not making any statements until she was sure. Progress.

The criminal trials—those of Marty, Willi, and Bucky, which took most of a year—made for a regular three-ring circus, owing largely to Willi's resurrection. His star just continued to rise. Even after the public discovered he was a goofball, they loved him anyway. Showed what Zoey knew. In exchange for his testimony, the prosecution allowed him to plea bargain to lesser charges and time served. The wheels of justice miss a few now and then, Zoey learned.

Fortunately, Bucky's celebrity didn't echo Willi's. The great American hero went down in flames. That fire did shed light on the Touchstone Houses, though. A new charity was established to oversee them, one that promised to keep tighter controls. Zoey was even given a place on the Board of Directors. Maybe those kids would finally have a chance.

Zoey didn't see Dale again until Marty's sentencing the following September, and then only from across the courtroom. They'd missed each other all summer. She did touch base with Carolyn and Lou when she came to town to testify or race, but she didn't try too hard to see Dale. She just didn't know what to say to him.

Marty received life without the possibility of parole. The DA decided not to try for the death penalty, but Lou warned her his sentence was only a formality. He wasn't expected to last long in prison. Apparently, the mob has some rule about making an example of people who steal from them.

Someday, when Marty finally bought it, Zoey vowed she would hoist one for Cindy. And yes, she admitted to herself, she'd grieve, too, because she remembered how it felt to be loved by him. Sure, she knew it wasn't real, but it could have been if only Marty hadn't been missing the little part that most of us call our soul.

After the sentencing, Zoey didn't think Dale saw her slip out of the courtroom, but he stopped her on the courthouse steps with a wolf's whistle.

"Look at you," he said. "Makeup, heels—the whole shebang. You look fabulous."

She felt herself blushing, but she did a little pirouette for him. She wore the dress she'd worn to Cindy's memorial service. Just seemed right, somehow.

But what a sight Dale was. He was back in the leather he wore when she first met him, still looked like a thug. How deceiving looks can be._They fell into walking together.

"Did Lou tell you? I'm living in San Diego now," Dale said.

"Really? I've moved here, too."

"Zoey, that's great. Since when?"

"Still unpacking. I'm renting Cindy's place. There was nothing left for me in Boulder." Zoey shrugged. "Anyway, it just seemed time for a change. Not everything that happened here was bad."

"Yeah."

They lapsed into a heavy silence that was only broken by the sound of their shoes tapping against the sidewalk.

To fill it, Zoey asked "How's Holly?"

"Doing real well. They think she's gonna make it."

"Dale, that's wonderful. I'm so happy for her, for all of you."

Silence came to rule again. The awkwardness felt so awful, Zoey practically threw herself on her Jeep with relief when they reached where she'd parked it.

But Dale seemed reluctant to leave. "It's great that we're both living here, Zoey." He kicked the heavy toe of his black boot against the dusty sidewalk. "I mean, after all we've been through, we should be friends."

"I'm not sure that's possible, Dale." Had she stammered? "I mean, when people have—" *Shit.* She almost said "gone all the way," like she was in eighth grade or something, not to mention conveniently forgetting the embarrassing technicality that they hadn't. Now she knew what she felt: this man knew too much about her. "You can't come back from…all we experienced…to mere friendship."

Dale gripped her hand in his, clutching it hard. "Sure, you can. We make every friendship from scratch each time, so we get to write our own rules."

Zoey didn't say anything. After a while, Dale just gave his head a sad shake. "I see." Hurt shaped his voice. "You'd probably never feel you could trust me."

He didn't see at all.

"Well, have a good life, Zoey Morgan. No one deserves it more."

Zoey felt something dying in her, as she watched him walk away. *Zoey, only a fool starts a forward journey by taking a step back.*

"Hey!" she shouted.

Dale turned hesitantly, seemingly unsure of whether she was talking to him.

"Texas is pretty flat, isn't it? I bet you never skied." She rushed on before he could correct her. "Now me, a native of the Rockies, I need to check out these puny California mountains. Not expecting much, mind you, but I gotta see for myself. If you're good to me, my boy, I just might take you."

Amusement, and a twirling toothpick she hadn't spotted before, tugged his mouth into a sardonic grin that made his scars stand out. How had that face ever seemed menacing to her?

"If you're good to *me*," Dale said, "I just might go."

Hope filled her heart until it burst free, filling her body with a joyous warmth. Zoey found herself grinning. Something told her this fall would see a lot of friends taking care of friends.

She couldn't wait to see what winter would hold.

About the Author

Kris Neri writes the Tracy Eaton mysteries and the Annabelle Haggerty and Samantha Brennan magical mystery series, along with standalone thrillers. In addition to being a three-time Lefty Award finalist for Best Humorous Mystery Novel, her novels have also been finalists for the Agatha, Anthony, Macavity, International Book Award, and the New Mexico-Arizona Book Award. Her latest mystery, *Revenge on Route 66*, was a finalist for the New Mexico-Arizona Book Award, and her most recent magical novel, *Magical Alienation*, won it. She teaches writing online for the prestigious Writers' Program of the UCLA Extension School and in private classes, and with her husband, she owns The Well Red Coyote bookstore in Sedona, Arizona. Kris welcomes readers to her website, www.krisneri.com.

www.ingramcontent.com/pod-product-compliance
Lightning Source LLC
Chambersburg PA
CBHW051410170626
46809CB00006B/2094